To PHIAN

Enjoy - if you dare!

2025

NOT BAD, BUBBA!

ROBIN ANDERSON

Copyright © ROBIN ANDERSON 2025

This book is a work of fiction. Names, characters, businesses, organisations, places and those other than those clearly in the public domain are either a product of the author's imagination or else used fictitiously. Any resemblance to actual persons, living or dead, events or locales is entirely coincidental.

Cover design by Michael Marsden

IN MEMORY AND HONOUR OF THREE UNPARALLED FRIENDS

BEESLE, BENEDICT & BOBBY

NOT BAD, BUBBA!

A FORETASTE

"Oh. you must have been a beautiful baby," crooned Warwick Laudanum-Standton proudly eyeing his latest handiwork, "but baby, look at you now!" He gave a snicker. "What's more, I've kindly allowed you to live, not only for you to *tell* your miserable tale, but for you also to weep and most certainly wail about your oh, so, inglorious future."

Warwick, a twenty-something Theo James lookalike, stood eyeing the naked, bleeding form of a former schoolteacher, Dick - the prick - McCausland lying on the kitchen table in front of him.

"Not bad, Bubba," he muttered, admiring the letters FYLWLS (Fuck you - love - Warwick Laudanum-Standton) freshly carved on the schoolmaster's forehead and pale, hairless chest. "A few more like this, but with different initials, of course, and they'll be begging me to hang - ha! - one of my wondrous works - a rival to Jusepe de Ribera's goriest - in the Royal Academy! As for Mr. McCausland's missing left foot and laughable willy, a sure-fire case of dribble, dribble hobble, hobble and the million-dollar question; was it worth the toil and trouble!"

Giving a soft chuckle, Warwick turned to the Jack Russell terrier sitting patiently next to him. "So, Vincent, the planet's most handsome pooch (named after Vincent Price, the sixties actor who, with Coral Browne his glamorous wife, were known in Hollywood as Mr. and Mrs Horror), a little something else perhaps? Something witty? A naughty double entendre? Why not a *boner* as it were. But, instead of the usual graffiti concept of a boner, a large *doggy* bone-r instead!"

Warwick gave Vincent a wink. "Furthermore, why not carve it not only on his forehead but above his former, seriously laughable personal boner as well? Agreed?"

On cue, Vincent gave a combination of a growl and a bark.

"Thank you, Vincent," crooned his master. "So, without any further ado, here's *cutting!*"

Two hours later Warwick, accompanied by Vincent, dropped the unconscious elderly man in all his naked, mutilated glory at a convenient bus stop for - quote-unquote - "Some idiot to find and no doubt faint or throw up! Or both!"

A LOCAL HOSPITAL

"Poor man," muttered Nurse Ingrid Lupino. "Not only has he had his penis plus his left foot cut off, whoever did this also carved some letters and what looks like a *bone* on his forehead, chest and lower down. God, imagine having to *live* with all this!"

"All this and without *it*," snickered Nurse Ivor Madden, a gangly, ginger-haired Ed Sheran lookalike. Tut-tutting, he added soulfully. "All I can say is that whoever did this must have been seriously pissed off with Mr. Mystery Man here. I pity the poor nurse who'll be with him when he eventually comes to. Moreso the doctor who will have to explain to him what's happened,"

SEVERAL HOURS LATER

"Where . . . where am I?" croaked Dick McCausland, his eyelids fluttering as he attempted to focus on his surroundings. "Jesus!" he cried on attempting to sit up. "Please answer me . . . is someone there?"

"Yes, sir, I'm here," cooed Nurse Viola Dawkins, a motherly Hattie McDaniel lookalike, taking hold of Dick's hand. "You're in hospital, sir, following a nasty accident. However, you didn't have any identification on you . . ."

"McCausland, Richard McCausland," croaked Dick. "What sort of accident? I feel as if my whole body . . . my head is on fire. What the fuck . . . what happened?"

"Please wait while I fetch Dr Dipesh, Mr. . . . err McCausland, as I feel it best if he explains what has happened to you."

"Please wait?" echoed Dick. Making a brave attempt to give Nurse Dawkins the semblance of a smile. he added weakly. "Of course I'll wait, seeing the marathon's still several weeks away . . ."

"Once Dr Dipesh has seen you and if you're up to it (*Jesus, unfortunate choice of words, Viola,* she thought) the police would like to talk to you."

*

Dick's anguished cries of "No! No! No! What are you saying?" reverberated round the small private room and through the nearby corridor before they managed to give him a further sedative. Having been informed of Dick's injuries, the police officer waiting to talk to Dick was heard to say. "Poor guy. I'd do more than scream. I'd bloody well top myself!"

1

FLASHBACK

"I don't give a toss about what you think, Standton," snapped Dick McCausland glaring at the defiant young boy. "If I tell you to dissect a guinea pig, you damn well dissect it!"

"And if I won't, don't?" replied Warwick Laudanum-Standton, a blond, angelic-looking fourteen-year-old, his still breaking voice a staccato of sharps and flats.

"What did you say?" roared McCausland, a red-faced, Ian Mckellan lookalike. "What did you just say? Repeat yourself, if you dare!"

"I said, *sir*, that I won't. Meaning I will *not* cut up an innocent guinea pig, whether you like it not. It's unfair and it's also cruel."

"It's unfair . . . and it's c . . . cruel?" stammered McCausland. "This is a biology class, Standton. B-i-o-l-o-g-y, and part of biology is studying the ins and outs of one's anatomy."

"There! You've just said it yourself, sir: of *one's* anatomy. So, sir, if you agree, I'll be more than happy to cut you open in order to study your innards. For the sole purpose of biology, of course." The latter said deadpan.

"Get out!" yelled McCausland, much to the amusement of the other boys in the class. "Get out of my class and go and wait for me outside the headmaster's office. Now!"

HEADMASTER PHILLIP TOWNSEND'S OFFICE

"Come in," grunted Phillip Townsend on hearing a light knocking.

"Excuse me, sir," said Warwick poking his head round the door, "I'm Warwick Laudanum-Standton and I've been sent to see you by Mr. McCausland who's on his way. He told me to wait until he arrived."

"So?"

"Well, before Mr. McCausland arrives, sir, can I say something, something which I know is out of order, sir, but I have to say it, sir."

"So, come in, Standton, and say what you seem determined to say."

"Mr. McCausland is going to say I was rude to him, sir, but what he *won't* say I was rude to him because of what he keeps on saying to me when he thinks the rest of the class can't hear him."

"And what was it he said, exactly?" replied Townsend, alarm bells ringing.

"Mr. McCausland . . . he . . . he keeps asking me to . . . oh, sir! Sorry, sir, but I don't think I can say it!"

"Yes, you can, Standton, lad! Out with it! What does Mr. McCausland keep saying to you?"

Giving the headmaster an embarrassed look, Warwick took a deep breath and said with a gulp. "He keeps asking me if I would like to play with his . . . his . . . his old man or, to use his exact words., his c . . . cock."

*

"He said *what*?" exploded McCausland, on having been hastily summoned to the headmaster's office. "He said *what*?"

"You heard me loud and clear," said Townsend grimly. "There's no need for me to repeat myself."

"But it's all lies, sir!" cried McCausland. "I'm not like that! I'm a happily married man and father of three children: you've met Belinda, my wife, for God's sake! Standton's doing his because he was instructed to dissect a guinea pig in my biology class and refused to do so. He became abusive which led to me sending him to your office where he was supposed to wait for me to arrive."

Dick McCausland gave an exasperated sigh. "It's his word against mine, Mr. Headmaster. What's more, I can guarantee you will not a single pupil who will back the little shit up. In fact, you'll find Standton to be one of the most unpopular - if not *the* most unpopular - student registered."

"No matter what you say. McCausland, this is serious accusation; very serious indeed. You may go, but let me assure you, you haven't heard the last of this!"

*

Two weeks later a smirking Warwick clambered into the chauffeur-driven Roll-Royce and was driven away without giving a backward glance at the school buildings.

On investigating Warwick's complaints against Dick McCausland, it soon became clear that his complaints were nether seconded or justified. Every boy questioned was adamant that McCausland was blameless whereas Warwick Laudanum-Standton was nothing more than a "lying, troublemaking little prick."

"Mr. Mc is *not* a paedo, not in a hundred years," was the general response, whereas Warwick was seen as "a worrywart, a worm and a loner with no real friends apart from old Shep, the groundsman's aged Labrador".

As the Rolls-Royce glided its way toward London. Warwick's only comment as a murmured. "Bye, Shep, old thing. I'll miss you. Hopefully matron will remember to give Harry, the groundsman, the bag of doggy treats I bought for you. If ever someone deserved a thank you present, you're the one and you will never be forgotten.

"As for the shits who made it their daily duty to make my life as unpleasant as they could, just you wait! It won't be tomorrow or the day after, but some unexpected day in the future. The day when I allow you to *live* in order to reap what you so gleefully sowed! However, for my first dalliance, as it were, it's *got* to be that bastard Giles Gordon, the head prefect back at that tribute to Belsen I've just left. Oh, Mr. Giles Gordon, am I going to have fun preparing and perfecting you for a *blighted* instead of a brilliant future! What's even more tantalising is that after I've dealt with Gordon, I'll take great delight in dealing with Roger Lincoln. Gordon's slimeball best friend."

"Did you say something, sir?" asked Peter Stiles, the unformed chauffeur (a sparky Jack O'Connell lookalike referred to as Pete the Wheel by Warwick and his parents) glancing at Warwick in the rear-view mirror.

"No, Pete, not really," sniggered Warwick catching his eyes reflected in the mirror. "Simply talking to myself; the first signs of losing the plot no doubt."

"If you say so, sir," replied Peter catching Warwick's eye again. *Something you started doing the day I found you trying to get Mrs Horsfall, the cook, to see if you could give the Christmas turkey the kiss of life after the nasty butcher man had killed it,* thought Peter with an inward chuckle. *Something cook and I were never able to understand is how sex on legs, Rex - our name for the butcher - ended up getting nicked for having unhygienic premises. To this day Rex swears blind the cockroaches found in certain peoples' orders - cockroaches and mouse droppings - had been deliberately placed within the orders so as to get him into trouble!*

As the Rolls approached the elegant white fronted Georgian house in elegant Chester Square, Warwick gave a start and said brightly. "Tell me, Pete, I know you have a finger in many pies, so, my question. Do you know of anyone who could kidnap a dog for me? Obviously, I'm prepared to pay, pay well for such a manoeuvre." He gave a conspiratorial snigger. "Another obviously! Shep will have to stay in the mews house you share with cook and her hubby until I can make other plans, but that shouldn't be a problem."

"Not for me, sir, but cook may object seeing we already share the mews house with her four cats and Bonnie and Clyde, her two budgerigars! So could be a bit crowded."

"Hm, I see what you mean." Warwick gave a snigger. "Oh well, as they, it was a nice thought but, as thinking caps were invented for thinking, we'll do just that. Thank you, Pete, and please don't hesitate in telling cook how you so cleverly thwarted a potential invasion!"

AN ELEGANT TOWNHOUSE - CHESTER SQUARE - BELGRAVIA

"Welcome home, Master Warwick," smiled Hilda Horsfall, the cook, a cheerful Mrs Doubtfire lookalike. "Peter told me about you asking if we could cope with an elderly *dog* living with us in the mews but, quite honestly, Master Warwick, as much as I'd like to say yes, it wouldn't be fair on Myrna, Matilda, Marilyn and Lilian, our cats." Giving Warwick a further smile, she added chirpily. "Humphrey said you would understand my concern." Humphrey being Hilda's burly husband and the Standton's butler and referred to as "Hangdog Humph" by Warwick.

"Understand? Of course I do, Mrs Horsfall," replied Warwick with a tight smile. "It *was* a bit presumptuous of me to have even asked. However, have no fear as I have already spoken to a friend of mine (*You have the cheek to say you have an actual friend?* thought Mrs Horsfall. *Now, there's a surprise if ever there was!*) and he was more than happy to do the honours. As long as old Shep doesn't mind living in a double-decker penthouse overlooking Canada Square at Canary Wharf; London's towering answer to Manhattan!"

"Oh, that *is* good news, Master Warwick! "And how kind of your friend!"

"I can assure you, Mrs Horsfall, my friend Nathan Leopold is one of the kindest and most generous people you would ever wish to meet!" Tongue in cheek, he added with a tighter smile. "Added to which, with his good looks, a real killer!"

"Goodness," tittered Hilda Horsfall. "Hopefully I shall meet this dashing Mr. Leopold at lunch one day! Do let me know if you invite him to lunch or dinner, and I will make sure my special crème brûlée is on the menu!"

"Lucky Leopold," replied Warwick as he made for the door. "I'm sure he'll *loeb* it!"

"Did he say loathe it?" snapped Hilda Horsfall, giving husband Humphrey a glare.

"No dear, I'm sure he said love it," grunted Humphrey, his eyes fixed firmly on *The News of The World* in front of him.

"Well, I'm sure he said loathe," said his wife. "Cheeky sod!"

"Tell me about it," replied Humphrey with a further disinterested grunt.

"And as for a friend taking care of that dog for him: utter codswallop!" snorted Hilda. "Kids like him don't have any friends, unless they're that sort!"

"You mean gay," grunted Humphrey. "That's if young Warwick even knows what being gay means seeing he's too up his own arse to think of any other arse."

"Humphrey! You know I won't tolerate such language in my kitchen!"

"Really?" said Humphrey drily. "I thought you'd *loeb* it. Any more tea in the old pot?"

*

"Stupid vacuous vagina," snorted Warwick on entering his private sanctuary or Dracula's Den according to the red enamel name plate on the door. His sanctuary occupying the complete top floor of the house apart from a large storeroom.

Glancing approvingly at his surroundings (red ceilings and woodwork throughout, along with black walls, black carpeting and black, red or red and black patterned upholstered furniture, Warwick flung himself onto the king size bed (red and black pattered cover). "If she's stupid to believe that I have a friend, a friend named Nathan Leopold living in a double-decker penthouse in Canary Wharf, then she needs serious help. As for her fucking crème brûlée, crème shitty not okay would be a better name for it!"

Warwick lay staring at the red ceiling for several minutes before hauling himself from the bed and going through to the sleek red, black and chrome kitchenette where he opened a packet of shortbread and poured himself a Coca- Cola. Perched on a stool he sat staring at the large Helen Steele painting dominating the breakfast nook and said to himself, in between chews and swallows.

"As Pete was quite happy for Shep to move into the mews whereas Madam Defarge and her hapless Hangdog Humphrey were not, the only answer is to get rid of the pair. Mother Dearest shouldn't be too difficult to bring round to my way of thinking. Not that it really matters seeing she's never, ever been sober long enough to put anything into its proper perspective. As for Father Dearest, he's too busy making money or trying to get into some new secretary's knickers it could be several months before he figured out the butler wasn't deaf nor was his name Humphrey!

"Which reminds me, I have to face him and Mother Dearest at six o'clock 'on the dot' in his study to explain my impromptu dismissal, expulsion or ejection whatever one wishes to call it, from bloody Bledisloe College." Warwick gave a resigned sigh. "Oh well, the plus side will be seeing their faces when I repeat words such as gay, buggery, cock and fuck in order to justify my shock, my horror and my anger toward McCausland."

*

"I can't believe what my poor darling has been through," cried Lutetia Laudanum-Stanton, a Lily Tomlin lookalike clutching her surgically enhanced bosom. "My poor, poor but such a *brave* boy to have had the courage to report that vile man!"

"Hmm," grunted Percival Laudanum-Standton, an overweight doppelganger for Mr. Bumble the beadle, regarding his smirking son with a disbelieving look. "I'm only going to ask you once, Warwick, and I want an honest answer. I do *not* wish to hear one of your usual flighty, fairy - err - fantasies. So, did McCausland say to you what you claim he did?"

"Percival!" admonished Lutetia in a shocked voice. "How could you ever *not* believe what our dear Warwick told the headmaster?"

"Quite easily," growled Percival. Pointing a thick, hairy finger at Warwick he said in a no-nonsense voice. "If he can call my secretary and tell her he knows what she and I were up to but, if she paid him one hundred pounds cash, he'd keep quiet about it: *despite* Sheila being in her sixties and a grandmother to boot! Then he is more than capable of saying McCausland propositioned him! So, I'll ask you again. Did he, or didn't he?"

"Of course he did," replied Warwick in a choked voice. Eyeing his father, he added defiantly, "Like George Washington, I cannot tell a lie."

"Well, as we're not talking about a felled apple tree here, I'll ask you once more. Did he, or didn't he?"

"Of course he did! How many times do you want me to repeat myself?"

"According to your fellow pupils, McCausland did not. Nor would he ever suggest such deceitful matters! However, knowing you as I do, *Warwick*, it should come as no surprise that I am on their side. I have already had Sheila Hardcastle, my *loyal*, harangued secretary, speak to one of the local schools: a school you will be attending as from next Monday. Pete the Wheel has already been informed and he will drop you off in time for your meeting with Mr. Teague, the headmaster, at nine o'clock sharp. Is that clear?"

"I look forward to meeting this Mr. Teague at nine o'clock sharp next Monday at some unnamed local school," replied Warwick deadpan. "Now, as I have an aged dog to deal with, please excuse me." Turning to face a bewildered looking Lutetia, he added smoothly. "And no, Mother Dearest. I won't be joining you and Father Dearest for dinner as I've already asked the accommodating Mrs Horsfall to make me a sandwich which I shall have in my room."

Looking stonily at Percival he said in a sonorous voice. "It may surprise you, *Father,* but having been so ruthlessly, never mind unfairly, ousted from school today, has completely thrown me. What's more, *despite* your hurtful comments regarding my honesty, what I said about Mr. Causland was the truth, the whole truth, and nothing but the truth. So, help me Satan."

Shooting his parents a poisonous look, Warwick upped and stalked out from the room.

"Did he just say so help me, *Satan*?" gasped Lutetia.

"Yes, he most certainly *did* say so help me Satan," harrumphed Percival. Eyeing his wife, he said grimly. "I'm more than convinced there was a mix up in the bloody nursing home where Warwick was hatched, and we were given someone else's baby. I mean, just *look* at Warwick. He doesn't bear the slightest resemblance to either of us!"

"Nonsense, Percival!" tittered Lutetia. "You know how everyone keeps saying Warwick's the spitting image of you!"

"Then Satan owes *me* an apology," grunted Percival. "Now, after all that I most *definitely* deserve another large martini; how about you?"

"*Touché* and *touché* again!" carolled Lutetia.

*

"Right," muttered Warwick on entering Dracula's Den. "Showtime! Which means out with the wretched Horsfalls and *in* with old Shep! With a new school to cope with, time is of the essence. Now, I wonder *just* how serious Pete was about having Shep to stay, or was it just a load of hot air? If it *wasn't* then he *won't* have to prick his balloon with what I imagine to be an impressive prick! Oh, Warwick Laudanum-Standton, such a wit! Anyway, there's only one way to find out."

Warwick reached for the intercom phone on his Rabih Hage black writing desk and punched in Peter's number.

"Yes sir?" said Peter on picking up.

"Pete, it's me. Warwick!"

"Yes, sir, I gathered that."

"Have you a few moments to spare as I need to talk to you about Shep, old Harry's dog."

"Err . . . I'd be happy to talk to you about . . . err . . . old Harry's err . . . dog. Tomorrow, some time?"

"No, I'm talking about right *now!*" snapped Warwick. "We can't talk here or at the mews in case we're interrupted, but there's a coffee place on Elizabeth Street where we could meet in fifteen minutes." Said as a statement: not a question.

*

"Let's not beat about the bush, Pete," said Warwick in a no-nonsense voice on eyeing Peter while taking a sip of his espresso. "You were totally correct when you said to me in the car that Mrs Horsfall would never agree to *you* having a dog living in the mews with you."

"Excuse me, it was you, sir, who wanted the old dog living in the mews with me and the Horsfalls. Not me!"

"Whatever. However, I've made up my mind and, as far as I'm concerned, whether Mrs Horsfall agreed nor not, Shep *will* be coming to stay. In other words, a sure-fire case of 'The cook is dead! Long live old Shep!"

Noting Peter's horrified expression, Warwick said cheerfully. "I wasn't suggesting we *kill* Mrs Horsfall. Pete, merely make sure she leaves, and you remain as king of the castle, as it were."

"Err ... and how do you propose to make sure the Horsfalls leave, sir? I take it we are talking about both for, if Mrs H goes, I'm sure Mr. H would leave as well."

"*What* a sharpie! Of course, Horsfall goes! As I just said, they both go whereas you, along with their replacements and Shep, stay."

"And how to you plan to make sure Mr. and Mrs H leave, *sir*?" asked Peter, a touch sarcastically.

"Easy-peasy. We all know Horsfall *dotes* on that vintage Vauxhall Viva of his. That ghastly blue and white effigy which I see as his substitute blow-up doll in preference to diddling Mrs H." Warwick gave a snicker. "God only knows what the car's back seat must look like having subjected to endless emissions from Horsfall's much wanked horse brass!"

"If you say so, sir," replied Peter. Eyeing Warwick for several seconds he said brusquely. "I wish you luck, *sir*. While you obviously see me as nothing more than the hired help, and what's more, hired help to do your every bidding, you are seriously mistaken as *this* hired help has just unhired himself. I shall hand in my notice to your father, *sir*, on my return the house. As for you, *sir*, you can go fuck yourself as I'm pretty damn sure, nobody else will."

Not giving Warwick a chance to respond, Peter rose to his feet, tossed a crumpled a £10 note onto the table and said with a sneer. "To cover my coffee, *sir*," before walking out.

"So basic," murmured Warwick watching as Peter stood aside to allow two gossiping women to enter. "As I said to the ghastly Giles Gordon, the last time he told *me* to fuck off. 'You're *such* a peasant, Gordon. Why not, for once, try to emulate the superior me and say *puck*, instead of the uber-common fuck. In other words, see *fuck* as barred. Pun most definitely intended!"

LATER

Warwick sat up in bed with a start. "Bloody hell! How could I?" he said to the darkened room. "How could I even *think* about kidnapping Shep when he's so obviously adored by old Harry, and vice versa! Shame on you, Warwick Laudanum-Standton! Shame on you!"

Turning on the bedside lamp, he tossed aside the duvet (red), hefted himself from the bed and shuffled through to his desk. "I *know* I have the old boy's number somewhere so let's have a looksee. Once I've found it, I'll give him a call first thing."

2

"Harry, good morning, it's Warwick Laudanum-Standton speaking. I'm quite sure me calling you comes as a surprise, but I need to talk to you about Shep. Yes, Shep, your fabulous pooch. Any chance of you being in London over the next couple of days? What was what? Oh, you're coming up to town tomorrow to see *Les Misérables*? That's brilliant! Is there a chance I could meet you before the show? Say that again? The Salisbury in St. Martin's Lane at around five? Double brilliant! Yes, Harry, I *know* it's a pub and thank you for the chuckled 'it's child friendly'. I'll see you there!"

"The Salisbury?" muttered Warwick putting down the phone. "But isn't the Salisbury basically *gay*? Jesus! How stupid of me not to realise old Harry is gay seeing he shares a cottage - ha! - in the school grounds with another old geezer: obviously the other adult. Well, well, well, this could complicate matters, but let's wait and see what happens."

THE SALISBURY - A POPULAR VICTORIAN PUB - ST. MARTIN'S LANE

"Hi, Harry!" crooned Warwick, looking decidedly more a young sixteen than thirteen in a tweed jacket and cords, on spotting Harry seated at a table with a distinguished looking, silver-haired Stewart Granger lookalike.

"Good evening, Master Warwick..." said Harry, a grey-headed Woody Allen lookalike, rising from his seat to greet Warwick.

"Warwick, Harry! Warwick! We're not at school here and now!" interrupted Warwick with a mischievous grin.

"Good evening, *Warwick*," echoed Harry with a chuckle. "This is my friend, Christopher Wren, No relation! Haha!"

"Good evening, Christopher," said Warwick shaking hands with the seated man. "I see you're both drinking pints so let me order the same again for you while I make do with a Coke, *despite* the grown-up garb as one can never be too sure!"

"No, please allow me," rumbled Christopher, in a deep bass voice, rising from his seat. "I won't be a sec."

On being told by Harry that Christopher was a "chef extraordinaire", Warwick gave out an exalted cry of "Bingo!" followed by an equally exalted "Q.E.D!" causing both men to give a jump.

Turning to face a startled Harry, he said excitedly. "Harry, in your long, varied career, have you, by any chance, ever worked as a butler before?"

"Yes, Warwick. I have. In fact, I was butler to Sir Desmond and Lady Denning of Didcottle for nigh on ten years."

"Double Bingo!" cried Warwick. "Because it just so happens my delightful Mother Dearest may well be looking for a new cook *and* a butler. The present cook and her butler husband live in a nearby mews house which, like the main house, has a garden; the garden to the main house is vast and, should you ever consider the position, would be idea for you two and Shep!" Ignoring the two men's startled expressions, he added excitedly. "At present, Pete, the chauffeur whom you briefly met the other day, has a room in the mews house, but he shouldn't be a problem." Warwick gave a snort. "If he is, I am sure we can face that little bridge when we come to it."

"Sounds good to me," chuckled Harry. "Christopher?"

"Sounds *very good* to me," rumbled Christopher. "Particularly as my present employers are definitely more second class than first class in the quality stakes."

"You said that that your . . . err . . . dearest mother . . . *may* be looking for a new cook, Warwick," said Harry. "Why only may be?"

"I obviously misled you there, Harry. What I should have said was *perhaps* my Mother Dearest could be *made* to look for a new cook and appendage butler."

"Care to explain?" This from Christopher.

"If I - we - could arrange for Mother Dearest to get rid of the two of them, then it would be a problem solved, wouldn't it?"

"Get rid of them both?" replied Christopher with a sardonic chuckle. "Am I hearing a suggestion of foul play here?"

"Yes and no," said Warwick smugly. "I don't know if it helps but Horsfall's pride and joy is a blue and white vintage Vauxhall Viva so, maybe a *puncture* of sorts to his pride and joy could result in him going into a decline of such extremes that his performance as our butler is no longer acceptable and Mother Dearest decides he has to go; meaning Mrs Horsfall goes too!"

"Calculating young man. Aren't you?" chuckled Christopher. "And before you take that as a criticism, it's not." Taking a swallow of his lager, he added thoughtfully. "Where exactly does Horsfall garage his pride and joy. This love of his life?"

"It's parked, usually under a tarpaulin, outside the mews house. I know he's spoken to Father Dearest about parking it in the garage attached to the mews house but there simply isn't room thanks to *his* Roller and Mother Dearest's Mercedes. Hence geriatric Mr. Vauxhall Viva having to slum it on the cobblestones outside."

"A *blue* and white coloured vintage car, you said," murmured Christopher. "Leave it to me."

*

Several mornings later a distraught Horsfall staggered into the kitchen of the main house to inform Mrs Horsfall that, having removed the tarpaulin to give his beloved car a loving polish, he found it to have been totally vandalised.

"Totally vandalised?" questioned a delighted Warwick who, by chance, was eating breakfast in the breakfast nook when Horsfall staggered in.

"The fuckers not only *gouged* the paintwork, they slashed all the seats, smeared what was left of the seats with dog shit and, on top of all that, removed part of the fucking engine!"

Clutching his tearful face in a parody of Edvard Munch's *The Scream*, Horsfall fell sobbing to his knees. "I don't believe it!" he wailed. "Not my beloved Viva! What will I do without her? What will I do?"

Take to drink, for one, thought Warwick giving the distraught man a derisive look. *On checking you out, Christopher was intrigued to discover you were a member of Alcoholics Anonymous which means, with luck, you'll be turning to Madam Bottle again to help you cope with your shock and disbelief. Once Madam Bottle is back in the fold as the most comforting of companions, it shouldn't take long before your standard of work slips to such a low that Mother Dearest has no alternative but to give you your marching orders; meaning wifey goes too! So, welcome Christopher, Harry, and Shep. As for Pete the Treat? Who knows? Only time will tell.*

*

As predicted, an exuberant Warwick gleefully telephoned Christopher to inform him that a "deliciously drunken Humphrey" had not only stumbled and dropped a tray of entrees at Mother Dearest's latest dinner party but gone on to douse one of the guests, the questionably titled Baroness Griselda von Schloss with a decanter of Napa Valley Merlot. As might be expected, the furious so-called Baroness and her lover, a spotty young Frenchman known only as Metre, did not stay for the remainder of the repast.

Warwick ended the call saying, "and despite Father Dearest saying the poor man should be given another chance, Mother Dearest said no. On hearing that the Horsfalls were no longer wanted on the voyage, Mother Dearest was delighted to be told by the loveable *moi* that Pete the Treat had come up the *your* name - having been suitably compensated for his role in the plot - and, as you were thinking of a change from his position as chef to Russian billionaire Timor Tretchikoff and his arm candy missus, the former Miss Something-or-other, should I get Pete to get you to ring her. Mother Dearest replied, a touch emotionally. 'Darling Warwick! A knight in shining armour!' So, without any further delay, do you have a pen and pad handy?"

"Not only handy, but poised and ready," chuckled Christopher.

*

Two weeks later a jubilant Harry and Christopher, accompanied by a tail wagging Shep moved into the mews house. A month later Peter, having rapidly morphed from Pete the Treat into Pete the Not so Sweet, moved out.

As Warwick confided in Shep. "Silly Pete no longer a treat having idiotically implied to a disinterested Mother Dearest that Mr. Horsfall's spectacular dive from the sober board was all her angelic son's doing and, surprise, surprise, found himself promptly dismissed. Give it a few years and then sweet, innocent Warwick, unaided and unabetted, will make sure Pete the now Obsolete learns, to his extremely painful cost that, in the end you *do* reap what you sow!"

*

"A question, Harry, how old is Shep?" asked Warwick.

"Despite being referred to as *old* Shep and despite him looking the part, I got him as a pup some five years ago which would make him in canine years somewhere in his late thirties I suppose."

"Late thirties?" chortled Warwick. "Gosh! He looks double that!"

"Hence me referring to him as *old* Shep," chuckled Harry. "I don't have to tell you that being here with me and Christopher in the mews with *two* gardens of his own, old Shep is in doggy heaven."

"You really love Christopher, don't you?"

"Yes, I do, Master Warwick," replied Harry warily. "So much so, that we're about to make our relationship official."

"You mean you guys are getting *married*?" exclaimed Warwick. His face breaking onto a grin.

"Yes, we are, Master Warwick," replied Harry, a touch sheepishly.

"It's *Warwick,* Harry; master being a thing of the past. Please stop from making me always having remind you!"

"Sorry, Warwick. In fact, we are getting married this coming Friday and would be honoured if you would care to be a witness at the official ceremony."

"Honoured, Harry? I'll not only he honoured but flattered and *proud* to be there as a witness. I take it I will be sharing the honour with Shep?"

"But of course, Warwick! Who else?"

*

To his surprise Warwick found himself delighted with Father Dearest's "local school".

The pupils are a fifty-fifty mix of boys and girls," he told Harry and Christopher. "And, despite some of their almost impossible to understand accents, the majority are great."

"Hopefully they say the same thing about you," snickered Harry. "An almost impossible to understand accent but great."

"Careful, Harry: careful," said Warwick crisply. "Anymore comments like that and you'll be back to addressing me as Master Warwick!" Noting Harry's shocked expression, he gave a light laugh. "Joke, Harry! Joke! I promise you I was only joking! Look at old Shep over there. If he ever thought I was being serious he would have been up in err . . . barks, instead of snoring away."

Warwick took a sip of coffee. "Getting back to the school, there are two pupils in my class whom I really seem to have clicked with. A rather fab girl named Tally McGuire, and a boy named Lance Sandson. In fact, I've invited them around for tea next week." He gave a snicker. "That's the second shocked expression to invade your usual tranquil visage within a matter of minutes, Harry. Have no fear as I have already described to them, in lurid detail, what to expect on meeting Mother Dearest. No, and before you ask, I did *not* say they would be meeting another Miss Havisham, I suggested a Lily Munster instead. As for Harold, our butler? A veritable double for Grandpa Munster; aka Count Sam Dracula!"

Once the laughter had died down, Christopher, tactfully changing the subject said, matter-of-factly. "Being curious, Warwick, what are your plans - if any - once you've completed your schooling?"

"A bit of travelling; *Bella Italia,* the Land of Machiavelli for starters and then perhaps the Land of poor Cio-Cio-San and all those sexy Samurai! Then, after all that culture, maybe Drama school! What else?" chortled Warwick. "I can already see myself accepting endless Oscars!" He gave a snigger. "And I don't mean of the *Wildean* sort! Haha!"

"Touché! Warwick!" chuckled Christopher. "So, an actor then?"

"See it as a permanently *resting* actor who will be making use of a substantial inheritance Grandma Dearest left me. So, as I just said, a resting actor with other far more interesting roles on his palette. Nota bene I said *palette* instead of plate seeing plate sounds a touch mundane."

"Whatever you say, Warwick," replied Christopher. "Another question, as questions appear to be the call of the day. How would you describe me and Harry?"

"Easy-peasy!" chortled Warwick. "If anyone asked, I'd describe you and Harry as Chester Square's answer to Freddie and Stewart in that old TV sitcom, *Vicious*!"

*

"I found your mother - or Mother Dearest as you kept on calling her - quite fab," giggled Tally (full name Tallulah, Edith, Ella McGuire, her mother being a devoted fan of mesdames Bankhead, Piaf, and Fitzgerald). "As for Harold your butler, I always thought people like that only appeared in films!"

"Like Tally, I found it all great," enthused Lance (full name Lancelot Arthur Sandson). The name Lancelot leading to endless teasing at school. "As for your house and your private sanctuary; unbelievable!" He glanced round approvingly round Colbert where the three were having an "after your visit" coffee of Coca-Cola. "As is this place!"

"*I* like it and that's why I suggested we come here in case the two of you needed somewhere to recover after meeting Mother Dearest," chortled Warwick. "But Lance, getting back to you, tell me more about what that creep

Norman Livingston said to you outside class the other morning as you seemed pretty upset."

"Oh, it was nothing really," replied Lance, a Ned Sheran lookalike, his face reddening. "Just something about someone like me probably enjoying being lanced-a-lot." Feeling an explanation was necessary, he added softly. "Livingston keeps telling everyone I'm gay."

"Are you?" asked Warwick, causing the two to stare at him as if he had asked Lance to undress there and then.

Catching their expressions, Warwick said hastily. "What I mean is, who cares? I think I could be gay but then I don't know. I mean I find Tally err . . . spot on, but then I find you, Lance, spot on as well!"

"Maybe you're bisexual," said Tally knowingly.

"Maybe I am," said Warwick nonchalantly. "Tell you what, if you're game, how about we try it out with one another and, if I find out I prefer doing it with Tally instead of you, Lance, we'd still be friends, wouldn't we?"

"Yes, of course," replied Lance with a snigger. "However, Tally and me, have already done it, just as I did it with Mikey Watson. Being honest, Warwick, I like you a lot but when it comes to a boy or a girl, Tally wins by a mile."

"Great," chortled Warwick. "So, as I won't be trying it with either of you, how will I know whether I'm gay or not?"

"Only one way to find out," said Tally all business. "I'll introduce you my friend Olivia's brother Henry. He's one hundred percent gay, so let me set it up."

"You do that," chortled Warwick. "Now, getting back to Norman Livingston: the guy needs to be taught a lesson. A lesson he won't evert forget and, if you're game, how about we do this?"

*

A week later a distraught Norman Livingston staggered into the Emergency Department of a local hospital after what the police described as a "nasty, but not unusual mugging". However, as one of the doctors on duty said to a colleague. "Some strange bloody mugging if it *was* a mugging. I mean, why the fuck cut of one of his ears and then carve the letter H on his forehead?"

"A bit of 'ear, 'ear, 'Enry perhaps?" said another doctor, causing the three to burst out laughing.

*

"We make a good team, don't we?" commented Warwick as the three sat in Dracula's Den having coffee while discussing the success of Livingston's "lesson for keeps". "So, anyone else being an arsehole?"

"No, nobody at the moment," pondered Tally. Glancing at Lance, she said with a giggle. "No! I sit corrected. How about that dreadful Isobel Parr?"

"You mean the arrogant, bloated cow who imagines she's another JK Rowling in the making?" snorted Lance.

"Yes! Her!"

"Another JK Rowling in the making? Tell me more," said Warwick.

Tally gave a brief description of the disliked Miss Parr. "She not only sees herself as another JK Rowling, she also sees herself as the ultimate disco queen and can be found dancing the night away in some dive. A place called Gadzooks being a firm favourite for showing off her dance floor capabilities!"

"After what you've told me, it shouldn't be a problem to ensure the unlovable Miss Parr becomes a touch more unlovable," snorted Warwick. "How about this for a *novel* that'll teach you?"

*

Three weeks later, Isobel Parr and several others suffered terrifying, disfiguring burns when some lunatic decided to toss a bottle of acid over the dancers enjoying themselves in Gadzooks, a popular nightclub. It was later reported that Miss Isobel Parr, a journalist, has lost the sight in her right eye along with severe damage to her right hand.

Six weeks later it was reported that the "brave" Miss Parr was considering devoting herself to carrying out good works in some remote, war-torn country.

"From wannabe bestselling author to a wannabe Mother Theresa," tittered Tally. "What next? A moon landing?"

"Any misgivings or feelings of guilt?" asked Warwick.

"No, not one iota," replied Tally firmly.

"Nor me," said Lance. Leaning over he gave Warwick a playful punch on the shoulder. "All I can say is that meeting you. Warwick Laudanum-Standton is the greatest thing since sliced bread!"

"Oh, good one, Lancelot! Is that because I use my loaf?"

3

PRESENT DAY

THE STUDY - A LAVISH DUPLEX PENTHOUSE - CHELSEA HARBOUR

"Wow! Just listen to this young Vincent," crooned Warwick looking at Shep's successor, a perky Jack Russell terrier. "A text from Tally and Lance wishing me a happy hatch day! Pucking cheek having decided to ditch me in lieu of potential marital bliss and with only two notches on our combined belts. Namely the odious Norman Livingston and so-called bestseller wannabe, florid, horrid Isobel Parr."

Giving a disinterested Vincent a quizzical look, Warwick gave a sniff. "Jesus, Vincent! If you insist of emphasising your lack of interest, at least have the courtesy of doing so via a growl as opposed to s silent, stinky snoopy!"

Warwick picked up his glass of early morning vitamin C (vodka and freshly squeezed orange juice) and crossed over to the vast, plate glass window overlooking one of several terraces and The Thames. Glancing at the spectacular view he said with a sigh. "Pity those two came to the rapid conclusion that producing a couple of uber-spoilt sprogs was preferable to the production of further mutilations: but such is life. And *what* a life!"

He gave a chuckle. "Here I am with a fabulous, multi-million-pound duplex penthouse, the star feature in endless design glossies, a fabulous Mercedes sports, and a wardrobe that would make even GQ magazine turn green, all thanks to Great Aunt Gertrude Dearest. Added to which there's also doting Aunt Clementine still treading water in sinking Venice whose admirable assets I'm also looking forward to coming my merry way.

"She used to adore my visits when I was still a sprog. Her *piccolo putti Perfetto* she always called me and, thanks to my almost religious, caring phone calls and the occasional surprise, flying visit, I am quite sure there is another suitable inheritance waiting in the wings. Or, dare I say it, *water wings*. However, this doesn't mean that the divine Warwick is a happy soul because after the adrenalin rush following our enhancements to Livingston and Parr, if the truth be known; the pampered, dilettante Warwick is b-o-r-e-d with a capital, neon-lit B!

"Okay, okay. I did manage to do another tribute to Vincent van G when in Venice, plus two *almost* suicides - or hara-kiri as they call it in Japan - where instead of disembowelling my two Tokyo triumphs, I simply gouged out the words *I AM FULL OF SHIT* across their forehead and chests instead!"

"Talking to oneself is one of the first signs they say," said a deep voice from the doorway. "And from the heady stench of *Aroma Vincente* doing its best to destroy the last vestiges of oxygen in the study it looks as if Vincent agrees with me,"

"Ah! The Incredible Bulk in all his Turnbull & Asser glory! Good morning, oh Mighty Schlong! Snore well?"

"Apart from having to earn my daily and nightly bread, your Incredible Bulk snored like a crashed out newborn bundle of joy," chuckled Kurt Cameron, a giant, blond Chase Hoyt lookalike. He nodded to where Vincent now stood eyeing him, his tail wagging. "Please don't tell me this lazy bugger has made you humiliate yourself with a make do poo on one of the extravagantly tiled terraces simply because he was too lazy to escort you downstairs and the pristine lawns just waiting to be desecrated by your delightful deposits?"

"If you *must* know, this ever-thoughtful, delicious yours truly of yours has already taken that Janus of a hound downstairs as well as witness him desecrating Bert, the porter's pride and joy, pacified Bert and brought him back, so his plea for another chance to upset Bert should be taken with a pinch of tarragon!"

"Did you hear that, Vincent?" said Kurt, stopping to give the adoring pooch a pat. "So, best you stop with the expectant looks, However, your devoted Bulk *will* take you for a walk, but only after he and your other daddy have had breakfast."

As if he had been waiting in the wings Christopher appeared in the doorway and announced cheerfully. "When you're ready, gentlemen, so is breakfast!"

Greeting Christopher with a cheerful "How're the stretch marks this morning, Christopher!" Warwick and Kurt sat down in the jungle-inspired breakfast nook and tucked into a handsome breakfast of poached eggs, kedgeree, toast, marmalade and freshly ground coffee.

"Tell me, Christopher," said Warwick between chews, "any luck in tracing those two names I gave you? That Giles Gordon and Roger Lincoln; two former school friends of mine?"

"I did indeed, sir. Giles Gordon is still at university studying law . . ."

"God! *Still*?"

"Well, it is a fairly lengthy course, sir."

"Of course. Haha! Anything on Lincoln?"

"Now working with a firm of architects with offices no more than a stone's throw from here, sir."

"Goodness!" chortled Warwick thinking. *And guess who's about to cast a very unpleasant first but not the last stone.* "I take it you have the name of this architectural firm?"

"Naturally sir. I'll have Harry leave all the details on your desk."

GLAZEBRROK & CROZIER - ARCHITECTS

"Glazebrook and Crozier, good morning," said a chirpy voice. "How may I help you?"

"Good morning," replied Warwick silkily. "Is it possible for me to speak with Mr. Roger Lincoln, please?"

"Of course, sir. Mr. Lincoln's about to go into a meeting but let me see if I can catch him before he does. May I ask who's calling?"

"Mr. Jumbo: like the elephant," said Warwick solemnly. "Plus, it's local and not a *trunk* call."

"Err . . . right, Mr. Jumbo, would you please hold on while I see if I can put you through."

There was a brief silence during which the receptionist must have told Lincoln about the strange Mr. Jumbo on hold, followed by a rasped. "Good morning, Mr. Jumbo. Roger Lincoln. You wished to speak to me."

"Yes, I did, Mr. Lincoln," said Warwick giving Vincent a thumbs-up. "I'll get straight to the point. Having viewed several of your organisation's splendid buildings now adding a touch of Manhattan to The Thames, particular your very own noteworthy Retorta Tower, I recently purchased an old property in Wapping and would like to talk to you about creating a similar structure there. I'm very much my own man, Mr. Lincoln, which means it's my money and mine alone: money I am more than willing to entrust to Glazebrook and Crozier on the condition they have you, and only you, in charge of the project from start to finish.

"What I'd like to propose is that you and I have an initial 'getting to know each other meeting' -nobody else at first - and take it from there. Before you ask, we're talking about a substantial invest me here, Mr. Lincoln: Millions in fact. Interested?"

"Of course I'm interested Mr. Jumbo! I'd be an idiot if I said I wasn't!"

"Good, Mr. Lincoln, good. If you are free tomorrow morning, let my secretary make the necessary arrangements with your secretary, for me to collect you tomorrow. Armed with enthusiasm and a thermos or two of coffee along with celebratory libation we can view the site and literally toss ideas about. Shall we say ten o'clock sharp." Presented as a statement, not a question.

*

"Another of your Greta Garbo moments?" quipped Kurt. "Or maybe another of those clandestine 'the love that dares to speak its name' meetings in some secluded spot. Not that *I* care!"

"Absolutely," chortled Warwick. "A rip-roaring gang bang in the hallowed sanctuary of Piccadilly Circus, no less, where only Vincent and a few dozen others are allowed to tread!"

*

"I appreciate it's a touch unfair to ask you, Christopher, but have you any idea as to what young Warwick *does* get up to on these mysterious away days and night, never mind the endless mysterious meetings at" - Kurt made several finger quotes - "an address or addresses unknown."

"No, Kurt. Harry and I have no idea, no idea at all. We've known Warwick for ten years or slightly more thanks to a loveable old pooch called Shep who sadly was run over by a drunken driver who - lucky for him - Warwick was never able to trace despite a manhunt of unbelievable proportions. What we *do* know is that Warwick owns a very elaborate houseboat moored somewhere in Little Venice. But where exactly remains a mystery and we feel it best that the houseboat remains just that: a mystery."

"Yes, he vaguely mentioned it to me." Kurt gave a chuckle. "You guys make it sound almost like a typical Agatha Christie-type murder, mystery novel but light on the murder, I trust. Christ is that the time?" he added, glancing at his watch. "Look, I'll catch you later."

What Kurt did not tell the two unassuming oldsters was that he was not only fully aware of what Warwick was up to, but an integral part of all taking place.

THE NEXT MORNING

"Nice wheels, Mr. Jumbo," grinned Roger Lincoln, a smug Daniel Craig lookalike admiringly sliding onto the passenger seat of the gleaming Mercedes sports after the two young men had introduced themselves.

"I like it," replied Warwick with a self-satisfied smirk. "I find it an ideal little runabout whereas the Roller is more suitable for what I describe as huff and puff occasions. Haha!"

"Err . . . right," muttered Roger. "Now, would you like me to enter the site details into your sat nav or will you?"

"Later, Mr. Lincoln -or may I call you Roger and you, me Walt?"

"Of course, Walt!" chuckled Roger. Staring at Warwick he said curiously. "You know something Walt, I am sure we've met before?"

"I don't think so, Roger," chortled Warwick sporting a black wig, a moustache, goatee and horn-rim specs for the occasion. He gave a snort. "I've obviously got one of those seen here, there and everywhere faces! Haha!"

"You said later, Walt?" said Roger as Warwick proceeded down King's Road. "What did you mean by that?"

"Oh, before we have a look at the site. I need to drop by a houseboat I have moored at Little Venice; my 'away from it all' bolthole where I keep details of my various projects. There are plans and sketches of a building I own in Cape Town. South Africa, I'd like to show you as I feel this is what I'd like you to recreate in Wapping despite Wapping not having a Table Mountain! Haha!"

"Err . . . sounds good to me," murmured Roger. *Why the fuck you couldn't have collected any plans or sketches prior to our meeting today and save us a bloody scenic trip to Little Venice defies all reason: but with that* ridiculous tash and goatee what would one expect. As for that irritating laugh ... but then, think of the money, honey!

"Here we are," crooned Warwick drawing to a halt alongside the leafy canal. "That's One Star, my hideaway houseboat over there. Haha!"

"One Star?" sniggered Roger and he and Warwick got out of the car. "All I can tell you, Walt, it looks more of a *five star* than a one! What the fuck?" he added as a hooded figure suddenly materialised next to Warwick and struck him soundly on the head with a cosh, causing him to crumple to his knees.

"Now you, arsehole," grunted the man before belting a frozen Roger across the face breaking his nose and knocking him unconscious. Stooping down the man quicky hacked off the remnants of Roger's nose. Tossing the bits into the canal he reached for the keys in Warwick's limp hand, snapped his lower arm and without as so much as a backward glance at the two unconscious figures, calmly climbed into the Mercedes and drove off. Heading toward a friend's scrapyard he used a burner phone to report the mugging to the local police: then tossed the phone into the canal à la Roger Lincoln's former nose.

LATER

"Jesus, Kurt! That was meant to be a *stage* effect knock on the head! Not the real McCoy!" chortled Warwick. "As for this pucking plaster cast - six to eight pucking weeks they tell me! But, my dear Kurt, it was worth it!"

"It sure was," rumbled Kurt. "As for your arm, I made sure it was a clean break, so I'd say four to six." He gave a chuckle. "There was a nasty moment when I had to think twice as to which hand you used for wanking!"

"That deserves a zillion puck offs; if not more!" chortled Warwick. "Now, how about we get Harry to bring in a bottle of fizz to celebrate Roger Lincoln's nostril-*damus*! Haha!"

"Good one! Warwick! Look! Even Vincent agrees! And before you ask, good old reliable Jess Rix assures me the revamped Merc will be on its way to Spain first thing tomorrow and what we agreed, fee wise, into one of my offshore accounts pronto so nobody, but nobody, can ever trace this back to you! And not only that but there will also be the insurance due to the car being stolen along with endless sympathy for poor you on being so brutally mugged!"

"Only fly in the KY is that *my* money is in one *your* offshore accounts which means I can never get rid of you!" tittered Warwick.

"Fear not, Warwick, dear," rumbled Kurt. "Remember the tale of *Beauty and The Beast.* Maybe, if I stick around long enough, I may even turn into a handsome prince!"

"There are fairy stories and stories about fairy bears," giggled Warwick, "so maybe I too will stick around for as long as a certain Kurt Cameron remains a furry, fairy bear, he's prince enough for *moi*! Despite him having a split personality."

"Split personality?" echoed Kurt.

"Well, according to dear to the dearly disfigured and obviously confused Mr. Lincoln he told the police there were two of you who attacked us! Hence you being seen as a split personality! Rather like those two holes in his face, a challenge to any plastic surgeon worth his plastic. Geddit?"

"I geddit!"

"Good, Now, go and get on your glad rags as we need to go shopping for a new car! Maybe a Lamborghini?" Warwick gave a chuckle. "I still can't get over Lincoln's secretary when I rang to say how sorry I was about Lincoln being attacked and her casual, 'Oh, he'll be alright Mr. Jumbo! But what about poor you. Hit on the head and your arm broken. One doesn't know what the world's coming to!' Obviously, there's no love lost there!"

4

A LAVISH DUPLEX PENTHOUSE - CHELSEA HARBOUR

"You know what we need," murmured Warwick snuggling up against Kurt's massive chest.

"Not another energetic, sweaty screw, I trust?" rumbled Kurt. "Seeing your Incredible Bulk - all thanks to a very demanding, young Mr. Standton - is well and truly knackered."

"No, that is something I'll eagerly anticipate," said Warwick with a giggle. "What we really need is another female mutilator: another Tally McGuire. To misquote Mae West. 'A good woman mutilator is hard to find!'"

"So, not a *Rose* West but a Mae," murmured Kurt giving Warwick a gentle kiss on his tousled head.

"Definitely a Mae with the telling mantra it's not the mutilators in my life, but the life in my mutilators," snickered Warwick.

"Well, my delightful, twisted friend I may well have the perfect answer to the much missed and lamented Tally," rumbled Kurt. "A longstanding friend of mine, a decidedly exotic lady and a stripper to boot. Stage name Delilah Divoon! Divoon as is in *Lorna Doone!*"

"A stripper named Delilah Divoon?" exclaimed Warwick sitting bolt upright. "I love her already! Tell me more?"

"Me and Delilah - correct name Daisy Metcalf - were at school together. Delilah - then Daisy - even at that early age were great movie buffs." Kurt gave a soft chuckle. "I will never forget how completely bedazzled, zonked and completely overwhelmed she was on seeing the film classic *Gypsy* starring Rosalind Russell and Natalie Wood. 'That's me,' whispered Daisy when Natalie was doing her stuff. That's what I'm going to be: a strip tease artiste like no other'."

Kurt gave a snort. "I didn't take her seriously until a few years later when I was invited by a friend to join him and a few others to see the latest stripper sensation, Delilah Divoon, at a popular nightclub they frequented. And there she was, Daisy Metcalf à la Deliah Divoon!"

"Very touching Kurt, but how does that help us with finding another Tally McGuire?"

"Help? I can assure you, Warwick, little Daisy went through hell at school because of her over large boobs and her height, the poor girl being almost as tall as I am. To top - ha - it all, she also had a slight squint which saw having to wear large remedial glasses, leading to certain insensitive little shits calling g her Four Eyes and Four Tits to her face. In between frequent, tearful conversations with a comforting me, she kept saying that one day she would make sure certain pupils would pay for their cruel taunts. So, why don't we see if she would like to help us make those dreams come true?"

"You have her number?"

"Of course."

"Then let's invite her to lunch today or whenever she can. As soon as she confirms, if it's today or another, I'll ask Christopher to whip up his special *bombe surprise* to go with the *bombe surprise* we offer her!"

*

"From the sounds coming from the entry lobby I do believe your answer to Gypsy Rose Leigh has arrived," said Warwick, "or else Harry is *so* overwhelmed by Miss Divoon he's now talking castrato!"

"God! Talk about *Architectural Digest* meets *House Beautiful*!" crooned Delilah Divoon, a statuesque young Sophia Loren lookalike swathed in furs as she swept into the sitting room followed by a star struck Harry. Spinning on her stiletto heels she added with a banshee-like cry. "*Darling* Kurt! Just look at you! The Jolly Green Giant would go lemon *curdle* if he saw you! As for the *scrumptious* young man next to you I take it he can only be the mysterious Mr. Warwick Laudanum-Standton."

"Correct, Miss Divoon, and welcome," said Warwick taking hold of Divoon's gloved hand, "and how generous of you to accept my invitation at such short notice."

"Oh, darling! Given the chance to come I jump to any sort of notice," replied Delilah deadpan. Glancing toward the main seating area she said curiously. "Tell me, darling, are those sofas *floating*?"

"Yes, in a way, thanks to their mirrored plinths or bases," chortled Warwick. "But please perch on one as I can assure you will *not* float away! Meanwhile, a welcome drink. Champagne, a martini or something else? You name it and Harry will produce it!"

"Ooh, champers, please," crooned Delilah making herself comfortable on one of the sofas. Glancing round the elegant room she said animatedly. "I spy with my mascaraed eye a painting which looks as I could only be by the magnificent Senor Joan Miró. Is that *really* by the great man himself?"

"Yes, Miss Divoon."

"Delilah, *per-lease*!"

"Yes, Delilah, and that wonderful splash of colour over there is a genuine Sandra Blow."

"Oh, I simply *love* Blow jobs!" quipped Delilah. "And *that* painting over there. Tretchikoff perhaps?"

"Yes, a bona fide Valdimir Tretchikoff."

"My, what a wonderful eclectic collection of artworks you appear to have Warwick - I take it I can call you Warwick as Mr. Sleeping Draught standing sounds such a mouthful, even for an expert such as I!"

"As long as its Warwick and never worrywart, that's fine," giggled Warwick, "I'd be delighted.

Settling himself on a sofa opposite he murmured a "Thank you, Harry," on reaching for a martini from a proffered tray and adding in a stage whisper: "Did *your* Mother Dearest never tell you it's rude to stare?"

"He's gorgeous, isn't he?" cooed Delilah as a red-faced Harry literally withdrew.

"Wait until you meet his other half, Christopher, the chef," rumbled Kurt. "He's equally as err . . . gifted!"

"So, tell me?" said Deliah having taken a sip of champagne, "how did the likes of you two, Mr. Chalk and Mr. Cheese meet? Somewhere suitably aboveboard I trust and not some sleazy bar."

"We met while browsing through the contents for an upcoming sale at Christies," said Kurt with a grin. "I was looking at some fore-edge paintings when I couldn't help but notice this handsome young man studying some framed manuscripts. We got talking; Warwick invited me for a drink where, discussing our likes and dislikes, we ended up talking about what I've already told you, Delilah dear, what we'd like to talk to *you* about. Retribution."

"Please tell me *this* could be my lucky day," said Delilah with a cat that got the cream look, "and, better still, the start of many more. Now, if the gorgeous Harry could top us up and before we gorge ourselves on what I am sure will be a delicious lunch, why don't you, Warwick, fully spill the Heinz, and nothing but the Heinz, no holds barred, and tell me how I may be able to not only help, but add several of my own irons in this intriguing fire?"

"Right, and without any more beating around the rhododendrons, and a recalling of both your schooldays," replied Warwick with a tight smile, "are there any pupils, boy or girl, who caused you grief, leading to a hidden itch - desire sounds a touch theatrical - that could only be satisfyingly scratched by subjecting him or her to an ongoing HH - namely a hideous happening?"

"HH? Hideous happening?" echoed Delilah.

"Something disfiguring and therefore a recurring reminder," said Warwick blandly.

"Goodness, Warwick," replied Delilah with a throaty laugh, "you're talking about a serious line-up here." Glancing at Kurt she said with a sinister smile. "Tell me, Kurty Baby (*Kurty Baby?* thought Warwick with an inward chuckle. *That's definitely a first!*), wouldn't you agree that first in line could only be that odious Mark Sikes, now a banker wanker based in Brighton?"

"Mark 'my cock's bigger than anyone else's' Sikes!" guffawed Kurt. "How could anyone forget him and that marked - ha! - measuring tape he carried round so as to prove his point! Talk about a cocky bastard!"

"Fine, I get the point," snickered Warwick reaching for his Mont Blanc pen and a notepad on the coffee table in front of him. "Now, two more names, please, as all good things come in threes."

"Cherry Leighton," purred Delilah.

"God yes! Cheralina Leighton or the Cherry who always wanted to be on top!" grinned Kurt. "According to all those who had the misfortune to bed her, it was more a case of Cherry the almighty flop!"

"Your turn, Kurt. A name, *s'il vous plait.*"

"Brian bloody Harkin," snorted Kurt. "Now a master tailor based in Mount Street or Savile Row, or knowing his predilections, *Jimmy* Savile Row!

Haha! Added to which he has a tongue that would give even the most vitriolic poison pen an inferiority complex."

"That, Kurt Cameron, was quite dreadful," tittered Delilah. "So, there you are, Warwick. Mark Sikes, Cherry Leighton, and Brian Harkin."

"Great, and I will get started on making a list of their likes and dislikes and their toing and froing immediately after lunch," said Kurt.

"You do that while I get into Machiavellian mode and think up some terrifying HH for each of the chosen three. Ah! Harry! I take it lunch in now being served?"

"Yes sir, your electric chairs await you," said Harry in a sonorous voice from where he stood in the doorway.

*

"So," said Warwick sat in the lower terrace enjoying their after-lunch digestifs, Delilah a crème de menthe while Warwick and Kurt each settled for a Courvoisier. "If we're going to become s trio of bona fide serial mutilators I feel it vital we should have a theme. Something not too obvious but something we three appreciate." He gave a chuckle. "Something some bright spark among the boys in blue could eventually put together."

Warwick focussed his attention on Delilah. "How squeamish are you, Delilah dear?"

"Squeamish?" echoed Delilah. "Darling, I'm about as squeamish as a gall stone!"

"And you, Kurt?"

"About as squeamish as the Rosetta stone," grunted Kurt. "Why?"

"Right, and which do you prefer, Chinese or Japanese?"

"If you're talking food, definitely Chinese," said Delilah. "But if you're talking about booze. Then I'm a one hundred percent sake slut!"

"Me too," rumbled Kurt, "*sans* the slut!"

"Brilliant! Because what I suggest is that we follow that old, tried and true, Japanese saying; see no evil, hear no evil and speak no evil; and on extra special occasions, a combination of all three."

"Love it!" crooned Delilah.

"Touché," rumbled Kurt. "So, who's going to be the unlucky winner in our first draw?"

"Why don't we, literally, pull the unlucky winner out of the proverbial hat. In other words, out of that decorative conch shell next to the ornamental lily pond. Here," Warwick reached for an always available note pad and pen, "let me tear a couple of pages into strips and then print your three suggestions along with a couple of my own: shake, rattle and roll them in the shell and then you, Delilah as politeness *always* insists on a stripper doing the honours. Take your pick."

Closing her heavily mascaraed eyes Delilah delved into the hastily procured and filled shell and gave the contents a brisk shuffle before pulling out a piece of folded paper. Opening her eyes, she unfolded the paper, stared at the printed name and said with a mischievous grin. "Oho! Cheralina pie, talk about an eye for an eye!"

"Fab, Delilah! Fab!" chortled Warwick. "And as it's almost November which means November the fifth, Guy Fawkes Day, why not a well-aimed rocket into a Cherry Leighton eye socket!"

"Bags I light the rocket!" yodelled Delilah.

"Not only will you *light* the rocket, Miss Delilah Divoon, you'll be the one to *hold* the lighted rocket right in front of Miss Cheralina's eye socket! A sure-fire example of an eye burning bright!"

"Tut-tut, Warwick," replied Delilah with an admonishing shake of a gold and red striped nail. "I can tell by your expression that was meant as a joke. And I agree with you. But how on *earth* could I - or anyone else for that matter - possibly aim a rocket a rocket at Miss Flat-as-a-Pancake's wretched eye?"

"Easy-peasy," chortled Warwick. "There are *endless* words beginning with e-y-e. Words such as eyelid, eyebrows, eyelashes, eyesore..."

"Which bloody Cheralina Leighton most certainly is!" cackled Delilah.

"And what about eyelet," said Warwick. "Just think of what eyelets are involved with."

"And what exactly *are* eyelets involved with?" asked Kurt, feeling it time for him to add to the conversation."

"If someone was a touch dyslexic or simply bad at spelling, they could be forgiven for spelling eyelet inlet," said Warwick knowingly. "Think about it?"

"Genius!" exclaimed Delilah. "Cheralina Leighton owns a bijou bungalow overlooking an inlet near to a popular seaside resort down south ...I can't remember where exactly."

"Hence me mentioning it," said Warwick smugly, "seeing I too have mentally crossed swords with Madam Leighton in my glorious past."

"So, now we have an inlet as opposed to an eyelet, how does that help us?"

"How about we do this," replied Warwick with a snicker.

*

Cheralina aka Cherry Leighton, a buxom Jessica Rabbit lookalike gave a wide, inelegant yawn, stretched, pulled on a Bonsoir robe and slid her feet into a pair of fluffy slippers before shuffling through to the small cosy kitchen overlooking the small bay sparkling in the early morning sunshine. Stifling a further yawn, she reached into a cupboard for a jar of instant coffee and laconically added three spoonsful into a mug labelled, *I'm The Greatest.*

Patting the small pile of £10 notes on the *faux* oak counter, she said with a smirk. "Not bad, though I must say Mr. Gent, or whoever he was, didn't seem too keen to stay for seconds. No doubt my expertise and wild contortions were too much for him."

"I somehow disagree with you," growled a voice from behind her. "If truth be told, he couldn't be bothered with a further attempt to inflate a deflated mattrass."

"What?" gasped Cherry on spinning round and coming face to face with a large figure wearing a Pluto mask. "Who the fuck are you?" Grabbing a knife from a nearby knife block she said as firmly as she could. "One step nearer and I'll damn well gut you!"

"Gut me, Cheralina?" growled Pluto. "Can't you see I'm a dog: not a fish, A friendly dog who's here to deliver a simple message: an eye for an eye."

Before Cherry respond, Pluto gave a bark and disappeared.

Without any hesitation, Cherry reached for the kitchen wall phone and dialled 999. Not giving the person responding a chance to enquire the type of emergency Cherry said with a shriek. "Help! I've just been threatened by Pluto!"

*

The next day a man taking his dog for an early morning walk came across the unconscious Cherry wearing pyjamas and her Bonsoir robe, an odd-looking necklace of sorts, her feet neatly bound in blood-soaked bandages, lying on the beach below the bungalow.

On further examination it was discovered both her big toes had been amputated: the two missing toes being attached via a pair of fishhooks threaded through a pair of eyelets on the black leather bondage style necklace around her neck.

All Cherry could remember was going to bed as usual and being wakened on the beach below by the startled dog walker. Her hysterical reference back to Pluto appearing in her kitchen the previous day and threatening her, leaving her and the police even more baffled than before.

*

"More an eyelet for a hallux than an eye for an eye," chortled Warwick on informing Delilah of Kurt's Oscar-winning performances as an avenging Pluto. "Or even a case of toeing the line. The great thing is that when Miss Leighton remembers the heady days of Louboutin heels and sexy, strappy Jimmy Choo sandals she will *not* be a happy wannabee bunny! Okay, she's still got her feet, but feet that will never be seen again for a fetishist footloose and fancy free and more than willing to pay an eye-watering toe-sucking fee!"

5

A PRIVATE PRACTICE - SLOANE STREET

"All I can remember is his bloody voice," said Dick McCausland staring defiantly as Dr Eric Warren, the psychiatrist he was seeing. "The police kept on asking me the same question, and still do whenever I demand an update into their *supposedly* ongoing search for the sick bastard who did this to me. And no, I didn't see anyone since I was attacked from behind.

"As I repeatedly keep telling you and the police is that I will never forget the man's voice, a *soothing,* velvety voice and the word baby and the name Vincent. And that's *all* I can remember. But I tell you this, Eric, if ever the police do get hold of the bastard who did this to me, I trust he'll be put away for the rest of his sick, miserable life. Better still, is that once his fellow prisoners learn of the reason why he's there, they'll do to him what I am unable to do myself!"

A LAVISH DUPLEX PENTHOUSE - CHELSEA HARBOUR

"So," said Warwick popping a wedge of mango into his mouth, "now we've had Cheralina Leighton for starters, who shall we have as the unlucky main course for our delicious mutilator banquet?"

"I'd like to suggest Brian bloody Harkin," grunted Kurt as he sat lathering a piece of toast with Fortnum and Mason's best chilli and tomato jam. "Unless you have a preference for Mark Sikes."

"No, I'm more than happy to give your Brian Harkin an unforgettable jolt or two," replied Warwick, slipping Vincent a piece of croissant. "Delilah's had her choice so now it's only fair that her Kurty Baby has *his* turn."

"I do wish you'd stop this Kurty Baby shit," grunted Kurt. His sharp, unexpected comeback causing Warwick to raise a sardonic eyebrow.

"Stop this Kurty Baby shit?" he repeated. "Goodness! So, big, bad Kurt Cameron, aka the Incredible Bulk, *does* have an Achilles heel? Well, I never!"

Warwick raised his right hand and said deadpan. "I hereby swear I, Warwick Laudanum-Standton, will never refer to Mr. Kurt Cameron as Kurty Baby ever again. So, help me, whoever happens to be eavesdropping."

"Very funny, Warwick," rumbled Kurt. "I'm sure you mean well. Back to Harkin. Any ideas?"

"We know he's a tailor so it positively *screams* that a stitch in time will be part of his decorative finish so let's talk about that. And when I say let's, I mean let *us*, that's the two of us, you, me and no Delilah."

"Why no Delilah?" retorted Kurt, "when your very words a few days ago were 'who needs another Tally now we have Delilah!'"

"I'm well aware of what I say or may have said, Kurt, but that doesn't necessarily mean that she must be included in all our forays. Added to which, she'll be away in Las Vegas for the next two months wowing them with her Hindenburg tits!" Warwick gave a snort. "Hopefully they won't burst into flames."

"Not funny, Warwick," said Kurt through gritted teeth. "Not funny at all."

"Oops! Naughty me and my wicked sense of tumour," said Warwick sarcastically. "However, let's - that word again - face facts, it's now only you and *moi*." (Warwick's use of *moi* becoming more prevalent in his every day speech.)

"I have to agree with you there, Warwick," grunted Kurt, "but please, my friend, no more cracks about me and Delilah, and no more second thoughts about her."

"Your wishes are my command, *Bulk*," snickered Warwick. "However, I can't help recalling an old Tom Jones hit. *Why, why, why Delilah*! Perhaps you should *hum* that to your grumpy self when not having a go at the hand that wanks and feeds you! But, before you decide to self-combust, this is what I suggest we do when tinkering with our master tailor."

As before, Kurt could not help but be impressed by Warwick's inventiveness.

THE MAIN PENTHOUSE TERRACE - LATER

"I have to tell you, Vincent, I am not at all happy about Kurty Baby's wavery," murmured Warwick giving Vincent's perked ears a gentle tweaking. "Talk about a veritable rewrite of Samson and Delilah; a rewrite in which it won't be Samson's hair the dubious Delilah could be cutting, but his throat as well. Therefore, my loyal, little friend, let her go and twiddle her torso in Vegas but, on her return, it'll be *our* turn: yours and mine, my magnificent, miniature Baskerville!"

Taking a decisive sip of his mid-morning martini, Warwick said to the blissful pooch. "I also ponder/wonder, and yet, for the life of me cannot understand what Kurty Baby - I love that! - Christopher and Harry get up to on those lengthy shopping sprees that appear to occur on an almost daily and not a weekly basis."

Giving Vincent's ears a further tweaking, he added softly. "You know what, Vincent, the more I think about it - them - the more I like the words 'one man and his dog'. What's more, I *know*, just know I was wrong to woo the likes of Kurt, Christopher and Harry. In fact, the more I ponder/wonder and think about it them, I realise just how pucking wrong I was!" Warwick drained the rest of his martini, plonked the glass down on the McGuire table and said to a startled Vincent. "Right! Enough of my prevaricating! In other words. time for you and me to go walkies so, how about a stroll along vibrant King's Road with all its tantalising smells sound to you? Was that a 'yes' waggle I saw? Yes, a definite yes waggle. Give me a moment while I don a pair of Signor Gucci's buckled best, grab a jacket, keys and wallet and then off we go!"

*

Warwick and Vincent were waiting patiently outside Waterstones for a break in the traffic before daring to dash across busy King's Road when Warwick noticed a sleek Jaguar saloon drawing to a halt and the barely visible driver gesturing to him to cross. Before Warwick and Vincent had reached the other side, the Jaguar sped away.

"I could be wrong, Vinnie, but I am sure that the driver of yon sleek automobile was none other than the former Pete the Treat! Or Janus the Anus, if ever there was. I'd quite forgotten about him. C'mon, let's cross the road again and head for Finns on Chelsea Green where I can have a coffee and you a delightful bowl of H2O. We then make it our vital business to find out where Janus the Anus now works and where he lives. In other words, *this* man and his debonair dog make sure the former Pete the Treat, now Janus the Anus, becomes an arsehole supremo obsolete!"

*

Back at the penthouse Warwick said to Vincent busy with a doggy treat. "Thank you, Ares, ancient Greek god of war, for the likes of Facebook and Linkedin. Within minutes I found the correct Mr. Stiles and current girlfriend, a pouting Barbie wannabe named Melody. *Melody*, for God's sake! More of a *discordant* melody from the looks of her. What's more, Janus the Anus now has his own chauffeuring business named Travel with *Stile* no less. Trust him to use such an obvious pun. Right, Vincent, time to don our magical thinking caps and see what we can come up with to make sure Mr. Travel with Stile never forgets his last journey!"

THREE DAYS LATER

"Travel with Stile, Melody speaking," cooed Melody Young on answering the telephone. "We're here to help you travel in style and arrive with a smile!"

"Good morning," replied Warwick giving Vincent a thumbs-up. "The name's Cotton, Charles Cotton, and I'd like to book a car for this evening. To be collected from The Waterway, Formosa Street, Little Venice and drop me off at The Criterion Theatre, Piccadilly. As I'll be dining at Le Caprice I'll ring from there when I require a lift back to Little Venice."

As requested, Warwick gave a card and mobile number (both false). "If you would prefer cash. I'm more than happy to pay in *feelthy* lucre," chortled Warwick.

"Cash and a card are both acceptable," replied Melody prissily.

Get you, thought Warwick. "I take it there is a Mr. Stile or Stiles with a I or a Y? If so, it would be a pleasure to be driven by him in person and, as I have just moved to London, open an account in anticipation of many more journeys with Travel with Stile."

"There is a Mr. Stiles and a Mr. Knight," replied Melody, "and I will do my best to see that Mr. Stiles is your driver."

"Thank you, Melody, and as I plan many future visits in style, why not begin with the big man himself. I look forward to meeting Mr. Stiles at six-thirty."

THE WATERWAY - LITTLE VENICE

"Mr. Cotton?" asked Peter on approaching the only solitary figure sitting near the entrance to the busy pub. "Peter Stiles, Travel with Stile."

"Aha! The stylish Mr. Stiles himself" quipped a suitably disguised Warwick. "And what's more, bang on time! I like that!"

Settling himself on the back seat of the sleek Jaguar saloon, Warwick suddenly let out a hissed "Damn!"

"Err . . . something not to your liking, sir?" enquired Peter staring at Warwick in the rear-view mirror.

"Would you believe it, just remembered I left the theatre tickets on the console in the hallway so that I wouldn't forget them which is exactly what I've gone and done. I'm currently renting a flat in the next street along so if you wouldn't mind, take the next left ahead and wait for me while I run in and collect them."

Telling Peter to stop outside one of the terraced houses, Warwick quickly leaned forward and deftly plunged a syringe into his neck. "*Puck*!" he added as Peter fell forward against the steering wheel, followed by a blaring of the horn, "Double puck!" grunted Warwick as he grabbed Peter by the shoulders, lifted him from the steering wheel and threw him onto the passenger seat. With a quick glance at the empty street, Warwick hastily moved from the back of the car and into the driver's seat, slipped the car into drive and continued sedately along the canal to where One Star was moored.

Hefting Peter's unconscious weight onto his shoulders, Warwick cautiously made his way onto the houseboat and let himself into the main cabin where, with a sigh of relief, he dumped Peter down on the dining-cum-operating table.

"Now, what shall we do to him in order to make sure it upsets him daily," said Warwick to Vincent, who had been left on board with a chewy bone while waiting for his master to return. "Do we do another Roger Lincoln nose job or a Dick McCausland cock job?" He gave a snigger. "Better still, why not both! And remember, Vincent, not a growl or a bark to Christopher, Harry or Kurty Baby - oh how I enjoy referring to him as that behind his delicious, brawny back - about me, and me alone, taking the smile out of the promised style with an I. *Capiche*? Good. So, with another doggy treat for you and without any further ado, let the mutilating begin!"

Minutes later Warwick's eyes darted from part of Peter's nose and former penis lying in a surgical dish, back to his bleeding face and lower torso. "Not bad, Bubba," he muttered with a grin. Turning to where Vincent sat looking at him expectantly, Warwick said with a chuckle. "You may look at me with those soulful eyes, Vinnie *non amour,* but his is one bone-r you are *not* having!"

*

Two hours later a wild-eyed woman ran screaming into the A & E unit of a local hospital having stumbled across a bleeding, unconscious Peter lying on a nearby pavement.

On coming round all Peter was able to remember was collecting a Mr. Cotton from The Waterway and nothing more. On being told of his injuries, he began screaming and had to be heavily sedated for several days before finally coming to terms with his fate.

As for his car, this was never found all thanks to the ever-reliable Jess, a wad of £50 notes guaranteeing his well-practised: "What sort of car did you say? No, mate. Haven't had one of those in here for yonks."

A LAVISH DUPLEX PENTHOUSE - CHELSEA HARBOUR

"Despite Delilah being away we two can still play, and I'm not talking about beddy-byes play, but mutilation play," said Warwick as he and Kurt sat on the main terrace enjoying one of Christopher's special cocktails, while Vincent lay happily chewing on a "cocktail" bone.

"Hmm," he added, smacking lips. "Christopher's delicious tribute to the late Nikita Khrushchev, a mix of vodka, champagne, Campari and a dash of raspberry cordial certainly tastes yummy. He really *is* a clever chef-cum-mixologist, wouldn't you agree. Kurty, big boy?"

Warwick gave a giggle. "Got you there, didn't I? Bet you thought I was about to say the banned other!"

"Forget Christopher's tribute to President Khruschev and see what you think when you taste *my* tribute to former Chairman Mao! An atomic mix of sake, Jing liqueur, champagne with a dash of angostura which will make your toenails curl!" replied Kurt with a grin.

"Curled toenails," echoed Warwick camply. "Imagine what Mr. Gunja, my podiatrist would have to say about *that* picturesque little anomaly! But, forgetting Mr. Gunja, here's what I suggest we do with your Mr. Harkin.

Forgetting the innuendo regarding him and *Savile* Row. A severe *tinkering* with your gossipy tailor should do the trick and give him something to think about in the least fashionable way,

"Jesus," muttered Kurt, "did nobody ever tell you a pun is the lowest form of humour."

"So *that's* how you see me," pouted Warwick, "nothing more than a low form of humour. Tumour, I could accept but humour? Never!"

"You know damn well what I meant," rumbled Kurt, "so without any further unnecessary campy-wampy shit, simply tell me what you have in mind for Mr. Tinker, Savile Row Tailor Harkin."

"I take it you know where Mr. Harkin resides and whether there is a husband or a blinkered Mrs Harkin?"

"He has a house near Parsons Green and there is a definite Mrs Harkin with a playboy or two scattered in dubious bedsits around London."

"A house near Parsons Green. How very comforting should he ever feel it necessary to beg forgiveness for his many dalliances away from the unsuspecting Mrs Harkin." Warwick gave a chortle. "Lucky for Mr. Tinkering Tailor Harkin, what I have in mind for his self-appointed remembrance service doesn't require him being deposited at the nearest A & E seeing a panicky call from Wifey Dearest should do the trick."

CHIDDINGSTONE STREET - PARSONS GREEN

Whistling cheerfully, Brian Harkin, a plump, immaculately dressed Norman Hartnell lookalike, stepped out from his gleaming Lexus, automatically locked the vehicle and walked the few steps leading to the front door of the red brick terrace house when he felt a sudden sharp sting in his fleshy neck before blacking out.

*

"Was that a thump I heard against the front door," muttered Freda Harkin, a sour-faced Hilda Ogden lookalike. "I'll *brain* that lazy Alfie! Why he can't simply leave the *Evening Standard* and the day's *Metro* on the doorstep, I'll never know!"

Hoisting herself from her favoured armchair, Freda walked briskly toward the front door and pulled it open. Expecting to find flapping copies of the two newspapers, she found the unconscious, crumpled figure of her husband leaning against the door jamb and bleeding profusely from his lips which had been crudely stitched together.

*

"Poor bastard not only had his lips sewn together but, on removing the stitches, we discovered that all his lower teeth had been pulled out! And when I say *all*, I mean the whole bloody shebang! Trust me," added the doctor in charge, "whoever did this to Mr. Harkin - that's the poor bugger's name - must have had one helluva grudge against him. A past misdemeanour perhaps?"

6

SOUTH DOME CAFÉ - CHELSEA HARBOUR

"Darling, 'tis *moi*, taking a well-deserved break in between twirling and stripping." Deliliah gave a gurgling laugh. "Those lecherous old geriatrics who flock to see my show may not be able to get it up, but God, can they drool! No doubt all those poor cleaners have to literally mop up gallons of the stuff after each of my mouth-watering - ha! - performances!"

"Just what I expected to hear you say," chuckled Kurt.

"And how are things with you, Kurty? (Kurt flinched, waiting for the "Baby" which, thankfully, was not forthcoming.) And how goes it with the warring Warwick:"

"Okay so far with Cheralina Leighton and Brian Harkin licking their eternal egos and wounds. Next on the list is Mark Sikes with the great exposé of how we deal with him taking place in approximately an hour and a half's time on my return to the penthouse."

"Where are you now?"

"Having a comforting coffee or two in the Dome café away from it all." Kurt took a deep breath before saying sonorously. "As per usual I have no idea as to what's going on in that slurry pit mind of Warwick's, but you should know that at this current point of time Delilah Divoon is *not* the flavour of the month."

"Me? Why for God's sake?"

"I don't know why, Delilah, but he specifically asked me - no, make that *instructed* me - not to tell you what we did with Harkin. I expect he'll do the same when it comes to Sikes."

"But why?" repeated a confused Delilah.

"As I said, I have no idea, Delilah, but rest assured that if push comes to shove, it will be the two of *us* doing the pushing and the shoving and *not* the unpredictable Mr. Laudanum-Standton."

A LAVISH DUPLEX PENTHOUSE - CHELSEA HARBOUR

"Regarding Mark Sikes, I've been thinking," said Warwick taking a sip of his martini. "Remember the nursey rhyme *Sing a Song of Sixpence* and the bit, *The king was in his counting-house counting out his money*? Well, how about we change that to Mark Sikes in *his* counting-house *unable* to count his money?"

"Meaning?" asked Kurt.

"Meaning we cut off all his eight fingers leaving just his thumbs making it something of a hindrance when he tries to count those elusive bank notes!"

Warwick took a further sip and said with a chuckle. "Sikes resides in some splendour in one of those mansions lining Melbury Road in Kensington. He's currently divorced but there is a chance the latest bit of fluff could be about and even is she is, who cares about a bit of muff fluff. So, my bulky friend, how about we do a bit of pruning this very night. Better we give those much-fondled bank notes a rest rather than allowing him to keep kinkily fondling them; wouldn't you agree?" He gave a snicker. "Not that you've any choice."

"You literally took the words out of my mouth, Warwick, *dear*," said Kurt brusquely.

"And not only your words, Kurt, *dear*, thinking back," replied Warwick foxily. "So, with morning blow jobs firmly back on the back burner, this is what I suggest we do with Mark Sikes, Esquire. We'll need a pair of secateurs for the finger and willy pruning along with a suitable marked ruler. Once the secateurs have done what all good secateurs do, then it'll be a another sneaky to the nearest A & E."

Giving Vincent's ears a gentle fondle, Warwick said in a suitably sloppy voice. "And *this* time Vincent joins us where he will be treated to a never-before-tasted-finger instead of his usual doggy chew! Will he, or won't he? That *is* the question!"

LATER

"Mr. Sikes?" quavered Warwick, resplendent in a grey wig, pince-nez, a voluminous raincoat and carrying a battered pet carrier, as a scowling Mark Sikes opened the front door.

"Yes, and you are?"

"The name's Harbinger, sir. Henry Harbinger, and I'm doing a house to house on the off chance someone may have seen my missing Muffy: my pet cat."

"Seen your missing Muffy?" snorted Sikes, a sinister Christopher Lee lookalike. "No, Mr. Harbinger, I haven't seen your missing Muffy and somehow have no wish to, either. Now, if you'll excuse me as I'm in the middle of watching a documentary . . ." He gave a sharp, startled cry as the bland Mr. Harbinger stuck a syringe in his neck; the syringe having been hidden in the left sleeve of his voluminous coat.

"Out like Elton's *Candle in the Wind*," snickered Warwick, "so come along Kurt, no need to skulk in the shadows, and help me get Mr. Sikes back into the kitchen."

"Is the bird here?"

"Not that I'm aware of. And as you insisted on wearing that ridiculous Pluto mask *again*, if she *is* about, simply knock her out so that we can get on with what needs to be done."

Two hours later an unconscious Mark Sikes's roughly bandaged, bleeding body was discovered lying near to the entrance of the local A & E department.

On being examined by one of the doctors it was discovered that all eight fingers had been amputated at the knuckle leaving only thumbs intact. On further examination the doctor was horrified to find part of his penis had been removed and what was left had been attached to a marked ruler by an elastic band.

On regaining consciousness and being tactfully informed of his injuries, Mark Sikes went into shock.

THE NEXT MORNING

"Happy birthday, Kurty *Bulky*," carolled Warwick as Kurt joined him and Vincent on the sunny terrace for breakfast. He pointed to a gold wrapped box sporting a large purple satin bow placed next to Kurt's place setting. "A small something from Vincent *et moi* to whet your appetite before I lead you through to study for a further whetting! All after your special birthday breakfast, of course!"

He turned to where Harry stood with a fixed smile on his face. "Harry, Mr. Kurt's birthday breakfast, if you please, but not until he's opened his little teaser of a present."

"What on earth can this be?" chuckled Kurt untying the purple ribbon and removing the wrapping. Gently taking hold of the top book of three, he carefully examined the first before looking up at Warwick, his rugged face breaking into a huge smile.

"A fore-edge painting? And not one, but *three*? Oh, my dear, dear Warwick, this is more than splendid; it's out of this world!"

"Well," purred Warwick, "not only are they a reminder of when we first met, but also a reminder of the best thing that's ever happened to me. I know of your unfulfilled interest in fore-edge paintings so, hopefully, these three will spur you into action to start a collection of your own, aided and abetted by *moi* and, of course, Vincent. "

He glanced to where Harry had reappeared pushing a hostess trolley. "As its your birthday, and a day where you deserve to be ridiculously pampered, today's breakfast is caviar served with boiled quail eggs and crème fraiche, accompanied by endless mimosas and blown kisses!"

Breakfast concluded, a grinning Warwick took Kurt by the hand and led him through to the study.

"If you ever saw them, you may have wondered what those two workmen were doing here the other day," chortled Warwick. "Well, take a look."

Kurt stood gazing round the study with a questioning frown. "Bookshelves," he said without hesitation. "There, next to the window. A new set of shelves with a smattering of expensive looking books."

"Bull's-eye!" chortled Warwick. "Now, check out the *smattering* of books."

Striding over io have a closer look, Kurt pulled out one of the leather-bound volumes from a shelf and gave it a cursory look before saying in a choked voice. "*Another* fabulous fore-edge painting," before examining the other leather-bound books. "Jesus, Warwick, a total collection of fore-edge paintings! Thank you, my darling. Thank you!"

"Now it's entirely up to you to continue adding to *your* amazing collection," said Warwick smugly, "so, don't let your collection down."

LATER

"I still can't quite believe your amazing present, Warwick, dearest," whispered Kurt as the two sat in the study having a cocktail before Christopher's special birthday dinner. "And I know it must sound boring to you having to hear me say it yet again but you, Warwick Laudanum-Standton, are one helluva guy and a guy who never fails to amaze me!"

"Likewise, Kurty *Bulk,* likewise," said Warwick smoothly. "After a splendid dinner to round off your birthday celebrations and the beginning of your new avocation . . ."

"God, I'd forgotten about Christopher's birthday dinner," grinned Kurt cutting in and patting his rigid six-pack. "My poor figure!"

"Yes, in a single day you've gone from Superman to Michelin Man," snorted Warwick, "and as your celebrations are about to go into hiding for another year, maybe we can get to your charming other half's avocation: namely his merry mutilations."

Looking as if Warwick had suddenly upped and slapped him, Kurt said sharply. "From that more snide than subtle reproach, I take it you already have a candidate in mind?"

"I have indeed," replied Warwick smugly. "Inspired by what we did with Mark Sikes and especially that witty addition of a *marked* before and after ruler it should be embarrassingly obvious to all and sundry who's next on my Mikado!"

"Your Mikado?"

"Think Koko in The Mikado who has little list," snickered Warwick.

"Of course," muttered Kurt. "How stupid of me."

"The sight of a *marked* ruler attached to Mark's somewhat reduced proboscis must have certainly got those mediocre medical minds whirring," tittered Warwick. "Which means next on *my* little list can only be the bogus Baroness Griselda von Schloss's Metre. A *metre* we will reduce to mere centimetres!"

"And where does this randy Baroness have her castle?" ask Kurt with a grin.

"Her castle," replied Warwick making finger quotes, "is a basement flat - *excusez moi* - a *garden* flat in Cadogan Gardens, so I think a different *Midnight in the Garden of Good and Evil* is the call of the day; midnight being a tad awkward."

"Jesus! Warwick! Yet another of your mindless references or ridiculous riddles. What *exactly* do you mean by bloody *Midnight in the Garden of Good and Evil?*"

"Being a literary phenomenon, I'm referring to John Berendt's deliciously nasty novel which was also made into a film starring the racy Kevin Spacey. However, forgetting my expansive brain, attempting to snatch him from there would be far too public, but I've been told by super sleuth Harry that the Baroness's daily divining rod religiously jogs along The Embankment every morning at six a.m. in preparation for another day of diddling the ghastly Griselda, no doubt. So, that's where we'll grab him before taking him across to One Star."

"One Star?" questioned Kurt.

"The proper name of my somewhat lavish houseboat moored near to where you so gently dealt with Roger Lincoln prior to his subtle enhancements and where you took great delight in coshing me and breaking my arm," replied Warwick deadpan.

"I assume this is another typical Warwick Laudanum-Standton wind-up," said Kurt equally deadpan. "Seeing I haven't the remotest idea what you're talking about."

"Touché, Kurty *Bulky*. Just like you never, ever, realised One Star, belonged to *moi.*" tittered Warwick. "However, a bit of caring Warwick advice. The next time you rent a clandestine car, don't pay for it with one of our joint credit cards as your wily Warwick always checks the revelatory statements. Now, no further talk about Monsieur About-to-be Mutilated Metre until the morrow and let's talk about *The Accident,* that gripping series on Netflix instead! What a conundrum!"

Bloody Hell, Warwick, nothing, but nothing escapes those deadly antennae of yours, thought Kurt. *Just as one will never, ever, know what you're really thinking.*

*

Later, on checking his messages, Kurt was delighted to hear a message from Delilah. Her message being a breathy rendition of *Happy Birthday to You* à la Marilyn Monroe when she sang the song to President J.F. Kennedy at his forty-fifth birthday celebration at Madison Square Garden in 1962. The song followed by a series of blown kisses and a breathy, "Love you, Kurty Baby. Call me when you can."

Glancing at his Rolex Kurt made a quick calculation. "It's eleven here so it's three on the afternoon over there. Hopefully she'll be able to take my call."

"Darling!" crooned Delilah on answering. "How does it feel to be twenty-one again?"

"It feels great despite the glamorous Delilah Divoon not being here to help me celebrate the inevitable milestone," chuckled Kurt. "But then beggars, even *aged* ones, can't always be choosers! How about you and how's the drool pool?"

"The ever-expanding drool pool could give the Hoover Dam a run for its money but, apart from that, things couldn't be better. And you?"

"Me? Well, with Warwick being even more waspish than usual, doing my best to keep my handsome head above water," replied Kurt with an audible sigh.

"Even *more* waspish?" echoed Delilah, "And here was innocent me thinking miracles only happened in Cecil B. DeMille movies. Care to explain?"

"My fault, really. Silly idiot I am having inadvertently used one of our dual credit cards when renting a car a few weeks ago."

"What were you doing renting a car when you have the use of a Mercedes or that other car?"

"I do, but I wanted to be anonymous - ha - seeing I've been curious as to what other little jollies Warwick's been getting up on these never discussed jaunts. Mysterious little jaunts which have nothing to with our usual, meticulously planned manoeuvres. So, I decided to do something underhand and tail him, all to no avail. Hence the screw-up with the cards."

"Did you find out anything exciting? A secret lover or another *House of Wax* in tribute to Warwick's Vincent and Hollywood's Mr. Horror, Vincent Price?"

"Apart from the fact that he must own that whacking great houseboat moored in Little Venice he never stops visiting; nothing else." Kurt gave a hollow chuckle. "Apparently, I will have the great privilege on being allowed on board tomorrow when we will be dealing with the latest of his ongoing mutilations. Some French guy named Metre."

"As in parking metre?"

"No, more as in length," chuckled Kurt.

"Say no more," giggled Delilah. There was a moment's pause before she added tentatively. "Any further news about you popping over to Vegas for a few days *sans* waspish Warwick?"

"Yes, there is!" exclaimed Kurt. "God, forgive me. I should have told you before I started rabbiting on about a mix-up with bloody credit cards etcetera." He gave a chuckle. "So, as some form of an apology, is there a chance that a lady of your calibre would be free to have dinner with lowly me after your show on Saturday?"

7

CADOGAN GARDENS - CHELSEA

Inhaling the cool morning air, Metre Gallois, clad in a dark blue track suit with matching trainers, set off on his daily run from Cadogan Gardens, through Sloane Square and along Lower Sloane Street before reaching his main goal: the Chelsea Embankment. Here he veered to the right and began pounding his way toward Chelsea Harbour, oblivious to the dark blue BMW tourer (courtesy of the always reliable Jess) trailing him.

"Oi! Mister!" called the front passenger from his side window. "Can you tell me if we're on the right road for The Chelsea Harbour Hotel, please?"

"Just continue straight ahead," panted Metre, running on the spot, "and when to reach the bend, take a left. You'll then see three large glass domes - that's the Design Centre - and the hotel is next to it." He gave the smiling man a grin. "As I'm headed that way for my usual restorative coffee prior to jogging back home, let me hop into the back of your car and I can take you to the door."

"There *must* be a God," muttered Warwick who was driving. "Tell him we'd de delighted to give him a lift."

THE NEXT MORNING - THE SOUTH DOME - CHELSEA HARBOUR DESIGN CENTRE

The piercing screams of one of the women cleaners reverberated through The South Dome as Doxie Moss almost tripped over a crudely bandaged Metre lying unconscious next to the service counter in the spacious coffee bar.

On being rushed to the nearby Chelsea and Westminster Hospital, the drugged and dopey Metre was able to give his name and address before the doctors gave him their full attention. Within half-an-hour a distraught Griselda von Schloss arrived at the hospital. On finally being allowed to see the dozy Metre and unaware of his exact injuries, she went into an angry tirade of: "See what happens when you disappear to God knows where not only for a day, but for the whole wretched night as well!" followed by a shrieked. "Who *is* she? Who is this mysterious bitch I know, just know, you've been seeing behind my back!"

"Madam, please," the doctor began, but was cut short by Griselda's imperious. "It's Baroness if you're addressing me."

"Right Baroness, Mrs or whatever," snapped the doctor physically taking her aside. "I strongly suggest you remain silent while I explain the gentleman's unfortunate injuries to you."

"Injuries? What injuries?" shrilled Griselda. "I was under the impression he'd been beaten up by his whore's other half!"

In clipped tones the irate doctor, sparing no details, explained Metre's injuries to Griselda, namely part of his penis being cut off along with his two big toes.

If the doctor along with the nurses on duty had thought Griselda' earlier shrieks had been excessive, her second ranting and raving proved them to be a very poor second indeed.

"Bloody hell," muttered one Don, one of the bemused male nurses. "If she behaved like that *before* the poor bastard lost his dick, imagine how she'll be treating him now!"

"She won't," sniggered Ralph, another nurse. He nodded to where s calmed-down grim-faced Griselda was talking to the doctor and one of his colleagues. "You know who she is, or don't you?"

"A fucking harridan, if nothing else," replied Don.

"She's some so-called Baroness who is always in the gossip columns and that poor bastard lying over there is her lover; or should that now be *former* lover seeing he's no longer got what it takes! Haha!"

Eyeing Don, Ralph added slyly. "Maybe you should, if you can, get in there, Donny boy. Give it a go. Although what you have to offer wouldn't be nearly enough: even *after* lover boy's amputation!"

"Piss off, Ralph. I've had on complaints. Unlike some *other* medic I've heard about!"

A LAVISH DUPLEX PENTHOUSE - CANARY WHARF

"Jesus! Kurt! Give me a break!" snapped Warwick. "The whole point to leaving bloody Gallois - pun deliberate - lying in the South Dome was to ensure that the boys in blue wouldn't *dream* of seeing the perpetrator or perpetrators as local. Added to which, *all* our mutilated mishaps have been dropped off at various hospitals scattered across the city and nobody, not one single plod, has even *remotely* had the acumen to put two and two together."

"If you say so," muttered Kurt.

"I do say so!" retorted Warwick "And not only do I say so, it's because I also know I'm pucking right!"

Glowering at Warwick, Kurt cleared his throat before saying a touch apprehensively. "I take it you *do* remember that I'm off to Las Vegas tomorrow and will be in The States until Thursday?"

"Of *course* I remembered," pouted Warwick reaching for his martini. "It's in my diary in red ink. *Kurty Bulk in Vegas to see his Baby*. Plus, I also have a little prezzie from *moi* for you to give to the diaphanous Delilah.!

"You have?"

"Yes, Kurty *Bulk,* I have. A DVD of Cecil B. DeMille's epic *Samson and Delilah* starring Victor very Mature and Hedy hood-winky, kinky Lamar. Somewhat in keeping, don't you think?"

"As long as *she* doesn't suggest I pull down Temple Laudanum-Standton, I'd consider it most appropriate," replied Kirt a touch sarcastically. "Anything you'd like me to bring you back from The Sates?"

"Only yourself, Kurty *Bulky*, only yourself," replied Warwick with a faux smile. "Meanwhile, rest assured Vincent and I will miss you on an hourly basis."

"Likewise," grunted Kurt. "Now, I need to take Wallace and Gromit out on their usual shopping spree so, if you'll excuse me."

"You're excused, oh bulky one," tittered Warwick. "Have fun with Messrs. W and G and *don't* forget a couple of packets of biltong for his *very* particular lordship."

*

Armed with a mug of coffee, Warwick sat in the study reading the latest JD Kirk, when the landline rang.

"Elucidate," crooned Warwick on picking up.

"Err... Mr. Laudanum-Standton?" said a gruff, Cockney voice.

"You are blessed, my son," giggled Warwick on recognising the voice. "Jess, my friend, how are you and to what do I owe this *very* unexpected call?" He gave a chuckle. "Please don't tell me Kurt scratched, scraped or dented the BMW before returning it to you the other day!"

"No, Mr. Warwick, the car was in perfect nick," grunted Jess. There was a brief pause before Jess Rix said in a conspiratorial voice. "Please don't take this as me speaking out of turn, Mr. Warwick, but I do think a discreet word with Mr. Kurt about what he lets drop now and then wouldn't hurt."

"Let's drop?" questioned Warwick, alarm bells ringing. "What do you mean by let's drop?"

"As far as I am concerned, Mr. Warwick, you and I are both businessmen and what you do is strictly your business, so I don't think it right that Mr. Kurt should go round saying things like 'you wouldn't believe what your BMW witnessed, Jess,' or 'another trip to Spain thanks to a not too willing donor'."

"Mr. Cameron actually said those very words?"

"Yes, Mr. Warwick. Those are his very words. And not only to me but several of the mechanics I employ. I am sorry if I've upset you, sir, but I thought it best I let you know."

"No need to apologise, Jess, your concern and exceptional loyalty is much appreciated. Bye for now, and thanks again for calling."

*

"Pucking kumquats!" exploded Warwick causing a dozing Vincent to jump and give out a startled bark. Glaring at the pooch Warwick said apologetically. "Sorry about that, Vincent, but you obviously didn't hear what Jess Rix just said to me. Not only is bloody Kury traipsing off to pucking Vegas to see the dubious Delilah it now appears he's taken to dropping hints regarding my somewhat indelicate divertissements."

Eyeing the mug of cooling coffee, Warick said with a grunt. "Puck the coffee. Why not a white bear instead while I think about what Kurty Baby, Bulk or spiller of beans could be up to. The mere suggestion - even to a stalwart like Jess Rix - will never do! Kurt, however, appears to be morphing into more of a fantasy than the firm, reliable fixture I need to fully trust and love. Meaning I now *need* to have a further word with Jess Rix before Kurt and those two caricatures return from yet another magical mystery tour."

Reaching for his mobile next to the little-used landline, he tapped in the relevant number.

"Jess, it's Warwick Laudanum-Standton." Warwick gave a light-hearted chuckle. "I'm calling back because I have to say to say your earlier comments have got my grey cells doing a merry old gavotte. We need to meet ASAP. Mention a time and a place and place that's convenient for you and I will meet you there."

Warwick glanced at his vintage Cartier watch. "If you don't mind a latish lunch and you don't mind eating above the clouds, may I suggest the Aqua Shard as The Shard itself is near to your business premises."

"Err... sounds a bit grand for old Jess, Mr. Warwick."

"Nonsense Jess! Nothing's too grand for a friend of mine. However, if you could suggest a place you'd prefer, please do and we'll meet there."

"There's a good little pub near me which does what I consider to be the best steak and kidney pies in the whole of London, Mr. Warwick. We could meet there."

"It sounds great, Jess. Give me the name, address and a time and I'll see you there. I'm already reaching for my car keys!"

"Oh, and Mr. Warwick, the pub's dog friendly which means Vincent will be welcomed with a juicy bone!"

"It sounds as if your suggestion has already got our approval before even trying it out. We're on our way, Jess! We're on our way!"

*

Greeting Warwick on his arrival at the cosy Victorian pub, Jess said with a beaming smile. "I'm having a typical un-Shard like pint so, what can I get you, Mr. Warwick, along with Vincent's promised bone?"

"A glass of house white would be fine and Jess, skip the mister, would you please, seeing we're not here to play nice, we're here to play nasty. In other words, as comrades in *harms,* which means politeness is not the call of the day."

"Point taken... err... Warwick," grinned Jess, a hirsute, Bart Simpson lookalike. "Now, let me get you your wine and Vincent his bone and then we can settle down and have a serious talk."

Once Warwick had finished expressing his concerns about Kurt's "somewhat erratic and questionable behaviour", Jess said with a grin. "Having anticipated what was worrying you, err . . . Warwick, I took the liberty off inviting a young lad - young by my standards, that is - to join us for a drink and, if you approve, maybe for lunch as well. His name's David Pegg, but everyone calls him Pegg. A ruthless ally when needed and a total contrast to the great love in his life, his personal school for training guide or seeing-eye dogs. Aha! Speak of the devil for here he is."

Glancing at the approaching young man. Warwick did a double take. *Christ,* he thought, *Apart, from when I first set eyes on Kurt in Christie's I've never experienced such a similar jolt. Until now! God, it's Tatum O'Neil and Dwyane Johnson rolled into one giant denim-clad package!*

"Hi, Pegg!" called Jess rising to his feet. "Come and meet Warwick (he deliberately dropped the Laudanum-Standton) who I told you about."

"Hi, Warwick," grinned David Pegg. Proffering a large, hairless, manicured hand he added in a spine -tingling tenor voice. "Call me Pegg. Pleased to meet you."

"As I am to meet you," purred Warwick, his eyes out on their proverbial stalks as he drank in the smiling Adonis. "Err . . . can I get you a drink?"

"No, I can do that," interrupted Jess with a mischievous grin. "Dubonnet and Coke, isn't it, Pegg?"

"As always," replied Pegg with a whiter than white smile. "Along with a brandy chaser, of course!"

Within minutes Jess returned with the requested drink and vital chaser. Settling back in his chair, he took a sip of his pint and said matter-of-factly. "Okay . . . err . . . Warwick, fire away. We both know that you and Kurt have been handing out what *I* feel are best described as long lasting, painful reminders in compensation for various painful recollections from your own past. Pegg and me are here to listen, not to pass judgement, so feel free to explain, in detail, how we can help in stopping Kurt doing any further damage due to his ensuing indiscretions."

"In other words, the whole truth and nothing but," snickered Warwick in a weak attempt to make light of the situation.

"If you please, Warwick," said Pegg, dropping a hefty hand to give Vincent, blissfully chewing on a large bone, a gentle fondle. (Vincent's earlier decision to settle down next to Pegg's size 19 feet causing Warwick to hiss a not at all subtle "traitor!") "If we're going to be working together, that's how things should be. No beating about the bush."

Not even your bush, thought Warwick with an inward snicker, *Pity! Though, looking at you I wouldn't be at all surprised if every delicious square inch of you is shaven and shorn, including your pubes guarding, no doubt, a mind-boggling horn of plenty.*

Pegg gave a chuckle. "Something else you should know about me, Warwick, is that I can also read minds. Now, if *you* would care to reveal all." The latter said with a mischievous twitching of his sculpted lips.

LAS VEGAS - A MUCH SOUGHT AFTER NIGHTCLUB

"So, what did you think of my revamped little performance?" crooned Delilah on joining Kurt at his VIP table.

"Spectacular; in all senses of the word," chuckled Kurt. Glancing round at the well-dressed, appreciative diners who kept glancing in their direction, he added softly. "Are you okay having dinner here or would you prefer somewhere else away from all your admirers? Some place where the gentlemen don't keep on mentally trying to undress the now dressed you!"

Kurt nodded toward the stylish cocktail dress Delilah was wearing. "Fabulous little number, by the way."

"Divine Mr. Tom Ford. Not only do I love him, but thanks to Vegas I can also *afford* him," camped Delilah.

"Ouch, Delilah Divoon, that hurt! Surely a Las Vegas super star stripper can do better than that," chuckled Kurt reaching for her hand and giving it a gentle kiss.

"It all depends on which Mr. Ford we're talking about," purred Delilah. "Mr. Tom Ford the designer or my gorgeous new friend, Mr. *Joel* Ford who's about to join us."

Glancing over Kurt's shoulder Delilah added with a cry and a wave. "*Joel*! You made it after all, despite being on call!"

Kurt blinked in disbelief at the handsome young man heading for their table. *Bloody Hell,* he thought, almost knocking over his martini. *If ever Jude Law had a double, it could only be this beguiling Mr.* Joel *Ford! If there is a God, please, please allow hm to be gay and, better still, turned-on by gob-smacked bulks and hulks.*

To his delight Kurt would go on to discover not only was there a God, but an aiding and abetting God when it came to him and Joel seeing eye to eye.

8

LAS VEGAS - TEN DAYS LATER

"It'll be a sure-fire act of get *me* to a nunnery if the two of you don't stop telling me how wonderful either of you are!" crooned Delilah to a grinning Kurt. "As for 'alas poor *Warwick*' - my apologies to the proper Willy - we've already had the thunder and lightning when you announced you'd be staying in Vegas for an extra week and now you're you've decided to stay for a further week, I dread to think of poor Vincent's eardrums!"

"I'll Fedex over a supply of Quies doggy earplugs for Vincent, if such things exist," quipped Kurt. "But, seriously, Delilah. I've never been happier since you, you sly old puss, introduced us the night of our so-called special dinner *à deux*. A dinner not only special but earth shattering."

"A little something I may have noticed," said Delilah dryly. "However, being serious, Kurt, darling, you'll have to return to London, sooner or later. Though, if you must know the truth, I'm all for the later. Which brings me to the zillion-dollar question. What *are* you and Joel going to do? God, he's even talking of seeing if he can get a position as a doctor over there despite a thriving practice here in Vegas."

"I know, and I promptly put the kibosh on *that* suggestion. If anybody is going to up sticks and move, that person has to be me."

"But what about visas, work permits and such? Won't there be all sorts of problems?"

"Not if Joel and I tie the knot," replied Kurt with a grin.

"Forget the stripping!" shrieked Delilah, "seeing I've just been knocked over by my stripper's feather boa! Congrats, my wonderful darling! Oh, this is the best news since losing my virginity to some lucky spotty, testosterone infused teenager! Kisses, darling and an extra-large flute of champagne to celebrate!"

She gave a start. "Really, Kurt, you can be such a ditz at times. Where oh where is the blushing husband to be as he too must be a victim to my hugs and kisses!"

"Right behind you, Delilah, dear," giggled Joel, "armed with a bottle of champers to celebrate our glorious news; or else to crown you if you didn't!"

"Only a bottle?" crooned Delilah. "All I can say to the two of you utter darlings is that not even a champagne house could provide enough fizz for your delighted Delilah to toast the two of you!"

Rapidly produced glasses in lieu of champagne flutes cheerfully raised, and toasts made, Delilah said coquettishly. "It may surprise the two of you to know that endless rumpy-pumpy is not yours exclusively and while you've been *hard* at it, so have I!"

"You mean you have a *beau* as well as a boa?" chuckled Kurt.

"A beau with a suitable *boa* constrictor, we trust," added Joel, not to be outdone.

"A six-foot six beau positively *bristling* with oil wells and, need I say it, an oil derrick spectacular!"

"You devious wench, you!" chuckled Kurt. "So, what is the name of this oil derrick spectacular and when are we two humble folks allowed to meet Mr. Sex-on-Legs?"

"His name is Seb; full name Sebastian Salamander, and he could easily pass as chiselled Mr. Clint Eastwood's twin brother. But a bountiful, bulky brother at that! Added to which"- Delilah paused for effect - "not only does he possess an oil derrick spectacular, just wait until you see his Stetson!"

Once the three had stopped laughing, Joel managed to gasp. "When do we have the honour of meeting this oil derrick spectacular topped by a magnificent Stetson?"

"At lunch if the two of you are prepared to take a break from what you've apparently not stopped doing since the night you met," tittered Delilah.

"And where will this memorable lunch be taking place?" This from a giggling Joel.

"At *Plata, Plata, Plata*. Seb's ranch near Houston," preened Delilah, "courtesy of his private jet. However, be warned. If you're expecting another Tara, forget it. Sebastion's besotted by anything French; the unique, lovely English *moi* being the exception. So, instead of your typical antebellum mansion be prepared for a replica of Château Le Petit Versailles outside Paris set in the middle of an oil field." She gave a throaty laugh. "Not only that, but the château faces one particular oil derrick, Sebastain's first, lovingly named the Eiffel Tower!"

A LAVISH DUPLEX PENTHOUSE - CHELSEA HARBOUR

"You're getting *what?*" screeched Warwick almost dropping his mobile phone. "You're getting bloody pucking *what?*"

"Married, married, *married!*" carolled Kurt cheerfully. "You know, husband and husband, that sort of old-fashioned thing. And before you ask, Warwick dear, no, you won't be asked to the wedding as Joel . . ."

"*Joel?*" shrieked Warwick "*Joel?*"

"As Joel - that's Joel Ford, my husband-to-be - and I are not prepared to risk giving you the remotest of chances to spoil our special day." Kurt took a deep breath. "So, there you have it, Warwick. It was good knowing you, but your ongoing spiteful, sordid and criminal activities no longer appeal."

There was a prolonged silence before Kurt said, tongue in cheek. "Delilah sends love, as do I, to you and Vincent. Now, I need to go as my new world awaits me. Take care, Warwick, and have fun destroying my fore-edge panting and any Kurty *Baby* bits and pieces you can vent your rage-cum-spleen on!" There was a distinctive click as Kurt terminated the call.

"Destroy your pucking fore-edge paintings and bits and pieces," hissed Warwick. "You wish!"

Turning to face a puzzled Vincent, he gave a derisive snort. "Our former friend and ally must think I'm a pucking idiot for not only will I be selling his fore-edge pucking paintings, but I will be using the substantial proceeds toward making sure Kurt Cameron rues the day he decided to ditch me for another! If you think the likes of Sikes, Lincoln and Leighton will never forget, to misquote Eliza Doolittle: 'Just you wait, Kurt Cameron, just you wait!' As for that strip teasing bitch, if she thinks Mr. F. Scott-Fitzgerald's *The Strange Case of Benjamin Button* was back to front, wait until Madam

Divoon is subjected to Warwick Laudanum-Standton's personal adaptation of *The Strange Case of Deliah Divoon's Missing Belly Button*! Haha!"

Glaring at his mobile Warwick said with a mutter. "Married, eh, to some gilded youth no doubt, but none so gilded as this fair lily who, despite Mr. Cameron's Hiroshima-like news, will remain a *gilded* lily as opposed to a *water* lily swimming in what would be blatant crocodile tears. What's done is done, so time to gird my frustrated loins and think of *ungirding* the mountainous Mr. Pegg who, despite Jess's comment that he is Ancient Greece inclined, he doesn't seem all that interested in enrolling *moi* in a history lesson or two. So, if the mountain won't come to Olympus, then Olympus best call the mountain! Here goes!"

"David Pegg," said the instantly remembered spine-tingling voice.

"David ... err ... Pegg, it's Warwick. Warwick Laudanum-Standton."

"Oh? Warwick, Jess's friend? You probably won't believe me, but I have been meaning to call you."

"Oh, so those echoes of 'I Rem-Mem-Ber-You-Ooh' *weren't* coming from Australia but from much closer by."

"From Australia? Much closer by?" said Pegg in a confused voice.

"A song made popular by Aussie crooner Frank Ifield back in the last century," snickered Warwick. "Mother Dearest was a devoted fan and used to totter around our humble abode, G and T in hand, yodelling same. I did suggest she get Phillip Tracey to make her a mink bush hat decorated with dangling champagne corks, but she wasn't keen on the idea."

"Mother Dearest?" echoed Pegg, sounding even more confused.

"My monster of a mother. Think Cruella De Vil meets Elizabeth Bathory and you'd still be way off key."

"I'm sure I would be. In fact, I still am," chuckled Pegg.

"You said you were meaning to call and as I've just saved you a further enhancement to your BT account, may I ask the reason for the aforesaid potential call?"

"To invite you to lunch." Pegg couldn't resist a snigger. "I take it you *do* lunch?"

About to gaily say "Don't *all* ladies lunch?" Warwick said instead. "Not only do I *do* lunch, I'm also a great advocate of the practice. Therefore, should such a lunch take place then perhaps a hint of when and where."

"Today, if you're free, that is. I'm a great fan of Daphne's on Draycott Avenue so, if you *are* free, let's meet there at one. I'll make a reservation."

"I look forward to it!" crooned Warwick. Placing his mobile back on the desk he turned to Vincent and said with a cat that got the cream smile. "If you and I wag our tails correctly, Vincent my loyal friend, who knows? Maybe, just maybe, a *square* Pegg in a round hole could be a happening after all! As for Mr. Square grandly offering to make a reservation; seeing I'm almost part of the furniture there, I'd better give them a ring, ask for my usual table and when a Mr. Pegg rings, make sure they assign him *my* table as it's a surprise."

DAPHNE'S RESTAURANT - DRAYCOTT AVENUE

"Good to see you again Pegg, not that you're easy to miss," said Warwick with a faux smile as his giant guest was shown to the table. Not bothering to stand, he proffered a limp hand which Pegg briefly took in his hairless ham-like hand and gave a cursory shake.

Warwick pointed at his glass. "I got here earlier - nice table by the way; you obviously have some clout - and took the liberty of ordering a de rigueur martini. I can't remember your poison."

"I'll have a gin and tonic, no ice," grunted Pegg to the beaming waiter standing expectantly by Warwick's chair.

"Another martini for you, Mr. Warwick, while I'm organising your guest's G and T?" asked the waiter.

"Yes, please, Carlos," said Warwick perkily.

Carlos? Your guest's, G and T? thought Pegg. *Bastard! I should have realised Daphne's was one of his regular haunts. Hence the effusive greeting when I arrived and said a Mr. Laudanum-Standton would be joining me and being told he was already at the table. Sly little sod, aren't you?*

"I trust my earlier not that you're easy to miss wasn't taken the wrong way. I was referring to your *size*, not a phone call. Haha!"

Saved by the obliging Carlos, thought Pegg as the beaming waiter arrived with their drinks.

Taking a fortifying swallow of his G and T, Pegg said blandly. "Been busy?"

"I'm *always* busy," pouted Warwick. "So up to my *neck* in it that the days never seem *long* enough."

Christ! Is it me or was that another of his sly innuendoes? thought Pegg.

"Those two over-glossed ewes dressed as lambs sitting to your left haven't stopped staring at you since you arrived," tittered Warwick, interrupting his thoughts. "They obviously must think you are a movie or TV star."

"You mean someone who always plays the bad guy," chuckled Pegg. "You're right. They always do." He gave a grin. "The number of times I've been called Dwayne as in Johnson, Vin as in Diesel or Jack as in Jack Reacher, beggars belief."

"Well, that certainly doesn't happen to *moi*!" giggled Warwick. "Seeing Mother Dearest is convinced she produced her very own baby Theo James as opposed to a Big Arnie."

"There's nothing wrong in looking like Theo James," chuckled Pegg, "I take it you've watched *The Gentleman*?"

"Endlessly!" tittered Warwick. "A true example of mirror, mirror on the wall!"

Taking a further swallow of his G and T, Pegg gave a frown and said matter-of-factly. "Being honest, I have to say it. I'm not at all comfortable sitting here with you err . . . Warwick. So, before we order - that's if I *do* decide to stay for lunch - let's cut to the quick. Jess, bless him, attempted to explain your - how shall I put it - sicko little predilections on the wild assumption I could be interested: be of help."

Ignoring Warwick's stunned expression, Pegg continued matter-of-factly. "He wasn't a hundred percent clear, but I was given to understand you take a perverse delight in mutilating people who have offended you in the past. Or, as Jess put it: a perpetual reminder of the fact that sooner or later, you *do* reap what you sow."

"Jess was able to tell you all that?" gasped Warwick. "While here I am thinking I was being discreet!

"You, yourself, may have been discreet, Warwick, but your colleague Kurt Cameron wasn't, and it was common knowledge what you were up to with him as your accomplice. So much so that Kurt Cameron's nickname in London's shadowy underworld is Pay dirt Kurt. Rather unfortunate, wouldn't you say?"

"I have no idea what you're talking about, *Mr.* Pegg," snapped Warwick, backpedalling furiously. "As for you having the audacity to say you may or may not stay for lunch: for your information, *I* most certainly will not be staying!"

Giving the smirking man a glare, Warwick calmly placed his table napkin on his side plate, stood up and with a further glare at his bemused host, turned on his heels and stalked away from the table.

"Just as Jess said he'd probably do, get up and leave," muttered Pegg. "Ah well, you can't win them all, However, when it comes to being spoilt, churlish and childish, Warwick Laudanum-Standton has no equal."

Aware of a figure standing next to the table he added offhandedly. "My apologies, but due to a change of plan I won't be staying for lunch as my guest has been . . ."

"Your guest has been what?" interrupted Warwick. "Called away? Stamped off in his usual spoilt, churlish and childish manner? Not at all. In fact, while looking for a taxi, your *guest* experienced what some would call an epiphany. So, Mr. David Pegg-cum-Johnson-cum-Diesel-cum-Reacher, shall we start again?"

"We could," came the quick reply, "but only if now *I'm* the guest! However, you're still on very thin ice, Mr. Warwick Laudanum-Standton, so tread carefully."

"Well, I'd better sit down again instead of having to watch where I tread," said Warwick impishly. Settling down on his recently vacated chair, he added with a grin. "Oh, and in my sudden seeing the light I ordered another G and T for you and a martini for myself in case you think the drinks about to land on the table have something to do with your two highly intrigued ewes dressed as lambs who can't seem to get enough of you!"

Reaching for the duly delivered martini, he added nonchalantly. "Regarding your probable role in helping me with my 'you reap what you sow remembers', were you shocked on learning what it entailed?"

"Shocked? It takes more than an amputated toe or two to shock me, Mr. Warwick Laudanum-Standton," snorted Pegg. "Though, I have to admit when Jess mentioned the other, I was a bit taken aback as I haven't come across cutting off someone's dick before. No, knowing your mind let me rephase that. I've never been *asked* to hack off somebody's penis before."

"There's a first time for everything, Pegg," said Warwick deadpan. "What's more I'm delighted to hear you now see it as a case of easy come, easy go." He gave a tight smile. "And now that's settled and before we order, a very *telling* question. Do you like animals?"

"Yes, I do like animals, Mr. Laudanum-Standton, and they like me," replied Pegg a touch sharply. "Added to which I find that question irrelevant seeing Jess must have told you about Peggs, my school for training guide dogs for the blind. if you're referring to Vincent, your Jack Russell terrier, I'm sure you must have noticed the mutual appreciation when we met."

"Yes, I remember. I also how remember his fascination for your somewhat large feet: couldn't seem to leave them alone," snickered Warwick. "One other thing, Pegg. When we three meet again, for Vincent's sake, please stop calling me Mr. Laudanum-Standton and call me Warwick otherwise he'll only get confused." Warwick gave a giggle. "I take it I am now back to treading on thicker ice than before?"

"See it as more of a glacier, *Warwick*," chuckled Pegg.

"Goody good!" crooned Warwick signalling for a waiter to come and take their order. "Let's order and then we can begin discussing my next - dare I say our first combined - mutilation."

Two hours later as Warwick and Pegg sat enjoying their brandies, Warwick glanced at his watched and said with feigned surprise. "Glory be to Brad! Is that the time? Doesn't time simply *fly* when one's enjoying oneself. So, just to recap what we've agreed, oh mighty Pegg! A suitable donation to Peggs, your organisation for helping train guide dogs along with a smaller taster, as it were, in anticipation of our working together on future projects impermissible."

Patting his breast pocket, Pegg said in a warm voice. "As I told you, I was happily prepared to settle on a taster or deposit for s future project, but then, out of the blue, you come up with this totally unexpected donation for Peggs, plus a hint of more to come if, hint, hint, you could become involved in the organisation. Well, it goes without saying Warwick, from this moment on, not only are you involved with us, Peggs, but, if you are agreeable, I'd be honoured if you'd be part of our committee."

Leaning back in his chair, Warwick said with a genuine smile. "The answer's a huge yes recurring! What's more I can hardly wait for Friday when I pay my first visit to Peggs." He gave a frown. "I take it Vincent will have to stay at the penthouse with Wallace and Gromit?"

"I have no idea who this Wallace and Gromit can be but there is no earthly reason for Vincent not joining us. A, he'll find playmates galore and B, Warwick Laudanum-Standton without *Vincent* Laudanum-Standton is tantamount to a large G without the T!"

9

LAS VEGAS

"This getting hitched seems to be contagious," crooned Delilah in her daily phone call to Kurt. "So, as from Wednesday on will you kindly address me as *Mrs* Salamander seeing my glorious Stetson simply couldn't hold back from telling me I was even more exciting than when he first struck oil, and would I be prepared to spend the rest of my days with him and his personal geyser!"

"You mean you and Seb are tying the hallowed knot?" exclaimed Kurt. "Forgive me for the pun, but geysers of congrats! Wait until I tell Joel. He'll be over the moon!"

"Shouldn't that be over the oil derricks?" crooned Delilah. "As you *well* know, on Saturday we're holding a party to celebrate the two of *you* tying the knot so now it's obviously going to be a *double* celebration. A celebration *Plata, Plata, Plata,* will never forget!"

"The ring! The ring!" exclaimed Kurt. "Tell me about the ring!"

"If you're thinking of a special wedding present for the blushing bride herself, may I suggest a portable crane."

"It's *that* big?"

"Darling," crowed Delilah. "They both are!"

A LAVISH DUPLEX PENTHOUSE - CHELSEA HARBOUR

"His nibs and his other nibs are spending the day at Mr. Latest's centre for training guide dogs," tittered Harry, "which puts Mr. Latest on a par with

Mr. Noah and his ark *despite* his ogre-like looks. As they so rightly say, you can't judge a book by its cover seeing Mr. Latest is all heart."

"Ogre-like looks. Can't judge a book by its cover. Mr. Latest is all heart! Bloody hell, Harry, you sound more like Warwick every passing day!" snorted Christopher.

"I know I do. Put it down to something hideously contagious that must be going around. Getting back to Mr. Latest, you cannot but agree that anyone so *passionate* about our four-legged friends helping blind people literally *to* see, deserves some sort of admiration."

"Well, he's certainly got our capricious lord and master well and truly hooked and as for Vincent, he'll need a tail replacement after all that wagging!"

"Are they here for dinner?"

"Yes. Warwick asked me to come up with - ha! - something special and to ask *you* to wear something less funereal." Harry gave a titter. "To quote his lordship. 'Something a touch more outré than the boring butler wore it'."

"Something a touch more outré?" snorted Christopher. "I've never had the desire to emulate a flipping Christmas tree, but who knows?"

"Now, now," chided Harry. "You don't need to be *too* over the top, so why not wear the pink velvet jacket and gold lamé trousers you wore for Dildo and Daniel's wedding?"

"A dazzling suggestion, Harry, love! However, I shall stick to my chef's whites along with my special chef's hat. The one you had dear Phillip make for me: the one swathed in crystal beads."

LATER

"That was some dinner, Warwick," announced Pegg patting his stomach. "Any more such dinners and I'll be giving the Michelin Man a run for his money!"

Reaching for his Drambuie, he added softly. "Thank you, Warwick, and may I say once again, when it comes to being a superstar, I've never met anyone more deserving of the accolade than you and the *way* you handled the trainers, the staff and especially the pups and the fully-grown dogs at Peggs today. Coli - Colin - the head trainer and all the staff adored you, especially Trish in charge of the kennels."

"I enjoyed meeting Trish the dish," chortled Warwick. "As for Coli - Colin -your head trainer; he can train me anytime!"

Eyeing Pegg over the rim of his brandy balloon, Warwick said coquettishly. "I take it you *will* be staying the night?"

"Only if Vincent insists," quipped Pegg,

"He not only insists he *demands*!" giggled Warwick. "Which brings me to the rather delicate, million-euro question. As you sport a pair of decidedly heavenly eyebrows but a billiard ball-like head and totally hairless hands and forearms, I don't think we're talking alopecia here, but is it the same everywhere else where there *should* be hair, glorious hair?"

"Yep. Apart from my eyebrows I am totally and completely hairless, thanks to the skills of Mr King Camp Gilette - I swear on my Scout's honour that's his correct name - expensive epilation and various depilatory creams."

"And the instigator behind this somewhat unconventional practice?"

"Me! It started as a joke when I decide to dress-up as Casper the friendly ghost for Halloween some years ago. Having decided to go the full hog, I shaved my head, face, arms and lower legs before coating myself with white grease paint. Draping a sheet over my torso I then stood studying my reflection in my mother's full length dressing room mirror. I can only say that my reaction to what I saw reflected would have even made Narcissus look a mere amateur. Hence the hairless hulk you see before you."

"Apart from the eyebrows, all pucking over?"

"Aha! The famous pucking! Jess did warn me! And yes, Warwick; apart from the eyebrows, pucking all over. Even my bum crack."

"Did you see what just happened?" yelped Warwick, his hands flying to his face *à la* Edvard Munch's painting, *The Scream.*

"No! What?" replied Pegg, his eyes widening.

"Vincent! On hearing you say, 'even my bum crack', I saw his ears stand to attention!" Warwick gave a theatrical sigh. "Please assure me, Pegg, when t comes to playing sniffins with your bum crack, the privilege will be mine and *not* Vincent's!"

"I think that can be arranged," chuckled Pegg, "So, without any further delay let's head for the bedroom so that you can start sniffing!"

LAS VEGAS

"Talk about an air of intrigue," chuckled Kurt. "Whatever you and Delilah have in mind for the great event two weeks on Saturday, I take it there *won't* be an eye boggling striptease as I have a feeling any of grey-headed dowagers on the guest list may never recover whereas their ogling old husbands will no doubt panting for more!"

"Okay, Kurt, a hint but only a hint," replied Joel with a mischievous grin. "Cast your mind back to when Delilah first invited us to *Plata, Plata, Plata,* so as to meet Sebastian."

"How could I possibly forget," chuckled Kurt. "It's not every day one sees a French château sitting in a landscaped park bristling with oil derricks."

"Apart from the house and the endless, run of the mill oil derricks, what else can you remember?"

"The gold painted oil derrick named Eiffel Tower marking Sebastian's first strike taking pride of place in the forecourt of the château."

"Precisely! Now, what does *that* call to mind? I'll give you another clue. Cast your mind back to a jamboree of sorts a couple of months."

"A jamboree of sorts a couple of months ago?" pondered Kurt. "Unless you're referring to Warwick's merry mutilations, I honestly have no idea what you're talking about."

"Think Eiffel Tower. *Think* Paris."

"Think Paris? Surely you can't be referring to the Olympics?"

"Hot! Hot! Hot! But not quite hot enough!"

"No! No way," chuckled Kurtm his face wreathed in smiles. "Please don't tell me Delilah is planning on doing a Celine Dion and sing to the guests while perched on Sebastian's golden Eiffel Tower?"

"A hundred out of ten!" chortled Joel. "Yes, the lovely Delilah will be up there singing her diamond embellished heart out!"

"Am I allowed to know the name of the song?"

"A take-off on Eartha Kitt's *Just an Old-Fashioned Girl.* Only this time the old-fashioned girl wants an old-fashioned *billionaire* with endless oil wells going slurp, slurp, slurp, into *his* barrels!"

A LAVISH DUPLEX PENTHOUSE - CHELSEA HARBOUR

"Talk about a night to remember," chortled Warwick as he and Pegg sat finishing breakfast on the main terrace. Muttering "Thank you" to a smirking Harry with a "I knew it, I just knew it" expression on his face as he topped up their mimosas. "You, Mr. Uber-smoothie Pegg are one tornado of a lover! What? Oh, forget Harry," he added noting Pegg's discreet nod to where Harry stood stacking the empty chafing dishes and plates. "He sees himself as a second Madame Arcati and no doubt thinks you spending the night was a *prediction* instead of the obvious!"

"Will that be all, Mr. Warwick, sir," carolled Harry as prepared to make his way back to the kitchen accompanied by a tail-wagging Vincent.

"Yes, thank you, Harry," crooned Warwick. "Please make sure that Vincent doesn't con you and Christopher into a double helping of *his* breakfast as he usually does. Deny, Harold! Deny!" He reached for one of the papers stacked neatly on the table.

"I always check out the various gossip columns first," he murmured, "as I love to see what all those self-promoting WOPOs and ZINTs are up to."

"WOPOs and ZINTs?" questioned Pegg.

"Wastes of pucking oxygen and of zero intelligence," came the murmured explanation as Warwick gave the front page to one of the lesser tabloids a cursory glance before turning to his favoured column.

"What the puck?" he muttered homing in on a particular article. "It can't be."

"What? What can't be?" said glancing up from his selected paper, namely the *Daily Mail*. "Bloody Hell, Warwick! You look as if you've seen a ghost!"

Warwick gave a hollow laugh. "No, after last night you're hardly a ghost, *Caspar.*" Tapping the page he said with a vehement hiss. "It's pucking this!"

"This?"

"This pucking article here! About someone attacked night before last before being dumped outside A & E at St. Thomas's Hospital. Not only that, it's here - in black and white - that the victim cannot be named for security reasons. However, it does say he suffered several *disfiguring* injuries: whatever the puck that's meant to mean."

"Please can you confirm your whereabouts night before last between the hours of eight p.m. and midnight, Mr. Laudanum-Standton," said Pegg in a sonorous voice. Switching back to his usual tenor he added brightly. "I can assure you, officer, I was cuddled up on the sofa, with Vincent, my handsome lover, watching telly!"

"If that's meant to be funny, David Pegg, it's pucking not! For all I know this could be someone who *knows* about me and my mutilations. Then again, they don't say what the disfiguring injuries entail. Not wishing to flatter myself, could this be a mysterious, copycat admirer? If so, who? Whatever one wishes to say about Kurt, this is so un-him. Not only that, he and Deliah are too involved to seriously play silly buggers with me. The same applying to Jess."

"Jesus, Warwick! Leave Jess out of it!" Pegg shook his head in exasperation. "He's not only a friend but also a business friend who knows everything there is to know about *all* your shady dealings. A friend whose loyalty is in a league of its own!"

"See it as a slip of a confused tongue," said Warwick. Turning his attention to the sliding door leading onto the terrace he said with a grin, "Aha! Harry! Perhaps a mystic after all!"

"Call on the landline for you, Mr. Warwick. A Mr. Walton saying he has some information regarding a Mr. Lincoln."

"A Mr. Lincoln?"

"That's what he said, sir."

"I'd better come and speak this mysterious caller," said Warwick getting up from his chair. "Plus, it will also give me the chance to give you, Vincent and Christopher the third degree and find out exactly was in Vincent's doggy breakfast bowl. If there the slightest hint of your favourite croissants or chocolate chip cookies. Heads-will-roll!"

Following Harry into the penthouse, Warwick skipped along to the study and picked up the landline. "I've got this Harry," he crooned, "so you can hang up." On hearing a click, he said cheerfully. "Mr. Walton, I presume? Warwick Laudanum-Standton in the flesh! You called me?"

"I have indeed, Mr. Laudanum-Standton," said a silky tenor voice. "The name is Walton, Bernhard Walton, and an associate of Mr. Roger Lincoln."

"Mr. Roger Lincoln?" repeated Warwick, alarm bells not ringing but jangling. "Did you say Roger Lincoln?"

"Mr. Lincoln, Mr. Laudanum-Standton, was a pupil at your former school who recently had the misfortune to be severely beaten-up, and not only be beaten up, but also have his nose and part of his penis cut-off. Still in the dark?"

"Most definitely in the dark despite it being bright sunshine outside and a delightful twenty-five degrees. Look, Mr. Walton, I haven't the foggiest idea what you're talking about. As for how you got my name and number, again, I have no idea, but I'm hanging up. Please delete this number from your phone or whatever."

Slamming down the receiver, Warwick hurried through to the kitchen. "Christopher! Harry!" he barked. "I need you to find out all you can about this Bernhard Walton character who just called. Every pucking thing even down to his shoe size, as he could be a serious problem."

"On it, Mr. Warwick," said Christopher. "Just let me rinse my hands and I'll get dialling."

Back out on the terrace Warwick quickly repeated to Pegg his brief conversation with Bernhard Walton.

"This Walton character sounds like trouble," agreed Pegg. "Serious trouble."

"Not waiting for the *arse* to fester or grow 'neath my Gucci shod feet, I've already asked Christopher to run a search on the bastard and see what he comes up with."

Eyeing Warwick, Pegg said grimly. "As soon as we have an address, I will deal with Mr. Threatening bastard Walton. The guy is beyond a mutilation and a warning, he needs to disappear."

"Any luck?" said Warwick, shielding his eyes and glancing up at Christopher as he stepped out onto the terrace.

"Yes, sir. Putting two and two together I telephoned Glazebrook and Crozier, the architectural company where Mr. Lincoln still works, and simply asked if I could speak to Mr. Walton. Bull's-eye! I was told Mr. Walton was out on an appointment and wasn't expected back until late afternoon, and would I like to leave a message. Telling the receptionist that I'd call back tomorrow - I didn't leave a name or contact number - I started hunting and got lucky." Christopher held out a piece pf paper. "It's all there, home address, phone numbers, car registration. The lot."

"No!" cried Warwick in feigned alarm. "Please hand that Hiroshima to Mr. Pegg, not *moi*! Well done, Christopher! Sterling work as always!" He gave a chortle. "Thanks to you and Mr. Pegg I can now relax knowing that any more unpleasant calls from Mr. Bernhard Walton are now a yuck from the past. If you catch my drift."

"Your drift is well and truly taken, Mr. Warwick, sir," replied Christopher with a smile. "To make sure Harold and I not caught unawares, will you be dining in or out this evening? I know Mr. Sex-on-Legs Rex at The Chelsea Fishmonger, is expecting a delivery of delicious lobsters today, and as Vincent enjoys saying hello to all at Chelsea Green, may I suggest lobster for dinner?"

"Sounds good to me, Christopher. How does lobster thermidor sound to you, Pegg?"

"Sounds more than good," grinned Pegg.

"Thank you, Mr. Warwick. And as I will be visiting the fishmonger, if Mr. Pegg is partial to kippers, shall I get kippers as well as I know they're a favourite of yours."

"Sounds doubly good to me, Christopher," sniggered Warwick, "so do add them to Mr. Sex-on-Legs Rex's list!"

"Cheeky sod," chuckled Pegg once Christopher was out of earshot.

"Hmm," said Warwick. "If you think Vincent and I enjoy playing sniffins, you can bet your bottom - ha - euro that those two had a good old sniff at the sheets when making our bed this morning. It's one of Harry's - read Harry's *and* Chrisopher's - happier chores."

There was a companiable silence until Pegg said matter-of-factly. "Something I told Vincent earlier and something I need to tell you, Warwick."

"Please God, not another Waltonism!"

"No, not another *Waltonism* but a serious Peggism. I think I'm falling in love with you, Mr. Warwick Laudanum-Stantdon."

"You know what, Mr. David Pegg, rather like your good self, I have a strange feeling Mr. Warwick Laudanum-Standton and Mr. Vincent Laudanum Standton are falling in love with *you*. Such a happening can only be confirmed by a flute or two the magical monk to seal the deal!"

"Magical monk?"

"You obviously don't know it, dearest Pegg, but the magician behind Dom Perignon champagne was a monk named Dom Pérignon who was cellar master in some Frenck abbey back in the seventeenth century."

"Now that's *two* things, I've learned today," chuckled Pegg. "One, where Dom Perignon champagne originated and, two, you and Vincent, could be falling in love with me!"

THE NEXT MORNING

"Thank God I am into strange sounds, rhythms and olfaction seeing I had you and Vincent snoring and farting next to me in bed last night." Warwick gave a titter. "Otherwise, I wouldn't have gotten a *wank* of unnecessary beauty sleep."

"I don't snore, and I most certainly suffer from flatulence," replied Pegg in what he took to be a suitably hurt voice. "Okay, I may be guilty of the odd draught now and then: but an explosive fart? Never!"

"Tell that to the Judge," giggled Warwick. "Now, back to things to do today. I take it I can leave the yucking of wise guy Walton to the faultless and flawless you."

"You most certainly can. I won't literally be *yucking* him today but getting everything up and running for his debut into the unknown." Pegg gave a chuckle. "Now if that didn't sound like a typical *Warwickism*, I rest my case! Give it a day or two and you'll find your yucky black cloud has turned to gold! Haha!"

"Oh, *very* E.H Benson. Pegg. I couldn't have plagiarised it better myself. Meanwhile, as you know, Vincent and I will be spending the day at Peggs, as so kindly arranged by your heaven-sent self. And whilst I'm having my first lesson in how one teaches a puppy to become an incredible, amazing, guide dog, Vincent will be in doggy heaven playing sniffins with all the other pooches not having lessons."

10

RANCHO PLATA, PLATA, PLATA

Sebastian Salamander, resplendent in a white tuxedo, his traditional white Stetson decorated with a diamond studded "Stetson" band, sat staring open-mouthed, a worshipful look in his wide-open eyes as he, Kurt, and Joel, along with three hundred star struck guests watched and listened to Delilah, dressed in a shimmering, figure-hugging gown, as she lustily sang her version of *Just an Old-Fashioned Girl* from where she stood on a specially-constructed platform a quarter of the way up the golden derrick.

On her final rendering of "an old-fashioned *billionaire*" the assembled guests burst into thunderous applause; their enthusiasm accompanied by an explosion of fireworks lighting up the night sky.

"That's my own darlin', not at all ol' fashioned lil' girl you've jes heard singin'," twanged Sebastian to the crowd below on joining Deliah up on the platform. "What's more, I need ya'all to know that this lil' girl has agreed to marry this ol' fashioned billionaire in a few weeks' time. An' folks, if ya'll think tonight's party is spectacular, wait until you see our weddin' party as nothin's spectacular enough for Seb Salamander's lovely Miss Delilah!"

*

"Wasn't my lil' Delilah jes wonderful," Sebastian kept on saying as guest after smiling guest came forward to congratulate him and Delilah.

"Isn't my handsome oil derrick husband-to-be too, too divine," crooned Delilah, not to be outdone. "And, dear friends, I can assure you Seb and I are going to slurp, slurp, slurp happily ever after!"

Once all the excitement had died down the guests sat down to enjoy a sumptuous dinner while an orchestra, specially flown in from Las Vegas, played a background melody of show tunes and jazzed-up popular classics.

"Talk about an evening never to be forgotten," whispered Kurt giving Delilah sitting next to him a gentle kiss. He nodded to Joel sitting opposite. "And, as Joel, lil' old me, and everyone else keeps telling you, you were amazing."

"I'm only amazing because I have a friend like you," whispered Delilah. "A friend always ready to help me pick myself up and dust myself down whenever I needed to. But now, thanks to my darling Stetson Sebastian, when I feel the need to dust myself down, it'll be gold dust you'll be dealing with."

"I don't bloody well believe it." muttered Kurt, his massive frame tensing.

"Believe what?" questioned Joel giving Kurt a concerned look.

"Over there, talking animatedly with Renato, the master of ceremonies."

"Oh, my God!" said Delilah, her face visibly paling the light of one of endless candelabra gracing the tables. "Please don't tell me that's bloody Warwick and your replacement?"

"I'm afraid to say it effing well *is*," growled Kurt, "and what's more, Renato's showing him to our table, but never fear, Delilah, dear. Seb and I had an inkling your party would be far too good an opportunity for Warick to miss an attempt at some form of sabotage."

"Everythin' okay, Delilah, lil' one?" asked Sebastian, now aware of the anxious conversation taking place between Delilah, Kurt and Joel.

"No, Sebastian," hissed Delilah, "because following Renato toward our table is bloody Warwick Laudanum-Standton!"

"No worries, Delilah, mah sweet," replied Sebastian with a tight smile, "as Renato, Kurt, an' I have it in hand, so leave it to us."

Rising to his feet, his Stetson still in place, Sebastian gave Renato a discreet nod before facing Warwick and Pegg and said with a Machiavellian smile. "Evenin', gents. I won't say welcome to *Plata, Plata, Plata,* because welcome ya ain't. An' now, before you attempt to cause some sort of lil' ol' rumpus, the four gentlemen now standin' behind ya will be only too willin' to escort you off mah property. So, which is it gonna be? Ya'all leave nice and quietly on ya own or else I have ya escorted out. Mah polite way of sayin' I'll have ya thrown out."

"Thank you for your kind offer of two such generous alternatives, Mr. Salamander," purred Warwick with a whiter than white smile. "And, as your first offer is obviously the more acceptable of the two, we'll see ourselves out. May I also say that Mr. Pegg and myself, were not given the opportunity of shaking your hand or kissing the bride-to-be and congratulating both of you on your engagement. Nor did we have any intention of upsetting your celebratory dinner. So, without any further *boo-hoo,* bad luck and puck you both."

Turning to face a beaming Pegg, Warwick said cheerfully. "So, c'mon, Pegg. Time for us to puck off before Mr. Stetson and his band of trigger-happy caballeros get nasty. Not that they should, seeing we happily accepted Mr. Stetson's kind offer to leave nice and quietly."

Taking hold of Pegg's brawny arm Warwick did an about turn and marched the two of them toward the entrance where their chauffeur-driven limousine was waiting.

"A question, Pegg," giggled Warwick as their limousine swept them away from the illuminated faux château with its glowing gold oil derrick. "Have you ever blown up an oil derrick before?"

"No, love of my life, but there's a first time for everything! Now, our late dinner in the Main Kitchen - don't look so alarmed, it's the name of the restaurant at the Marriot where we're staying - should be interesting. Bam Crocker, our guest is an old mate and a mine of information on most illegal queries. I therefore suggest you bring up the question regarding the blowing up of an oil derrick. Not only will this be s sure-fire way to get his gonads going, but he's sure to have the answer."

"What, if I may be so bold, is Mr. Crocker's profession apart from being a probable blower-upper of an oil derrick?" tittered Warwick.

"He's a florist."

"You mean a florist about to become a fully blown floribunda blower-upper!" chortled Warwick rocking with glee. "As you said, there's a first time for everything!"

THE MARRIOT HOUSTON DOWNTOWN

"I take it that must be our potential floribunda blower-upper sitting over there," whispered Warwick nodding the direction of a lone Sebastian Flyte lookalike sitting by himself at a cocktail table. "He *breathes* the name, floribunda!"

"Wrong, Warwick! *Wrong!*" sang Pegg. "The Jolly Green giant sitting on his lonesome ownsome at the bar is our Mr. Bam Crocker and *not* your *Brideshead Revisited* Mr. Flyte sitting by himself." Pegg gave a soft chuckle. "Despite him being very much my type until a certain Mr. W L-S entered my life."

"Goodness! Just as well you insisted on me wearing a chastity before our disastrous attempt to seduce all and sundry on our surprise, surprise descent upon *Plata! Plata! Plata!* earlier! Like you, Mr. Crocker is exactly the sort of mating call that gets *my* gonads going."

"Hmm. But remember Warwick, love of my life, Dave Pegg is the one and only holding the key to your chastity belt. So, let's go and say hello to Mr. Universe meets Mr. Bam Crocker but remember, if you misbehave, I'll simply *swallow* the key and then you'll really be in the capital S-H-I-T!"

"Dave Pegg! You old reprobate, you!" boomed Bam Crocker sliding from his bar stool to greet Pegg with a warm hug. "And this delectable young man," he said turning to face Warwick, "can only be my great friend's happy husband!"

Well, that was easy, thought Warwick. *However, on a closer look dear Pegg need* not *swallow that key as you, Mr. Crocker, have a serious tribute to tempestuous testosterone and ancient acne scribed all over your otherwise turn-on face and that will never do!*

"Shall we go into dinner as it's getting late," suggested Pegg, "Then we can both catch-up on old times, before discussing this and that."

"*Not* until you both have had a 'good to see you and a good to meet you' drink with me here at the bar," boomed Bam. "So, gentlemen, name your poison!"

*

"So, getting down to basics, you want me to blow up Seb Salamander's prized golden derrick," grunted Bam in what he assumed akin to a whisper. Taking a large bite of his steak, he chewed pointedly before taking a swallow and with a ponderous nodding of his shaggy head, said cheerfully. "Shouldn't be a problem. I'll take care of it once you're back in Charlie boy and Camilla land so that no one can point an accusatory finger at you. And, before you ask, my fee for this little favour will be . . ." Bam reached inside his jacket, pulled out a small notebook and a pen. His massive forehead creasing into a frown he printed a figure before turning the notebook round so that Warwick and Pegg could see the amount he was asking for. "That's in dollars, of course, paid into a Caymans account."

Bloody Hell! thought Warwick. *Thank the Good Lord for Auntie's legacy!*

As expected, thought Pegg. *Now all we need is for Warwick to fuck it up by trying to renegotiate the bloody price.*

"Done!" crooned Warwick, reaching across the table to shake Bam's proffered hand.

Thank Christ for small mercies, thought Pegg discreetly exhaling. "Thanks, Bam. I know you'll do us proud."

"As I said, no problem for me," guffawed Bam. "Pity poor Sebastian Salamander when he learns, to his cost, that the term 'pie in the sky' can also mean 'oil derrick in the sky.' Haw! Haw! Haw!"

A LAVISH DUPLEX PENTHOUSE - CHELSEA HARBOUR - THREE DAYS LATER

"Today's the day! Hip, hip hooray for today's the day!" yodelled Warwick as he and Pegg sat down for breakfast. "Today's the day when dastardly Sebastian's prized oil derrick is blown away!"

"And tomorrow, we'll know for sure that threatening Mr. Bernhard Walton is no more," sang Pegg in an off-key tenor.

"Thank you, passionate Pegg!" tittered Warwick. "In all the excitement of the past few days plus a soupçon of jet lag I'd literally forgotten about Mr. Bernhard Walton. As he's about to become another 'no more', what have you got planned? I trust you'll make triple sure he's made *painfully* aware that his end - rear or otherwise - is nigh."

RANCHO PLATA, PLATA, PLATA - THE SAME EVENING

"What a charming couple," purred Delilah snuggling up as the luxurious black Cadillac Celestiq (the standard Cadillac emblem replaced by a miniature gold-plated oil derrick) glided smoothly toward the floodlit château and its glowing oil derrick.

"Almost as charming as us, though not quite," rumbled Sebastian giving her hand a loving squeeze. "And now," he said proudly, "my favourite view of all time, my view of my pride and joy . . ." He gave a chuckle. "Oops, make that my *second* pride and joy as you, my glorious Delilah, are now most definitely my first. My golden derrick and glorious Château Plata, Plata, Plata, soon to be *our* home."

"It sure looks wonderful, Seb, honey," twanged Delilah, Mae West style. "As for my former stage, it sure glows."

The words were barely out of her mouth when Delilah, Sebastian, and Earl, the chauffeur, watched in horror as the glowing gold oil derrick appeared to disintegrate in front of them.

"Jesus Christ!" bellowed Sebastian, grasping hold of Delilah.

"Oh my *God*!" screamed Delilah.

"Bloody hell!" shouted Earl as he jammed on the brakes and skidded to a stop. The three watching in disbelief as the small flames on what was left of the broken oil derrick flickered and died. The silence within the limousine eventually broken by Sebastian's heart-rendering sobs.

GLAZEBROOK & CROZIER - ARCHITECTS

"Thank Christ today's over," muttered Bernhard Walton, a smooth John Cusack lookalike on approaching his parked car. About to activate the locks on the gleaming Lexus, he stopped midstride and said exasperatedly. "If I thought I would get away with it, I'd really strangle that effing Ruth Lloyd. Why can't the stupid cunt get it into that thick head of hers that we will *not* get permission for an underground swimming pool in a second basement because it is simply not feasible due to house having been built on clay."

"That's strange," he added. "I could have sworn I locked the car earlier. Out of habit, if nothing else. As for bloody Lloyd. I need to have a word with Colin Glazebrook first thing tomorrow and see if we can ditch the bitch as nobody on the building site can stand her. Even old Eric, one of the painters, is threatening to walk off the job."

Sliding onto the driver's seat, he immediately froze on catching sight of two masked men sitting calmly in the back of the car.

"Not a word, Mr. Walton," rumbled one of the men. "So, be a good little architect, start the car and leave the parking area. Once we're in the street turn left and them follow my instructions."

"Who . . . who . . . are you?" stammered Bernhard doing as instructed. "If it's money you want, take my wallet. If it's the car you want, take it and let me out!"

"No money and no car, thank you, Mr. Walton, as it's *you* we want. So, drive!"

"Drive where?" snapped Bernhard, his initial fear quickly dissipating.

"My, you *are* a curious one," said the second masked man in a strong Scottish accent. "They say curiosity killed the wee cat, Mr. Walton, but me and my friend here will give you at least a half-hour's grace before killing you seeing we're first going for a wee drive. Not very generous, we know, but like most supermarket products, Mr. Walton, today's the day you've reached your sell by date."

Half-an-hour later Pegg and his burly associate, a Glaswegian known as Psycho Sporran, stood impassive as they slowly fed a frantically struggling, screaming Bernhard into a large, industrial wood chip machine.

"*Very* Jackson Pollock," quipped Pegg eyeing the scattered pieces of glistening flesh and bone lying about

"Jackson who?" questioned Psycho.

"Jackson Pollock, an American artist who made splattering famous," chuckled Pegg. "However, he did it with paint as opposed to a human being."

*

"I love it! Simply love it!" crooned Warwick clapping his hands with glee. His handsome face breaking into a broad grin, he added jubilantly. "Maybe I should start calling you Chucky Pegg?"

"Chucky Pegg? Why?"

"Why not? After all, how much would a woodchuck Pegg chuck if a woodchuck Pegg could chuck wood?" chortled Warwick. "Answer? Easy-peasy. A woodchuck Pegg would chuck as much wood as a woodchuck Pegg could chuck if a woodchuck Pegg could chuck wood!"

"Now, *that*, if nothing else, deserves a *very* large drink; if not a distillery," laughed Pegg, applauding wildly; much to the consternation of Vincent seated nearby.

"Please not a distillery," crooned Warwick, "as it would never do if too much of the delicious, demon drink *did* make the woodchuck Pegg chuck up." He raised a hand. "Sorry! No more woodchuck jokes from now on, I promise. Plus, no more oily Derek jokes either!"

"You promise?"

"On my Scouts dishonour!"

11

A LAVISH DUPLEX PENTHOUSE - CHELSEA HARBOUR

"That was Bam calling," said Pegg wandering buck-naked into the study. "Just as well I take my mobile into the shower with me, just in case."

"So?" said Warwick, his eyes wide.

"To quote him, Seb's narcissistic monument is no more." Pegg gave a chuckle. "Talk about killing two bastards with one stone."

"Genius, Pegg! Pure pucking, undisputed genius!" crooned Warwick. "What I'd give to see Delilah's and Sebastian's faces this merry morn! As for Bernhard Walton, I wonder how long it will be before his office finally realises that he's *not* out on an early morning appointment and will never, ever be returning, but eternally vanished!"

"Well, my love, not a word to anyone," said Pegg, "Especially Wallace and Gromit."

"Despite what I cannot help but spy with my lascivious eye, and despite my wish you'd say, 'open sesame', my lips are well and truly sealed," giggled Warwick. "Goodness! Aren't we having such fun! Now, tell me all about the second bird who, according to you, could easily be a contender for the Tate Modern!"

THREE MORNINGS ON

"Aha!" crooned Warwick glancing up at Pegg as the two sat having breakfast (Vincent sprawled at Pegg's feet) and going through the morning papers. "The dreaded Bernhard Walton has been reported as missing.

Apparently, his wife and two brats are *devastated.* God, how I *loathe* the word!"

"Anything else?"

"No, *nada,* nothing." Warwick took a sip of coffee. "In the meantime, anything from across the Atlantic?"

"Same old, same old. Oil billionaire Sebastian Salamander remains outraged by the callous and cowardly attack - his words, not mine - on his historical - perhaps that's a typo and it should have said 'hysterical' - oil derrick, while his fiancé, glamorous cabaret star Delilah Divoon - cabaret? - having cancelled all her Las Vegas performances, remains at his homestead, *Rancho Plata, Plata. Plata,* comforting him."

"I bet. By having her suck on his *flesh*-coloured oil derrick," snickered Warwick.

"Uh-oh," muttered Pegg. "Another copycat from the looks of it. Here. I'll read it out to you. *'Gerald Thompson, a part-time caterer and dog walker, was left, unconscious, outside A & E, St. George's Hospital, Tooting yesterday evening. Mr. Thompson, who was found by a passing nurse, is believed to be suffering from several severe disfiguring injuries. This is the second attack of a similar nature reported almost two months ago. Could we be seeing the emergence of a serial MUTILATOR as opposed to a SERIAL KILLLER? Only time will tell'."*

"Bloody Hell!" exploded Warwick. "Who the *puck* can this guy be as he needs to be found and stopped. Pronto! Not only because of any such further attacks, but because he's also stealing my - our - thunder!"

"Hear! Hear!" grunted Pegg. "Once we finish breakfast, I'm on it. I'll get those jungle drums beating."

"It's a pucking liberty," said Warwick with a pout. "Talk about an understudy thrown into the limelight and receiving a standing ovation!"

VICTORIA STATION

They met in a local Starbucks.

He: "I take it you've seen the mention in several of todays' papers? With luck it should get those alarm bells well and truly ringing."

She: "Well, my friend, let's keep them ringing as we're only getting started. With a mere *two* punches below the belt, there's a lot more body left to punch. According to one of my sources, the tactful reference to disfigurements covers such nightmares as missing fingers, toes, noses, hands and in one case, half of some poor guy's whatnot!"

He: "Ouch!"

She: "There was hardly a mention of carved letters, but that could have been easily overlooked."

He: "So, ready for the next one?"

She: "Most certainly. And as we've been given the accolade of being a potential serial *mutilator,* let's keep on mutilating. The more we keep on upsetting the real McCoy, the better it will be. As for our avaricious, but discreet helpers, they are more than ready for more readies!"

He, after a contemplative pause: "Are you still okay with all this? No second thoughts? After all we don't have any real proof that the guy and those two creeps are a hundred percent responsible for what happened to us."

She: "Am I a hundred percent sure about this and the fact that he - or all three - may or may not be guilty?" She gave a tight smile. "I'm about as sure about him, them, being guilty as I am about Venus de Milo being a pickpocket! In other words, no, I'm not a hundred percent sure, merely ninety percent sure. I've spent the last years wracking my brains as to who the culprits responsible for our attacks could be or who would have guts and be sick enough to do such a thing and, strange as it may seem, the unwavering finger of suspicion always comes back pointing at that smug, supercilious Standton and his two minions."

He: "Well said." He gave a snigger. "And if we *are* mistaken, at least we're having fun!"

A LAVISH DUPLEX PENTHOUSE - CHELSEA HARBOUR

"My guys are still looking into it," confirmed Pegg. "But rest assured, whoever this so-called copycat is, he's leaving no tracks. Even the police are baffled. As for his victims, they're apparently no help, both saying they can't remember anything apart from coming to in hospital."

"I've been cudgelling my brains as to who this person, or persons, could be, but nobody springs to mind. I had thought it may have been Roger Walton, but that thought has been well and truly scotched. Haha! However, instead of being a deterrent, I see if more as a challenge. In other words, a pathetic attempt at anything you can do, I can do better."

"By that, I take you have another person in mind?"

"I have indeed," chortled Warwick. "Again, it's connected to my schooldays, not quite *The Happiest Days of Your Life* as claimed by a certain Mr. John Dighton. Whilst at my so-called punishment school where I had the good fortune to meet Tally and Lance, there were two more pupils, close friends of Norman Livingston, who really got my goat. A pathetic sycophant named Giles Gordon, and his equally pathetic equivalent named Frank Boreham. Therefore, let's get Christopher Googling and work his magic in order to find these odious, little pricks."

"Little pricks?" chuckled Pegg. "Reminds me of something Aussie actress Coral Browne said to some queen at a cocktail party she had been bamboozled into attending."

"Coral Browne?"

"Married to actor Vincent Price; the couple known in Hollywood as Mr. and Mrs. Horror."

"Sounds suitable."

"At this party, here in London in the eighties, the host, some flamboyant queen who saw himself as a connoisseur of the arts, came over to where a disgruntled Coral was sitting on a sofa between to frail, awe-struck gays and said brightly. "Darling Coral, look at you, a rose between two thorns!"

"Yes," replied Coral deadpan. "And wondering which one has the bigger prick."

"Brilliant," snickered Warwick. "From what I've heard, Miss Browne was known for her witty, acerbic comebacks. I would have liked to have met her. However, coming back to the twenty-first century, let's get Christopher in here and ask him to see what he can find out regarding Gordon and Boreham."

*

"Sir, if you have a moment," said Christopher having knocked gently on the study door.

"For you, Christopher, I always have a moment," crooned Warwick. "Aha! I see you've brought along the usual bribe for his nibs."

"Not a usual bribe at all, sir," grinned Christopher handing an excited Vincent a doggy treat, "as Vincent sees it as his right and our humble awareness of his majestic presence."

"That His Majesty most certainly does," giggled Warwick. Taking a sip of his de rigueur mid-day martini, he said glibly. "Now, you obviously have some news."

"Yes, sir, I do."

"Then, Sherlock Holmes Christopher Wren, take a pew and tell all."

"Thank you, sir," replied Christopher sitting down a touch embarrassed on the edge of the sofa. "Now, about your former school botherations" - he handed Warwick a slip of paper - "Giles Gordon, following an abortive attempt to study law, is now a questionable second-hand car dealer with a showroom in Barnet. While Boreham is the manager of a hardware shop in Bayswater."

"My, talk about a pair of achievers," tittered Warwick. Eyeing Vincent h busy with a second doggy treat he said softly. "On hearing the term 'second-hand car dealer' the most delightful connotations spring to mind. As for being the illustrious manager of a hardware store in Bayswater, the skies the limit. Now, when Mr. Pegg returns - where is he, by the way? - let's have a pow-wow in order to discuss our two latest mutilations." He gave a snicker. "Be warned, Christopher, for what I have already spinning in my technicoloured mind will have you, Harry and Mr. Pegg reaching for your safety helmets!"

LATER

"I somehow never saw my elegant study as a teepee," giggled Warwick eyeing Pegg sitting on an adjacent chair along with Harry and Christopher on the sofa. "But here we are for a mega powwow. Me, Big Chief Warwick and his braves." He gave a further giggle. "Just as well I didn't say feather headdresses to be worn as you Harry, no doubt, would have turned up wearing a feather boa! Haha!"

"But I haven't," replied Harry, not best pleased. Turning to face Christopher, he said crisply. "Christopher, please tell Mr, Warwick what more *we* found out about the two so-called gentlemen."

"Ahem," said Christopher, nervously clearing his throat. "Let's deal with Giles Gordon first, shall we? As I've already said, after an abortive attempt at studying law, he owns a second-hand car dealership based in Barnet. What I didn't know until Harry, and I, had another look about an hour ago, apart from selling cars he's seriously into sky diving."

"Sky diving?" echoed Warwick. "Now that *is* interesting. However, attempting to mutilate Gittings at ten thousand feet could pose a teensy-weensy bit of a problem: so, this is what Big Chief Warwick suggests we do to him on good old terra firma."

"A drive instead of a dive to remember," sniggered Pegg.

"A drive to remember and a drive to regret is what I'm sure you meant to say, Pegg," said Warwick with a tight smile. "So, do my loyal braves agree?" Not waiting for a response, he said cheerfully. "Clearly, I'd like this taken care of ASAP. As Gordon has never met any of you, I suggest Pegg does the necessary with Christopher as his helper whilst Harry takes a sabbatical."

"You mean I'm out of the picture?"

"Yes, for this particular picture, Harry old friend," said Warwick with a syrupy smile. "After all, it only takes two to tango. However, when it comes to Frank Boreham, you'll be given a free hand. Knowing you, former occupation I can't wait to see what you'll do with something like a roller or a power mower! By the way it may amuse you to know that forehead-carving is now back on the agenda."

THE NEXT MORNING

"Bit of a flash bugger," observed Pegg as he and Warwick drove into the small parking area outside the showroom. The single story building surmounted by half a dozen fluttering banners emblazoned with the words GILES GORDON FOR THE CAR OF YOUR DREAMS.

"Not for long. Pegg. Not for long," replied Warwick with a sardonic smile. "Right. Off you go and do your Oscar winning performance while I back out and wait out of sight before following you when, hopefully, you take the car of your choice for a test drive. Christopher will then follow me as he'll have to return the other car and bring it back and park it nearby."

"I can see Christopher crammed into what looks like a grey VW."

"It's what I call the staff charabanc," tittered Warwick. He gave a snort. "Dear Harry wanted an *orange* VW, but I said no matter how hard the old queen tried, he'd never look good enough to eat! Now, enough of the chitchat. Time for your close-up, Mr. De Mille."

"Good morning. sir," chirruped the receptionist, a Mitzi Gaynor lookalike as Pegg entered the car showroom. "How can I help you?"

"The name's Hunter, John Hunter said Pegg smoothly. Giving the perky woman a whiter that white smile he added equally as smoothly. "I take it there *is* a Mr. Giles Gordon?"

"There is, indeed, sir," said a cheerful voice as Gordon appeared in the doorway to what was obviously his office. "Good morning, sir. I take it you are here for Giles Gordon to help you find the car of your dreams?"

"That I am," replied Pegg, all business. "I'm looking for a saloon. A Mercedes preferably, but I can't go above a certain figure."

"And that is, sir?" replied Gordon cooly; mentally rubbing hands in anticipation of a sale.

Pegg named the figure.

"So, Mr. Gordon, show me a couple of cars and if the price if more or less within the figure I mentioned, we can then talk business."

On selecting a car, a dark blue Mercedes-Benz EQA, and after a cheerful bit of haggling over the final price, Gordon suggested the de rigueur test drive.

"I'll just collect the keys and then we can take a spin in your new Giles Gordon car of your dreams car!" he said wittily. "Won't be a sec!"

Leaving the car dealership, Gordon said cheerfully. "I always suggest to a potential customer that we do what I call my scenic route, if you don't mind, Mr. Hunter."

"Not at all," replied Pegg, the word "bingo" lighting up in his mind. "When you say scenic, may I suggest Little Venice? It's a favourite of mine and not too far."

Little Venice? thought Gordon irritably. *Bloody cheek. However, if you do buy this not at all reliable heap, so be it."*

On approaching the part of the canal where One Star was moored, Pegg, glancing in the rearview mirror, caught a glimpse of Warwick in the Mercedes and Christopher in the VW close behind. *Right,* he thought. *Showtime!*

"What the fuck!" yelped Gordon as Pegg suddenly jammed on the brakes, slewing to a stop.

"Just testing the brakes, Mr. Gordon!" said Pegg cheerfully as he jabbed a syringe previously kept hidden inside his jacket pocket into the startled man's scrawny neck. "A perfect prick for a total prick," he chuckled, sliding open the window as a grinning Warwick approached.

"Goody good," chortled Warwick eyeing the unconscious man. "I guarantee yon sleeping beauty won't be much to look at once we get him on to the houseboat and I slip into Sweeny Todd mode and give him a one-off super-duper Warwick L.S. shampoo!"

"And that is?"

"C'mon, Pegg! Get that grey matter going," chortled Warwick. "As Gordon *is* a second-hand car salesman, it's pretty obvious to *moi* that a notorious barber like Sweeny Todd, when washing his hair, would use his special car salesman shampoo. His unique *battery acid* shampoo! Or, sulphuric acid to give it its correct name."

Giving a sigh, he added disparagingly. "It won't leave much of a base on which to create a shining example of our return to forehead carving. But then. rather like beggars, even the most sophisticated mutilators cannot always be choosers."

*

Several hours later an unconscious Gordon was discovered outside the A & E Department of a local hospital, his head and face covered in painful acid burns. Adding a further element of curiosity to the heinous event was the fact that the car in which Mai Zitt, the receptionist had seen both Gordon and the mysterious Mr. Hunter set off in for a test drive was found parked near to the boastful GILES GORDON FOR THE CAR OF YOUR DREAMS showroom.

12

RANCHO PLATA, PLATA, PLATA

"I know, I just know, bloody Warwick Laudanum-Standton must have been behind that act of sabotage," said Kurt in a no-nonsense voice. "Just as I know Delilah agrees with me one hundred percent. His uninvited and therefore unexpected presence at your gala party the other week is sure-fire proof of this."

"And you, my darling Deliah, agree with Kurt?" grunted Sebastian.

"Totally," pouted Delilah, giving Sebastian's hand a loving squeeze.

"Right," growled Sebastian. "So how do we deal with this. Kurt, any suggestions?"

"His Achilles heel is his dog, Vincent," replied Kurt.

"Jesus, Kurt! You surely don't expect me to allow you to do something to an innocent dog, do you?" questioned Sebastian. "Not only is that an insult to my intelligence, but an insult to my first oil derrick. The replacement of which they will begin installing tomorrow."

"That's brilliant news, Sebastian," replied Kurt. "As for my out of order suggestion we get to Laudanum-Standton via his dog; I apologise." He gave a tremulous smile. "I take it the replacement derrick is again coloured gold?"

"Of course," replied Sebastian deadpan. "What other colour is there?"

"Well," crooned Delilah. "Once the new derrick is in place, *I* plan to christen it by clambering up part of it and sing for my darling Sebastian. My song on this *second* memorable occasion being the Supremes' *Back in My Arms Again.*"

"Hear! Hear!" yodelled Joel, followed by an off-key. *"I've got him in my arms again. I'm satisfied, so satisfied!"*

A LAVISH DUPLEX PENTHOUSE - CHELSEA HARBOUR

"Today it's *my* turn" carolled Harry as he finished helping Christopher put away the breakfast dishes. "Today *I* pay a never to be forgotten visit to Mr. Frank Boreham at his Olde Curiosity - read hardware - Shoppe in Bayswater. Haha!"

"And what exactly do you plan to do with Mr. Boreham?"

"Something hideous that will make even our blasé young Warwick go cross-eyed with disbelief," carolled Harry. "Just you *all* wait and see."

"And you're quite sure you don't me or Pegg to give you a helping hand?"

"Give me a helping hand?" trilled Harry, waving his hands. "Why would I need a helping hand for *this* particular exercise when I have two adequate hands - *as you well know* - to do my bidding!"

F. BOREHAM - SUPPLIER OF HARDWARE ITEMS

"Good morning, sir," croaked Frank Boreham, a doppelganger for Jiminy Cricket in what sounded to Harry like a twenty-five to thirty cigarettes a day voice. "Frank Boreham, the man himself, at your service. How may I serve you. Haha!"

"Good morning, Mr. Boreham," replied Harry affably, having donned a black wig along with a handlebar moustache, steel-rimmed glasses and, his piece de resistance, a large wart applied to his chin for the occasion. "Fine display, I must say," he added looking around. "So much so, that I'm sure you'll have precisely what I'm looking for."

"And what *precisely* are you looking for, sir?" simpered Boreham. "As you so rightly say, I am quite sure we'll have what you're after. If Frank Borham can't oblige, we'll make sure we can get the item for you within a day or two. Try me!"

"It's nothing special," said Harry matter-of-factly, "simply an electric screwdriver as I have some shelves and pictures to put up and hang up."

"Not a problem, sir," smirked Boreham. "I am sure we have what you're looking for. If you'll follow me to those shelves over there, you can try out the one of your choice and. if it meets with sir's approval, better still."

"I rather like this one," said Harry reaching for one he had seen on Google. "Can I give it a try?"

"Absolutely, sir," croaked Boreham. "All the samples on display are fully charged - my daily *bore* as I call it - Haha! All one has to do is press this button..."

"Here, let me," interrupted Harry reaching for the screwdriver in question.

Seconds later the shop was filled with Frank Boreham's agonised screams as Harry rammed the active screwdriver into each of the shop owner's kneecaps."

Leaving the screaming man writhing in agony on the floor, Harry walked calmly away from the shop. Pausing in a convenient doorway, he quickly removed the wig, glasses, moustache and wart and dropped them inside a nondescript carry bag he'd brought with him, before boarding a bus bound for Marble Arch.

RANCHO PLATA, PLATA, PLATA

"I've got it!" announced Kurt in a phone call to Delilah. "Or at least, aided and abetted by my lovely Joel here, *we* got it after Joel, a great Shirley MacLaine fan, suggested we watch one of her early films on Prime. The film being - you won't believe it - *The Trouble with Harry*, directed by the one and only Hitchcock, no less. And there it was, loud and clear. It won't be as effective as involving Vincent, but why not go for old Harry, Warwick's butler-cum-Nurse Ratchet-cum-Mrs Doubtfire. The we can even go for Harry's husband, Christopher Wren, Warwick's chef. In other words, old Harry for starters with Wren as the main course, with a pudding in waiting!"

"I *love* it!" shrilled Delilah. "And what trouble do you have in mind for Harry?"

"With his other half being a chef, the obvious answer is to come up with something *culinary*, something showy, something like a Harry flambé!"

"A Harry flambé sounds quite delicious!" crooned Delilah. "Hold on a sec while I tell Sebastian about your suggested do unto Warwick after his heinous do unto us! Better still, let me call you back within the hour as I know, just know, whatever you have in mind will see my darling, depressed Sebastian, go into a much-needed overdrive! Love ya!"

*

"Your diaphanous Delilah calling her sumptuous Samson back as promised!" crooned Delilah. "Needless to say, Sebastain is both thrilled and fascinated by your gourmet suggestions, so tell me more."

"Since we last spoke, I have been sitting here while wearing a mega thinking cap," chuckled Kurt. "Instead of two separate gourmet courses it would be far easier if it were simply one large main course. Therefore, I suggest two *chateaubriand* steaks, namely Harry and Christopher, which would guarantee a tremendous impact. When Harry is out and about, it's usually when he's out with Vincent on what Warwick wittily describes as a 'widdle and watch where you step' walk."

"Typical Warwick," interrupted Delilah.

"However, you know Sebastian's feelings about involving a dog, so best we deal with the two old dodderers as one. In the old days I would have asked Jess Rix for his help but as we both know, that's no longer on the cards. However, I do have another contact back in London; a totally ruthless, yet totally reliable young man, named Joseph Heyday, known in London's seamy underside simply as Mayday. If anyone can produce those steaks rare and sizzling, Mayday's the man. I plan on calling him as soon as Sebastian gives me the go ahead."

"Hold on, Kurt. You're on speaker phone so I'll let Sebastian answer that!"

"Good morning, or afternoon, Kurt," boomed Sebastian. "Simply do what it takes, mah friend, as you have mah an' mah lil' Delilah's blessin'. An', as I said before, make sure you don't harm the pooch!"

"Leave it to me, Sebastian," replied Kurt. "I can assure you Heyday Mayday and I will not let you down."

CHELSEA HARBOUR - LOTS ROAD - TWO DAYS LATER

"As his lordship, Pegg and Vincent have taken the BMW to visit Peggs, and as we're not permitted the use of the Merc and the VW is in for a service, us plebs will simply have to make use of your ancient Ford Mondeo," tittered Harry. "I take it Miranda will manage to take us as far as Harrods without collapsing?" (Miranda being the nickname of Christopher's twenty-year-old Ford Mondeo.)

"Thank you, Harry! Fortunately for us, Miranda is catching up on her beauty sleep in the building's underground car park, otherwise she could have easily refused to start as a result of your derogatory comment!"

Oblivious to the solitary, leather-clad figure sitting astride a powerful Kawasaki motorcycle who had been watching the building and the entrance/exit to the underground carpark for the past two days, Christopher cautiously steered Miranda up the ramp and onto the sunny street.

"About fucking time," growled Joseph Heyday, a grizzled Chips Rafferty lookalike reaching for his helmet before double checking the contents to the two panniers attached to the motorcycle. Firing up the powerful motorcycle he gave a sadistic chuckle. "So, Mayday, time to get cooking. Having seen Standton plus some bruiser and the dog leave earlier in the BMV and not the Merc, it's just as well I sussed out all the vehicles belonging to the poofter household!"

Christopher was about to accelerate from Lots Road into King's Road when a dark figure on a motorcycle drew up alongside and shouted. "Your rear tyre! Your rear tyre!"

Braking sharply, Christopher wound down the driver's window and called out. "Sorry! I couldn't quite hear you! What did you say?" his words greeted by a petrol bomb - ignited seconds beforehand - hitting him in the face and bursting into flame. The first firebomb swiftly followed by a second before Heyday roared off. The strength of the combined explosions of the two bombs and the car damaging nearby shop windows and setting off endless car alarms. The noise completely obliterating Harry's and Christopher's agonised screams as they were burned alive.

*

Joseph Heyday's text to Kurt was a simple three words. "Heyday now Mayday."

"It's done," announced a grinning Kurt to Joel. "I'll give Delilah a quick call and then you and I, my randy, well-hung, insatiable glorious husband can then go and treat ourselves to a celebratory lunch! Whoever said this is as good as it gets, obviously never got the chance to meet Kurt Ford-Cameron, Joel Ford-Cameron and the sensational Salamanders for whom it gets better by the minute!"

PEGGS

"They've been *what*?" exclaimed Warwick on receiving a call from the police. "Err ... could you please hold on whilst I inform a great friend of the two gentlemen as to what has happened. Better, still, let me call you back once I've gotten over the initial shock. Yes, I've noted the number. Thank you."

"What was that all about?" question Pegg who was sitting nearby enjoying a cup of tea.

"That was the police," muttered Warwick. "Jesus, Pegg!" he exploded. "Someone just firebombed Christopher's pucking car and he and Harry are both *dead*! Incinerated! Jesus Christ! Have that pucking Sebastian Salamander and that pucking Kurt Cameron got something to answer for"

"Harry and Christopher *dead*? Firebombed?" gasped Pegg.

"Yes, in their car at the junction of Lots Road and King's Road. Pucking Hell, Pegg! Whatever next?"

"It's okay, Warwick, it's okay; calm down," said Pegg rising to his feet and embracing Warwick in his brawny arms. "Here, sit down while I fix you a stiff drink."

He turned to Trish who had been watching Warwick with increasing concern. "It's Harry and Christopher, Warwick's sweet old butler and lovely chef. Some ruthless bastard firebombed their car an hour or so ago."

"Oh, my God!" cried Trish, her hands rushing to her face. "I heard you say something about people being dead, Pegg. But old Harry and Christopher? That's terrible!"

"It's more than terrible," muttered Pegg. "It's a fucking liability! Look, Warwick and I were planning on taking you and Coli out lunch, but we need to get back to Chelsea Harbour."

"Of course," replied Trish. "At a time like this, words seem so pointless, but I am so, so sorry, and I know Coli will be too. Do you feel you need to leave Vincent with us for the rest of the day, even the night, or will you be taking hm with you?"

"Thanks, Trish, but we'll take him with us." Giving Trish the semblance of a smile, and making sure Warwick was out of earshot, Pegg added wryly. "After all, rather like his master, he enjoys a good drama!"

*

"I still can't pucking believe it," muttered Warwick as he and Pegg headed back to Chelsea Harbour; Pegg driving with Warwick and Vincent on the passenger seat. "But as Mother Dearest always says; one must look on the bright side. So, doing just that, at least one's been spared the expense of not one, but *two* cremations."

"Jesus! Warwick!" snapped Pegg. "That's a bit sick! Even for you!"

"Really?" crooned Warwick, spoiling for a fight. "Well, Mr. Goody pucking Two-Shoes, it's more than a glaring fact, we're talking about me and my *chequebook* here, so don't you *dare* start getting so high and nighty with me. In fact, if the truth be known, living in such luxury as *my* penthouse and, up until today, waited on hand and foot, seems to have gone to your not exactly Einstein-inspired head. There's always a front door and nobody is going to stop you should you wish leave."

He gave a snort. "Strange, isn't it, how quickly love dies. Almost as quicky as it must have taken that firebomb to snuff out Harry and Christopher."

The remainder of the journey continued in a strained silence apart from a few whimpers from Vincent, the pooch immediately aware of the growing frigidity within the BMW.

*

"Yes, yes, I've already been informed," said Warwick soothingly as a grim-faced Bert came forward to meet him as he entered the main lobby. "It's terrible news, Bert. Absolutely terrible. Give me a few minutes and then why don't you join me and Vincent in the penthouse for a much-needed drink."

If Bert was aware of the fact Warwick has not included Pegg's name in his conversation, he gave no indication of the fact whereas Pegg, acutely aware, was inwardly seething.

"Will do so, sir, and thank you sir." Tut-tutting, Bert, adding grist to the mill, said in a sonorous voice. "Mr. Harry and Mr; Chistopher will be sorely missed."

"What pucking poppycock," snorted Warwick as the lift whooshed its way up to the penthouse floor. "People are such hypocrites. Bert and co *loathed* Harry and Christopher, calling them Evadne Hinge and Hilda Bracket being their backs."

Glancing at Pegg staring straight ahead, Warwick bent down and, giving Vincent's ears a fondle, said with a chortle. "Goodness, Vincent, I almost forget spongy Pegg is no longer speaking to *moi* seeing he's already left the building."

On exiting the lift Warwick called over his shoulder. "If you're still in a poncey, woncey, flouncy, wouncy mood and wish to start packing, please use your *own tacky* suitcase and *not* my Gucci or Louis Vees."

"You-are-fucking-unbelievable," said Pegg through gritted teeth. "You don't give a fuck - oh, *excusez moi* - a *puck* about anyone else, do you? Vincent being the only possible exception. In a matter of minutes: not hours, not days, the person I fell in love has disappeared in a Rumpelstiltskin-like spiral of smoke."

"As far as I'm concerned, I am *still* that exalted person," replied Warwick loftily. "Added to which, if you weren't so pucking Hell-bent on being such a self-centred drama queen yourself, you'd still see it!"

Glaring at Warwick, Pegg gave a sudden roar and lunged forward. Within seconds the two were rolling about on the floor, tearing off each other's clothes. Stark naked, Warwick and Pegg began hugging and kissing, as if there was no tomorrow.

Cocking his head as he watched the panting couple. Vincent gave a small bark of approval before trotting through to the kitchen to check if, by some magical chance, Christopher had left a doggy treat in his bowl before setting out on his fatal journey,

13

A LAVISH DUPLEX PENTHOUSE - CHELSEA HARBOUR

"Good morning, Warwick, it's Jess Rix calling. I'm not too early, am I?"

"Heavens to Betsy Wetsy, Jess. Pegg, Vincent and I have been up since sparrow part!"

"Sparrow part?"

"My elegant alternative to fart," tittered Warwick. "So, how may I help you seeing it's usually *moi* calling Mr. Fix Rix. Not the other way around."

"First of all, Warwick, I was appalled to hear about what happened to Harry and Christopher. Dreadful, quite dreadful. My condolences."

"Thank you, Jess," replied Warwick. "And now the 'and'."

"Haha! Of course, the mysterious 'and'," chuckled Jess. "The 'and' in this case being you'll obviously be looking for another chef, major domo, whatever."

"I am, so, back to the recurring 'and'."

"*And* I could have the perfect solution for you."

"Gadzooks, Jess! That was quick!" camped Warwick, "Wait whilst I tell Pegg. It's Jess saying he's already found us a replacement for Harry and Christopher." Speaking back into the phone he said chirpily. "Please continue with this good sounding news."

"Instead of two gay guys, these two are a couple pf lesbians."

"I *love* lesbians!" crooned Warwick, "Think Lily Tomlin and Jane Wagner! Tell me more?"

"They're known - and I kid not - as Punch and Judy. Judy being the one who should be called Punch and Punch the one who should be called Judy.

Haha! Punch's correct name being Julia Mander and Judy's correct name, Wilma Davis. And, before you ask, Julia is a five-star female chef and Punch, a five-star housekeeper-cum-major domo in a skirt. In addition to those plaudits, should you ever have a problem that needs to be resolved discreetly, these two can be a veritable Anne Bonny and Mary Read. The two formidable women pirates who terrorised the Caribbean in the late seventeenth century."

"Punch and Judy? I love them already!" crooned Warwick. "Please tell me that if they *do* end up working here, I won't have to refer to them as *Funch* and *Fudy*?"

"Funch and Fudy?"

"My lame attempt at a joke, Jess," giggled Warwick. "So, when can I meet these two Harry and Christopher wannabes?"

"Later today, if you're around. Luckily for you, they're looking for a new position - ha - as their former employer has now wafted off to that happy hunting ground in the sky."

"Could you try and see if they could be here by noon today for an interview? That gives them four and a half hours to make themselves presentable."

"I am quite sure they could be there by noon," chuckled Jess. "Give me a couple pf minutes and I'll call you back."

Jess's return call came within minutes. "You're on!" he announced. "Good luck and let me know how you get on."

TWELVE NOON SHARP

"A Miss Mander and a Miss Davis here to see you, Mr. Warwick, sir." announced Bert over the house phone.

"Thank you, Bert. Please send them up." Replacing the receiver Warwick couldn't resist a giggle. "Unfortunate choice or words there, Mr. L.S!"

"They're here," he hissed at Pegg. "I'll go and greet them at the lift with Vincent as my safety net and, If I'm not immediately consumed amidst wild cries of 'isn't he gorgeous" or 'he looks good enough to eat', I'll bring them through to where you'll be sitting on the terrace as planned!"

Before Pegg was even halfway out of his chair, Warwick, accompanied by an excited Vincent, raced through to greet the visitors.

"Here goes, Vincent," he muttered. "These two ladies could be the new source of endless doggy treats and pats so, best behaviour, please."

Warwick stood with a ready smile as the lift door slid open. "Good morning, ladies," he crooned. "Welcome to my humble abode in the sky."

"Mr. Warwick Laudanum-Standton. I presume," announced the Lola Bunny lookalike. "Wilma Davis otherwise known as Judy and the lady with me, Julia Mander, otherwise known as Punch."

"Hi!" squawked the Olive Oil lookalike stepping briskly from the lift. Glancing down at a tail wagging Vincent she gave a cry. "Oh, my *God*, Mr. Laudanum-Standton, Jess Rix told us *you* were a handsome young fellow, but who is this *uber-handsome* fellow at your feet who puts anybody else described as handsome to shame?"

"His name is Vincent, err ... Punch, and the *real* ruler of this penthouse-cum-roost."

"And I can quite see why," chortled Julia aka Punch, stooping to take hold of Vincent's proffered paw. One of the many tricks taught to him by Trish when visiting Peggs.

"Oh, my goodness, such manners," she cried, gently shaking Vincent's paw. "Good afternoon, handsome Vincent. My name's Julia - or Punch - and, if there's any room left, I'd simply *love* to join your fan club!"

"I'm sure that can be arranged, *Punch*," crooned a delighted Warwick. "Now, please come through to the main terrace where Pegg, my partner, and self were having a mid-morning martini. Pegg may have just made a fresh pitcher but, should you prefer anything else. You only have to ask."

As Warwick led a smiling Punch and Judy (Julia and Wilma) out onto the terrace, Pegg jumped to his feet to greet them with a cheerful "Hi, there. ladies!"

"Punch and Judy, meet Pegg, my other half. And Pegg, before we even *offer* Punch and Judy a welcome drink, I'd like to offer them a *congratulatory* drink as Vincent agrees with me one hundred and ten percent that, without doubt, you are the heaven-sent solution to our little problem!"

What the hell? thought Pegg raising a quizzical eyebrow. *God only knows what sort of magic dust those two must have sprinkled over you Warwick on exiting the lift; but it certainly worked!*

As the four sat enjoying their martinis despite Julia aka Punch stating her preference for a G and T but, as the pitcher of martini looked so enticing, why not? Warwick suddenly said, all business. "Jess told me of your charges, fees, salaries, whatever. All of which are fine, plus I know he also informed you accommodation was also included. When we finish our drinks, allow me to show you the flat you'll be using. The flat it only has one bedroom, I'm afraid, and is situated on the floor directly underneath the penthouse."

He gave a chortle. "Harry's idea of interior decorating is somewhat Pollyanna meets Disney meets Hicks, but please free to make any changes you deem necessary. I know an interior desecrator - Haha - Hector Hopkins - who is there to do your every bidding."

"Sounds wonderful, doesn't it, Punch?" said Wilma.

"Absolutely, Judy," simpered Julia. She gave a light, scratchy laugh. "I take Vincient *is* allowed the occasional sleep-over? Hee-hee!"

"Punch has anyone ever told you you're a 'livin' doll' Elvis Presley style, because you *are*!" crooned Warwick. "So, after you've had a look at the flat and you would like to make various changes to the décor, Pegg will arrange for you to stay at the Chelsea Harbour Hotel."

Oh, I will, will I? thought Pegg. *Since when have I become your fucking lackey-cum-secretary?*

Ignoring Pegg's angry look, Warwick added cheerfully. "Now, the million-euro question. When can you start?"

"Tomorrow," announced Wilma. "We could start tomorrow. I would like to check out the kitchen once we've had a dekko at the flat. If there's anything Punch and I need, we'll give you a list before we leave."

"Sounds good," said Pegg for want of something to say. "I see your martinis are almost ready for another round, so why not let Warwick show you the flat while I organise another pitcher along with a G and T for the having made do Punch!"

"That sounds perfect," giggled Julia looking down at a blissful Vincent as she continued fondling his ears. "And tell me, Vincent," she added in a little girl voice. "Would you like to some along with Punchy Wunchy while she and Judy have a look at the flatty watty? I do hope so."

Jesus! thought Pegg. *No wonder the likes of Spitting Image went into a decline.*

What a charmer, thought Warwick. *And as Vincent is so taken by the scatty, somewhat batty Punch, then so am I!*

RANCHO PLATA, PLATA, PLATA

"Not only fried but *rari*-fried!" guffawed Sebastian to a delighted Delilah. "Serves that double-barrelled little bastard right!"

"And no *hotdog* included?" asked Delilah.

"No, lil' girl. No hot dawg included, as Vincent - damn stupid name for a dawg if you ask me - an' his master were visitin' master boy's lover's training school for guide dogs. A bit of an anachronism if you ask me, but somethin' he could be given credited for."

"A very *rare* credit," snickered Delilah. "Almost as *rare* as those two former old retainers!" She took a genteel sip of coffee. "So, magnificent, macho, love of my life; what's next on our ongoing campaign against the odious Warwick?"

"Well, lil' one, today is the day the replacement oil derrick is delivered an' tomorrow night is the celebration party. Once these are done an' dusted, I must leave it up to you and Kurt to advise me regarding the next 'that'll teach you" for the little prick." Sebastian gave a chuckle. "Apart from blowin' up that penthouse of his, Imma kinda outa suggestions."

"No way. José!" carolled Delilah. "Despite his attitude toward us, Warwick is quite popular. One of his most favourite of 'cosy ups' is another rich, elderly aunt, Aunt Clementine, who lives in great style in Venice and, according to hearsay, devotes her whole time doing her utmost to outshine the legendary Peggy Guggenheim. Needless to say, Aunt Clementine, a countess no less, lives in a grand palazzo simply bursting with valuable paintings, tapestries and more. All of which Warwick, no doubt, will inherit."

"A Clementine-cum-wannabe Guggenheim," chuckled Sebastian. "The ol' gal sounds ideal for what Ah have in mind and therefore a must meet. So, my lil' darlin'. Fancy a trip to Venice with Kurt an' Joel as chaperones?"

"Goodness," said Delilah with a throaty laugh. "I thought you'd never ask."

*

"Kurt, it's Sebastian Salamander. "How ya doin'."

"Ah, Sebastain, a very good morning to you. I - we - are fine, thanks. Loving the work and cannot thank you enough for the opportunity (Kurt now part of Sebastian's PR team). It's a dream come true!"

"Great Kurt, glad to hear it," boomed Sebastian. "Now, reason for callin'. I'ma plannin' a surprise for mah lil' gal, a lil' surprise to which you and Joel are an integral part. So, how about a lil' trip to Venice, Italy, next week? I say Venice, Italy, because a few years back when I wanted to surprise someone else. The arsehole of a travel agent booked us to *Lil' Venice,* London, England! Haw! Haw!"

"A trip to Venice, *Bella Italia,* sounds great, Sebastian . . . but?" questioned Kurt. "And I'm sure you'd know there would be a 'but' waiting in the wings."

"There sure is," chuckled Sebastain. "The 'but' being A'll need ya to take care of a lil' problem while there . . ."

"The 'lil problem' being a Warwick Laudanum-Standton type problem," interrupted Kurt matter-of-factly.

"Spot on, as always, Kurt! Her name is Clementine Lorenzo, *Contessa* Clementine Lorenzo, an' apparently another rich, devoted an' obviously blindfolded geriatric aunt."

"In other words, you want me to find a suitable lire-seduced gondolier willing to paddle Aunt Clementine along to the Grand Canal in the sky?"

"No, nothin' like that, we don't want Aunt Clementine barbecued but we sure do her ol' palazzo an' its priceless contents. In other words, not barbecued but seriously broke," boomed Sebastian. "So, how about we leave a week from today, check in at The Gritti Palace, an' take it from there?"

"Sounds good, Sebastian. Joel will be over the proverbial moon as he's never been abroad."

"Well, as they say Kurt, there's always a first time."

A LAVISH DUPLEX PENTHOUSE - CHELSEA HARBOUR

"It's time once more for another of my *darling Zia* Clemmie calls to the old girl in Venice," said Warwick to Pegg lying spread-eagled on a nearby sun-lounger. "Or, better still, pay her a surprise visit armed with a jar or two of Fortnum and Mason Platinum caviar for her to get her ill-fitting dentures in to." He gave a chortle. "As I keep reminding Vincent, when I think of her elegant palazzo and her mountains of lire, it's best to continually *endear* her."

"A solidifying trip to Venice: Why not?" yawned Pegg, stretching his rippling arms above his shining head. "I'm a great fan of Harry's. As for their bellinis? *Bellisima!*"

"Right, I'll get Punch to book our flights for the coming weekend. There's no need to check if Zia Clemmie in residence seeing she spends her days emulating former party doyenne, Elsa Maxwell, entertaining endless pompous ex-pats and WOPOs made up of never-been writers and artists whilst gathering mildew inside what will soon be mine." Warwick gave a chortle. "Apart from the glorious *moi*, what tickles your fancy: The Gritti or The Cipriani?"

"Oh, The Gritti," chuckled Pegg. "I've always wanted a good fuck in a palace."

"God! At times you can be *so* gross, Signor Pegg," giggled Warwick.

"Yes, I know," chuckled Pegg. "And, should you have any complaints, I suggest you write a letter as I've obviously misunderstood your cries of 'Harder! Harder!' and 'yes, yes, *yes!*'"

"Per-lease! *Not* in front of Vincent, Maestro Massive *Zizi*! You *know* how sensitive he is! So, is this coming weekend okay with you?"

"A weekend in Venice - particularly a dirty one - is always okay with me!" chuckled Pegg. "Oh, and Warwick, before I forget."

"What?"

"Like Vincent, I too see you as a superstar!"

"As opposed to the *falling* star a day or two ago, you mean?" quipped Warwick.

"As Perry Como sang back in eighties," replied Pegg in a singsong voice. "*Catch a falling star and put it in your pocket; never let it fade away.*"

"Please stop with the caterwauling Pegg otherwise this resuscitated star could easily stop twinkling," tittered Warwick. "Aha! And here she is! Another star! The lovely Julia-cum-Punch- with a pitcher of martinis! Thank you, Judy. I take it everything is still to your liking?"

"To our liking, Mr. Warwick?" croaked Julia. "Forgive me for being so corny, but Wilma and I are as pleased as *punch*! Hee-hee!"

"Goody good!" said Warwick with a faux smile. "Now, Mr. Pegg and I have decided to spend a few awaydays in Venice - I'll give you the dates in a minute - and Vincent, of course, will be staying with Trish and Coli at Peggs. Therefore, if you and Julia wish to take a few days break; please do."

"Oh, Mr. Warwick, that would be lovely," rasped Wilma. "It sounds as if the break could coincide with Judy's little godson's birthday which means we attend his birthday party! He's going to be six!"

"A celebration *not* to be missed," replied Warwick with another faux smile. "Now, let me check those dates and call Tamara, my uber-efficient travel agent."

"Is there anything I can do?" asked Pegg.

"Yes," giggled Warwick. "Save your strength for all the *poling* you'll be doing in Venice, my about to be gondolier! Plus, I can show you the imaginary X marking the spot where I did a Vincent van G and sliced off the ear of a tiresome of friend Zia Clemmie's who tried to have his wicked way with innocent, lovely *moi*."

Pegg couldn't resist a snicker. "And what, may I ask, did you do with the poor sod's ear?"

"Why, tossed it into The Grand Canal, of course! What else would one do with an errant ear! Oh, and as Zia - I must remember she now prefers aunt - as *Aunt* Clementine will doubtless invite us to dinner, make sure you pack your dinner jacket as black tie is de rigueur!"

14

THE GRITTI PALACE HOTEL - VENICE

"*Buongiorno,* Dario, 'tis Signor Warwick calling. Is the Contessa available to speak to me, *per favore?*"

"*Buongiorno,* Signor Warwick," boomed Dario, the butler. "*Si,* I know the Contessa will be only too delighted to accept *your* call, Signor, seeing almost everyone is trying to get an invitation to the Contessa's party this evening!"

"Party this evening?" echoed Warwick. "Talk about a coincidence. Dario, as I happen to be here in Venice staying at The Gritti!"

"Then I know I shall see you this evening, Signor Warwick," boomed Dario. "Please hold. Signor, while I connect you."

"My now grown-up, precious *Putti?*" trilled Countess Clementine Lorenzo. "What a *heavenly* coincidence, your being here in *Venezia* as I am having a little gathering at Palazzo Lorenzo this evening which you, my darling Warwick, simply *have* to attend!"

"I'd love to Aunt Clementine," replied Warwick, "though there goes my planned surprise visit along with my two usual companions, Signor Fortnum and Signor Mason, plus, one more."

"Plus, one more precious *Putti?* What do you mean by one more?"

"A very charming gentleman named David Pegg, Aunt Clementine and, when I say charming, Signor Pegg would make even Italy's Inspector Salvo Montalbano look plain and in need of several plates of fattening pasta!"

"I love him already!" crowed Clementine, "but if Signor Pegg's with *you,* my precious *Putti,* then he wouldn't be at all interested in a lecherous old title like me, would he? Haha! Still, I simply *have* to meet what I've obviously missed. So, tonight at eight." Said as a statement, not a question.

"See you then, Aunt Clementine . . ."

"Before you hang up, my grown-up *Putti,* a quick question. Does the name Kurt Cameron mean anything to you?"

"Kurt Cameron?" gasped Warwick. "How on earth did *his* name come up?"

"It's simply because he called - he's also staying at The Gritti - and introduced himself saying he was a friend of yours and he and his companion would love to meet me and, if possible, have a tour of my little palazzo."

"And what did you say, Aunt Clementine?" said Warwick, alarm bells ringing.

"Why, I said I'd be delighted to meet him and his companion Noel, Joel or something like that, and invited them to this evening's get-together!"

There was what some people would call a dramatic pause but what Warwick saw as a worrisome moment. "Anything else, Aunt Clementine?"

"I wasn't going to tell you until I saw you tonight, but I got married last week, my new husband being Paulo Pablo. The film star," said Clementine coyly. "So, not only do you have a delicious new uncle you have two delicious cousins as well. Sophia, aged nineteen and Stephano, aged twenty."

There was a break during which a stunned Warwick could hear Clementine talking to someone in the background. "Darling, I *must* go so *ciao* and I'll see you and your lovely Signor Pegg later."

"You okay, Warwick?" asked Pegg as Warwick slowly replaced the receiver, his face tuning an unflattering puce in colour.

"No, I'm *not* pucking okay," snapped Warwick, "seeing that pucking old witch has not only gotten herself another husband, the pucking film star Paulo Pablo, but he's also the pucking father of two pucking kids from a previous marriage! Jesus Christ! I need a pucking drink! Pronto!"

PALAZZO LORENZO - LATER

"I take it that's the unexpected blemish on my anticipated inheritance," murmured Warwick nodding to where a tall, silver-haired Marcello Mastroianni lookalike stood next to a graciously smiling Clementine Lorenzo, a Claudette Colbert lookalike.

"It sure looks like it," muttered Pegg. "I take it the two grinning miniature Mastroianni lookalikes with him can only be your freshly minted stepbrother and stepsister."

"Doubtless," whispered Warwick. "Little do they realise that in no way are they or their conniving papa going to puck up my *La Dolce Vita* in any which way, so, Pegg my love, perhaps the time has come for us to change from simple mutilators to fearsome *annihilators*. Meaning that for cherubim one and two there are no mutilations but a very telling final exit. Now, let's go and introduce ourselves to the pucking threesome."

*

"Warwick! At last!" beamed Paulo Pablo on being introduced by a coquettish Clementine. "I've heard so many good things from my darling Clementine. I'm delighted to meet you and, please, let me introduce you to my other darlings; my daughter Sophia and my son, Stephano."

"The delight's all yours," replied Warwick crisply ignoring the three proffered hands. As if unaware of their bewildered expressions, he said brusquely. "The gentlemen next to me is Mr. Pegg."

"Pleased to meet you, Paulo, Sophia and Stephano," said Pegg shaking hands with the startled three while flashing Warwick a "was that prime bit of bitchery really necessary" look.

"I can already see that we're all going to be one big happy family," trilled Clementine giving Warwick and Pegg a concerned look. "Ah, the two gentlemen approaching can only be your friend Mr. Cameron and his friend, Mr. Ford."

"Kurt!" exclaimed Warwick. "Talk about a lukewarm surprise seeing Aunt Clementine had already told me you would be here this evening. And *this* can only be the other groom: Mr. Joel Ford." He gave a snicker. "And now we've met, I'm delighted to say I no longer feel like a second hand rose but a prize bloom instead."

"Jesus, Warwick! What the fuck's got into you?" hissed Pegg grabbing Warwick by the arm and forcibly leading him away from the visibly taken aback group. "We're supposedly here on a major mission: not a major fuck up!"

"As far as I'm concerned it's already a major puck up," retorted Warwick. Turning to face Pegg he said matter-of-factly. "You said you're an aficionado of Harry's Bar, so let's heigh-ho there for a bellini or three and puck this lot of WOPOs. As for Clementine? Typical! She may now be the blissful Signora Pablo on a certificate but to the world she still is, and always will be, the Contessa Clementine Lorenzo *married* to Signor Pablo-Marcello Mastroianni lookalike movie star and her latest plaything."

Walking in the direction of Harry's Bar, Warwick said nonchalantly. "When we get back to The Gritti, I'll get the concierge to book us on the first available flight to London. Then and only then, will the ravishing begin!"

*

"*Merda*," said Stephano Pablo, a younger version of his father, to his sister as they watched Warwick and Pegg leave. "If anyone wished to meet a total prick, we've done just that! Who the hell does that pretty boy upstart think he is!"

"A very *camp*, pretty boy upstart," giggled Sophia, a pert, pouty young Brigette Bardot lookalike. "Although, when it comes to handsome, bald *macho* men, David Pegg wins by several lengths. If you see what I mean!"

"Lascivious tart! As if I wouldn't," chortled Stephano. "What's the betting he and his testosterone infused lover boy return to London ASAP. The shock of meeting Papa and us, obvious rivals for Clementine's affection, being too much for him."

"Yes, it must be," giggled Sophia. Gazing around the sumptuous ballroom with its frescoes and priceless tapestries plus the well-groomed guests she added calculatedly. "He obviously sees us as an unexpected challenge to him inheriting all this and more but is far too full of himself to see that we see *him* as the challenge. What's more, I know, *just* know, Papa will agree with us."

HARRY'S BAR

"Change of plan, Pegg," announced Warwick after his second bellini. "Instead of running back to London, tail between my legs. I've now decided I - we - stay in Venice and thoroughly check out those decidedly flaky Mastroiannis. There's something very wrong there, very wrong indeed, and I fear Aunt Clementine is the intended victim."

"Great minds think alike, Warwick, and I totally agree with you." replied Pegg. "For all his charm, Paulo Pablo reeks of BO - BO on this occasion meaning bloody opportunist - and as shifty as a feather in a hurricane."

"So, let's have another bellini or three and make a plan for how we can bring down the feathered three."

"Attaboy! Warwick!" chuckled Pegg, "No wonder I remain a devoted fan! Remember Kurt Cameron and his other half are also staying at The Gritti, so brace yourself as bumping into the two of them again is inevitable."

"*Nessun probleme,*" chortled Warwick. "I'll simply slip into Warwick Laudanum-Standton super charming mode and stun them with best wishes and congratulations for a dismal future." He gave a snicker. "What's more, as this Joel creep must have the same taste as *moi* in men - i.e. macho, butch and demanding - maybe, just maybe - *you* could seduce little Joel. Now, wouldn't *that* put the proverbial cat among the pouter pigeons!"

"I'll pretend I didn't hear that!" snapped Pegg.

"But you *did* hear it," said Warwick with a tight smile. "If we're going to fight dirty with the likes of the Mastroiannis, we may as well fight equally as dirty with Kurt Cameron and his little hubby. *Nèst-ce pas?*"

"So be it," said Pegg a touch sulkily, reaching for his bellini.

"Getting back to Paulo Pablo and his conceited offspring," said Warwick smugly, "I have a delicious, nasty idea festering in my Einstein topknot. How about *this* for starters?"

Five minutes and a bellini later Pegg said with a chuckle. "I've got to hand it to you Warwick, for when it comes down to what you've just suggested, you do yourself and Vincent proud."

PALAZZO LORENZO

"I'm delighted to meet you Mr. Cameron and Mr. Ford," said Clementine graciously. "However, sad to say, you've just missed Warwick and the delightful Mr. Pegg." She gave a light laugh. "I've no idea what's going on with dear Warwick - he was always a highly strung child - but for some strange reason known only to himself, he decided he didn't like Paulo, my husband of a few weeks, nor his son or daughter, and left. I'm not only embarrassed but deeply humiliated by his behaviour. Behaviour he will live to regret."

Pulling herself together, Clementine added brightly. "But, enough of that. Come and meet Paulo, Sophia and Stephano who are standing talking over there."

"Well done, Warwick, and typical you," muttered Kurt, loud enough for Joel to hear as they followed Clementine. "It looks as if you've not only blotted your copy book as far as your aunt's concerned; you've also gone and dug a mega hole in your anticipated inheritance as well."

Within a matter of minutes Kurt and Joel were enjoying a sparkling conversation with Clementine and her new family, so much so that Clementine and Paulo had to excuse themselves in case their other guests felt they were being ignored.

"As Big Arnie Schwarzenegger almost said, '*we'll* be back'," said Paulo cheerfully. "So don't go away!"

"I think your dad's a poppet and simply *love* his films," said Joel to Sophia and Stephano.

"So do we, don't we, Steph?" giggled Sophia. "But then, we could be somewhat prejudiced!" Her comeback causing Kurt, Joel and her brother to burst out laughing.

"We're back," said Clementine as she and Paulo reappeared. "Now, if you two haven't any plans for dinner, why not join us for a light supper once all the other guests leave. It's only a light supper - if I know Lucia, our cook, it will be more of a banquet than a light supper - but you're more than welcome."

"We'd love to!" chorused Kurt and Joel, leading to more cheerful laughter.

Such was the success of the evening that Kurt and Joel invited the four to lunch the next day at a restaurant of Clementine's choosing.

After much cheerful banter it was Paulo who finally came up with the suggestion of lunch on the island of Torcello, adding with a delighted chortle. "And as you two are paying, may I suggest we lunch at *Osteria Al Ponte del Diavolo* as my darling Clementine and I are far too mean to ever treat ourselves to a spoiling lunch or dinner there! And before you ask, we'll take you there in *our* motor launch which means you'll at least be spared the fare!"

"Apart from the other fare!" shrilled Clementine. Her pithy comeback leading to further laughter.

"Needless to say, and in case you're worried that if I do happen to see Warwick at The Gritti, after what I told you about what happened between him and me prior to my marrying Joel, there is no way he would be asked to join us," said Kurt with a tight smile.

"At your peril!" added Clementine. "After his appalling behaviour this evening my nephew is going to have an enormous problem finding enough humble pies to gorge on!"

"And, so say all of us!" chorused Paulo, Sophia and Stephano.

PALAZZO LORENZO - MIDNIGHT

"Come in," called Sophia softly on hearing a light knocking on the door to one of the seemingly endless guest suites.

"Sophia, it's Papa and Stephano; may we come in?"

"Of course, Papa. After tonight's earlier little debacle with Clementine's ghastly nephew, I've been waiting for the two of you to join me."

Settling himself in a chair facing Sophia while Stephano simply sprawled across the bed at her feet, Paulo said in a low voice. "Signora Midas is asleep but keep your voices down just to be safe. Now, any suggestions for what we do about the interfering Warwick? I could tell, from the moment we were introduced that he's trouble with a capital T. Before marrying his irritating aunt, I made damn sure that half of her estate was willed to me and you two, which means that bloody little pest still gets fifty percent when we decide it's time for her to go."

"Not if Sophia and I have anything to do with it, he doesn't," said Stephano grimly.

"I *knew* you'd say that my always reliable son," chuckled Paulo. "Clementine, quite rightly, is pissed off with the little shit which means - for the time being, that is - he's persona non grata. However, that's not infallible. Standton and his super stud are staying at The Gritti but I have a feeling they could be leaving for London later today following his fall out with Clementine."

"Which means we'll have to deal with him when he's back in London," said Sophia.

"Which is far better than dealing with him here," said Paulo pragmatically. "So, *I miei amati figli,* it so happens I will be filming in London in a couple of weeks' time, so we'll deal with Signor Warwick Laudanum-Standton then. You both enjoy your visits to the capital, and I can assure you *this* visit will have a bit of extra oomph to it!"

"And Papa, you *know* how Stephano and I enjoy anything with a bit of extra oomph to it, don't we Stepho?"

"That we do, little sister!" agreed Stephano with a cackle.

THE GRITTI PALACE HOTEL

"Sebastian, it's Kurt. Not too late, am I?"

"No, Kurt, we're jes startin' on cocktails here," boomed Sebastian. "Sorry we had to cancel at the last minute but, as Ah always say, business - especially *oil* business -before pleasure. Haw! Haw! Outa interest, how *is* the sinkhole?"

"Sinkhole?"

"Venice. It's meant to be sinkin', ain't it? Haw! Haw!"

"Oh, it's still floating, Sebastian," replied Kurt with a forced laugh. "However, a change of plan could well be on the cards. Were you unaware that that Contessa Clementine Lorenzo, Warwick's aunt, had recently remarried?"

"Remarried?" boomed Sebastian.

"Not only remarried but married to Paulo Pablo, the film star and, get this, the father of two grown-up offspring. Joel and I have just had dinner with them, and, from all appearances, they epitomise the term 'one big happy family'. Nota bene, the happy family does *not* include Warwick, far from it, seeing he's well and truly blotted his copy book with Clementine due to his unforgivable rudeness to Signor Pablo earlier. With luck, Warwick's anticipated inheritance is either severely reduced or, better still, no more."

"Now, *that's* the sorta news I like to hear!" guffawed Sebastian. "However, I still expect you to do a Feniche on her palazzo destroying not only the interior but all the valuable contents as well but, as Ah said, do not, under any circumstances, barbecue the old biddy herself. Let that bloody Standton realise havin' an ol' aunt suddenly go broke ain't oke! Haw! Haw!"

(Sebastian's reference being to the magnificent Venetian opera house - The Feniche - which burned down in the mid-nineties. The fire seen as arson with two electricians convicted for the crime.)

"Let me assure you, Sebastian, the kindling as well as the new buttering-up is well and truly in hand with the four Pablos having lunch with me and Joel tomorrow: now today. During lunch I'll make sure I come up with several fun but decidedly unflattering tales from Warwick's murky past! Haha!"

"Good man!" boomed Sebastian. "Oh, an' Delilah sends her love. Hold on. What's that, lil' honeybun? Ah, Delilah says go easy with the clippers; whatever that means?"

15

VICTORIA STATION

They met, as usual, in a convenient Starbucks.

He: "Do you, like me, get the feeling we've been a bit complacent of late?"

She: "I'd say more stagnated than complacent." Her comment accompanied by a sardonic grin.

He: "Well, there's an easy answer to that. Time for another hit and fun."

She: "Hit and fun? You can be so corny at times, accomplice dear. Any suggestions so as to get us out of our complacent rut?"

He: "I would have suggested his two live-in staff, but someone also thought of them and subsequently firebombed their car. A bit of a bore if nothing else."

She: "What about their replacements? I can't see the dreaded Warwick in a pinny or pushing a hoover."

He: "Haha! Well said, and I agree! The good news is that the two old queens have been replaced by two pansies without stems, no less..."

She: "Pansies without stems?"

He: "Dykes or lezzies, in other words."

She: "Oh, very funny! A real Oscar Wilde if ever there was. Bring a tear to a glass eye, you would."

He: "Touché! So, we're agreed. The ladies in leather as opposed to ladies in lavender?"

She: "Agreed! And this time we make sure that both their foreheads are suitably enhanced or engraved."

He: "Your word, as always, is your demand!" Reaching for his cup he took a sip and added meditatively. "Two instead of our usual one? A bit obvious, don't you think? I mean, one proves a point whereas two together - to my mind, anyway - seems a bit much. Another one will keep Warwick waiting for the next mutilated shoe, as it were, to drop. Whereas a *pair* of mutilated shoes - Haha! - could lose their impact or 'oomph' in your sort of speak."

She: "You could be right. Two could well be too much."

He: "So, back to another *single* mutilation now that Gertude and Alice have been spared from their unexpected facelifts and stitched fannies?!

She: "Stitched fannies? That's a first! Talk about a 'No Entry' sign with a difference! But being serious. Who else?"

He: "We could always *dognap* his dog."

She: "Oh? And who would take care of it? Not me, that's for sure."

He: "Nor me. So, let's get another coffee and ponder. I won't be a sec."

She, on his return: "As they say, time to look abroad instead of your own backyard, or something to that effect. I don't mean that literally, but why not somebody he doesn't actually *know* but sees on a regular basis. His hairdresser for example."

He: "Brilliant! His hairdresser's a mince called Phillip and has a salon near Sloane Square. So, why not an old-fashioned Native American scalping with the words 'totem pole' carved onto his bewildered brow?"

She: "Hair today! Gone tomorrow! I love it!"

THE GRITTI PALACE HOTEL

"As I thought," muttered Warwick from where he stood staring down at the activity taking place at the hotel's jetty below. "My aunt, fortune hunter Paula Pablo and his two odious offspring have just drawn up to the jetty below in a somewhat spectacular motor launch and being greeted - make that *effusively* greeted by Signor Cameron and Signor Ford no less! What's more, Signor Cameron and Signor Ford are now clambering aboard!"

Turning to Pegg who had joined him, he said triumphantly. "Just as well as I told you to get your act together and be ready to dash out if necessary. They're obviously heading off somewhere special for lunch and we, my comrade in harms, are going to follow them. C'mon!"

On reaching the hotel's jetty Warwick quickly beckoned one of the waiting water taxis. As he and Pegg jumped aboard Warwick said with a mischievous grin. "I've *always* wanted to yell this but have never had the chance so, here goes!"

Turning to face the waiting driver Warwick gave a whoop followed by a yodelled. "*Capitano*! Follow that boat!"

*

"Any idea where they could be heading, *Capitano*?" asked Warwick restraining himself from giving the man a mock salute.

"Torcello, signor, they're obviously heading for Torcello," replied the bearded Joe Manganiello lookalike. "Very popular; very good restaurants."

Christ! thought Warwick with an inward snicker. *Are there any Italian men who don't look film stars? Even the concierge at The Gritti looks as if he's just stepped out of the silver screen.*

"Warwick! Warwick!" snapped Pegg, bringing him back to earth or, in this case, back to the canal. "If they're going to Torcello for lunch, isn't it a bit bloody obvious if we appear in whatever restaurant as well? Far better we change course and head for the Lido instead."

"I hate to admit it, but you're right," replied Warwick with a scowl. "I'll inform the captain. This means we can discuss over a leisurely lunch what we do about Kurt and his husband-cum-stab." He gave a derisive snort. "If that Joel's meant to replace me then I am both mortified and insulted beyond comprehension."

"Let me assure you nobody, but *nobody*, could ever replace you, Warwick, *dear*," chuckled Pegg. "See Kurt's choice as one of desperation; nothing else."

"You say the sweetest, strychnine sweet things, Pegg, *dear*," snickered Warwick. "Thankfully, as Scarlet O'Horror said. 'Tomorrow *is* another day'. Another day before Kurt and his blissful groom receive a resounding comeuppance!"

TORCELLO

"Your choice of restaurant is a delight, Clementine," said Kurt to Clementine as the group sat enjoying their food. "My pasta with mussels and sea bass is truly out of this world." He gave a conspiratorial chuckle. "Then it would have to be to lure you away from your enchanting palazzo. Tell me honestly, do you ever leave Venice for a break somewhere else?"

"Oh, yes," gushed Clementine. "In fact, Paulo and I, accompanied by darling Sophia and darling Stephano will be leaving in a few weeks' time for a month in Tuscany. Julian Craggs, the writer and dear friend, has a wonderful villa there which he lets me use when he's back in America visiting his family. A yearly visit which he thoroughly enjoys."

"I take it Dario accompanies you," chuckled Kurt. "I can't imagine the Lorenzo menage with Dario."

"Oh, no, not at all. *He* in turn visits his family in Liguria which means that Palazzo Lorenzo also has a break," replied Clemetine with a tinkly laugh.

Bingo! thought Kurt not daring to even glance at Joel. *Talk about a perfect opportunity for a rival La Feniche, added to which it gives us time to plan everything with Joe Heyday. I'm pretty sure he has a contact here in Venice who is willing to literally wipe out Palazzo Lorenzo and all its contents while Clementine and her sponging brood are living in up in sunny Tuscany.*

"A month in Tuscany?" repeated Kurt with a faux laugh. "Goodness, Clementine, when it comes to a charmed life I doubt if there is anyone else as charmed - *and* as charming - as lovely you!"

*

"Good evening, Sebastian and good news to accompany it," said Kurt cheerfully. "To quote a certain Julius Caesar. *Veni, vidi, vici!*"

"Veiny? Vicki? VD? Forget what fuckin' Julius Caesar said! What the fuck are *you* trying to say?" boomed Sebastian.

"I'm trying to say that what we thought was going to be a major problem has literally resolved itself and is a problem no longer."

Kurt quickly gave details of Clementine's impending departure for Tuscany with Paulo, his son and daughter, along with Dario's visit to his family in Liguria. Apart from sporadic visits from the housekeeper, the palazzo would be unoccupied.

"This gives us a whole month in which to arrange the burning down of the palazzo and its contents," enthused Kurt. "Plus, dare I suggest, it gives you and Delilah a golden opportunity to visit Venice seeing you couldn't make it this time round. I've already emailed you the definite dates the palazzo will literally be ours so, if you and Delilah wish to come along for the fireworks and bonfire night, let me know and I'll reserve the Royal Suite here at the Gritti Palace for you."

"A week at the Gritti Palace Hotel with fireworks an' a bonfire night thrown in?" boomed Sebastian. "Why, mah lil' Delilah will be cartwheelin' with joy!" There was a moment's pause before Sebastian said shrewdly, "Anythin' else you need to tell me?"

Taking a swallow, Kurt briefly explained Warwick's fallout with Clementine the night before.

"Gets fuckin' better by the fuckin' minute," said Sebastian matter-of-factly, "but that doesn't see any change in our plan. Knowin' how those gals love a kiss an' make up, what's the bettin' that ol' Miss Clemmie an' that lil' shit won't be all a lovin' an' a dovin' again by the time we get there." Without saying another word. Sebastian hung up.

"Well, at least he didn't end up bellowing like some demented Minotaur," chuckled Kurt. "Fancy a bellini at Harry's?"

"A bellini or two at Harry's Bar followed by a night of lust and thrust with my devoted husband?" chortled Joel. "Who said there wasn't a God?"

A LAVISH DUPLEX PENTHOUSE - CHELSEA HARBOUR - A DAY LATER

"Talk about a waste of pucking time and space," grumbled Warwick reaching for his glass of orange juice. "How right you were, Pegg, to suggest we come back to Old Blighty and give it a rest."

"Glad to hear it," muttered Pegg, his eyes fixated on a morning paper, "and doubly glad to hear you agree with me for once."

"I *always* agree with you Pegg, once you agree with *moi* point of view," snickered Warwick. Noting Pegg's expression he added tersely. "Now what?"

"This," replied Pegg, slapping the newspaper lying on table in front of him. "There's been another pf those copycat mutilations. However, the details are sketchy. They mention he's a popular hairdresser, but they haven't given a name."

"A *hairdresser*?" exploded Warwick slopping his orange juice over the table and part of the newspaper. "What's the betting it'll be Phillip Hoxton, *my* pucking hairdresser! Who the *Hell* is behind this? In no way can it be directed toward me - us - as the precautions we took would have made even Al-Quaeda jealous! Do they mention the name of the hospital where whoever is responsible dumped him?"

Pegg read out the name.

"Where's my pucking mobile when I need him?" stormed Warwick springing up from the table and almost colliding with Wilma carrying a tray of scrambled eggs and bacon out onto where the two were having breakfast.

"Sorry! Judy! Crisis time!" yodelled Warwick as he dashed indoors.

Five minutes later he was back.

"As I thought," Warwick said triumphantly. "I called the hospital and, taking a wild chance, said I was a relative of Phillip Foxton, the man who had just been rushed into A & E there after being seriously mugged, and simply wanted to know how he was. Having been passed on to at least three idiots I was eventually told that Mr. Foxton was stable but suffering - and I quote - severe head injuries."

"That could mean anything," snorted Pegg.

"*Including* something carved onto his forehead," muttered Warwick. Glancing at Pegg, he said in a strained voice. "Who the *puck* can be responsible for this? It can't be bloody Kurt as he and his gormless stab are still in Vencie. So, who then?"

"Do you know Foxton well enough to pay him a visit?"

"I would think so. That's if he's allowed visitors, but I somehow doubt it. After we finish breakfast, I'll give the hospital another call . . . yes, Judy?"

"I've brought you a fresh plate of scrambled eggs and bacon, Mr. Warwick," replied Wilma reaching for the plate of congealed eggs in front of him and setting down a fresh plate. "After all, we can't have you catching a nasty case of tummy wobbles, can we?" Staring at a bemused Warwick, she added in a concerned voice. "Will you be collecting Vincent from Mr. Peggs' kennels sometime today?"

"Yes, Wilma. I'll have him back here by lunchtime: I promise!"

"Oh, good," tittered Wilma. "I'll let Julia know so that she can start preparing a batch of pancakes for him. As you well know, Vincent *adores* his pancakes with a slathering of Marmite"

"No wonder he's beginning to look like a *fat* dog instead of a hot, handsome dog," chortled Warwick. "You and Julia never stop spoiling him so instead of a *fat*, hot handsome dog, maybe a *diet* dog should be on the cards!"

"I think that's up to Vincent to decide," trilled Wilma as she wafted back inside the penthouse.

*

"At least I have the comfort knowing that you're a *zillion* percent loyal," murmured Warwick giving Vincent a resounding kiss on the snout. "I also know that you're passionately in love with Punch and Pegg but remember it's me, the one and only lovely me, who pays for all those lovely doggy treats! Now, I need to ask you a favour. Tomorrow I will be visiting Phillip, my hairdresser who's in hospital, and you'll be accompanying me. I know Phillip adores you and with your additional charm working on both the nurses and especially Phillip, hopefully I'll be able to glean a bit more information about this meddlesome, copycat piece of shit. So, uber-charm, woofs, snuffles and licks tomorrow, please and, if you're successful in *any* way at all, it'll be raining doggy treats for you and all those hard-working pooches in training at Peggs.

"Obviously, if I am *not* allowed to take you in to see Phillip, I'll make a great play on how you send loving licks and woofs which should help in jogging the idiot's hair sprayed mind and, hopefully, give us a lead as to who this copycat could be."

Giving a blissful Vincent a further kiss followed by a fondle of his ears, Warwick added sotto voce. "However, getting back to equally as pressing other matters, what the *hideous* Hell is Aunt Clementine think she's up to? As the saying goes if you want a puck, rent it. There's no need to buy it or, in her misguided case, marry it! I always thought she was a willy old bird and would never, *ever* allow herself to be taken in a by such an obvious gold-digger-cum-gigolo as pucking Paulo Pablo! So, Vincent, my friend, what do we do about Pablo and his two condom escapees?

"As for Pegg, why, oh why, do I have that sinking feeling that, at the end of the day, he'll end up in a similar gondola to that of pucking Kurt Cameron. Ha! Such a wit am I. even in my hour of desperate need. I'm also having second thoughts about Jess Rix. Pucking hell! As baldy Brynner *sprechgesang* in *The King and I*, it's 'A Puzzlement'. Which brings me back to our two residents, Punch and Judy; aka Anne Bonny and as Mary Read! The mind boggles! And why not? I cry!"

Ten minutes later Warick picked up the house phone. "Hi Wilma. Have you and Julia got a minute? I need you both to pop along to the study." He gave a chortle. "And in case you think it has anything to do with your work here, don't, as it's about something else entirely. And yes, you know better than anyone else Vincent would never say no to an unexpected doggy treat or two!"

Giving Vincent's ears a further fondle, Warwick said with a soft chuckle. "Not bad, Bubba! Not bad at all! And tomorrow being another day, it can also be seen as a day for eating humble pasta. Meaning I'll even give Aunt Clementine a kiss and make up call *including* an apology for my behaviour toward her gigolo husband and his two brats. Ah!" he added as Vincent hurtled toward the door to greet the two concerned looking women. "Julia and Wilma, please come in and take a seat."

Barely giving the couple time to sit down (Vincent having made a beeline for Julia and, having happily accepted a doggy treat, settled himself next to her feet while chewing contentedly on his present), Warwick said cheerfully. "No need to look so worried, ladies. Just a simple question with a simple yes or no answer please. What would you say, *Anne* and *Mary*, to a new, blood thirsty and exciting game of pirates versus landlubbers?"

16

A LAVISH DUPLEX PENTHOUSE - CHELSEA HARBOUR - THE NEXT DAY

"*Buongiorno,* Dario. It's Signor Warwick. May I speak to *la Contessa, per favore.*" Warwick gave a chuckle and said conspiratorially. "However, knowing she probably doesn't wish to speak to me as I've been a *ragazzo cattivo* - ha! - I'll call back but don't answer so that *la Contessa* will finally have to answer the call herself."

"*Si,* signor," replied Dario, well aware of Warwick and Clementine's minor spats. "As you wish, Signor Warwick."

Three minutes later an exasperated voice said sharply. "Contessa Lorenzo. *Chi è questo?*"

"*Zia* Clementine, it's Warwick."

"Ha!" snapped Clementine. "Cajoling poor Dario again! Plus, it's back to *Zia* instead of Aunt *and* even more suspicious, all said in a hurt, little boy's voice."

"*Si, Zia* Clementine," replied Warwick solemnly. "It's all of that, as well as a very apologetic Warwick asking your forgiveness for his atrocious behaviour the other night. Put it down to jealousy and shock."

"Jealousy and shock?" echoed Clementine.

"Yes, *Zia* Clementine. Jealousy and shock on finding you had remarried and not only that, married a famous film star; father to a grown-up son and daughter!"

"Hmm," muttered Clementine. "I suppose I should be flattered but Warwick, *dear,* instead of apologising to me, you should be apologising to Paulo, Sophia and Stephano."

"Okay, I will," said Warwick giving the empty study an emphatic V-sign. "If they're about, I'll be happy to do so now."

"On, they're not here," replied Clementine smugly, "but I'll certainly pass on your message. Now, as you've had the courtesy to call me and to apologise, let me have the courtesy to say that your apology is accepted. However, Warwick, be warned. Anymore displays of such childish, temper tantrums and *Zia* Clementine won't be so malleable. On a totally different note, I *did* like your friend, Mr. Cameron and *his* friend - like most of my generation I can't get used to saying husband. The two being totally charming. So much so, Paulo and I have invited them to stay with us in Tuscany where, as you well know, I have the use of Julian Craggs's glorious villa for a month each year while he's in The States."

She gave a titter. "Dear Stephano, was quick to say that at long last he'd be able to get his skateboard out of mothballs; something Venice didn't exactly encourage!"

"How nice for all of you," said Warwick through gritted teeth. "A month in Tuscany in Julan Craggs's sumptuous villa overlooking those endless vineyards? As long as it isn't totally alien to Mr. Steinbeck's bestseller, I am sure you'll all have a wrathful time!"

Before Clementine could respond, Warwick hung up.

Staring at the silent telephone, Warwick said with a growing Machiavellian smile. "Dear *Aunt* Clementine, you've just gone and solved a problem for the lovely *moi*." Reaching for the housephone he said to Juila who happened to answer. "You'll be delighted to know that the problem of what to do with Paulo Pablo and his brood has now been resolved. So, ladies, get ready for a terror trip, two weeks from now, to tranquil Tuscany of all places."

VILLA DIRUPI MONTANI - TUSCANY - TWO WEEKS LATER

"Dear Julian, he is so naughty," giggled Clementine holding onto her large straw hat as an unexpected gust of playful wind decided to play with it. "Of course, you three still have to meet him, which I'll make sure you do on his return." She gave another madcap giggle. "Only he, a miniature Mr. Magoo lookalike, would name his villa set among the gentle vine covered plains pf Tuscany, Villa *Dirupi Montani,* or Villa Mountain Craggs, for the unenlightened!"

Her cheerful denouement leading a triple eyerolling from Paulo, Sophia and Stephano which she luckily failed to notice; the three having joined her on the main terrace for breakfast.

"*Scusatemi, Contessa,*" interrupted Alfredo, Julian's butler, "a telephone call for Signor Craggs. I did tell the lady that Signor Craggs was in America so perhaps she would like to speak to you instead."

"Can you ask her to call me back in an hour's time if she would like to speak to me, Alfredo. Explain to her that l and my houseguests are in the middle of breakfast."

"*Si, Contessa.*"

By chance, Clementine happened to be in Julian's study to collect a copy of his latest book which she had promised to read during her stay, when the telephone rang.

"This must be the woman who rang earlier," she muttered reaching for the phone. "Villa *Dirupi Montani. Contessa* Lorenzo speaking."

"Er . . . oh, dear . . ." said a distinctive English woman's voice. "I called earlier to speak to Mr. Julian Craggs and was told he was in America and then, after a brief pause, was told to call back if I wished to speak to the Countess Lorenzo who is staying in the villa while Mr. Craggs is away." Julia gave a chuckle. "I take it I *am* speaking to Countess Lorenzo?"

"You are indeed," tittered Clementine. "As Alfredo, the butler said, Julian is away for his usual yearly month's visit to America. Julian's an old friend and kindly lets me use the villa while he's away. If it's anything urgent I am sure Julian won't mind me giving you one or two of the telephone contact numbers in The States I have for him."

"No, no, that's very kind of you, Countess, but it really isn't necessary. It's simply because I did meet Julian . . . Mr. Craggs . . . when I, too, was over in America, and he did say that if ever I found myself in Tuscany, *Bella Italia* - his very words. Haha! - I was to give him a ring. Oh!" gushed Julia. "My manners! My name, Countess Lorenzo, is Bonny; Bettina Bonny, and I'm travelling with a lady friend, Rosanna Read. In fact, would you believe, we're saying in a charming *pensione* in the village near to the villa! Talk about a coincidence!"

"Goodness," crooned Clementine, "then it's obvious that you simply *have* to come and meet Julian's squatters Haha! By squatters, I'm referring to my husband, Paulo Pablo, and his two *very* grown-up children, Sophia and Stephano. Haha!"

"Ooh! You don't mean Paulo Pablo, the film star, by any chance?" gasped Julia. (She, Wilma and Warwick having really done their homework when it came to the three Pablos.) "We did hear he'd recently married a glamorous Countess with a palazzo in Venice."

"Guilty as charged," replied Clementine coyly. "Oh, your call is so unexpected and such fun! Please, *please,* say you and your friend can join us for lunch today!"

"If I said we couldn't, I'd be telling *the* most enormous fib!" cried Julia.

"Wonderful!" crooned Clementine. "So why don't you and your lady friend join us here, at the villa, at one o'clock or thereabouts."

"Love to, Countess."

"Clementine, *per favore,*" trilled Clementine, "as I know we're going to be friends, Bonny! Julian will be delighted we met! So, see you two at one, then." She gave a giggle. "I take it you do know where the villa is?"

"Oh, yes, Clementine, we most certainly do," came the cheerful reply. "We have already been introduced to Tino, the one and only taxi driver, so we'll get him to bring us up to the villa. *So* looking forward to meeting you. *Ciao!*"

*

"Who on *earth* was that?" exclaimed Wilma as a helmeted figure on a skateboard flew past them on his way down the road leading up to the villa.

Tut-tutting, Tino, the elderly taxi driver shook his grizzled grey head. "It's the young signor staying at the villa, *signore.* He spends all his time skateboarding up and down the road, paying no attention to anyone or anything else on the road."

"Gets better by the second. Doesn't it?" whispered Julia to Wilma.

"It certainly does," whispered Wilma. "What a blessing that Wilma Davis wasn't known as Whizzing Wilma for nothing in *her* skateboarding days!"

*

On meeting Julia and Wilma, Clementine's immediate thought was. *Talk about Mesdames Little and Large,* while Paulo's immediate thought was. *Hmm, I wonder which one wears the trousers or, better still, which one wears the dildo.*

"How lovely to meet you," trilled Clementine. "Now, come and meet Paulo and Sophia, his delightful daughter. Stephano, Paulo's son, should be around somewhere and, as he's never been known to miss a meal, he should be here any minute. Now, what would you like to drink? Alfredo makes a wicked martini. I'm having a bellini, but please ask for whatever you wish from what is known as Julian's 'Bar None'. Haha!"

"A bellini sounds grand," said Wilma with a smile.

"I second that," said Julia cheerfully.

"Oh, my goodness! And *who* is that handsome fellow!" squeaked Julia pointing toward a tail wagging, golden retriever who had pattered his way onto the terrace.

"Oh, that's *Roccio*. Full name *Roccioso,* and wicked Julian's witty answer to Sylvester Stallone. To go with the name of the villa, *Dirupi Montani*, or Rocky Craggs in English." Clementine gave a titter. "I too, at first, didn't 'geddit', but dear Julian soon put me right!"

"Hello, Roccio," purred Julia sinking to her knees and beckoning the curious dog with outstretched arms. "Just as well my other doggy, great friend Vincent isn't here as I am sure he'd be extremely jealous to meet another pooch as handsome as he!"

"Please forgive my friend." chuckled Wilma. "She's mad about dogs of any sort."

As Alfredo proceeded to serve Wilma and Julia their bellinis a cheerful tenor voice called out. "Sorry I'm late, but skating back *up* the hill is a helluva lot tougher than skating down!"

"Ah! *Caro* Stephano, come and meet our luncheon guests, Wilma and Julia."

"Hi. Stephano," smiled Wilma, proffering her hand. "You could say we've already met in a way seeing it was you tore past our taxi on your skateboard when we were our way here!"

"Aha! I *thought* the passengers could be our lunch guests," replied Stephano with a dazzling smile. "I trust I didn't startle you. Haha!"

Looking up from where she was busy fondling a blissful *Roccio's* ears, and before Julia could answer, Wilma said with a titter to what she would later describe as a heaven-sent cue. "Not at all, Stephano. I'm a great skateboard aficionado myself, and simply adore it'"

"You are? You do?" exclaimed Stephano eyeing the Lola Bunny lookalike in disbelief. "Err . . . I don't know how long you're planning on staying in the village but maybe, if you're here for a few more days, I could show you one or two really great rides."

"I'd love that," giggled Wilma. "But sadly, I didn't pack my skateboard! Haha!"

"*Niente probleme,*" replied Stephano with a grin and thinking. *Stupid cow. Skateboard aficionado indeed. Let's make you eat your words.* "I brought several boards with me so you can happily borrow one." He gave a chuckle. "Apart from Zoom-Zoom, my pride and joy!"

He nodded in the direction of a neat shed adjacent to the terrace where they were sitting. "I keep all my boards and a couple of spare helmets in that toolshed over there seeing Clementine won't have them cluttering up poncy Mr. Craggs's villa." Leaning forward Stephano gave a snigger and said, sotto voce. "Her words, not mine, apart from the word 'poncy', that is."

"You're on!" cried Wilma. "And if I can select a skateboard and a helmet after lunch and borrow it for a practice run or two, then I'll be more than ready to challenge you to a race either tomorrow or the day after!"

"Let's make it *domani,* that's tomorrow," sniggered Stephano. "Can you arrange for Tino to bring you to the villa around tennish? Explain to him he'll then have to take us on to another place before returning to the village while we make our own way back. I mean, while we *race* back! Haha!"

"Take it as done. Stephano," giggled Wilma, giving Julia a discreet thumbs-up.

LATER

"Talk about biting off more that you can chew," grunted Julia as she and Wilma crept silently across the terrace toward the toolshed containing Stephano's skateboards. "The wretched road seemed to be twice as long to walk as opposed to drive. Hopefully the wretched shed isn't locked."

"If it is, it won't take me a sec to open it," said Wilma matter-of-factly.

On reaching the shed, she said in a relieved voice. "It's open and thank goodness I can see Zoom-Zoom in all his glory!" She gave a giggle. "See, I was right, and you were wrong. Despite being an out and out smug weirdo, and despite what new mummy Clementine says about clutter, Stephano does *not* sleep with his skateboard!"

"Thank whoever it is we should thank that I was wrong. Okay, me hearty, time to do your damnedest!"

THE NEXT MORNING

"*Grazie,* Tino," said Stephano with a vindictive grin on telling the taxi driver to stop. "Signora Rossana and I will be skating back to the villa from here. Signora Rossana wishes to call it a race, but I think it should be called a foregone conclusion! Haha!"

Watching the taxi drive away he turned to Wilma and said cheerfully. "Ready, Rosanna?"

"As ready as this Rosanna will ever be," replied Wilma with a seraphic smile.

"Okay! Let's go!" yelled Stephano, hopping onto his skateboard and setting off. "I forgot to warn you about a rather nasty - even lethal - bend about half a mile on," he called over his shoulder as he raced ahead. "Plus, there's an equally nasty ditch alongside! So, watch how you go!"

"No need to try and teach this wily, worldly bitch any new tricks," snorted Wilma as she watched Stephano race ahead, hellbent, as if to teach Wilma a lesson for having the audacity to challenge him. "It should happen any second now," she hissed, followed by a triumphant yelled "Yes!" as the wheels to Stephano's skateboard which she had loosened earlier, flew off followed by a screaming, cartwheeling Stephano.

"Poor, arrogant Stephano," muttered Wilma as she slowly approached the groaning young man lying in a crumpled heap inside the so-called nasty ditch. Grinning weakly on seeing Wilma, he said with a sob. "Christ, Rosanna, it hurts . . ."

"Well, let's put an end to that, shall we?" cooed Wilma as she crouched down, took hold of his Stephano's bleeding, helmeted head and, with a well-practised, vicious twist; broke his neck.

Glancing down at Stephano's lifeless form, Wilma calmly got to her feet, readied her skateboard and set off for the villa.

"I should have plenty of time to gear myself up for my Oscar-winning performance of a distraught, bewildered, shattered soul," murmured Wilma with a smile as she roller skated her way toward the villa, the wind gently ruffling her hair. "As wily Sir Walter Scott so rightly scrawled. 'Oh, what a tangled web we weave, when first we practice to deceive'. Not that this is my first neck breaking. Not by a longshot!"

*

"Brilliant, and well done, ladies," crooned Warwick on being told the news. "I take the posturing piece of celluloid, his daughter, and particularly my twitter of an aunt, are all in a suitable twitter?"

"You can rest assured, Mr. Warwick, that not even the Wailing Wall could hold a candle to the reaction of the three leftovers!" chortled Wilma. "Meanwhile, the Countess is on her way back to Venice - Stephano's funeral will take place at San Michele Cemetery on the island of Isola week after next. Paulo Pablo – the callous so and so - is back in London filming the final scenes of his latest film but will be back in Venice for the funeral. We don't know what Sophia is up to, but you can bet your bottom dollar, it'll be something devious and involves her father."

Wilma gave a chuckle. "As for what you have in mind for Papa Pablo - what did you just call him? A posturing piece of celluloid? I love it! And even if what you have in mind for the posturing piece of celluloid doesn't take place immediately, when it does, we're sure it'll make *Carnivale di Venezia* look like a damp squib!"

"A very damp squib indeed when compared to *my* proposed sacking of the Paulos' uber-comfortable, hedonistic, self-centred Rome abode!" crooned Warwick. "Alaric. King of the Visigoths, eat your heart out!"

17

VENICE - A FEW DAYS LATER

"*Mia cara* Clementine, it's Paulo!"

"I know who it is," said Clementine coyly doing her best to suppress a yawn. Glancing at the small clock on the bedside cabinet. "Goodness, it's late. Is everything alright over there in London?"

"Everything's fine, my love. The film is on schedule which means it should be wrapped up by next Thursday at the latest and I should be back in Venice by Friday evening, However, apart from calling to give you the good news and to tell you how much I love you and miss you, I've also taken the opportunity to do some snooping on your nephew..."

"Oh, please, Paulo, you promised..."

"I *know* what I promised," interrupted, "but Stephano was *my* son and despite the medical and police reports, I do not accept the fact that he was killed because of an unfortunate accident." There was a pause before Paulo said in clipped tones. "Somehow I think it won't come as a surprise when I tell you that Bettina Bonny and Rosanna Read are, in fact, a Julia Mander and a Wilma Davis."

"So?" snapped Clementine. "Maybe they preferred to remain incognito. There have been numerous occasions when I've introduced myself as Christine Clements!"

"Aha! But wait for it!" crowed Paulo rather like a magician about to pull a rabbit from a hat. "To top it all, I then went on to discover that Juila Mander and Wilma Davis were employed by a Mr. Warwick Laudanum-Standton. Mander as a chef and Davis as his major domo; female version!"

"Oh, my God!" gasped Clementine almost dropping the phone. "Oh, my God . . . you're not suggesting . . . you can't possibly can't even begin to think . . ."

"I *do* think, Clementine, dearest. After all, why would the women have gone out of their way to meet us in Tuscany and more to the point, why the aliases?" Paulo gave a derisive snort. "After all, a cook and a housekeeper are somewhat different to a countess."

"But they said they were friends of Julian," gabbled Clementine, her voice rising.

"I very much doubt it," said Paulo ignoring Clementine's growing hysteria. "I fact, I've been trying to reach Craggs in The States on both those numbers you gave me and was told that he was somewhere in the Florida Keys and wouldn't be back in New York for another ten days."

"I still can't believe . . . No, make that I *don't* - and I *won't* - believe that Warwick, despite his idiosyncrasies and failings, would stoop so low as if to ever do what you're suggesting," replied Clementine with a virulent hiss. "And how *dare* you, a mere; no, make that second-rate film star, contradict the findings of the police and doctor who examined your unruly son!"

"And how dare *you,* a mere countess, of which, in Italy, are two a penny, mock my dearly, departed son!" bellowed Paulo. "Believe me, *Contessa,* you and that sicko nephew of yours haven't heard the last of this but one thing that *is* certain is the fact I am now terminating my last, and I mean my final ever conversation with you. Any further contact will be via lawyers regarding a divorce." Paulo hung up.

Glancing again at the bedside clock. Clementine said angrily. "I don't care how late it is, but young Warwick and I are about to have an extremely serious conversation."

*

"Elucidate!"

"Darling, it's Clementine! Hopefully I didn't wake you, but I need to talk to you urgently!"

"Urgently? Goodness," carolled Warwick, "sounds exciting! As for waking *moi,* you didn't, dear *Zia* Clementine seeing I'm in the middle of reading a bedtime to Vincent and Pegg."

"What? *The Hound of the Baskervilles?*"

"No, *The Sleeping Beauty,* which each of them is claiming to be! However, curiosity has certainly killed the hound, Aunt Clementine so please, an uncensored version of this disruptive emergency?"

"It's Paulo Pablo! He's just informed me he's divorcing me!"

"Goodness," chortled Warwick. "Despite the lateness of the hour, some exceedingly news, and . . . there's always an and."

"In a ridiculous and obscure way, he's partly blaming you!"

"*Moi*? This paragon of virtue. Surely Mr. Movie Star's not saying I'm into old ladies and or incest?

"I *knew* you'd cheer up this ancient soul," tittered Clementine. "No, it's to do with Stephano's accident: yet again." She gave another titter. "Goodness! I've just realised if Paulo *does* divorce me, it will spare me from having to refer to the dreaded Sophia as my stepdaughter!"

"Attagirl! Auntie! However, I still have idea as to what has brought about this amazing redemption happening or package?"

"As you well know there were those two women staying in the village, one of whom was taking part in a race with Stephano, the two on skateboards, when the accident happened."

"Yes, Julia Mander and Wilma Davis, or Bettina Bonny and Rosanna Read as you knew them. Julia being my cook - and a darn good one - and Wilma my housekeeper, chatelaine, whatever."

"Well, Paulo's now saying you sent them to spy on him, me, us at the villa. Is that true?"

"Absolutely, Aunt Clementine! On first meeting Paulo Pablo I took an instant dislike to him with his aura of flashing, neon signs shrieking gold digger recurring. And, because I *adore* my *Zia* Clementine, I asked Julia and Wilma who it so happened had already planned a visit to Tuscany *before* coming to work for me, to see how *your* visit to the villa was faring."

Warwick gave a chuckle. "When I asked the ladies why Tuscany, their reply was to visit Florence, see The Ponte de Vecchio and suss out David's *poco* willy!"

"David's *poco* willy?" echoed Clementine.

"Michel Angelo's David's little doodah!"

"*Really,* Warwick," giggled Clementine. "You're better than a snort!"

"I didn't hear that, *innocente Zia* Clementine," snickered Warwick. "So, back to Signor Paulo Pablo. Please don't tell me he really *is* going around saying I had something to do with Stephano's accident?"

"No, not exactly. *Inferring* would be a better way of putting it."

"Well, I don't. However, I won't say I'm at all upset that he's asked you for a divorce. but I will say, and I've said it before, I will never understand why you married him in the first place." Warwick gave a giggle. "What happened to your old adage, a gentle cruise around Piazza San Marco and one's guaranteed to find a sparkle?"

"I *never, ever* said that!" shrilled Clementine before dissolving into peals of laughter.

"I know you didn't! I just made it up!" chortled Warwick. "But, as Albert Einstein said, great minds think alike!"

"Oh, I *do* love you, Warwick, dear," cried Clementine. "Please, please don't leave it for too long before you come and stay."

Yeah, and gloat over all which, thanks to the unwieldy machinations of Mr. Movie Star, are safely back in the hands of their rightful owner.

"Would this coming weekend be too long for you?" chuckled Warwick.

"Almost. But, as a wanton San Marco sprite, how can I say no to such a delicious suggestion?" cooed Clementine. "Will the divine Signor Pegg be joining you?"

"Not this weekend, Aunty," said Warwick with a mischievous giggle. "However, as I'm in a definite 'spoil *Zia* Clementine' frame of mind, after my visit *this* coming weekend, why don't Pegg and I return the week after in order to attend poor Stephano's funeral with you?"

"Would you, dear? That would be a blessing as I really do not wish to stand next to Paulo Pablo playing the grieving stepmother or about to be *ex-*stepmother. Stephano was always cold in his attitude toward me. As for his sister? The less said about her, the better."

"Consider it done as both Pegg and I will be there to support you, *Zia* Clementine. You may not be aware of the fact, but Warwick Laudanum-Standton *always* enjoys having the last laugh!"

"Of course you'll stay here at the palazzo; no more Gritti! After all, Palazzo Lorenzo will be yours one day, so it gives you a further opportunity for getting used to living in your own palace!"

RANCHO PLATA, PLATA, PLATA

"She's gone an' done fuckin' *what?*" boomed Sebastian.

"Cut short her stay in Tuscany and returned to Venice following the sudden death of her stepson," repeated Kurt.

"Death of her stepson? What death."

"Stephano, Pablo's son, was killed while taking part in some skateboarding race the day before yesterday. Pablo himself is filming in London and may or may not have returned to Italy to deal with matters regarding the funeral et cetera." Kurt gave a derisive snort. "From what I've heard about the guy, he's most probably left it up to the poor bloody Countess to see to the funeral arrangement's seeing his self-promotion-cum-adoration apparently has no rival."

"Forget about the bloody Countess! What about me havin' to tell mah darlin' Delilah that a second trip to fuckin' Venice has been cancelled," boomed Sebastian. "She'll chew mah fuckin' balls off!"

"Why cancel, Sebastian? See this for what it is, a temporary glitch. Whatever happens we *will* burn down the wretched palazzo and its contents sooner or later, I can assure you."

Kurt gave a snigger. "And, as it wouldn't do for you and Delilah to be a couple of flies on the wall at the young man's funeral, why not pay a visit to the Bridge of Sighs instead as I am sure it'll help the two of you shed a crocodile sigh or two!"

"Haw! Haw! Good one, Kurt! Crocodile sighs on the Bridge of Sighs? Delilah will like that! Haw! Haw! Ah will speak to her an' see what she says. So, when will you an' young Joel be back?"

"I'm actually calling from Rome as Joel was determined to see The Colosseum and no doubt fantasise over all those grunting, sweaty gladiators!"

"Sweaty gladiators?" boomed Sebastian. "Please don't tell me he's now got your wearing a loincloth an' sandals like that Aussie guy in the movie? Haw! Haw! Meanwhile, I'll leave you two guys to battle it out while Ah go an' tell Delilah that despite you an' Joel not bein' there, our visit to Venice is still on. An' Ah can tell you, here an' now, us bein' in the sinkin' city without you two guys could easily be seen as a 'no go' with a helluva lot o' sighin' goin' on here at Rancho, Plata, Plata, Plata! Haw! Haw!"

A GUEST SUITE - PALAZZO LORENZO - AFTER THE FUNERAL

"I must say I expected a bigger turnout and more of a furore at Stephano's funeral," commented Pegg as he and Warwick were dressing for dinner.

"Trust me, *mon amour,* had it been his devious daddy's funeral instead, it would have been a different canal of fish with the Isola di San Michele literally bursting at its tombstone seams!" chuckled Warwick.

"I give Clementine ten out of ten for her poise and serenity, despite having to stand next to Paulo Pablo and the snivelling daughter. He, of course, looked as if he was suffering from an attack of acute indigestion rather than conveying an expression of grief."

"I think he was put out by the small gathering of mourners more than anything else, along with the stringent diet of flashbulbs," snickered Warwick. "It'll be interesting to see how long the divorce proceedings will take." He glanced to where Pegg was studying himself in a mirror while struggling with his bow tie. "And now that dear Aunt Clementine has again confirmed that one day this idyllic palazzo and its contents will all be mine, dear Paulo must be girding his loins in readiness for another rich widow hunt, but a hunt where the widow isn't a mere *millionairess,* but a hoodwinked *billionairess!*"

"And snivelling, sulky Sophia?"

"A sure-fire case of 'and daughter came too'. And now you've finally managed to make a complete mockery of your bow tie, let us now descend so that we can join the gay divorcee for a cocktail or three before dinner."

THE ROYAL SUITE - THE GRITTI PALACE HOTEL

"I love it! Simply love it! I's magic, pure magic," crowed Delilah from where she and Sebastian stood, arm in arm, on the balcony surveying the twinkling lights reflected in The Grand Canal. Giving Sebastian a kiss on his freshly shaven, Gucci Guity enhanced cheek, she added softly. "Thank you, my darling for bringing me here. I *know* it was a stumble through a jumble for us to be here. Not only do I love you for bringing me here. I simply love you for you being you."

"Aw shucks, lil' darlin'," boomed Sebastian giving Delilah's hand a gentle squeeze. "Now, how about a stroll to the famous Harry's Bar for one or two of their famous mixes of champagne an' peach juice, an' then dinner at that lil' restaurant Kurt recommended."

"*Si! Si*! Signor Handsome Prince," purred Delilah. Giving Sebastian's hand a reciprocal squeeze, she said candidly. "I appreciate it was her stepson's funeral today, but will you still be introducing yourself - us - tomorrow to Countess Lorenzo, saying we're friends of Kurt's, and would like to offer our sincere condolences at her tragic, sudden loss?"

"Yeah, definitely," grunted Sebastian. Giving Delilah a kiss on the cheek he said with a mischievous grin. "With luck the ol' gal will invite us to her palazzo for a drink which will give us a chance of have a look at Warwick fuckin' Laudanum-Standton's inheritance before we burn it down or blow it to fuckin' smithereens! Haw! Haw!"

THE NEXT MORNING

"*Buongiorno*, 'ave a nice day, Tommaso speaks," said a tremulous male voice. "'Ow can you 'elp me?"

"Tommaso speaks? 'Ow can you 'elp me?" boomed Sebastian. "You can 'elp me by putting me through to Countess Lorenzo, for starters. Tell the Countess it's Signor Salamander from Texas calling."

"Signor Texas Calling? 'Old on, Signore Texax Calling, *per favore*."

"'Old on to what?" muttered Sebastian. "My dick?"

"Good morning, Countess Lorenzo speaking. I say good morning as Tommaso assured me it was an English-speaking gentleman on the telephone." Clementine gave a giggle. "As you must have gathered his English is somewhat erratic but please excuse him as he's my butler's nephew and standing in for Dario, his uncle, who is currently on holiday."

"Not a problem, Countess," boomed Sebastian. "The name's Sebastian Salamander *visitin'* from Texas." Sebastian was about to give a deep, booming "Haw! Haw!" but restrained himself on remembering that the Countess Lorenzo was obviously in deepest mourning. "Ah'm a friend of Kurt Cameron who said Ah should give you a call if Ah eva visited your lovely floatin' city."

"Floating city?" giggled Delilah from where she was sitting. "Whatever happened to sinking?"

"Ah yes, dear Kurt spoke about you most fondly," cooed Clementine. "Welcome to Venice, Mr. Salamander."

"Thank you, Countess. Before I say anything else, Kurt told me about your stepson's unfortunate accident, so our condolences. That's me an' mah lovely wife."

"Thank you, Mr. Salamander."

"Sebastian, please!"

"Thank you, *Sebastian*. That's so kind of you and Mrs Salamander. Poor Stephano. A terrible shock to all who knew and loved him."

Yeah, Ah bet, thought Sebastian. *Ah would have said a very welcome shock from what Kurt told us about your self-indulgent stepson, so no need to overdo the grievin'; step-mama!*

"However, life goes on," continued Clementine, more matter-of fact than resigned, "just as I am sure you have a very busy itinerary seeing, according to dear Kurt, such a charming man, this is your first visit to Venice. However, if by chance you and Mrs Salamander . . ."

"Delilah, please."

"You and *Delilah*. What an enchanting name. So *biblical*!" tittered Clementine. "If you and Delilah are free for dinner this evening, I'd be delighted if you could join me and my two houseguests for a 'welcome to Venice' dinner at Palazzo Lorenzo."

"Join you for dinner an' your houseguests at your *palazzo* for dinner, Countess?" boomed Sebastian. "It would be our pleasure!"

"Lovely," cooed Clementine. "Let's say eight o'clock for cocktails and, if you have pen and paper handy, let me give you the address. You already have my telephone number!"

"Thank you," boomed Sebastian making a note. "Err . . . Countess, as we're dinin' in a *palazzo*, 'ow formal do you want us to be?"

"Oh, casually elegant as there'll only be five of us," crooned Clementine. "Myself, my nephew and his friend who flew over especially for the funeral. I look forward to seeing you and Delilah at eight. *Arrivederci.*"

"Casually elegant?" boomed Sebastian looking at a bemused Delilah. "So, what do you think Ah should wear. Delilah mah sweet? Mah Stetson with mah Calvin Kleins?"

"No, no, Sebastian, darling, that's *far* too dressy," chortled Delilah. "Why not simply wear a sign above your delicious willy saying. 'Below proves that all *is* bigger and better in Texas!'"

Staring at a grinning Sebastian, Delilah did a double take. "Did I just overhear her say her *nephew* and his friend would be joining us for dinner?"

"That's what the ol' gal said."

"Her *nephew*, Sebastian," said Delilah with a virulent hiss, "is none other than bloody Warwick Laudanum-Standton, my bête noir, and the odious creature who walked out of our celebration party at *Plata, Plata, Plata!*"

"Fuckin' jumpin' Jehoshaphat!" boomed Sebastian. "No way are we gonna be attendin' that fuckin' dinner! In no fuckin' way! Warwick fuckin' Laudanum-Standton? It never crossed mah stupid mind!"

"Well, it certainly has now," snapped Delilah. "So, what do we do?"

"What do we do, mah darlin'? We leave it until the last minute an' then Ah telephone Clementine an' tell her mah lil' darlin' musta eatin' somethin' nasty at lunch an' is not feelin' well so we won't be able to join her for dinner. As for viewing the palazzo, we can do that *next* year. As Kurt so rightly said, the stepson's death was an unfortunate hiccough but a hiccough that can be resolved same time next year when ol' Clementine's back in Tuscany." Sebastian gave a chuckle. "Look on the bright side, Delilah, darlin', for everythin' we would have admired this evenin' will still end up in bits and pieces or ashes! Haw! Haw!"

"Ha! All thanks to your darlin' Delilah coming down with a Venetian version of a gippy tummy," giggled Delilah. "I love it!"

"Yeah, an' to help you to cope with yah poor, ailin' tum-tum, Ah suggest a lavish dinner at The Cipriani Hotel set on its own lil' island."

"Sounds like an ideal solution for my impending condition," crooned Delilah. Giving a beaming Sebastian a tight smile, she added waspishly. "Here's hoping Mr. Warwick Laudanum-Standton not only *chokes* on his dinner, but fatefully so!"

"That's mah lil' gal!" boomed Sebastian. "An' so say all of us! Haw! Haw!"

PALAZZO LORENZO - LATER

"You mean you actually invited Texan Sebastian Salamander and his wife to dinner, but they've had to cancel at the last minute, Clementine?" chortled Warwick giving Pegg a knowing wink. "Just as well seeing they are not exactly your cup of Earl Grey. He epitomes the term crude, nouveau, very riche buffoon, and she, an ex-stripper-cum-gold digger-cum-oil well slurper who finally staked her claim!"

"Goodness," tittered Clementine. "Just as well they *did* cancel, for, unlike Dario, poor Tomasso would never have had the perspicacity to check the silver!"

Her sharp comeback causing Warwick and Pegg to rock with laughter.

18

VICTORIA STATION

They met, as usual. in a convenient Starbucks.

He: "It's been a while since we were here, and I must say you're looking remarkably chipper! Love the scarf."

She: "A chip off the old block, you mean. Haha. As for the scarf; a self-spoiling something from Signor Gucci. How was Barbados?"

He: "Rather like taking a step back into colonial times or, as I imagine, colonial times would have been. However, they *do* have an abundance of good bars and traffic lights. And how was Holland?"

She: "Very Dutch. And now we're back and our batteries supposedly recharged, I am sure, like yourself, no reminder nudges are necessary regarding what we do next with Mr. W L-S in our pursuit of him and, hopefully, a further playing with his worry beads."

He: "*Very* journalistic, I have to say. According to my always reliable source, our rival to Niccolo M . . ."

She: "I take it by Niccolo M you're referring to Niccolo Machiavelli?"

He: "Oh, very sharp! Particularly as, according to my source, our nemesis, has paid two visits to Italy within recent weeks for a funeral, sadly not his own, and no doubt to further pursue and glue his Italian inheritance!"

She: "Pursue and glue his inheritance? Now who's the one being journalistic? So, what are you suggesting?"

He: "Someone Italian but someone anonymous; someone with no connection to the dreaded whatsoever.

She: "I do so agree with an anonymous Italian he, as he also means we have more to play with!"

He: "You wicked wanton woman, you! But you're right. A tribute to Michelangelo and his David's little fellow!"

She: "*Bravo!* Signor! Continue like that and you'll have me walking down the aisle!"

He: "Not a bad idea! I may even hold you to that! Double entendre or not! Being serious, Signorina, where shall we look for our newest paraesthesia?"

She: "Paraesthesia?"

He: "I would have said itch, but as we're being *so* journalistic, I thought it better to use paraesthesia."

She: "Idiot!"

He: "Guilty as charged. Now, if you are free for dinner this evening, there's a new Italian restaurant near to where I live, why don't we give it a try and where better to start looking for our potential paraesthesia? What's more, he may even be on the menu! Oh, in order *not* to put you off your dinner, may I now make a further suggestion regarding the letters we carve on our latest nudge's head, why not a *mirrored* version of Standton's actual initials? A back to front version WLS. In other words. SLW with a back to front L and S?"

She: "I take back the idiot!"

A LAVISH DUPLEX PENTHOUSE - CHELSEA HARBOUR - BREAKFAST - THREE MORNINGS LATER

"Bugger! There's been another one," growled Pegg glancing up from the paper in front of him. "But, this time, a somewhat more finger pointing one from my reckoning!"

"Show me! Show me!" yelped Warwick, almost spilling his coffee.

"Jesus, Warwick! Keep your bloody hair on!" snapped Pegg swivelling the paper round and pointing at the relevant article. "It's not on the front page, it's on page four. But there it is, some other poor bastard dumped outside an A & E, bleeding from wounds to hands, his main fingers cut off, and from cuts to his forehead."

"'A twenty-six-year-old Italian waiter from a popular Italian restaurant,'" Warwick read out loud. He gave a snicker. "Ex-waiter they should have said seeing he'll no longer be able to carry a plate!"

"Bloody Hell, Warwick! A bit of sympathy for the poor guy isn't too much to ask for. Or is it, from the likes of Mr. Laudanum-Standton?"

"Sorry, Pegg. See it as my nervous reaction to the article." Staring at the hazy photographs accompanying the article, Warwick gave a gulp and said in a whisper. "Jesus, Pegg! Have a proper look at the photo of his face which some sneaky nurse or one of the ambulance crew must have taken and sold to the paper! Look at the pucking markings on his forehead!"

"Hmm, I can't quite decipher them, but they look like hieroglyphics or something."

"Hieroglyphics or something?" snorted Warwick. "Are you pucking *blind*? To me they look *exactly* like my initials WLS as seen reflected in a pucking mirror; the letters shown back to front! What's pucking *worse* is that it won't take long for some pucking plod, wannabe Hercule Poirot or wannabe Piers Morgan, puts two and two together and works out what WLS stands for!"

Springing to his feet, Warwick stormed across to the protective railings attached to the lower terrace. Glaring at the placid river below and the buildings lining its banks, he took a deep breath followed by a frantic yelled. "Who the puck *are* you and why are you doing this to me?" His unexpected reaction causing Vincent to spring to *his* feet and give his master several supportive barks.

"Calm, Warwick Calm," said Pegg soothingly on joining Warwick and taking him in his arms. "Take a few, slow deep breaths and calm down. You're here, safe with me, and everything will sort itself out and be alright; that I promise you."

"Err, thank you Pegg." murmured Warwick visibly relaxing within Pegg's warm embrace. "In fact, let's get back to the table and ask Wilma to bring out a bottle of vodka to add a calming balm to our glasses of orange juice."

Seated back at the table with their enhanced glasses of juice, Pegg made a show of clearing his throat and said firmly. "Warwick, I need you to think back, *seriously* think back, to anyone of your previous, puerile, vindictive mutilations - for that's what they are; puerile and vindictive - who could now be looking for some sort of reprisal?"

"But how would they know that I had anything to do with their initial mutilations," replied Warwick in a hurt voice. "And why now?"

"Why now?" exclaimed Pegg. "Jesus, Warwick! Enough with the hurt, little boy act. You not only *disfigured* them *physically* you disfigured them *mentally* as well!"

"I'm well aware of all *that*," snapped Warwick, "But what I don't understand is what makes any of them think their attacks had anything to do with me. We were all so careful. So *pucking* careful!"

"Well, someone does, or some do," said Pegg grimly. "As for your ridiculous 'why now', if you were in their shoes, I'm sure you'd see it as a blatant 'why not?'" He gave a snort. "May I remind you, Warwick, of one of your favourite sayings . . ."

"What? Well done, Bubba?" snickered Warwick.

"No, another. Revenge is a dish best served cold. What's more, I can assure you, Warwick, these copycat mutilations will continue until the police get a break or you *mentally* break," growled Pegg. "And in order for you *not* to break and the police not getting a break, I strongly suggest is you start delving into your former 'isn't this fun' mutilations and do some *serious* thinking."

"And once I've *done* some serious thinking and made a list of my past mutilations past and present, what then?" replied Warwick sarcastically. "Send them a note of apology? Something along the lines of 'sorry I halved your dick but then you *did* you did upset me: *once upon a time!*"

"No, Warwick. You then do what you should have done in the first place. You now kill them!"

"When you say 'you', you surely don't mean *moi* on my lonesome ownsome," tittered Warwick.

"Why not?" said Pegg. "To quote you yet again. 'Strange, isn't it how quickly love dies?'. And as your love for me seems in the process of doing precisely that, I suggest you once more approach Jess, cap in hand, and ask him to find you another Kurt or yours truly to step into my shoes."

"You said it, so I'll happily do it," replied Warwick with a tight smile. "Now. if you wouldn't mind making yourself redundant by pucking out of *my* study tout suite, it would be appreciated seeing I need to make a phone call."

Striding into the kitchen Pegg said calmly to Julia, busy preparing dinner, and to Wilma, cheerfully polishing the silverware. "Continue the good work, ladies. Sadly, I won't be enjoying what I am sure will be another delicious dinner, Julia, aided and abetted by Wilma's gleaming cutlery, but I have a feeling dashing David Pegg may have just been given his marching orders; dashing David Pegg having unintentionally suggested it!"

"Given your marching orders and you unintentionally suggesting it?" repeated Julia. "That will never do!"

Setting down the knife she had been using for chopping parsley, she briskly wiped her hands on a dishcloth before walking purposefully from out the kitchen."

"Bloody Hell," muttered Pegg, raising an eyebrow.

"Poor bloody Warwick, you mean," giggled Wilma. "Just as I recently proved to be a Whizzing Wilma, let's see what Julia, sometimes known as the Gorgeous Gorgon, comes up with!"

"The Gorgeous Gorgon?" chuckled Pegg. "This I've got to see."

Five minutes later Julia came striding back. "To quote our dear *Mr. Moi, Moi. Moi,* Warwick, Pegg. He's deeply upset as his latest little temper tantrum, owes you an apology so could you please, pretty, *pretty,* please, go back and have a word."

"What else can a dashing bit of rough do when you put it like that, Julia, dear," chuckled Pegg making for the door. "Looks as if I could be enjoying your delicious dinner after all!"

"Another of their endless tiffs?" quizzed Wilma.

"Maybe, maybe not," murmured Julia. "As I said to the little twerp, if it wasn't for the love and loyalty from the likes of Pegg - I also mentioned Kurt Cameron and our somewhat debatable selves - if he continues treating everyone in the thankless way he does, he'll find himself ending up in the most horrendous doo-doo with nobody there willing to help him out of it! I also said we know where some of the bodies are buried and all it would take was an anonymous phone call or two!"

*

"I *knew* it, Vincent, I just knew it," muttered Warwick sitting at his desk with Vincent of his lap. Fondling Vincent's ears, he gave a snicker. "Tell me I look like James Bond's Blofeld and you, my cat in the disguise of a pooch. Haha. Okay, okay, being serious for a moment, Pegg may see himself on some sort of temporary reprieve, *very* temporary, nota bene. As for pucking Julia Mander and her titty sidekick, they too, could soon be carted away en route to the guillotine. Since when does a wannabe Madam Defarge start telling *moi,* Warwick Laudanum-Sandton, what he can and cannot do!"

Fondling Vincent's ears with one hand while drumming his fingers on the desk with the other, he murmured softly. "Psycho Sporran. Okay, the guy assisted Pegg in getting rid of that tiresome Bernhard Walton, but that doesn't mean he and Pegg are cojoined. Far from it. So, perhaps a cautious word with Mr. Sporran regarding Mesdames Mander and Davis and their murmurs of discontent would not necessarily go amiss. I've never met the mysterious Mr. Sporran so why not remedy that. Thank Hades that when Pegg and I were discussing Walton's demise, I jotted down his various numbers." Warwick gave a snicker. "As they say there's no time like the present so why not."

Opening a nearby cabinet, Warwick flicked through several files before pulling out a file labelled *Culinary Treats.* Opening the file he said in a relieved voice. "And here they are, just begging to be used."

Reaching for one of three landlines. Warwick gave Vincent a pat and said with a giggle. "What do think our Scottish Mr. Sporran looks like, Vincent? Another Sean the Brawn - i.e. Sean Connery - or, God forbid, a sprig of heather with a penchant for leather! Only one way to find out."

The first number Warwick dialled had a recording saying the number was no longer valid, with a similar response to the next number he tried. "Fingers crossed it'll be third time lucky," murmured Warwick on dialling. "Aha! It's ringing. Hopefully our friend will answer, If I get a machine and told to leave a pucking message, that's it and you can go puck yourself, Mr. Sporran!"

"Andy MacPherson speaking," said a rich, baritone voice with a pronounced Scottish burr.

"Err ... Mr. err ... MacPherson, sorry. I must have a wrong number. I was trying to get hold of Mr, Sporran. A Mr. *Psycho* Sporran."

"And who might ye be?" said MacPherson.

"The name's Standton. Warwick Laudanum-Standton. I'm an associate of David Pegg."

"Goodness me, a call from Mr. Warwick Laudanum himself," chuckled MacPherson. "I'm honoured. David not around, I take it?"

"He is, but isn't, if you see what I mean, Mr. MacPherson. Or would you prefer me to address you as Mr. Sporran?"

"Andy will do just fine."

"Thank you. In answer to your question, *Andy*. I say he is but isn't because there is a matter I'd prefer to discuss with you, one to one."

"In other words, face to my ugly face," chuckled MacPherson. "Right you are, Mr. Warwick, suggest a time and a place."

"Warwick, please."

"Right you are, Warwick. As I said, suggest a time and place and, if it's convenient, I'll meet you there." Andy MacPherson gave a further chuckle. "To put your mind at ease, Warwick, in spite of my nom de plume, nickname, whatever, I don't look like a Hollywood psycho nor a sporran, so the other diners shouldn't run screaming. If it's of any help, your *associate*, David Pegg, always says I'm a dead ringer for Sean Connery. With hair."

"Thank God for the hair!" tittered Warwick. "I was half expecting you to say a Fred West or a Freddie Kreuger. Haha! Scalini's will be relieved!"

"You said Scalini? It's one of my favourites and, as I do not look like a relic from a horror film, I never have never any trouble when visiting the restaurant."

"How about lunch today?" trilled Warwick.

"I'll see you there at one," said Andy. "Oh, afore ye go, a quick question. How will I recognise you?"

"Simply look out for a twenty first century Beau Brummel-cum-Little Lord Fauntleroy dressed in Henry Poole's finest and waving a handful of luncheon vouchers, and that'll be me." crooned Warwick. "See you at one!"

SCALINI - WALTON STREET - CHELSEA

"That's got to be him," muttered Warwick on seeing s cheerful, dead ringer for Sean the Brawn Connery talking to smiling maître 'd before heading toward the table. Noting the big man's tweed jacket, cream shirt, plain maroon tie and neatly pressed calvary tweed trousers he added with a snicker. "Put him in a kilt and he'd look exactly like one of those groaning giants tossing the caber. And, if Vincent was here, I'm sure he'd agree with me if I said I wouldn't say no to tossing *his* caber!"

"Warwick? Andy MacPherson," beamed the big man proffering a giant, hirsute hand. "Sorry I'm a few minutes late but you know how the traffic is round here." He gave a chuckle. "Like the suit. Lavender, is it?"

"I prefer lilac," tittered Warwick. "As for being late. Better late than never!" Reluctantly pulling his hand from the giant's warm grasp, he nodded at the bottle nestling in an ice bucket next to the table. "I ordered a bottle of

Pinot Grigio, it's my favourite, but please order whatever tickles your fancy! Haha!"

"I'll have a martini, very dry, no ice," said Andy to the smiling wine waiter. Turning his attention back to Warwick he said with a penetrating stare. "So, Warwick, you wanted to see me *without* Pegg. Care to explain as I was under the impression that the two of you were a team, an item."

"It's not only Pegg I need to talk to you about; it's also the two women who look after my apartment," replied Warwick shifting uneasily on his chair.

"Okay, so something's bugging you about Dave and your two domestics," grunted Andy followed by a quiet "Thank you" to the wine waiter setting down his drink. "If that's what we're here to discuss may I suggest you give me the gist of what you *wish* to discuss *before* we order. Frankly, if its anything to do with what I think you're going to say: forget it, as I'm not interested."

"And what *exactly* what were you thinking I was about to say?" said Warwick loftily.

"That you're having problems with David Pegg and want me to get shot of him, along with your two domestics."

"I wasn't thinking of getting *shot* of Pegg in the true sense of the word," snickered Warwick. "I just want him out of my life."

"To me that's more or less the same thing," replied Andy. Taking a contemplative sip of his martini, he said matter-of-factly. "Surely you can simply give Pegg his marching orders and dismiss the two women?"

"It's not that simple. Pegg says he's genuinely in love with me and therefore could be a recurring problem, while the two women know too much about my previous wrongdoings." Staring at Andy, Warwick said coolly. "Are you gay?"

"Am I gay?" repeated Andy, somewhat taken aback by the out of the blue question. "No, Warwick, I'm not. However, rest assured the fact that you and Dave are gay doesn't concern me one bit."

"Not even gay for pay?" giggled Warwick.

"Not even gay for pay or a generous retainer," chuckled Andy.

"Pity," pouted Warwick. "Not even if I asked you to name your price?"

"For fuck's sake, Warwick!" snapped Andy. "Keep your voice down. Dave Pegg told me you were a manipulative little shite, but I underestimated just how manipulative you are! Now, if you'll excuse me, I'll leave you to finish your bottle of Pinot Grigio. Thank you for the drink."

Rising to his feet, Andy looked down at the smirking young man and said, deadpan. "I wish you the best of luck, Warwick, with whoever and whatever you decide to do. You'll both need it."

"Well, puck you, you useless lump of rancid haggis," muttered Warwick as Andy marched away from the table. Taking s sip of wine he said with a chortle. "Oh, well, as they say, as one closet door closes another closet door opens. Now, what shall I order? I think a plate of their delicious *Fettucine al Ragu Bianco and Tartufo Nero* accompanied by Signor Grigio will suit this discarded, undefeated mutilator, admirably!"

LATER

"Who the puck can be calling at this time of night, or early morning," grizzled Warwick fumbling for the phone on the bedside cabinet. Glancing at a gently snoring Pegg and Vincent lying next to him, he said with a virulent hiss. "Yes?"

"Warwick, it's Andy. "I've been thinking. How much are you prepared to pay for me to, A, to deal with Pegg and your two ladies, and, B, if you can convince me, pay for me for having a go at being gay for pay. Call me in the morning with your answers." There was a click as the line went dead.

"Who was that?" asked Pegg sleepily.

"Some drunken idiot having obviously misdialled," replied Warwick softly. "Go back to sleep."

*

As promised, Andy called back several hours later.

"I have two prices for you," said Warwick said without preamble. "Five grand for getting shot - ha! - of Dave Pegg and the same again for silencing the two women in the nicest, possible way."

There was a moment's silence before Andy replied. "Fine. Here are my bank details for today's transaction - any future dealings will be strictly cash - and, as soon as the money is transferred, we're in business."

"Then we're in business as from today," chortled Warwick, "for as soon as you hangup I'll give my bank a call."

19

TWO MORNINGS LATER

"Missing *moi* already?" crooned Warwick on recognising the number for Peggs, Dave having left for the kennels less than an hour ago.

"Missing you? More like murdering you!" snarled Pegg. "You, Warwick Laudanum-Standon take the term devious little shit to a new low! How *dare* you collude with Andy MacPherson, whom I considered a friend, behind my back! And before you ask: yes, he has been one hundred percent successful in making sure I will never see you again. How did he do this? By threatening to destroy Peggs school for guide dogs if I didn't agree!

"So, two things, you loathsome excuse for a human being. A, I will never set foot in your wretched building ever again and any possessions I do have there can be binned, and B, do not even attempt visit Peggs as Trish and Coli have now been instructed to call the police and have you removed."

Before a startled Warwick could respond, Pegg slammed down the phone.

Seconds later one of the landlines started to ring.

"Warwick. Andy. Simply to let you know your former paramour is now your *ex*-paramour."

"So, I've just been told, in an extremely definite way," chortled Warwick. "Well done, Andy, and an extra thank you for not harming any of the dogs."

"Why would I have harmed any of the dogs when its humans - e.g. Dave Pegg and those two women - who are the real culprits," replied Andy with a chuckle. "Expect to hear from the gorgon gals later today or first thing tomorrow. Let me know how *they* react, and I'll take it from there."

*

"*Entrer*," crooned Warwick on hearing a sharp knocking on the study door. "Goodness! Julia *and* Wilma! Has something happened?"

"You know *exactly* what's happened!" barked Julia. "Andrew MacPherson's what's happened. Therefore, *Mr.* Laudanum-Standton, Wilma and I will be leaving as soon as we've packed our belongings. Have no fear, Mr. Laudanum-Standton, not a word will ever be said about your sordid, miserable little shenanigans. As for any monies owed, I - we - suggest you simply stuff this up your poisonous little rectum. Despite the irritating fact you'll no doubt enjoy the sensation."

"One last thing, if I may," added Julia. "You do *not* deserve the loyalty and love given to you by Vincent. In return for this underserved love and loyalty I would ask you to have the decency - a word not familiar to you - to make sure *he* comes to no harm because of you."

Giving Wilma a nod, the two women marched from the room.

Picking up Vincent, Warwick gave him a resounding kiss on his muzzle and then started to sing.

"*Oh, Vincent, I'm in trouble,*" he sang, à la Peter Sellers in the spoof song he sang with Sofia Loren in conjunction with the Sixties movie, *The Millionairess*. "*Goodness, gracious, me. For every time I meet a man, that man is not to be!*"

Giving Vincent a further kiss before putting him down, Warwick said with a snicker. "That's *three* little birds with one stone! What a clever Warwick I am! However, no matter how clever I'm back to the same old, same old dilemma, how on *earth* do I find another compatible cook and housekeeper? Perhaps the now uber-popular Andy can come to the rescue. Plus, we still have to discuss if he *is* still prepared to have a *try* at going gay for pay!"

*

What Andy MacPherson did not tell Warwick was that instead of telephoning Pegg he arranged to meet him in person at the kennels where he then explained what he had been requested to do. "Your so-called friend, Laudanum-Standton is not only paying me to supposedly threaten you: he is also paying me to make a similar move against Julian Mander and Wilma Davis. As I said, the ladies, you and I, Dave, go back a long way. I suggested they play the wounded domestics to the hilt and leave. Once you, Julia and Wilma are out of there, may I suggest we meet tomorrow either at my flat in Ladbroke Square or at your flat which you kept despite Standon's promises of living together happily ever after."

Pegg's reaction, along with those of Julia and Wilma, was a combination of disbelief and relief, the three agreeing to meet at Andy's flat at noon the next day to "discuss the situation".

A COMFORTABLE GARDEN FLAT - LADBROKE SQUARE - NOON - THE NEXT DAY

"My, oh my, *very* stylish," commented Julia eyeing the large sitting room with its dark blue ceiling and carpet, burnt-orange walls, two green leather Chesterfield sofas, a couple of comfortable armchairs upholstered in Macpherson tartan with matching Roman blinds topping a pair of French doors opening onto an outside terrace. She gave a giggle. "You wouldn't be Scottish, by any chance?"

"There's a rumour," chuckled Andy, proffering s large hand "Good to see you again, Dave, especially on *our* terms."

"Likewise, Andy, likewise," replied Pegg. Glancing around stylish room and contents subtly lit by a series of artfully placed ceiling spots and dark green ceramic table lamps, he nodded approvingly. "Very *Architectural Digest,* Andy; but then you've always had a flair."

Turning to a smiling Julia and Wilma, he added mischievously. "There's rumour - rumour, nota bene, as I can't personally say the proof in the haggis is in the viewing. Haha! The rumour being that our friend here wears MacPherson tartan patterned underpants to keep the home fires burning, as it were!"

"Oi! Enough about my privates when not on parade," chuckled Andy. "Ladies, what would you like to drink? Like any red-blooded Scotsman, I have a well-stocked bar, so simply name what you'd like. Pegg, I know, enjoys a very dry martini, as do I, but the choice is yours."

"A glass of white wine, preferably dry, for me, please," smiled Julia.

"And the same for me, please," echoed Wilma from where she now stood by the French doors. "Oh, Andy!" she crooned, "I simply *love* what you've done to the outside terrace! Julia! Come and have a look. Like me, I bet you've never seen a terrace patterned in tartan mosaic before with a billiard-like bit of verdant green lawn to give it that bit of extra oomph!"

"It really is quite magical, Andy," said Julia having joined Wilma. "I know it sounds a touch forward, but may I see the rest of the flat?" She gave a giggle. "Maybe your bed's a coracle!"

"Not quite," laughed Andy. "As I'm one of those people who really *does* enjoy a good night's sleep, I'm a loyal supporter of Mr. Sleepeezee. As for Mr. Coracle, two smaller *ceramic* versions of the hardy gentleman serve as fruit bowls in the tartan patterned kitchen! As you may have guessed, my bedroom is both *walled* and curtained in MacPherson tartan. A most reassuring sight to wake up to. Plus, it seems to keep the nightmares at bay. Somewhat of a surprise is the bed linen; all virginal white."

*

Drinks duly served and the four comfortably seated; Julia and Wilma on one Chesterfield sofa facing Andy and Pegg on the other, Andy said cheerfully. "Lunch is a selection of cold meats and salads followed by Key lime pie, so, we have stacks of time to talk about you know who without having to worry about anything being burnt or spoiled. Pegg, who don't you go first seeing you're more au fait with Warwick than any of us."

"Before Pegg takes the floor, or carpet," tittered Wilma, "I'd like to ask him a quick question, if that's okay."

"Please, ask away."

"Regarding your predecessor in Warwick's weird and mixed-up worlds, a man named Kurt Cameron, how well do you know him, if at all?"

"I don't," replied Pegg, "but I can see what you're getting at, Wilma, and I whole heartedly agree. What I *do* know is that he left under what I'd call a typical Warwick cloud and now lives in Texas and is very much part of Mr. Sebastian Salamander's team. Both of which do not sit well with Mr. WLS. So, the zillion dollar question, should we or shouldn't we contact him and see what *he* has to say - if anything - about Warwick."

"Good idea," said Andy, "and I think the person to contact him should be you, Dave. After all, you've both been smitten and bitten, as it were." His wry comment causing Pegg and the two women to burst out laughing.

"Okay, okay, point well and truly made and taken, in all sense of the words!" chuckled Pegg. "So, I contact Cameron and then what? Julia?"

"Tell him we are well-aware of what Warwick's been up to regarding him and now us," said Julia. "How he seems to be hellbent on a personal vendetta against the world in general: his associate Sebastian Salamander being a prime target!"

"I'm happy to do as you suggest," continued Pegg, "but first things first and something much closer to home. I take it you'll all read those strange attacks that have been taking place recently. People attacked and mutilated and then left outside some convenient A & E?"

"I most certainly have," said Julia. "Don't tell us . . ."

"They've been scaring the bejesus out of Warwick," said Pegg, "So much so that the report of the attack had him crying to the heavens and asking why *he* was being persecuted by a copycat!"

"Typical!" snorted Julia. "For when it comes to being a hundred percent narcissistic, Warwick Laudanum-Standton leads the pack!" She took a deep breath. "Like all of us sitting here, I'm embarrassed to say we're all guilty of helping Warwick with his twisted paybacks, but what's done is done and cannot be *undone,* and something we simply have to live with. Talk about an unfortunate millstone round one's neck

"If any of you took a good look at the photographs of the poor guy one or two of the papers managed to run, did you notice anything strange about the cuts on his forehead?"

"My God!" exclaimed Wilma. "You mean the strange looking markings? I remember thinking they looked - to me that is - like letters back to front."

"Ten out of ten, Wilma! They were," chuckled Pegg. "SLW. Warwick's initials as if reflected in a mirror!"

"Make that ten out of ten along with a well-deserved medal, Wilma Jessica Fletcher!" chortled Julia giving Wilma's hand an affectionate squeeze,

"On that laudatory note," chuckled Andy, "may I suggest we adjourn to my tartan tented dining room where we can sit, eat and be merry while we discuss what happens next."

HOUSTON - TEXAS - THE SAME DAY

"Good morning," said a cheerful voice. "Joel Ford-Cameron speaking."

"Err . . . good morning, Mr. Ford-Cameron," replied Warwick spikily. "Is Mr. *Kurt* Ford-Cameron about?"

"He's about and in a lather in the shower," chortled Joel. "Can I take a message?"

"No thank you, I'll call back later."

"Can I tell him who called?"

"No thank you, *Mr.* Ford-Cameron. As I distinctly said, I'll call back later," snapped Warwick slamming down the phone.

"Who was that?" asked Kurt entering the comfortable sitting room, dressed in a tiger print bathrobe and sporting a pair of Gucci slippers.

"Some lah-di-dah sounding guy wanting to speak to you and only you," replied Joel with a grin. "*Very* Noël Coward but without any manners as he simply put down the phone on me!"

"Hmm," muttered Kurt taking a sip of coffee. "Very Noël Coward, you said. How odd."

"He said he'd call back," said Joel nonchalantly. "Meanwhile, I see we both have busy schedules today so, if this *Mad Dogs and Englishmen* type *does* call back, he'll have to deal with the answering service which should *really* piss him off . . . unless that's him," he added as the landline started to ring. "Do you want to take it or shall I?"

"No, leave it to me," grinned Kurt reaching for the phone. "Good morning, Mr. Coward," he said, giving Joel a wink. "Sorry we couldn't talk earlier but, as Joel explained, I was in the shower."

"Sorry, this is not Mr. Coward," said Pegg smoothly. "The name's Pegg, David Pegg, and I was hoping to speak to Mr. Kurt Cameron. Is he there by any chance?"

"He is. Hold on and I'll get him for you. You did say your name was Pegg?

"Yes, David Pegg calling from London, England."

Kurt allowed for a few seconds to pass before he said jocularly. "David Pegg, Kurt Cameron! Although we've never met, I do know your name. However, a call from you, Warwick Laudanum-Standton's former err . . . associate *is* a surprise. How may I help you?"

"Maybe not that much of a surprise if I tell you, like your good self, I too consider *myself* a former associate-cum-whatever of Warwick Laudanum Standton," replied Pegg dryly.

"Ho! Ho! Ho!" hee-hawed Kurt. "Welcome to the club! So, Mr. Pegg, what seems to be the problem because if it has anything, *anything* at all, to do with a former associate-cum-whatever of wilful, wily Warwick's, it can only be a problem!"

"Can you give me a couple of minutes?"

"Just let me pour myself another cup of coffee, Mr. Pegg, and then I'm all yours,"

"Dave or simply Pegg, please."

"Pegg it is, much more stylish, and I'm Kurt. Let me get that coffee and then we can talk without any further interruptions."

"Before you do your coffee run, Kurt. This mysterious person who called you, it couldn't have been Warwick, by any chance?"

"My thoughts *exactly*, Pegg. With luck I could even have a name and number we can check out, should he speak to my answering service later today."

There was a moments silence before Kurt retuned to the phone. "I'm back so please continue."

"I shouldn't think there's been anything in the papers, whatever, over there, but someone here appears to be doing a replica - or replicas - of those unfortunate disfigurements we're both guilty of assisting our former friend carry out."

"Christ!" exclaimed Kurt. "No, I've seen nothing! You mean mutilations such as amputating fingers, ears and such?"

"By 'and such' I take it you mean cocks," interrupted Pegg. "Yes, the whole enchilada. However, and this is the most interesting factor, whoever's doing this made a clear statement regarding his, or their, latest victim by carving what appear to be Warwick's *mirrored* or reflected initials, SLW, on the victim's forehead."

"Bloody Hell! No wonder the little turd's shitting his pants," crowed Kurt. "Now I'm totally convinced it must have been him who called. Talk about scraping the barrel. Tell you what, Pegg, let's keep in touch twenty-four seven - I mean it - regarding anything to do with this Janus. I'll call you back, regardless of the time, as soon as I've spoken to Mr. Coward-cum-Standton - I'll explain later - and we'll take it from there."

"Thanks Kurt. Andy MacPherson says 'hi', as do Julia Mander and Wilma Davis, two ladies who have also been on the receiving end of Warwick's twisted largesse."

"I commiserate with them and trust we'll all meet one day," chuckled Kurt. "Speak to you later, my friend."

HOUSTON - TEXAS

"Good morning, Sebastian. I had an interesting talk last night with David Pegg, my replacement and now another Standton cast off," said Kurt in the first of their daily phone calls. "Talk about shooting yourself in the foot; I'm surprised he's got any feet left to shoot!"

"Tell me! Tell me!" boomed Sebastian, "or, better still, shoot! Haw-haw! Delilah's right here an' you're on speaker phone."

"Good morning, Kurty, *baby*!" crooned Delilah mischievously, "and a good morning to Joel if he's there."

"Good morning, lovely Delilah! No, Joel's out jogging but I'll pass on your salutations!"

Kurt went on to repeat what Pegg had told him about the mysterious attacks similar to Warwick's previous machinations, his instant dismissal along with Julia and Wilma, and how they had subsequently teamed up with Andy.

"Which means Warwick is now running solo with even his usually forgiving Aunt Clementine running a touch anti."

"Which brings me to what me an' mah darlin' Delilah have been discussin'," boomed Sebastian. "As the poor, lil' ol' Countess has never done *us* any harm, apart from havin' that lil' turd as a nephew, we both agree why upset the ol' gal by burnin' down her lil' ol' palazzo while she's still aroun' to enjoy it. So, we're doin' nuthin' until the ol' gal kicks the bucket!"

"I heartily agree with you and Delilah, Sebastian," replied Kurt in a relieved voice. "Countess Clementine is really an old sweetie so it would have been both cruel and unkind to make her suffer due to her nephew's abhorrent antics." He paused for a moment before saying. "Maybe a fire in his penthouse?"

"Too obvious an' too dangerous as there are other people livin' there," rumbled Sebastian, "so keep those thinkin' caps thinkin'. Haw-haw!"

"In the meanwhile, Kurt, what do you think Warwick will do to find another you-cum-David Pegg?" asked Delilah.

"To find another me would be impossible," chuckled Kurt. "As for another David Pegg, who knows. Maybe a hunt through some old copy of the former Yellow Pages. Haha!"

Little did Kurt realise how right he was.

20

A LAVISH DUPLEX PENTHOUSE - CHELSEA HARBOUR

"I tell you, Vincent, my cloak and dagger friend, I must be close to pucking losing it," muttered Warwick to a disinterested Vincent busy with a doggy chew. "What the purple *puck* was I thinking when I tried to speak to Kurt loser Cameron last night. However, as I didn't leave my name, hopefully his battered bride never mentioned the call."

Glancing at the sunny vista outside the study window, Warwick took a deep breath and said tetchily. "Right, it's pretty pucking obvious we need to find another God's big as opposed to little helper so there're two things I can do for starters; neither of which involve Jess Rix as he too is under a somewhat questionable cloud. One, I can ask good old Mr. Google for assistance or, better still, see if one of those cretinous porters' downstairs still has a copy, or copies, of the old Yellow Pages lurking about. Why the puck they had to stop printing Yellow Pages is typical of how the twenty-first century in regressing instead of advancing!"

Picking up the house phone, Warwick tapped in the number for the porters' desk.

"Good morning, sir," said a lachrymose voice. "Tim here. How can I be of help?"

"Good morning, Tim down there!" trilled Warwick. *Of course, it would have to be old misery guts Tim Matter instead of Bert on duty,* he thought. *However, buggers can't always be choosers, but one never knows.* "It's Mr. Laudanum-Standton from the penthouse calling."

I can bloody see who's calling," thought Tim Matter, the porter on duty. *What now? Wanting a new bit of rough seeing your last big mate's been given the heave-ho?*

Taking a deep breath, Warwick said cheerfully. "I know it's no longer available, *Tim*, but you wouldn't, by some remote chance, have an old copy of Yellow Pages lurking about, would you? I think the last volume was printed in 2019."

"It may come as a surprise, sir, we do have a copy in the porter's lodge," replied Matter with a giggle-cum-gurgle. "It's been propping up our tea table for yonks!"

"Well, I wouldn't like to upset the tea table, Tim," chortled Warwick. "But would it be possible for me to borrow your old copy for a couple of hours? I'll take good care of it and make sure I don't spill *my* cuppa over it! Haha!"

Ten minutes later Matter, a woebegone looking figure in his ill-fitting porter's uniform dropped off the copy. "There's no need to return it, sir," he mumbled deadpan, "seeing I've replaced it with a brick."

Seated at his desk, Warwick began to flick through the thick out of date directory. "Private Investigators? Maybe. Handymen? Maybe. Ha! As this is going to take some time, maybe a half pitcher of martinis to aid and abet the lovely *moi* wouldn't be a bad idea."

He turned his attention to Vincent. "And as you can hardly wait to help, I take it you'll be expecting another doggy chew!"

Fifteen minutes and one martini later, Warwick gave a chuckle. "I don't know who you are, sir, but anyone under the category of private eye who bills himself as Harold Hastings, Private Eye and a Man for All Reasons, simply *has* to have the same sense of tumour as *moi*, or else be a real thicko! So, let's give Mr. Harold Hastings a - dare I say it? - a quiver. Right, Vincent! Here goes!"

As the number kept on ringing and ringing, Warwick was about to hang up when the call was finally answered,

"Harold Hastings, Private Eye," said a cheerful baritone voice. "My apologies for the delay."

"Good morning, Mr, Hastings," crooned Warwick. "The name's Laudanum-Standton. Warwick Laudanum-Standton. Before we talk, a quick question." His question followed by a distinct silence. "Hello? Are you still there?"

"Yes, I'm still here, Mr. Laudanum-Standton and waiting for this quick question."

"Oh? Yes, Sorry. Here it is. When you refer to yourself as a man for all reasons, what does that entail, exactly?"

"It means I undertake most commissions as long as they don't involve the clink," replied Harold Hastings, followed by a deep, rumbling belly laugh. "For example, if you wanted me to help you to steal the Crown Jewels, I'd have to say no."

"As even *I* would look ridiculous decked out in the Crown Jewels, Mr. Hastings," chortled Warwick, "that is not the reason for my call. Would you, and it's a pretty wild 'would you', and despite it not being anywhere near Halloween, would you be prepared to don a costume, and some stage makeup and then scare the shit out of someone for me?"

"If you saw me as is, maybe you'd think I don't need any costume or makeup, Mr. Laudanum-Standton," replied Hastings with a further deep belly rumble. "When and where would you suggest we meet?"

"How are you placed today?"

"I'm completely unplaced, as you put it."

"Are you au fait with Scalini's in Walton Steet?"

"Totally au fait."

"Good, I'll see you there at one o'clock. I will be wearing an emerald-green blazer so I shouldn't be too difficult to spot. Plus, I'm well known there. And you? How will I recognise you?"

"Oh, I think a couple of horrified screams from the other diners will verify my arrival."

"Right," said Warwick with a snicker. "I look forward to meeting you, Mr. Fright Night!"

What Hastings did not tell Warwick was that the number he had dialled was that of an earlier scam. The number was only used by a select one or two and by Hastings for the odd outgoing call. His latest number and identity being listed as Arnold Agincourt, Financial Advisor.

SCALINI RESTAURANT

"Mr. Laudanum-Standton? Harold Hastings," said the familiar baritone voice.

Glancing up, Warwick did a double take on seeing the smiling David Niven lookalike - a touch more spivish than English gentleman - complete with pencil moustache.

"*Excusez moi,*" tittered Warwick, standing up and proffering his hand. "My hearing must have been temporarily afflicted seeing I never heard any accompanying screams."

"Put it down to one of my endless disguises," chuckled Hastings. "Today I'm Harold Hastings. Who knows who I'll be tomorrow."

"I like you already, Mr. Hastings."

"Harold."

"I like you already, *Harold*. Please sit and tell and tell the wine waiter your preferred poison. I'm currently poisoning myself with a large martini."

"Your poison is my poison," quipped Harold.

"Not only do I like you, Harold, I can see we're also going to get along. Please call me Warwick."

Having ordered Harold's martini and another for himself despite the three already consumed back at the penthouse, Warwick said briskly. "Shall we order before we start to waffle, or shall we waffle before we order?"

"Order and then waffle," said Harold in a no-nonsense voice.

Lunch and wine ordered, and martinis duly served, Warwick sat back, took a deep breath and said casually. "I'm currently being spooked by someone who appears to know more about me than they should by carrying out a series of minor attacks on a couple of people which appear to be identical to attacks I was supposedly responsible for in the past."

"You say identical to attacks which you are *supposedly* responsible for, Warwick," said Harold. "Please describe these attacks, no holds barred."

"How open can I be with you, Harold?"

"Anything you tell me is strictly confidential," replied Harold with a smile. "I am not wired, and my lips will be duly sealed, should you wish me to sound like one of those shifty sleuths on TV."

You, Mr. Hastings appear to be okay. Or in WLS talk, not bad, Bubba. Not bad at all, thought Warwick.

"Right, here goes." Taking a fortifying swallow of his martini he said in a whisper. "The truth is that I *am* responsible for several nasty little pranks made against former pupils who were pretty lousy toward me at school. Along with one or two others."

"These nasty little pranks you refer to. What do you mean by nasty?"

"Oh, one or two minor disfigurements; nothing life threatening. More like unpleasant reminders of their cruel attitude and behaviour than anything else. Oh, on one or two occasions I did inscribe my initials, back to front as if viewed in a mirror, on their foreheads." Warwick gave a hollow laugh. "I particularly remember the first time I did this as I also included a not really noticeable back to front W followed by an L for 'with love'."

"Very picturesque," muttered Harold.

"As you may have read over the past few weeks, there have been reports of several attacks of this sort. One against my hairdresser and one against an Italian waiter, and a complete stranger as far as I'm concerned. What's even more frightening is the fact that in the published photograph of the waiter's marked forehead, the initials, despite being back to front, are pucking mine!"

"Pucking?"

"Instead of the F word, I prefer the Laudanum-Standton equivalent: my very own P word," said Warwick loftily. Ignoring Harold's amused expression, he added sotto voce. "Getting back to what I was saying, I'm determined to find out who's behind these disturbing incidents and this where you, hopefully, come in."

"You appear to be an organised person, Warwick, so I assume you have a list of the recipients of your nasty little pranks?"

"I do, indeed," smirked Warwick, reaching inside his blazer and pulling out an envelope. "Here are all the names and addresses, though some of the addresses may be out of date." He added sharply. "It can only be one of the names on my list."

"Or maybe two or even three," said Harold with a dismissive shrug. Pocketing the list, he added matter-of-factly. "I'll take a look at this later, but first, before I do anything, I need you to agree my terms. If you agree, I will give you details for an account into which fifty percent of the agreed fee must be paid, tout suite." He gave Warwick a wolverine smile. "You can use my phone to make the transfer, if it helps."

"No thank you," snapped Warwick. "Pray, continue."

"From what you tell me this is an extremely complicated matter and once I find the culprit, or culprits, we will then need to discuss a further fee for what I see as phase two of your dilemma. In other words. a final nasty reminder before a final blissful oblivion. Give me a sec."

Reaching inside his jacket pocket, Harold took out a gleaming Mont Blanc pen and a neat Asprey notebook. Staring at the other diners, he sat thoughtfully for what seemed to Warwick an eternity as opposed to a couple of minutes before printing the words, Phase One and Phase Two along with the requisite fees. "My fees," said Harold tearing off the sheet of paper and handing it to Warwick. "Not negotiable."

Glancing at the figures, Warwick raised what he considered a sardonic eyebrow. *Pucking Shylock! Hopefully you're as good a Sherlock!* he thought.

Giving Harold a tight smile, he said through gritted teeth. "Not bad, Bubba! Now, if I may borrow your phone due to my, about to be, severely depleted funds, I'll quickly call my bank and have your fifty percent transferred as it looks as if they're about to serve our first course."

"Clever, wasn't I, to suggest we order before we waffled," chuckled Harold as he watched Warwick dealing with the bank, "otherwise lunch may have been reduced to starters, a bottle of mineral water and nothing else!"

"Nonsense," crooned Warwick handing Harold back his phone. "After all, you did save me the expense of a phone call. Now, what about this extraordinary weather we're currently experiencing?"

His slick change of topic causing the two to burst out laughing as smiling waiter proudly placed their plates of steaming *Canestrini Nettuno* on the table while another smiling waiter filled their wine glasses with chilled Pinot Grigio.

*

Harold called back the next morning. "Good morning Mr. People Hater Mutilator," he said cheerfully. "My, you have been a busy boy! Talk about an unpleasant, everyday reminder! I should imagine all those people on your little list simply loathe waking up. knowing they have to face another scarred day!"

"My point exactly," replied Warwick, deliberately ignoring the people hater, mutilator jibe. "So, does my expensive private eye have any overpriced suggestions to make or break my day?"

"I've been studying your little list - *very* Gilbert and Sullivan if I may say so - and after several hours or searching I have ruled out several names. Your Dick McCausland for example who, as a result of his attack, is now vegetating in a care home as is your Mr. Peter Stiles."

"Go on. As for your reference to Messrs. G and S and their witty *The Mikado.* Very sharp!"

"Thank you. The others on your list are possibilities and will require further investigation. However, I couldn't help thinking of the old proverb, hell hath no fury as a woman scorned, which I promptly switched to hell hath no fury like a woman burned. In other words, Isobel Parr who, in addition to being badly burnt in a nightclub fire, also lost an eye. Having spent some time abroad emulating Mother Theresa, she's now back here, and instead of emulating Mother Theresa, she's switched roles and in now more an Atilla the Hun than a nun."

"What? A female Atilla on her lonesome ownsome," scoffed Warwick. "Never!"

"I didn't say on her own, did I?" rumbled Harold. "So please stop interrupting."

Interrupting? thought Warwick. *Keep talking to me like that and I'll be reaching for my bow and arrow and aiming for your pucking private eye! King Arsehole!*

"Parr obviously has an accomplice," continued Harold. "Therefore, I have taken the liberty - see it as an additional expense - of putting a tail on her, a woman named Holly Golightly - no relation - the female equivalent of Mr. Wells's, *The Invisible Man.* Holly will be coming back to me with her first report later today." He gave a derisive snort. "Parr is so glaringly obvious a candidate that I can't understand how you, Warwick, with your quicksilver mind, didn't pick it up."

"Do I detect a hidden compliment or sorts, *King* Harold?" snickered Warwick. "Lord, have mercy on this grateful being!"

About to add a further pithy comment, Warwick was cut short as Harold terminated the call.

*

Harold called back after - what for Warwick - could be described as two nail biting days.

"Holly, as expected, has turned up trumps," he said with a chuckle and no preliminaries. "As a result of her excellent work the name of Miss Parr's clandestine comrade in arms can now be revealed. And yes, he *is* on your list. Mr. Norman Livingston."

"Pucking Hell!" gasped Warwick. "Norman pucking Livingston! Talk about a pucking surprise! Where is a martini when one needs one!"

Harold gave a chuckle. "Typical Holly, she now refers to Parr as VS or Vintage Steuben because of her scars and glass eye, and Livingston as VG or

Van Gogh because of his glaringly obvious false ear. Latest info is that VS and VG met up at a Starbucks near Victoria Station late yesterday where they sat in a conspiratorial huddle for a good hour obviously planning something. I now have a tail on Livingston as well as Parr."

"Not bad, Bubba!" crowed an ecstatic Warwick. "My 'not bad, Bubba' being the highest compliment I could ever bestow on you and Miss Holly Golightly. Plus, I am sure when I tell Vincent of the latest developments in 'find the miserable miscreant' his woofs will exceed my cries of 'not bad, Bubba!'"

LONDON - LADBROKE SQUARE

"Pegg? It's Wilma Davis. I take it this merry morn finds you equally as merry!"

"Not nearly as merry as you sound, Wilma! What's up?"

"Your newest best friend, Kurt Cameron. Julia and I have been talking. We've also discussed our idea with Andy who totally agrees with us. In order to get wretched Warwick to well and truly discolour his Y-fronts, would it be possible for Kurt, aided and abetted by Sebastian Salamander, to arrange a similar copycat happening to those happenings here to *happen* over there in Houston or even Las Vegas, and somehow be brought to Warwick's attention?"

"Hmm, I don't see why not. It would have to be a name, someone fairly prominent, otherwise such an attack on a derelict or mere nobody wouldn't be considered worth mentioning. However, don't despair. I'll have a word with Kurt and he, in turn, can have a word with Sebastian. I'll call you back. Is this the correct number?"

"I'm calling on Andy's landline. Julia and I are staying with Andy for a few days so call me here."

"Staying with Andy, eh?" chuckled Pegg, "The plot thickens!"

"Not exactly, Pegg. We don't get the keys to our new flat until Friday, and while Andy is into ladies he's not into ladies such as Julia and I. Toodle-oo!"

Pegg called back within ten minutes.

"That must be Pegg," said Andy, "so why don't you take it. If it's for me, simply hand me the phone. Pegg? That was quick!"

"Bingo! Wilma! Kurt had a quick word with Sebastian and to quote the big man's eloquent response to what we suggested . . . I joke not, 'Two shithole copycats would be better than one. Ah know several bloated, arrogant pricks whose unexpected facelifts with all the trimmins' - Haw! Haw! - will please a great many fellow Texans. Me and mah lil' Delilah send love an' winnin' kisses. So, big lad an' lassies, as they say, watch this space."

"Wow!" cried Wilma.

"Double wow!" enthused Julia.

"This definitely calls for a celebration," rumbled Andy. "Where are you Pegg?"

"At my flat and, as you say, this definitely calls for a celebration. So, if you can bear with me for twenty minutes or so, I will be there along with a couple of bottles of the very merry Widow Clicquot!"

*

Kurt called Pegg back early the next day. "It's already underway," he said, brimming with bonhomie. "The honour of being Texas's first mutilation-cum-amputation going to a guy called Buzz Klondike-Kripps - that's Kripps with a K - who Sebastian charmingly described as a bloated, arrogant, politico prick. As soon as soon as anything appears in print over here - the attack obviously won't make international headlines - I'll email all copy to you so that this can be passed on to our friend."

"Any idea when this Kripps guy will be paid such a memorable visit?"

"I do believe it could be happening as we speak," chuckled Kurt. "I'll call you with an update once I hear anything and, as soon as anything appear in print, this will be emailed to you."

Pegg immediately telephoned Andy. "It's all happening," he said excitedly. "Sebastian Salamander has well and truly gotten the bit between his molars! As soon as I receive copies of any press reports I'll alert you and the two ladies and send you copies of the copies! Haha!"

"That's great, Pegg. As soon as I have the copies. I'll have them duplicated and sent anonymously to Warwick. Kurt confirmed that whoever Sebastian selected, he would make sure the reflected WLS was carefully and clearly carved on the guy's forehead. As Wilma and Julia yodelled yesterday à la Peggy Lee. *Every morning, every evening. Ain't we got fun!*"

21

A LAVISH DUPLEX PENTHOUSE - CHELSEA HARBOUR

Warwick stood wild-eyed and open-mouthed as he reread the copies of cuttings taken from several prominent Texas tabloids.

TOP POLITICAL FIGURE ATTACKED, MUTILATED AND SCARRED! screamed one headline. BILLIONAIRE BUZZ KLONDIKE-KRIPPS IN FREAK ATTACK! screamed another.

"Pucking Hell!" shrieked Warwick hurling the print-offs to the floor. "What pucking next! A Royal pucking decree?" His action causing Vincent to give a startled woof.

Reaching for his mobile with a trembling hand, he barely managed to tap in Harold's number. "You'll never believe it, King!" - the nickname had stuck - shrieked Warwick as soon as Harold answered. "But I've just received copies of several newspaper cuttings regarding another copycat attack. Not here in London, but in pucking Houston, *Texas*!"

"Calm down, Warwick," replied Harold soothingly, "and I'll be with you as soon as I can. If you haven't done so already, pour yourself an early morning martini and do nothing, apart from sip your drink, until I get there."

*

"So, what happens now, King?" shrilled Warwick before Harold was even halfway through the front door. "We - no, *you* - have to do pucking something!"

"First thing *you* must do, Warwick, is take a grip of yourself, pour *me* a martini and give me a few minutes to actually take a look at what was sent to you. *Capiche?*"

"*Capiche*," muttered Warwick sulkily.

After reading and rereading the articles, Harold said matter-of-factly. "Before we do anything else, I need you to make copies of what you were sent and *post* the copies to Isobel Parr and Norman Livingston. If that doesn't put the fear of Hammer Horror up them, then nothing will!"

He picked up the envelope in which the copies had been sent. "A West End postmark? To quote you, Warwick. 'How pucking inconvenient'."

VICTORIA STATION

They met, as usual, in a convenient Starbucks.

She: "Not exactly what I expected to find in Postman Pat's delivery today."

He: "Nor me."

She: Do you think it's him? It can't be!"

He: "Definitely not. Nor do I, for a moment, believe it to be one of his other victims trying to make ripples, especially with this Texas connection. I'd stake my claim on the sender of these cuttings being either that Kurt Cameron or that David Pegg. Cameron not only lives in Texas and works for Sebastian Salamander and now with Pegg the latest stud to be given the boot by his nibs, what more can I say?"

She: "Well, *I* say instead of becoming all meek and feeble and lying low, we find another unknown patsy and do the necessary which should see not only wretched Warwick but Mr., Miss or Mrs Anonymous sender not only taken aback but well and truly confused."

He: "Has anyone ever told you, Miss Isobel Parr. That you're a genius?"

She: "Often, Norman. A genius with a glass eye in lieu of a crystal ball!"

Norman Livingston: "Despite my false ear, that came over loud and clear! Another coffee?"

Isobel Parr: "In a sec. Any suggestions where we find our latest Mr. Confusion?"

Norman Livingston: "Easy-peasy! My postman or your postman. Serve him right for delivering such upsetting mail!"

A LAVISH DUPLEX PENTHOUSE - CHELSEA HARBOUR - THREE DAYS LATER

"No! No! *No!*" shrieked Warwick tossing the newspaper aside and almost causing Simon Salway (he and his wife, Cynthia, being Julia and Wilma's replacements) to drop the tray he was carrying. Glaring at the startled man, he added with a further shriek. "Just leave the pucking tray! I need to be alone! I'll call you when I need you!"

Call me when you need me? thought Salway glaring at his distraught looking employer. *Think again, arsehole! A week of you and your tantrums is more than Cyn and I need. Cyn's already packed and as soon as I get a chance to talk to you once you've calmed down, we're outa here!*

Giving Warwick a further glare, Salway turned on his heel and marched from the room while Warwick, having reclaimed the tossed paper, remained staring at the offending news article with disbelief.

The article, headed POSTMAN BRUTALLY ATTACKED, went on to describe how Clive Roberts, a local postman, had been savagely attacked on his rounds, his "mutilated body" casually left outside a local A & E. Details were sparse, but the article did mention that there had been several recent attacks of "a similar nature". Whether it was meant to be taken seriously or simply a case of tongue in cheek reporting, the article ended asking whether the attacks were the work of a serial *mutilator* as opposed to a serial killer.

Reaching for the coffee pot Salway had left, Warwick poured a cup (no cream or sugar) and took a swallow. "And now even the pucking coffee's pucking cold," he hissed. Taking a deep breath he added with a yell. "Salway! Get back here!"

Turning back to the upsetting article, he took a further sip. Making a face, he gave a further yell. "Salway! Where the puck *are* you?"

On getting no response, Warwick stormed through to the kitchen which he found to be empty. "Salway?" he screeched. "Mrs Salway?"

"We're here, sir," said a grim faced Salway as he and his wife entered the kitchen. Holding out an envelope Salway said with a sneer. "We were downstairs finishing packing as we're leaving. The envelope contains our official notice. As for any money we're owed, Mrs Salway and self suggest you shove it down your poisonous gullet and, with luck, choke."

Before Warwick could respond, the couple had disappeared.

Warwick's immediate reaction was to return to his study and break the news of the latest saga in his tortured life to a disinterested Vincent while mixing an edifying martini. After a couple of healthy swallows. he telephoned Harold.

"Harold! Have you seen that *horrendous* article in today's *Mail?*" he shrilled. "It's all falling apart! I need you here! *NOW!*"

"You need *me* to be there for you NOW?" replied Harold in a voice dripping sarcasm. "Let me remind you, *Warwick,* I am not some dog you can command to sit or play dead. I happen to be in the middle of a meeting and once the meeting is over and I have a moment to spare, then, and only then, will I be able to call you back." He quietly hung up.

LADBROKE SQUARE - THE NEXT DAY

"Andy, it's Jess. Jess Rix. Quick update on Standton as you know I never miss a trick. Pun not intended. Apparently, there's a new ruffian on the block. Some so-called private eye called Harold Hastings. Again, no pun intended! Oh, and did you see there'd been another of those attacks?"

"We all did," replied Andy cheerfully. "As for Mr. Hastings, thanks for that. It'll be interesting to see how long it takes before *he* is given his marching orders."

He gave a chuckle. "I know you very rarely grace our part of the world with your questionable presence, but, if you happen to be in the Chelsea area around lunchtime, why not join me, Pegg and les girls at The Ivy Garden. King's Road. We're meeting there at one."

"Don't collapse, as I'd love to," chuckled Jess. "It so happens I have to meet a new client in the Baccarat Bar at Harrods at four, so lunch with you and your ladies will be a pleasant prelim before I have to face this hardass! See you there!"

THE IVY CHELSEA GARDEN

"It gets even more interesting, even more cloak and dagger-ish," announced Jess to the four once they were seated and drinks ordered. "For example, Harold Hastings, Private Eye, no longer exists.

In fact, he appears to have vanished into thin air approximately five years ago,"

"So?" interrupted Wilma with a grin. "There must be a so!"

"Sharp lady," chuckled Jess. "So, I got one of my endless contacts to check out the vanished Mr. Harold Hastings and was amused to discover he is now known as Mr. Arnold Agincourt. Battles of Hasting and Agincourt! Geddit?"

"It gets better by the second," chortled Pegg. "More, please, Jess!"

"Clever clogs Warwick, bless him, has been well and truly duped by whatever Hastings now Agincourt has told him or tells him. little realising it's all a load of - excuse me, ladies - bullshit. To ensure no harm comes to your kennels, Pegg, I have arranged for a couple of" - Jess made air quotes - "documentarians, a guy nicknamed Wingman and a girl named Bunti to deal with this. Bunti and Wingman will be calling you to set up a meeting. Before you ask, he's an ex-cop and she an ex-soldier and judo gold medallist. In case you're worried about what Trish and Coli might think, simply explain that the two are there for a week or so, getting the feel of things for a documentary they're about to make on guide dogs."

"Another so," interrupted Julia. "So, what do you think Mr. Phony will do next?"

"Another so and another discovery by one of my endless sources. It appears Mr. Hastings-cum-Agincourt could have traced those responsible for the recent copycat attacks. I say 'those' because I understand there are two former victims responsible. I could be gilding the lily, as it were, but I wouldn't be surprised if Mr. Agincourt, having been paid a substantial sum for his sleuthing, doesn't do another disappearing act and then reappear somewhere else in some other conning role. Silas Swindler Investments, perhaps?"

*

Around the same time the five were enjoining a carefree, gossipy, cheerful lunch at The Ivy Chelsea Garden. a startled Warwick received an unexpected visitor to the penthouse.

"As I explained on the phone, it was vital I see you," said Harold on being greeted by Warwick. "I can't stay but I am sure you will be more than delighted when you see what I've brought you."

Glancing round the impressive entrance hall he muttered. "Very impressive. How the other half live, eh?"

"You said you had something to show me," replied Warwick meekly, knowing how volatile Harold could be. "Sounds exciting. Let's go into the study and let me have a looksee. Please follow me."

Inside the study Harold, watched by a nervous Warwick and a curious Vincent, placed his briefcase on the desk, clicked it open and said teasingly. "The proof of the pudding is in the two envelopes."

Holding out one of the envelopes, he said encouragingly. "Go on, open it. It won't bite."

Taking the unsealed envelope from Harold, Warwick peered inside. "It's a glass eye!" he cried. "Tell me it's hers'?"

"It most certainly is," chuckled Harold, "and in the second envelope you'll find Livingston's grafted ear. Happy?"

"Ecstatic!" crowed Warwick. "Dare I ask what happened to the donors?"

"Let's just say that you won't be having any further problems regarding, how shall I put it, nasty reminders from Miss Parr and Mr. Livingston. Now, as I *am* in a hurry, could you do the necessary with the bank before I go, I'll be out of town for a day or two and then we can meet up and discuss what other little delights you may have for me to help you with."

"Of course!" cried Warwick reaching for the telephone. "Remind me."

"Here," said Harold producing a card. "I printed these for you to keep as I knew you wouldn't have remembered them."

An impatient Harold remained standing while Warwick spoke to the bank.

"Done," said Warwick cheerfully. "Thank you again, *King*! I know you're in a hurry but have you time for a celebratory drink?"

"A celebratory drink sounds tempting, Warwick, but I really have to go," replied Harold reaching for his briefcase.

"Right, I'll see you out," carolled Warwick. "Gosh, King, you really *have* made my pucking day!"

Giving Harold a cheerful wave as he entered the lift, a whistling Warwick returned to the study. Giving a cheerful whoop he glided over to the desk to take another look inside the two envelopes. Giving a startled cry, Warwick turned to where Vincent sat chewing contentedly on what he thought was a doggy chew brought for him by Harold.

"Oh, no! Vincent, please tell me you pucking haven't! *Not* Livingston's replacement ear!" cried Warwick before collapsing into shrieks of uncontrollable laughter.

VICTORIA STATION

They met, as usual, in a convenient Starbucks.

Isobel Parr: "You know what. Norman. At the end of the day the arrogant sod's bloody head is *so* in the clouds that I don't think he even cares about what we're doing."

Norman Livingston: "I have to agree with you, Bell, but *we've* had fun, haven't we?"

Isobel: "At a price! Me with an eye and you with an ear. So, what are you suggesting? We simply leave it. No more nasty copycats."

Norman: "No more nasty paybacks, Miss Parr. In fact, I have an important question for you. Would you ever consider going out with a one-eared chump?"

Isobel: "Isn't this a sort of going out?"

Norman: "Not really. I see it more as a not very nice sort of going out."

Isobel: "I'd love to have a very *nice* going out with you, Norman."

Norman: "Great! So, how about tomorrow evening? Let's make it as a kind pf farewell but welcome back dinner. Let's live it up and let me take you to dinner at the Aqua Shard, thirty-one floors above London!"

Isobel: "I thought you'd never ask!"

NURSES STATION - ACCIDENT & EMERGENCY DEPARTMENT - A SOUTH LONDON HOSPITAL

"That was an unusual one the other night, Di," said one of the duty nurses to her companion. "I've never had to deal with some poor old drunken tramp on that condition before. I keep asking myself what sort of sicko would ever want to cut off a helpless old drunks' ear in the first place?"

"No one *I* know, that's for sure," giggled Di, peering at her notes.

22

HOUSTON - TEXAS

"Time for another?" asked Kurt in his regular catch-up call with Sebastian.

"Why not?" boomed Sebastian. "Fuckin' Klondike-Kripps's lil' attack certainly got them hornets buzzin! Haw! Haw! Now, someone else who could also do with come facial enhancement is a rancher named Tim Bigshot Biggins. A total wanker if ever there was." He gave a further guffaw. "Maybe a horny steer to help him raise them bushy eyebrows in surprise? Haw! Haw! Leave it to me. Kurt, an' I'll get the lads to 'rustle up' somethin' newsworthy!"

PEGGS - SCHOOL FOR GUIDE DOGS - A WEEK LATER

"Kurt. Dave Pegg," said Pegg cheerfully. "Regarding the latest; Andy, self and les girls haven't stopped laughing! Did Sebastian really have a genuine ox horn rammed up this Biggins guy's rear as well as add the graffiti to his forehead?"

"Morning, Pegg! And yup, he sure did," chuckled Kurt sounding more Texan than ever." As Joel so rightly said, that's one kinda horny he never wants to know about!"

"Copies of the incident have already been posted off to our bête noire. From what we hear, he's now living in splendid isolation with not even a live-in couple to keep him company."

"He's still got Vincent, though."

"Oh, yes, he's still got Vincent. Talk about a dog being a mad man's best friend! His latest stud, helper, whatever, appears to have done a midnight flit.

Just as we all predicted." Pegg gave a chuckle. "A Hastings/Agincourt hasn't suddenly appeared in your neck of the woods, has he? If you hear of a dicey character setting up shop with connections to filthy lucre near you, let us know. Haha!"

"Will do!" chuckled Kurt. "Sorry, Pegg, I must go. Joel and I are off to a premiere at one of the galleries here. I'll give you a call in a day or two. Love to all! *Ciao*!"

Pegg promptly telephoned Andy to give him Kurt's update.

"Amazing," chuckled Andy. "Hold on while I tell les girls."

A grinning Pegg sat listening to the ensuing shrieks of laughter audible over the phone.

"Pegg!" giggled Wilma appearing on the line. "What happened, more or less, to that Mr. Biggins, reminds me of a schoolboy - or school person to be politically correct - rhyme which you simply have to tell Kurt!"

"Oh, dear, must I?" camped Pegg. "Okay; let's have it."

"It doesn't *exactly* involve a tiresome Texan," giggled Wilma, "but here goes.

>'Little Miss Muffet,
>
>She sat on her tuffet,
>
>Her panties all tattered and torn.
>
>It wasn't a spider that sat down beside her,
>
>But Little Boy Blue and his horn'."

"Jesus! Wilma! You don't seriously expect me to repeat *that* to the likes of Kurt?"

"Why not seeing he, like you and Little Boy, has a horn! Byeee!"

"I give up," chuckled Pegg eyeing the silent phone in his hand. "But no matter what, I love you all!"

A LAVISH DUPLEX PENTHOUSE - CHELSEA HARBOUR

"Mother Dearest, 'tis your doting, one and only darling son!"

"Warwick! Darling!" exclaimed Lutetia, à la Lady Bracknell and the offensive handbag. "What's happened? My God! Are you alright? The last Father and I heard was that you were a guest of dear Clementine's while attending some film star's funeral!"

"Not *his* funeral unfortunately, Mother. His son's. Aunt Clementine's stepson."

"Whatever," replied Lutetia, adding mordaciously. "So sad you can manage a funeral in distant Venice but not a visitation to your parents in nearby Chester Square."

"But, Mother Dearest, funerals are much more entertaining, especially a watery one," replied Warwick, equally as mordaciously.

"Do you wish to converse with your father?"

"Not particularly. It was *you*, Mother Dearest, whom I really need to speak to. In fact, it's to ask you a favour."

"I overheard that!" harrumphed Percival Laudanum-Standton in the background. "A favour spelt c-h-e-q-u-e no doubt!"

"No, Father Dearest, I do not need a c-h-e-q-u-e. thank you very much," snapped Warwick, his voice rising. "What I *do* need is a cook-cum-housekeeper and, if she's married, even better as he could be an odd job man-cum-butler-cum-whatever men of his ilk do. In other words, another Hilda and Humphrey Horsfall."

"What happened to that charming old Harry and Christopher who used to look after you?" fluted Lutetia.

About to say someone blew up their car, Warwick said nonchalantly. "Old age. They retired."

"Damn well flew the nest, more likely," harrumphed Percival within earshot. "Unless they were a pair of practicing masochists."

"I'll have a word with Hilda," said Lutetia. "I believe her cousin was looking for a new position."

"It all depends on what sort of new position she's looking for," snickered Warwick.

"What was that?"

"Japanese for a grateful thank you, Mother. I'm having lessons. Please ask Mrs Horsfall to have her cousin give me a call."

"Will do, darling. Oh! Before you disappear for another year or so, we're having some friends in for drinks on Thursday next. It would be lovely if you joined us."

"In other words, a 'goodbye friends do' once they've met our son and heir - I did say heir," harrumphed Percival directly into the mouthpiece.

"How kind of you, Mother!" crooned Warwick deliberately ignoring his father's jibe. "May I bring a couple of friends?"

"Now it *will* be a 'goodbye friends' do," snorted Percival. "Talk about another Jonestown! Pshaw!"

"I won't bother to send you an invitation," fluted Lutetia, "and there's no need for you to RSVP as you won't turn up anyway! Hee-hee!"

You should be so lucky, thought Warwick after Lutetia had put down the phone. *Not only will I turn up and, despite the debatable Harold, I still have one or two jarring strings to my lethal bow!*

*

Having put the phone down on Warwick, Lutetia sat staring at Percival. "Curiouser and curiouser," she murmured. "We don't hear diddly-squat from Warwick for weeks, if not months and now, out the blue, a phone call. It can't be anything to do with money as he's rolling in it thanks to gaga Great Aunt Gertrude leaving him all those unknown millions."

"Maybe he's finally run out of people to annoy," harrumphed her husband.

"Oh, Percy!" trilled Lutetia. "You *are* awful!"

THE IVY CHELSEA GARDEN

The four met up again a week later for a another cheerful get together and to discuss any new shenanigans regarding Warwick.

"No matter how much we dislike the guy, there *is* a redeeming side to him," said Pegg. "It's a well-known fact that dogs are true indicators of a person's character. Take our guide dogs for example. If, after a six-week period the dog shows signs of not getting along with his new owner, we then replace the dog with another and so on. However, look how devoted Vincent is to his maddening master and, I have to say, that whenever Warwick came to Peggs, my kennels for guide dogs, *all* the dogs would flock to greet him."

"Maybe it was his aftershave," quipped Julia.

"Could be," chuckled Andy. "Perhaps we should Google dog enhancer aftershaves or cologne and see if anything comes up."

"What? Something called *Sniffins* or *Undertail Aromas*?" giggled Wilma. "Maybe I'll see if I can get you and Pegg a bottle of each for Christmas!"

"Charming," chuckled Andy. "Maybe, while you're busy Googling you could also check out and see if they do a scent named *Eau De Bitch* or *Eau De Cow*!"

"But, Andy," replied Wilma in a hurt voice. "I'm already *drenched* in *Eau De Bitch*! Can't you tell?"

A LAVISH DUPLEX PENTHOUSE - CHELSEA HARBOUR

"Vincent, we have a problem," camped Warwick. "From the look of things, and apart from you and the lovely *moi*, our spaceship *Nasty Co-ordinators* appears to be alarmingly empty of a Kurt, Pegg, Andy, or even a Harold! The four miscreants now lost in outer space."

He took a long, thoughtful sip of an always present martini. "So, thinking caps, Vincent. Where, oh where, do we find another comrade in harms. Yellow Pages were a joke which, in a way, did pay off, but that was simply a lucky dip."

Warwick sat for a few minutes gently stroking Vincent's head as he lay dozing on his lap, before saying in a no-nonsense voice. "Enough of this wallowing. *Warwick*! Time for a definite girding of the loins, and time to have a serious t-h-i-n-k with a capital neon-lit T."

He sat pondering for a few more minutes before saying, with a snapping of his fingers. "Thank you, Mr. Eddison!" Giving a startled Vincent a soothing pat, he added excitedly. "A perfect 'seeing the light', and how stupid of *moi* not to have come up with the idea until now.

Pulling out a drawer to his desk - Vincent having been set down on the carpet - Warwick began shuffling through endless scraps of paper and business cards. "Aha! Here it is!" he crowed picking out a card. "With luck, Vincent, the solution to my - our - current alienation."

Noting Vincent's quizzical look, Warwick said with a chortle. "No, I am *not* a believer but there's no harm in trying, is there? So, let's call the mysterious-sounding Medea Monte Cristo of *New Multi-Coloured Magic* and see what she has to croak!"

"New Multi-Coloured Magic. How may we help?" lisped a lilting voice.

"Err . . . good morning," said Warwick. "Is it possible to speak to Medea Monte Cristo?"

"*Everything* is possible when you call New Multi-Coloured Magic," lisped the voice. "May I ask who's requesting the privilege?"

"The name is Warwick Laudanum-Standon," replied Warwick, a touch amused by the receptionist's flowery language.

"Would Mr. Warwick Laudanum-Standton please hold while I see if I can conjure up Medea Monte-Cristo for him."

"Yes, of course," snickered Warwick. Covering the mouthpiece he said to Vincent. "I don't know about new multi-coloured magic for it sounds as if I've got through to some nuthouse here."

"Mr. Warwick Laudanum-Standton?" said a voice, a mixture of contralto and baritone. "Medea Monte-Cristo. You wished to converse with me?"

It is a pucking nuthouse, thought Warwick supressing a giggle. "Ah, Miss Monte-Cristo, thank you for taking my call. Allow me to briefly explain my reason for calling you and, if all appears of interest to your good self, I then would we should meet; face to face."

"Medea Monte-Cristo is listening so, pray begin."

AN IMPRESSIVE ARTIST'S STUDIO - GLEBE PLACE - CHELSEA - THE NEXT DAY

"Good morning, I have an appointment with Medea Monte-Cristo for eleven o'clock," announced Warwick on entering a small reception area decorated entirely in purple; ceiling, walls, carpet, sofa, a pair of chrome Wassily chairs with purple leather seats and back straps, and a purple lacquer desk serving a Kewpie doll lookalike dressed in a purple velvet jumpsuit with curly purple hair to match.

"So, you have," lisped the Kewpie doll. "Pray, take a seat whilst I inform Medea Monte-Cristo of your on-the-dot arrival."

Inform Medea Monte-Cristo of my on-the-dot arrival? thought Warwick. *If Medea Monte-Cristo is anything like this suffocating infusion of purple, maybe I'm about to meet Medea Monte-Cristo, Purple People Eater! As for you, Miss Kewpie doll, I have a strong suspicion you are a very pretty boy as opposed to a lisping lady!*

"Mr. Warwick Laudanum Standton?" said a throaty contralto-cum-baritone. "Medea Monte-Cristo."

Springing to his Gucci clad feet (sans socks) Warwick avoided doing a double take on seeing the tall. elegant figure dressed in a purple velvet jumpsuit, a pair of purple coloured snakeskin boots, her purple hair a perfect chignon, walking toward him, her hand held out in greeting.

"Miss Monte-Cristo; Warwick Laudanum-Standton," he said smoothly as they shook hands. Warwick's hand completely engulfed in a large smooth hand, the little finger bearing a silver skull ring. "A pleasure to meet you and thank you again for agreeing to see me at such short notice."

"Likewise, Mr. Laudanum-Standton. Please come through to my bower; but not before you tell Larry what refreshment he can bring you. We have everything from coffee to hemlock."

"A sip of hemlock sounds tempting," chortled Warwick not to be outdone. "However. I wouldn't say no to a martini, straight up, despite it being a touch early."

"A man after my own heart," said Medea with a dazzling, whiter than white smile. She turned to face the Kewpie doll. "Two of your delicious, lethal martinis, straight up, please, Larry." Turning her attention back to Warwick, she added throatily. "Now, if you'd please follow me, martinis in our wake, we can then get down to business."

You, Medea, thought Warwick as he followed the elegant figure, *must be the most elegant transvestite to grace these shores and I know, just know, you will be answer to all my problems! Plus, I was right about lisping Larry. Aided and abetted by an uber-glamorous tranny and a veritable Tinkerbell, it looks as if the lovely moi could be about to win the pucking lottery!*

"More purple," said Warwick glibly on entering the spacious studio area which served as Medea's office: the only items not coloured purple being his and Medea's faces and hands, along with Warwick's navy-blue blazer, lemon rollneck and cream-coloured cords.

"But, of course," replied Medea. "The colour purple is synonymous with magnificent moguls, emperors and kings, so why not Medea Monte-Cristo!" She gave a throaty chuckle. "Added to which purple is preferable to pink as favoured by the majority of imperious queens."

Gesturing for Warwick to take a seat on a Platner lounge chair (upholstered in purple linen) she muttered a "Thank you, Precious Heart" as Larry placed the martinis on the circular Platner coffee table, Medea then sat down facing Warwick. Reaching for her glass she took a satisfying sip. "Delicious! And now, Mr. Laudanum-Standton . . ."

"Warwick, please."

"Warwick, and please call me Medea. And as Larry has happily delivered our drinks and he knows we have no wish be disturbed, please elaborate on what you so wittily described as similar to painful piles residing in other - I love it - quarters!"

Warwick wasted no time telling Medea about his suspicions concerning Isobel Parr and Norman Livingston. On noting her genuine interest. he went on to explain his ongoing feud with Kurt and Sabastian Salamander plus his latest fall-out with Pegg. "And that's it, in a fairly large nutshell," he concluded wryly. "The ongoing Laudanum-Standton saga with more irritating episodes to follow, no doubt."

"And, without *any* doubt, a perfect conundrum for New Multi-Coloured Magic to handle," replied Medea reassuringly. "On that note, I think we both deserve another fortifying martini after what you've told me and over which I and the team shall ponder."

Reaching for a small, stainless steel hand bell which appeared to disappear in her large hand, Medea gave it a brisk shake.

"Two more of your delicious martinis, please, Precious," purred Medea as Larry poked his head round the purple lacquered door. She glanced at the purple Swatch watch on her sizeable wrist. "No, sorry, cancel that as we don't have time for another drink as Jasper Judicious should be arriving any minute from now," she added firmly.

Rising gracefully to her feet, Medea said with a smile. "Leave it to us, Warwick. Larry will get back to you regarding another meeting and, of course, inform you of our fees." She nodded toward the sheet of paper Warwick had left lying on the coffee table. "Now we have names and addresses of Isobel Parr and Norman Livingston over which to ponder, give us a day or two before Larry gets back to you. When he does, please confirm our terms and conditions with him - he will email these to you before he calls you - and if all is acceptable, arrange where we should meet."

*

Larry telephoned two days later to thank Warwick for his confirmation to New Multi-Coloured Magic's terms and their fees along with details of his next meeting with Medea. Instead of meeting at the house in Glebe Place, the meeting was to take place at The Berkeley Hotel in Knightsbridge the same evening if convenient. Warwick promptly agreed.

"The Blue Bar at The Berkeley at six-thirty," he said to Vincent with a giggle. "I wonder what she'll be wearing. Maybe another velvet jumpsuit as before or something even more outlandish, a purple sari! And instead of a chignon, sporting a fringe! In other words, Medea Monte-Cristo in a *sari* with a *fringe* on top! Haha! Gianni Versace, eat your heart out!"

23

THE BLUE BAR - THE BERKELEY HOTEL - KNIGHTSBRIDGE

"Warwick, Michael Monte-Christo," said a familiar voice. Glancing up Warwick gave a visible start on seeing a well-groomed Alain Delon lookalike dressed in a dark grey, well-tailored suit, pale blue shirt and sporting a colourful Romero Britto tie and complimentary pocket handkerchief, before realising he was looking at Medea Monte-Cristo.

On noting Warwick's startled reaction, Michael/Medea Monte-Cristo said with a mischievous grin. "Sorry for the confusion, Warwick. Precious . . . Larry . . . should have mentioned to you that I'd be in Michael mode today as I had a business meeting with our accountants earlier."

"Wow! Medea - I mean Michael - what can I say?" Warwick gave a giggle. "What I *can* say it that I'm going to call you MM for today, if that's okay with you. Wow, wow and another wow! Talk about a surprise! I found you pretty spectacular as Medea but, in your other persona as Michael, you're *incroyable*!"

"Flattery will get you everywhere," chuckled Michael. "As for MM. you're not the first to call me that, so join the club." He turned to the hovering waiter. "A martini, please, straight up, and another drink for my guest." Giving Warwick's glass a quick glance, he said curiously. "Not your usual martini?"

"No, I'm having a Harlow stinger."

"I know a stinger, but not a Harlow stinger."

"It's your basic stinger but made with white crème de menthe with a splash of Pernod which, when floating down, is said to represent Jean Harlow's blonde locks!"

"Very you, Warwick, if I may say so," chucked MM. "However, I think I'll stick to my tried-and-true dry martinis!"

Drinks served, MM leaned back in his chair and said in a no-nonsense voice. "First of all, thank you for agreeing to our terms and transferring the requested deposit so promptly. Secondly, as from midnight tomorrow, your problem with Parr and Livingston will be a thing of the past. I won't tell you what we have planned until our 'blotting of the blemishes" has taken place."

He sat staring at Warwick who appeared to have lost all colour to his face and about to have a major heart attack or a stroke. "Hey, Warwick," said MM almost snapping his fingers. "Are you okay? You look as if you've just seen a ghost."

"Make that not one but *two* apparitions," replied Warwick in a strangled voice. "One named Isobel Parr, and the other, Norman Livingston, who have just entered the bar." Clenching his fists, he added with a virulent hiss. "Pucking Harold Hastings. Are *you* going to pay for this!"

"Warwick! Instead of hissing vitriol and dropping dead on me before you've finished your Harlow stinger, care to explain what's going on?"

Rewarding MM with a tight smile, Warwick said softly. "Did you ever happen to see a film titled *The Return of The Living Dead*? Whether you did or not is irrelevant. What's interesting is that two of the leading characters were those two I mentioned entering the bar. Oops! Forgive me if I duck while they pass by, and then I'll explain."

"Danger over," announced MM with a chuckle. "So, have a hearty swig of Miss Harlow and explain all. The uncensored version being preferable."

"Right," said Warwick having done as suggested. "Herewith the uncensored version and, whilst revealing all, I wouldn't say no to another slurping of the delicious Miss H."

"So, all in all. this duplicitous Harold Hastings not only duped you into believing he'd dealt with the two sitting over there by showing you a glass eye and an ear as proof, and you, true to your word, paid him?" commented MM once Warwick concluded his sorry tale. "Well, my friend, before we assist you with anything else, let me put it this way. New Multi-Coloured Magic is a firm believer in an eye for an eye; glass eye or not, so leave it up to us. It's right up dear Larry's *strasse* . . ."

"Larry?" interjected Warwick. "You can't mean Kewpie doll Larry, your receptionist? Why, he looks, to me, as if he wouldn't harm a fly!"

"Larry, our Larry Pinkerton, not harm a fly?" scoffed MM. "Let me tell you a little something of interest, Warwick. *All* the team at New Multi-Coloured Magic - and I do mean *all* - refer to Larry as our answer to Armin Meiwes, aka the cannibal next door, the German guy who cooked and ate his friend." He gave a chuckle. "Word has it round the office that if Larry invites you to dinner and serves up a stew, say you're a vegetarian! Now, back to the two lovebirds seated over there. I say lovebirds because they haven't stopped pawing each other since they sat down. Let me have their details, addresses et cetera, so that I can advise Larry accordingly. I'll also ask Petrus, aka Petra, our computer whizz, if he can trace the whereabouts of your Mr. Hastings. Meanwhile, after all that, I think it's time for a follow up drink!"

*

Medea telephoned Warwick a week later.

"Good morning, Warwick. You'll find me in Medea mode today should you wish to call by for a celebratory drink. The good news being that Miss Parr and Mr. Livingston are now two definite, one hundred percent, guaranteed problems of the past."

"How? When? Tell me!" crooned Warwick, followed by a loud "Wahoo!"

"It's all thanks to Larry who, having switched from an Armin to a Walter..."

"A Walter?"

"As in Sir Walter Scott. Let me explain. To quote Larry. 'Miss Parr is now an understudy for Sir Walter Scott's *The lady of the Lake* and Norman Livingston another *Lochinvar* sans any wedding feast'. Medea gave a throaty chuckle. "Should you call by for a drink - we all hope you do - Larry can explain what he has in mind for Harold Hastings whom he believes is alive and kicking in sunny South Africa! However, have no fear, as we know several aggregable voodoo spirits over there!"

"Talking about spirits, a quick question, *Medea*. Where does the name New Multi-Coloured Magic come from?"

"Put it down to today's obsession with political correctness," replied Medea with a throaty chuckle. "It would never do had had I decided to call us *New Old Black Magic.* Would it?"

AN IMPRESSIVE ARTIST'S STUDIO - GLEBE PLACE - CHELSEA

"Congratulations, Larry," said Warwick smoothly. "I hear Isobel Parr and Norman Livingston are now aged members Mr. Kingsley's *Water-Babies* brigade."

"Absolutely, Mr. Laudanum-Standton."

"Warwick, please."

"Thank you, Warwick. Please call me Larry or, if you prefer. Lola. Only Meda is allowed to call me Precious," lisped Larry.

"Lola? I think I'll stick to Larry," chortled Warwick. "So, pray tell me, what did you actually *do* with my former nemeses?"

"Easy-peasy," lisped Larry. "Another member of New Multi-Coloured Magic team named Amazon Amore - her name speaks for itself - having watched Miss Parr's abode for several days in order to establish some form of routine, noted that she and Mr. Livingston were prone to spend most evenings in along with Netflix, a pizza and a couple of bottles of wine. All Amazon and I did was waylay the pizza delivery man - a sharp tap on the topknot - with me then donning his uniform and then ringing the doorbell. As Miss Parr was about to pay me, enter Amazon, literally, who hurtled through to the sitting room where she knocked Livingston unconscious and I, Miss Parr. Several hours later, Amazon and self, chucked the wide-eyed, gagged and suitably weighed-down couple into a convenient reservoir." Larry gave a titter. "But *not* before passing on your message. Namely, Mr. Warwick Laudanum-Standton is delighted to note that this little happening will not be appearing in print'."

"All the more reason to drink Hildon Spring or Perrier," chortled Warwick. "Again, my congratulations." There was a moment's pause before Warwick said casually. "Any ideas regarding Harold Hastings, now in Cape Town, South Africa? MM-cum-Medea said you have several capable voodoo spirits out there."

"We have indeed," lisped Larry. "Our main spirit - hee-hee - being a formidable lady known as Serendipity Shaka. Serendipity's righthand man being a magnificent, giant black spirit named Amos Agja." He gave a titter. "*Meneer* Agja's hobby is collecting skulls, human and animal, and he's forever adding to his impressive collection!"

"Talk about skulduggery!" chuckled Warwick. "I love it!"

"Amos Agja enjoys playing a unique type of machete *Chopsticks* with his human victims by chopping his way up from their feet to the penultimate. Having finished with *Chopsticks,* he gently removes the head and leaves it to soak in a bucket of acid until Mr. Head morphs into Mr. Grinning Skull!"

"I *doubly* love it!" yodelled Warwick.

A PRIVATE HOUSE - DE WATERKANT - CAPE TOWN

"Have you got all that, my handsome Impi warrior?" questioned Serendipity Shaka, a towering black transvestite dressed in a colourful silk kaftan decorated with protea and flame lily flowers and sporting a splendid Afro hairdo sparkling with diamond hairpins representing miniature assegais (spears).

"Ja, ek got it all," beamed Amos Agja, a giant black genial Sidney Potier lookalike. His smiling face, a brilliant decoy as to what went on in his twisted mind. "*Meneer* Harold Hastings, now calling himself *Meneer* Harold Hanley and living at the address you've just given me, is to painfully vanish, with an emphasis on the painfully. B. D and A photographs required."

"*Perfek*," replied Serendipity from where she sat at a desk made from a stolen tombstone set on a pair of steel trestles: the desk in keeping with the graveyard theme of the black ceiling, black walls, and black bookcases filled with a kaleidoscope of brightly coloured books: the curtains, carpet and upholstery in a colourful batik fabric of yellow, orange and blue. "Those before, during and after photos are important seeing *Meneer* Hastings previously conned our client by showing him an eye and an ear which did not belong to the supposed donors! Imagine the client's surprise on spotting his victims alive and kicking in some bar, ear and eye very much on view!"

"Not only will I supply you with photos, my sexy Serendipity," rumbled Amos. "They will be, as always, accompanied by one of my brilliant poems."

"*Ag,* you and your blerry poems," scoffed Serendipity good naturedly. "You must have dozens on file by now."

"Dozens," chuckled Amos. "With dozens more still to write!"

Three days later Amos telephoned Serendipity. "All done," he rumbled happily. "If you are home this evening, I'll call by with a copy of my latest poem and prints of the before and during photographs. It'll take another day or two before Hastings's skull is totally cleansed in order to be photographed."

Amos gave a rumbling chuckle. "My latest poem is one of my best. Do you wish to hear it?"

"Not now, *danke*!" giggled Serendipity. "Let's wait until this evening when I have a large drink in my hand!"

*

"Nasty, very nasty," murmured Serendipity on taking a further look at the photographs spread out on her desk. "Very nasty, but very satisfying. Medea will be pleased."

"*Goed*! *Baie goed*!" said Amos with a wide grin. "Now, are you ready to hear my latest *meesterstuk*?"

"*Ja*, but before you totally destroy me with you latest masterpiece, I suggest you pour me a large G and T before you begin. You know where the drinks cupboard is! Tonics and ice, as usual, are in the small fridge."

Having poured the drinks, Amos made himself comfortable in an armchair facing Serendipity before teasingly unfolding a piece of foolscap paper retrieved from his briefcase. "I have called my latest poem, *Totsiens, Meeneer Hastings.*"

Making a great show of theatrically clearing his throat, Amos began to read aloud.

> "Panga, panga, panga!
>
> Two feet for my cousin in Inyanga!
>
> Pinga, pinga, pinga,
>
> Two lower legs for my cousin in Chipinga!
>
> Machete, chete, chete,
>
> Two hands for my cousin in the Serengeti!
>
> Bolder, bolder, bolder,
>
> A shoulder for my cousin in Ndola!"

Noting Serendipity's glazed expression, Amos added hastily. "Okay, point well and truly taken so I'll skip the rest apart from the final lines which read:

> As you can see, it's never, ever dull.
>
> And last, but not least, we remove the skull.
>
> Another perfection for my growing collection!"

"On that *beautiful* note, I wouldn't say no, so off you go, and pour me another G and T. to celebrate your poem's originality," chortled Serendipity. "Antjie Krog (top South Afrikaans poet) you have been warned!"

*

Serendipity telephoned Medea with the good news. "I've also emailed you a copy of dear Amos's poem in celebration of the occasion," she said with a throaty chuckle. "I am sure your generous *Meneer* Laudanum-Standton will find it as amusing as I do!"

On viewing the emailed copy of Amos's poem, Warwick said with a jubilant cry. "Another Simon Armitage if ever there was! (Simon Armitage being the current UK Poet Laureate.) Hopefully, one Puccini fine day, they will have the privilege of being thanked by *moi* in person!"

One fine day? thought Medea staring at Warwick with disbelief. *More a case of 'That'll Be The Day!'*

24

A LAVISH DUPLEX PENTHOUSE - CHELSEA HARBOUR

"I am sure you will agree with *moi,* Vincent; you're about the only living creature that does, thanks to your uber-intelligence, understand the endlessly tormented *moi.* After those disastrous Salways, the only sane thing to do is we go back to Mr. Google and see if he can help us in finding a gay cook and a gay man of all sorts. Preferably a couple like Harry and Christopher. So, without any further ado; let's get Googling!"

Having spoken to several agencies and explaining what he was looking for, Warwick said to Vincent (busy with a doggy chew). "As Bette Davis *almost* said to Paul Henreid in *Now Voyager.* 'We may not have the moon, but, with luck, we may have two new domestic stars!' We'll simply have to wait and see."

Warwick had just poured himself a de rigueur early morning martini and presented Vincent with a further doggy treat, when one of the landlines started to ring.

"Warwick Laudanum-Standton speaking," said Warwick crisply on answering. "Elucidate."

"Elucidate?" quavered a voice. "You mean explain?"

"Aha! A Webster or Oxford!" chortled Warwick. "Yes, pray explain who's calling."

"Err ... the name's Louis Rue. Mr. Laudanum-Standton, and I'm calling reference your enquiry for a cook and a major domo, preferably a gay couple. My husband and I (*How very Elizabeth the Second,* thought Warwick with a snicker) feel we may be the very answer to what you require. I am a cordon bleu chef and Clarke, my husband, is a butler-cum-chauffeur and general handyman. In other words, A man for all seasons. Hee-hee!"

I like you already, thought Warwick giving a disinterested Vincent a thumbs-up. "Tell me, Mr. Rue, do you like dogs?"

"Do I - we - like dogs, Mr. Laudanum-Standton? Clarke and I *adore* dogs. However, I have to tell you, we are the proud parents of a *very* possessive doctored ginger tomcat named - would you believe - *Ginger*! If we did get the position, would Ginger be a problem?"

"If you do get the position, Ginger will have his very own domain to survey," snickered Warwick. "I'm sure the agency must have told you, your personal accommodation would be a separate apartment in the building."

"Yes, the agency did, Mr. Laudanum-Standton," quavered Louis Rue. There was a moment's silence before he asked tentatively. "Would you care to grant us an interview us, Mr. Laudanum-Standton? My husband and I would be delighted to call by your apartment - I mean penthouse - at any time to suit you."

"Noon today would be most suitable," replied Warwick loftily. "Namely in an hour and a half. Make yourselves known at the porter's desk to they may alert *moi*."

"Wonderful, Mr. Laudanum-Standon!" quavered Rue. "We'll see you then. Thank you again. Byee!"

"Well, Vincent, let's see how Mr. and Mr. Rue turn out," said Warwick to a now snoozing Vincent. He gave a chuckle. "Clarke and Louis Rue? Please don't tell *moi* we're about to meet our very own Clarke, as in Kent, along with our very own Lois Lane as in Louis Rue!"

*

"Two gentlemen, a Mr. Rue and a Mr. Rue to see you, sir," said Bert the porter with a snigger. "They say they have an appointment, *sir*."

"Brilliant, Bert! Send them up," crowed Warwick.

I'll leave that for you to do, sir, thought Bert with a grin as he directed the couple toward the private elevator serving the penthouse.

"Mr. and Mr. Rue!" crooned Warwick on opening the front door, a vigilant Vincent by his side. (As Warwick had explained to the likes of Kurt, Pegg. and others. "Vincent is my litmus paper. If he senses a person could be up to no good, he immediately ignites!")

Eyeing the couple Vincent glanced up at Warwick, the cocking of his head accompanied by a "they're okay, master," wagging of his stubby tail.

"*Do* come in," added Warwick stooping to giving Vincent a quick "Thank you" pat. "Not being *totally* hopeless in the *cucina*, I could offer you a cup of instant coffee - Haha - but it would be far easier if you accepted a mid-morning drink. A glass of vino or something stronger."

"If you show me the kitchen I can see to the coffee," said the shorter man in a no-nonsense voice. "I'm Louis Rue, and this is Clarke, my husband."

Well, you ain't no Lois Lane, Louis Rue, that's for sure, thought Warwick supressing a snicker. *More of a Marge Simpson in drag. As for hubby Clarke. More of a Homer Simpson than a Christopher Reeve.*

"That sounds like a good start, err ... Louis. If you'll both follow me, I'll show you the kitchen." Glancing back over his shoulder Warwick added cheerfully. "And if you're not having a cup of Lois's - I mean *Louis's* instant coffee - Clarke, there's wine or beer in the fridge."

"Ta! I'll have a beer, if I may," grunted Clarke.

"One beer and one instant coffee coming up!" crooned Warwick as the three entered the gleaming state-of-the-art kitchen. "The kettle is somewhere over there," he added airily. "As for the jar of instant coffee, *Louis* ... if my radar serves me well, it's in one of those cupboards by the window. Clarke, that gleaming edifice over there is a fridge, so please help yourself. Whilst you're about it, please grab hold of a bottle of white wine and pour me a glass. Glasses are in the tall cupboard next to the fridge. You should find a corkscrew in one of the drawers where Louis is standing."

Well done, Clarke, thought Warwick as he watched the couple busily doing their appointed tasks. *You happily passed the Vincent worthy test which means Lois - oops, excusez moi, Louis - will no doubt also be accepted into the fold.*

Half an hour later, having been given the grand tour of the penthouse and the elegant two- bedroom staff apartment below, the duly impressed couple graciously accepted Warwick's generous terms of employment and announced they would be delighted to take care of Mr. Laudanum- Standon, as from the following week.

"I have several pieces of furniture I treasure that I will be bringing," announced Louis in a "don't you dare say no" voice. "I should imagine a block like this has storage facilities so that any of the furniture we won't need can be stored there?"

"Of course, Louis. To each his own," purred Warwick thinking. *Talk about a tiresome old queen. Maybe poor Clarke, having to put with the likes of Madam Defarge, really is another Superman in disguise!*

"As for Clarke's furniture rests, they'll enjoy sitting on the windowsill to the sitting room and looking at the Thames," said Louis firmly.

"Furniture rests, Louis?" questioned Warwick.

"Small porcelain heads backed by a ledge on which furniture used to rest so that someone could easily clean around the piece," explained Clarke. He added proudly. "I have, so far, managed to purchase eleven pairs and still searching,"

"Sounds fascinating," murmured Warwick, "and I wish you happy hunting." Eyeing the couple sitting opposite he said mischievously. "I am delighted that you will be here taking care of us, namely Vincent and *moi,* but now, the zillion-euro question. What will *Ginger* think? Maybe he'll also enjoy sitting on the windowsill with the furniture rests and gazing at the Thames!"

"Oh, Ginger will simply *love* it, won't he Clarke?"

"Oh, yes, Ginger will simply *love* it!" echoed Clarke. "Like Louis and me, he'll be full of admiration for your good taste and compelling style, Mr. Laudanum-Standton."

"As Mr. Laudanum-Standton is a bit of mouth full, as I've often been told," tittered Warwick. "Mr. Warwick is totally acceptable."

"Thank you, Mr. Warwick," replied Louis and Clarke in unison.

The three sat for a further fifteen minutes before the Rues left, making what began as polite, conversation but rapidly thawed with Vincent having made firm friends with a stroking and fondling Clarke and Warwick, an ally In Louis on discovering that he too was a great fan of "that *divine* Raoul Bova!"

TWO WEEKS LATER

"New Multi-Coloured Magic, how may we help?" lisped Larry on answering the telephone.

"Larry! Hi!" crooned Warwick. "Is the lovely Medea about?"

"The lovely Medea most certainly is, Warwick," lisped Larry, "but today we're in Michael mode as we have a meeting with a new client who specifically asked for Michael."

"What a conundrum!" tittered Warwick. "I don't know how you cope with the 'him and her' part of your organisation, Larry. You must have been a juggler in a former life!"

"Oh, I can juggle alright, Warwick," giggled Larry. "You name it, and I can juggle it! Hold on while I put you through to Michael."

"Medea! I hear you're on Michael mode today," said Warwick on hearing Medea's throaty "Good morning, young man." "A quick question. As you know I have now employed yet *another* new couple to look after Vincent and *moi*. A couple named Louis and Clarke Rue." He gave a giggle. "Behind their backs we refer to them as the Tweedles. Or to be more accurate. Tweedle not at all dumb and Tweedle not at all delicious! Louis has turned out to be the most marvellous cook; a positive gem, whilst hubby Clarke, a semi-precious stone in his role as man about the house. Now they have proved themselves worthy of a free apartment and their exorbitant wages, I am hosting a small dinner here tomorrow night. I appreciate it is all very last minute, but I would be delighted if you could join us."

"As Medea or Michael?" came the throaty reply. "I know, for certain. *Medea* would love to, seeing Michael is taking a welcome break from having to don male attire."

Before he could stop himself, Warwick said cheerfully. "Do you think Larry would like to join us?"

"Larry, join us?" repeated Medea. "I'm sure he would."

"See it as an extra thank you for his handling of the gruesome twosome," added Warwick diplomatically.

"Of course, what else?" chuckled Medea. "I'll get him to call with a yes or no. As it's a dinner party do you wish us to be formal or casual?"

"Oh, what I deem cocktail casual," chortled Warwick. "In other words, gold lamé and Gucci loafers and other such baubles. Eight o'clock for cocktails with dinner, a feast fit for queens, at nine."

"I look forward to it," replied Medea. She gave a throaty chuckle. "It gives me a chance to dust and flaunt the Monte-Cristo diamonds and, yes, Warwick, I'll make sure Larry calls you back with what I am sure will be a resounding yes!"

*

"Trish and Coli! How *woofy* to see you both!" crooned Warwick as a beaming Clarke, resplendent in a red jacket, red rollneck and black and red striped trousers ushered in the young kennel assistants from Peggs. "And not only Trish and Coli but with the dashing Mr. Jess Rix and a *very* glamorous lady hot on their heels!"

"Warwick!" cried Jess, full of bonhomie. "This is Ivana, Ivana Bomba, my lady friend I was telling you about!" Patting the hand of the smiling Zsa Zsa Gabor lookalike swathed in lime green silk clinging to his arm, he added proudly. "Ivana, as I told you, is a research scientist for Gluck, Gluck and Gluck, the pharmaceutical company." Giving Ivana's hand another pat he said equally as proudly. "Warwick, our host, is the amazing young man I was telling you about!"

"Welcome Ivana!" crooned Warwick. "What a lovely surprise. When Jess told me he was bringing a *lady* scientist I had no idea she would be a *gorgeous* lady scientist!"

"Ha-ha-ha!" brayed Ivana, her loud, unexpected response causing Warwick to visibly jump. "Jessie nefar said you was so funnee! I *lof* your icky pink jacket! So *gay*! Ha-ha-ha!"

"Naughty Jessie," replied Warwick with a tight smile. "I'll have to have a word with him about such a glaring omission."

"Champagne, madam," interrupted Clarke, coming to the rescue.

"I *lof* champagne!" gurgled Ivana. "Za bubbles, zey go straight to my 'ead and I become, what you English zay, a bubble 'ead! Ha-ha-ha!"

Jesus, Jess! thought Warwick. *With all the lunatic names you have in your hat, whatever made you pull out this loony tune.*

Glancing toward the doorway he was relieved to see a smiling Medea, resplendent in a gold lamé trouser suit, topped with a gold turban and wearing strappy, gold fuck-me sandals, standing next to Larry. A smiling Larry looking more angelic than assassin in a silver lamé jacket, aqua velvet trousers and aqua patent leather loafers.

"Mr. and Mrs Glister! Welcome! Welcome! Pray come in and join the mini fray!"

"Where is he?" hissed Trish sidling up to Warwick, a champagne flute in her hand. "Surely he's been invited to your glamorous dinner party?"

"*He* is watching television in the study as *he* has no interest in small talk and cocktail gabble," replied Warwick sternly. "However, I can assure you *he* will be joining us lesser mortals for after-dinner liqueurs and general woofs."

"I sincerely hope so seeing *he* is sorely missed by his friends at Peggs." said Trisha. "So much so that Coli and I have brought him a 'we miss you' card and a box of doggy treats from all the pooches at Peggs."

"Oh, Trish! I can assure you we both miss our visits to Peggs, and I promise you we will pay you all a visit sooner than later."

"You'd better," growled Trish. "Otherwise, Coli and I will set all the hounds - Baskervilles or not! - on you! You have been warned!" She added softly. "What's more, I know Pegg would love to see you."

"Did I hear you mention Peggs?" interrupted Medea. "That wonderful school for guide dogs?!

"You did indeed," replied Trish. "I'm part of the team there, as is my friend Coli."

"Medea Monte-Cristo," said Medea proffering her hand, first to Trish and then to Coli who had joined her.

"A friend of mine has one of your wonderful guide dogs," said Medea with a smile. "All I can say is that since meeting Taurus, he has taken on a whole new lease of life. The two adore each other and are always out and about having *the* greatest fun!"

Leaving Trish and Coli talking to Medea, Warwick approached Larry standing eyeing the small group. Pulling him aside, he said with a grin. "Love the twinkles, Larry. A bona fide twinkle, twinkle, assassin star! What a conundrum you are! Plus, I have to thank you again for the magical way in which you dealt with those two poison pens. You really are the tops."

"Thank you, Warwick," lisped Larry, "and yes, I am the tops as well as being the top."

"As in top of the pops?" quipped Warwick.

"As being top to those who prefer being bottom: top my preferred position which always comes as a bit of a surprise to most partners," lisped Larry. "Now where is that charming post box with the drinks tray?"

*

Eyeing the cheerful group enjoying their lemon pudding with lemon meringue ice cream, Warwick signalled to Clarke who, giving a discreet thumbs-up, quietly left the dining room.

"My friends, may I have your attention please, as I have a serious question to put to you," crooned Warwick, tapping his glass with his spoon. "Regarding your dinner. One hundred percent or zilch percent?"

There was a moment's bewildered silence before Medea cried throatily. "One hundred percent doesn't even begin to cover it! I'd say five hundred percent, and that's only for starters!"

"Well then," said Warwick with a grin, "I'd like you all to meet the gentleman responsible for tonight's delicious dinner. Mr. Louis Rue; chef extraordinaire!"

A coy, giggly Louis was led into the dining room by a proud, beaming Clarke, as Warwick continued. "And, of course, the man responsible for serving Louis's delicious repast. The one and only Mr. Clarke Rue!"

Once the applause and cheers abated Warwick added mischievously. "And now if you would care to join me on the terrace where Clarke will be serving liqueurs and where you will be meeting my other half; the one and only Vincent. Canine friend supreme!"

The second round of cheers and applause could easily have been described as thunderous.

*

As the guests were preparing to leave, Larry nonchalantly approached Warwick and said in a whispered lisp. "Would you mind if I stayed for another teensy-weensy nightcap as I know Medea has a car waiting to ferry her home and I can always ring for an Uber."

"Stay for a nightcap?" giggled Warwick. "Why not stay for the night as I would be fascinated to find out for myself is you really *are* top of the pops!"

SEVERAL HOURS LATER

"Pucking Hell," murmured Warwick drowsily. "Not only are you *truly* top of the pops; but a top of the pops and proud possessor of a pucking anaconda!"

"You mean a touch more capable than a Kewpie doll," lisped Larry.

"Kewpie doll?" giggled Warwick. "More of a Matryoshka doll than a Kewpie after what *I've* just experienced!"

"A Matryoshka doll?"

"Those Russian stacking dolls. You uncover one only to find a totally different doll underneath. The different doll in your case being a rampant super stud!" shrieked Warwick as Larry hefted himself on top yet again.

25

A LAVISH DUPLEX PENTHOUSE - CHELSEA HARBOUR

"Hmm, I wonder whose blood he sucked out last night," snickered Louis having read the note Warwick had left on the central island. "Breakfast for two on the terrace at eight-thirty. Omelettes preferable."

"A victim from last night's tacky list?" exclaimed Clarke. "Surely not, seeing they were all spoken for. Unless, of course, little Lord Fauntleroy rang out for room service. Haha!"

"You don't think it could be that frail flower who turned up with that Medea whatchamacallit? The towering tranny."

"What, the Miss Barbie-cum-Miss Kewpie? Not on your nelly, *Nellie*! All I can say is that it can only be that burly Mr. Rix. I mean, let's face it, Lou, *anything* would be an improvement on that bleached airhead he brought along. Talk about a blow-up doll with a severe brain leak!"

"Hush! I'm sure I just caught the sound of approaching fairy footsteps," tittered Louis camply covering an ear. "In other words, his little lordship is about to appear with his mysterious night rider in tow!"

"I'm surprised you didn't say his little lordship and his night rider *cometh*," giggled Clarke.

"Good morning, gentlemen," said Warwick brightly on entering the kitchen. "I trust you saw my note, Louis. Clarke, could we have two coffees in the study, cream and sugar on the side as I have no idea if my night rider takes it black or not." His vacuous remark causing Louis and Clarke to give each other a nervous glance. "As soon as breakfast is ready, let us know and we'll make our way to the terrace. Where's Vincent?"

"He's out on the terrace along with a nice big bone, sir," replied Louis, his face impassive, "having already had his bowl of daily Top Life milk."

"Well, we'll make do with a simple coffee instead of a vitamin drink whilst you busy yourself with our omelettes instead of a nice big boner or two," said Warwick snidely before turning on his heels and leaving.

"Bitch!" hissed Louis on making sure Warwick was out of earshot.

"Double bitch," hissed Clarke. "I wonder how much he actually overheard."

"Far too much," muttered Louis. He gave a giggle. "Now hurry with that coffee, Mr. Rue, as - like your curious self - I cannot *wait* to find out Mr. Night Rider's true identity!"

*

"Who? Who?" hooted Louis excitedly on Clarke's return.

"You could have knocked me over with a feather boa when I saw who it was," tittered Clarke. "For, perched out there like some ghastly, glittering bauble was . . ." Clarke, clutching his face, paused dramatically before adding in a sepulchral voice. "None other than Rebecca of Sunnybrook Farm! Namely that frightful Larry from that questionable agency. Talk about a Hiroshima moment!"

"You don't mean that lisping accoutrement accompanying the towering transvestite?" gasped Louis clutching *his* face à la Clarke.

"I do indeed," snickered Clarke. "And not only that, but he was charm itself on greeting me."

"Well, I never," muttered Louis.

"Something else that took my Listerine-enhanced breath away was the sight of Vincent sitting on Rebecca's lap!"

"Well, at least the sky is blue today," tittered Louis. "Wily Warwick and lisping Larry-cum-Rebecca spending the night together? A sure-fire case of watch this space!"

*

"Delicious omelette," lisped Larry pushing his plate aside. "As for those segments of orange in Cointreau. Wunderbar!"

"Goody. good," grinned Warwick, "as I'm sure, after last night's performance your lithesome frame needs all the vitamins you can swallow. Now, down to some serious business breakfast talk. As I keep saying, you were brilliant in dealing with Parr and Livingston so, what would you say if I asked you to do carry out a few more such happenings?"

"You mean repeat performances," lisped Larry, reaching for his coffee. "Yes, I'd be more than happy to *star* once again. All you have to do, is let me and Medea know who these wannabe actors are, how many, and whether they simply require a scare or seeing to or else a definite, lights out, agree a fee with Medea, and then let me deal with it."

"Does Medea have to know?"

"Does Medea have to know?" hissed Larry. "Yes, Warwick, Medea has to know or else it's a no go. Medea is one of the most important people in my life and, if you wish to remain a friend, I strongly advise you to remember that."

"I apologise," murmured Warwick. "I only thought that after last night . . ."

"Last night was devoted to fucking!" snapped Larry. "This morning we're talking about threats, scaring and even murder."

"Again, I apologise," muttered Warwick averting his face in order for Larry not to see his furious expression.

"Good," said Larry. "Now we've cleared the air, who are these people you wish New Multi-Coloured Agency to deal with?"

"David Pegg, who's local," replied Warwick without hesitation, "plus a Kurt Cameron, a Joel Howard and a Sebastian Salamander all who, rather inconveniently, reside in Texas."

"I've never been to Texas," giggled Larry, any earlier upset obviously forgotten. "Is it true that everything's bigger and better?"

"Oh, I think it's safe to say, Larry, dear, that even the biggest in Texas would find it difficult to compete with you," sniggered Warwick. *As for you, you Janus-faced pooch,* he thought eyeing Vincent snoring contentedly next to Larry's chair. *Nobody, but nobody talks to Warwick Laudanum-Standton the way your new best friend just did. However, no need to throw out the bastard-cum-baby with the bath water until my personal bastard babies are dealt with, and then it will be your turn. In the meantime, let's keep you on as a bed-warmer until an alternative raises his glans as it were!*

HOUSTON - TEXAS

"Good morning, Sebastian," said Kurt cheerfully at the start of his daily call. "Something of interest. According to Pegg, Warwick Standton has a new assistant-cum-stab seen by the majority as a frail flower but. according to a reliable source, is a lethal player when it comes to exit skills."

"Meanin'?" boomed Sebastian.

"Meaning one of us, and that includes Delilah and Joel, could be in danger as I wouldn't put it past that little bastard and his new friend to be plotting something catastrophic against any of us folk who he continues to bear one of his endless, inexplicable grudges against."

"So, instead of fuckin' *talkin'* about it, Kurt! Let's fuckin' *do* somethin' about it!" boomed Sebastian. "Any ideas?"

"Several," chuckled Kurt. "And as long as I know I have your backing you can leave it to me."

"Oh, you have mah fuckin' backin' alright, Kurt," boomed Sebastain. "Make that mine *an'* mah lil' Delilah's!"

A PRIVATE HOUSE - DE WATERKANT - CAPE TOWN

"That was Medea on the telephone, Amos, dear, saying, among other things, yet again how delighted Mr. Warwick Laudanum- Standton is in the way we - you - dealt with the problematic Mr. Hastings. So much so, there's now an additional five thousand rand in our account!"

Serendipity gave a throaty chuckle. "Something else you should know. He *insisted* Medea let him have a copy of your poem for his files!"

"*Goed. Baie goed,*" chortled Amos. "Each time you mention this Warwick bloke, I like him more and more."

Serendipity sat studying Amos for a moment before saying matter-of-factly. "Amos, tell me. have you ever been out of South Africa?"

"Nah, *niks,* never," replied Amos. "But, if and when I do, I will make sure I visit to of my favourite curiosities or places of interest."

"Curiosities or places of interest?" repeated Serendipity. "And what are those, if I may ask?"

"Two towers I've been fascinated by since my schooldays," replied Amos a touch sheepishly. "The Tower of London in England, and the Eiffel Tower in Paris, France."

"What a man of mystery you are, Amos Agja, as well as a dear, loveable and highly professional one." Serendipity took a sip of wine before saying thoughtfully. "As an extra bonus or additional celebration, why don't you and I take a short break from our commitments; fly to London where we can meet Medea, and you can visit your hallowed tower. We can then take Eurostar to Paris where we can both view the Eiffel Tower and even spend an evening at the Moulin Rouge and see the legendary French Cancan!"

"*Eish*!" exclaimed Amos. "Do you really mean that Serendipity? No bullshit?"

"No bullshit, *Meneer* Agja," chortled Serendipity. "Let's check the diary and, if we can find a week that suits both of us, it's to London and Paris *ons sal gaan*! In London we'll stay at The Dorchester Hotel on Park Lane where anyone who's famous always stays, and in Paris we'll stay at the equally exclusive Ritz Hotel on the Place Vendome."

Having agreed a date, Serendipity telephoned Medea.

"That's wonderful news!" crooned Medea. "You said you've already reserved a suite at The Dorchester. How very grand! No doubt Warwick L-S will be delighted to hear of your impending visit." She gave a throaty laugh. "So much so he'll be wanting to give an extravagant 'welcome to London' and a 'thank you' dinner for the two of you!"

"No thank you, Medea. No cocktail or dinner parties, per-lease! However, we would like to meet *Meneer* Warwick L-S. So, maybe lunch at one of those trendy eateries?"

"Leave it to me, Serendipity. Now, I insist on having Triceps, the company chauffeur meet you on your arrival at Heathrow - It's the *least* I can do - and take you to The Dorchester. The great thing is that due to the miniscule time difference the two of you will arrive as spry as you were on leaving Cape Town! Now, if you'll let me have your flight details, I can take it from there! I am *so* excited! What was that again? You'll be taking the BA overnight flight? Good. After Triceps has seen you checked in, it'll give you time to freshen up - not that you'll need to. Haha! - before he brings you to a very cosy and fun restaurant for our catch-up lunch!"

On hearing Larry entering the reception area, Medea called out. "Larry! Precious! *The* most exciting news! Serendipity Shaka and Amos Agja will be arriving in London on Monday! They're only here for a couple of days before heading off for Paris. They'll be staying at The Dorchester and would love to see us!"

"Serendipity to see you again, with Amos Agja to meet you and me, you mean," said Larry sauntering into main studio. "All I can say is that I can't wait to meet them as they sound exactly my cup of *Rooibos* tea! Hee-hee!"

Perching on the edge of Medea's desk. He added chirpily. "So, what's it to be? A cocktail party? A dinner? A lunch?"

"Serendipity was adamant. No cocktail or dinner party; just a cosy lunch, but a cosy lunch in some trendy place! Whatever that means! Maybe The Ivy Chelsea Garden?"

"Good thinking, dearest!" fluted Larry. Making a face he added spikily. "I take it they'll be wanting to meet Mr. Warwick Laudanum-Standton."

"Oh-oh! After your elevated night please don't tell me we've return to office earth with a bump!"

"A resounding bump, more likely. However, Medea dearest, in a way it came as no great surprise when, over breakfast, he had the audacity to ask me to carry out a few more commissions for him *without-your-knowledge*!"

"I trust you told the little shit what he could do with suggestion?"

"In no uncertain terms. The way Laudanum-Standton's mind works, he'd make Shakespeare's Iago a convincing Saint Francis of Assisi! God only knows why that dog appears to like him! Maybe it's a werewolf in disguise!"

MONDAY

"We're here, Medea, dear," crooned Serendipity over the phone. "And I must say, dear, your man Triceps, despite looking like King Kong, could not have been more welcoming and helpful. What's more, he said he'll be back to collect us and bring us to the exotic sounding The Ivy Chelsea Garden."

"Yes, he will," replied Medea with a delighted laugh. "As for Larry Pinkerton. He can't wait to meet my bosom buddy!"

*

Goodness! thought Medea as the smiling maître d' escorted a smiling Serendipity and a beaming Amos to the table. *Obviously, Serendipity must have found herself a witchdoctor with a formula for eternal youth! As for Mr. Agja, a delicious giant chocolate éclair if ever there was!*

Goodness! thought Larry watching the approaching couple. *I always thought Medea a stunner, but ebony Miss Serendipity Shaka is a double stunner! As for Mr. Amos Agja. A chocolate god walking on what I am sure can only be the most sensational pair of muscular chocolate legs!*

Giving Medea a nudge, he said with a mischievous whisper. "I've just done a mental Olympian somersault. Mr. Amos Agja is *gorgeous!*"

Medea Monte-Cristo looks exactly as Serendipity described her, a beautiful Amazon, thought Amos on reaching the table. *As for Larry Pinkerton. Not only does he look like a white male version of Walt Disney's Princess Tiana, but I simply cannot believe he's the lethal killer Serendipity says he is! Whatever happens, I'm going to do my best to find out if this innocent looking Mr. Pinkerton is also a killer between the sheets!*

Halfway through lunch Medea turned to Serendipity and said in a no-nonsense voice. "Sorry, Serendipity, but it can't be helped. Knowing Warwick as I unfortunately do, if he doesn't already know of your visit rest assured, he soon will, and in order not to ruffle any feathers. I've invited him for a drink at Glebe Place this evening."

"Something I would have done, dear Medea, were I in your shoes," replied Serendipity calmly. "And, may I *also* say, like Amos, I am more than curious to meet the capricious - if that's the correct word – Meneer Laudanum-Standton who seems to take a fiendish delight in taking a life, whether necessary or not."

Rather like me, Medea, you and your Mr. Turn-on, thought Larry with an inward snicker. *And if that isn't a prime example of calling the kettle black - pun not intended - then tell me what is!*

"So, you're not upset?"

"Why on earth should I be upset?" crooned Serendipity. "Ignore the saying 'curiosity killed the cat' for, as I'm always telling Amos, satisfaction brings life back!"

"Now *that,* if nothing else," responded Medea with a relieved chuckle, "most certainly calls for another bottle of wine!"

Atta girl! Serendipity. thought Amos proudly. *Never short of an answer. However, I have to admit the thought of meeting my first Beefeater at the Tower of London tomorrow is far more appealing than meeting this Standton bloke later! However, whatever Bwana lady Serendipity says, loyal Amos does!*

26

LADBROKE SQUARE - LATER THE SAME DAY

"I had an interesting call from Jess just before you two ladies arrived," said Andy taking hold of their coats on their arrival for drinks before going on to dinner with him and Pegg; the two women having finally moved into their new apartment. "Very interesting," he added leading them into the sitting room where an open bottle of iced Pinot Grigio, their favourite, was waiting.

"Oh?" giggled Julia accepting a glass of wine. "Don't tell me he's finally accepted defeat and has agreed to get rid of that ridiculous goatee he was hellbent on cultivating?"

"Jess will never get rid of that," said Wilma with a grin, "despite the goatee being akin to the Agave succulent which means it will take at least twenty-five-years before blossoming into an acceptable beard!"

"A veritable goatee van Winkle!" giggled Julia.

"Hi you two!" said Pegg cheerfully. "In case you haven't noticed, I'm also here!"

"Oh, Pegg, darling!" cooed Julia. "Forgive me but I didn't see you standing there despite that frightful tie! Now, had you been sporting a goatee like dear Jess..."

"Okay! Okay! You two! That's enough," chortled Andy. "Make yourselves comfortable and I'll attempt - attempt, nota bene - to bring you up to date."

"Ooh! Sounds as if it could be important," giggled Wilma, making herself comfortable.

"Maybe it is, maybe it isn't," replied Andy, "but, according to Ivana Bomba who has having lunch today at The Chelsea Ivy Garden..."

"Please don't tell me Miss Airhead can actually find her way into a restaurant unassisted?" quipped Wilma.

"If so, that's a first!" quipped Julia.

"Now, now, ladies," said Andy with a chuckle. "I can assure you there's more to Ivana Bomba than her looks."

"Yes. It's called silicone," tittered Julia.

"More to her than her looks," continued Andy ignoring the interruption, "and immediately reported back to Jess that sitting at a nearby table was none other than Medea Monte-Cristo and her righthand poisonous apple, Larry Pinkerton, along with a stunning black Amazonian lady and what Ivana described as a giant black man built like Mike Tyson but with the looks of Sidney Potier or Denzel Washington!"

"So?" choused Julia and Wilma.

"So," replied Andy patiently. "A quick phone call from Jess to another of his endless sources revealed that the couple lunching with Monte-Cristo and sidekick had literally flown in from Cape Town and were staying at The Dorchester. Adding grist to the mill was the info that these new arrivals were behind the mysterious disappearance of Harold Hastings, days after his arrival in South Africa!"

"Which we all know had something to do with the dreaded Warwick," added Pegg. "Please don't tell me we're talking of an assembling of a further *disassembling* involving bloody Warwick?"

"No, I don't think so," said Andy. "Otherwise, surely he would have been there as well."

"Maybe he was otherwise engaged," snorted Wilma.

"According to the ever-vigilant Jess, the only 'otherwise engagement' wretched Warwick's been involved with was a one-night stand with Cristo's poisonous apple which was simply that, a one-night stand, but I can't see that deterring Warwick from not being there."

"Let me give Kurt a quick call and see if he's heard anything new regarding Warwick and his never-ending ploy and plots," said Pegg rising to his feet. "Give me a couple of minutes and I'll be right back."

Five minutes later Pegg returned to the sitting room after calling Kurt from the privacy of Andy's study.

"Kurt is unaware of anything new regarding the dreaded Warwick," announced Pegg, "but he agrees we should keep a sharp eye on the questionable foursome. Kurt was pretty sure the couple with Cristo and Pinkerton could have easily been a lethal duo from Cape Town: a Serendipity Shaka and Amos Agja who, according to Kurt, would make the doings of the Spanish Inquisition mere child's play."

"Ouch!" giggled Wilma.

"Double ouch!" tittered Julia.

"Whatever the ouches, I strongly suggest we watch our backs," said Andy sombrely. "They say a worm can turn and if the worm in question *turns* out to be wormy Warwick, you can bet your bottom-dollar it won't be a single turn but a series of vicious wormy cartwheels!"

AN IMPRESSIVE ARTIST'S STUDIO - GLEBE PLACE

"Warwick! At last!" crooned Medea. "I was beginning to think I'd been stood up!"

"Not at all, MM, Medea," replied Warwick with a faux smile. "And look who I've brought with me. I trust you'll have noticed that Vincent is sporting a sparking purple collar and yours truly, a shimmering purple jacket, shirt and trews in honour of your purple abode."

"As if I *wouldn't* have noticed!" cried Medea, stooping to give Vincent a pat. "*Dear* Vincent! Welcome to Glebe Place! Naughty Daddy Warwick never told me he'd be bringing handsome you otherwise I would have had a bowl of doggy cocktail treats and water waiting!"

"I am sure *dear* Vincent will survive, *Medea,* dear," said Warwick with another faux smile. "Now, where are the blowpipes?"

"Blowpipes?"

"The two bushmen with their blowpipes and poison darts," quipped Warwick. "Otherwise known as Serendipity Shaka and Amos Agja."

"Silly me; of course," replied Medea jauntily. "They're in the studio, along with Larry, enjoying s flute of The Widow while waiting for the guest of honour to arrive!"

How appropriate that they should be drinking Widow Clicquot champagne, thought Warwick, *little realising the term 'widow' a portent of things to come!*

"Goody, good!" chortled Warwick. "Lead on, Medea, Michael, Macduff!"

He may be another Hannibal Lecter in the making but, God, isn't he good looking! thought Serendipity as Warwick and Medea entered the studio.

Eish! thought Amos. *That is one good-looking bloke, but he isn't a patch on my lekker Larry!*

"Delighted to meet you, Serendipity, and you, Amos," said Warwick proffering his hand while deliberately ignoring Larry. "And, once again, my sincere thanks for helping me get rid of that irritating itch."

Irritating itch? thought Serendipity. *How quaint!*

Irritating itch? thought Amos. *An irritating itch which required more than a scratch, you mean!*

"Dear, Warwick, your usual martini?" crooned Medea.

"What else?" said Warwick with a faux smile. "Unless you're offering something exotic like *skokiaan* in honour of your South African guests."

"*Skokiaan?*" questioned Larry.

"A noxious, self-made alcoholic beverage served in shebeens, read night clubs, over there unless I'm wrong," replied Warwick airily. "Otherwise, a martini would be *perfecto.*"

"I heard he could be difficult," murmured Serendipity to Medea. "But after a minute or two in Mr. Standton's company, I'd say that was putting it mildly. As for his attitude toward your friend Larry ... talk about Rikki-Tikki-Tavi meeting a cobra!"

"Hear, hear," muttered Medea. "The good news is that he won't be staying long as he has some other reception to attend."

"Lucky them," replied Serendipity dryly. "Uh-oh, he, plus dog, have now homed in on poor Amos. This could be fun."

"So, Amos, I hear you're here on what I'd describe as an 'in and out' visit to London, before Euro-starring to gay Paree," said Warwic silkily.

"*Ja*," said Amos with a whiter than white smile. "Tomorrow, I plan on visiting the Tower of London. Something I've always wanted to do since I was a kid, and then the next day we go onto Paris where I will visit the Eiffel Tower. Another thing I've always wanted to do." He gave a chuckle. "I can't wait to see a Beefeater. I take it you've seen a Beefeater?"

"Only in a martini," quipped Warwick.

On seeing Amos's puzzled expression, he added spikily. "I'm referring to Beefeater *Gin*. Geddit?"

Eisa! Talk about a total prick, thought Amos. Giving Warwick a further whiter than white smile, he said cheerfully. "No, I didn't *geddit*, *Meneer* Warwick, but *dankie* for your explanation. Now, if you'll excuse me, I'd much prefer to go and talk to *Meneer* Larry. Geddit?"

Giving Warwick another dazzling smile, Amos spun round and crossed over to where Larry was talking to Serendipity and Medea, leaving a startled Warwick alone with Vincent.

"Mind if I join you?" he said cheerfully to the trio. "Somehow, I have a feeling that as far as *Meneer* Standton is concerned, I didn't come up scratch, so I thought it best I left him to talk to his dog."

"I know exactly what you mean," snickered Larry. "If ever one needed a pungent fart to pollute a party, all that have to do is invite Warwick Laudanum-Standton!"

"You know what, Serendipity and Medea," chuckled Amos. "One could really get to like this bloke!" Giving a giggling Larry a high five, he added with a deep belly laugh. "You're okay, Larry! And, if you're not doing anything tomorrow morning, why not join me when I visit the Tower of London."

"I'm already there," giggled Larry. "Or, and wickedly plagiarising your surname. *Ag ja,* Amos!"

THE DORCHESTER HOTEL - THE NEXT EVENING

"How was your visit to the Tower followed by a very long lunch?" asked Serendipity mischievously.

"*Fabelagtic*!" grinned Amos. "Absolutely fabulous! Larry certainly knows his London! We had lunch at The Aqua Shard, a restaurant thirty-one floors above London. Incredible!" Still grinning, he added nonchalantly. "Seeing Larry was *so* enthusiastic and informative about the Tower and appears to know *all* there is to know about the Eiffel Tower, I've invited him to join us in Paris. He'll also be taking us to see Versailles as well as showing us all sorts of naughty nightspots!"

"Darling Amos!" crooned Serendipity. "If you're expecting me to be surprised, I'm not!" She gave a throaty laugh before saying with a wink. "The moment I saw your reaction on seeing Larry Pinkerton, I knew you were hooked and vice versa!"

"It was that obvious, was it?"

"Obvious?" exclaimed Serendipity. "It was as obvious as a charging bull elephant!"

*

"To make doubly sure Amos doesn't change his mind and the two of you board Eurostar tomorrow without me," grinned Larry as he and Medea joined Serendipity and Amos for a drink in their suite at The Dorchester before dinner, "I've brought along an overnight bag which also contains a change of clothes for an overnight stay in Paris. So, *Meneer* Amos, if you could show me where to dump it, I'll take it we're still in business!"

"*Ja*, we're still in business," chuckled Amos. "Very much so. Now, if *Meneer* would follow me I'll show him where he can leave his bag."

"To quote my colleague," said Medea with a throaty laugh once the two were out of earshot. "People may think Larry Pinkerton flighty, but not, it seems, if it means spending a naughty tonighty plus a *tomorrow* nighty with the one and only *Meneer* Amos Agja!"

"I heard that!" chortled Larry as he and Amos re-entered the sitting room. Turning to face a beaming Amos he said in mock alarm. "Please don't tell me I've been wickedly led astray and my packing an overnight bag has been vain!"

"Only if you packed your pyjamas!" chuckled Amos. "For tonight and tomorrow night I can assure you, *lekker* Larry, pyjamas will *not* be worn!"

*

"I think we may have a problem there," murmured Serendipity to Medea later when they were in the restaurant's powder room.

"A problem? Why?"

"Because Medea, dear friend, Amos is talking about your Larry about joining him in Cape Town!"

"Serendipity dear, let me tell you something. I've known Larry for ten years and consider him the ultimate friend. However, in all that time I have never seen him so deliriously happy as he has been since meeting Amos yesterday. Talk about love at first sight!" Medea gave a small sigh. "So, if my darling friend thinks moving to Cape Town to be with Amos is his destiny, so be it. I'll be distraught to see him go, but as Larry said, Cape Town is only a phone call and an eleven-hour flight away."

Giving Serendipity's arm a gentle squeeze, she added with a smile. "And Larry, being Larry, couldn't resist saying think of the business the four of us could do together!"

A LAVISH DUPLEX PENTHOUSE - CHELSEA HARBOUR - EARLIER

"Unless, unbeknown to me, I'm experiencing a heavy dose of amnesia," sniped Warwick on seeing the table on the terrace set for two, "as I have no recollection of leaving a note saying there'd be two for breakfast."

Giving Clarke a disparaging look he gestured toward the second-place setting. "Get rid of that, toute suite and, in future, kindly look before you assume."

PALAZZO LORENZO - VENICE - TWO WEEKS LATER

"*Grazie,* Dario," cooed Clementine as Dario handed her the day's post on a sliver salver.

"Hmm, this looks interesting, she mused taking hold of a heavy envelope. "A wedding invitation perhaps?"

On opening the envelope and reading the heavily embossed card, Clementine couldn't resist a tinkly laugh. "Not quite a wedding invitation but an invitation to the premiere of Paulo Pablo's latest film in Rome next month. Well, I never! If that isn't a bit cheeky, tell me what is!" She gave a giggle. "But then, why not? And, as the invitation if for two, I'll invite darling Marissa Mildew as she'd simply *love* a few days shopping in Rome plus the idea of attending a glamorous first night! We'll stay at The Excelsior, my treat, and thoroughly spoil ourselves. And, if we *do* happen to meet Paulo, I shall be charm itself!"

27

A LAVISH DUPLEX PENTHOUSE - CHELSEA HARBOUR - TWO WEEKS LATER

"Oh, *Warwick*!" wailed Lutetia over the telephone. "The-most-ghastly-news! Poor, dear, Clementine's been run over by a taxi!"

"Run over by a taxi?" chortled Warwick. "What on earth was my dizzy aunt doing swimming in a canal?"

"Not a *water* taxi!" shrilled Lutetia. "A taxi on that Via Veneto in Rome!"

"Oh. Then I apologise Mother Dearest, as I didn't realise that she was in Rome." Warwick gave a snicker. "Hence a taxi with a difference, as it were. Haha! A sure-fire example of first look left, then look right and then look left again!"

"She's *dead,* Warwick!" said Lutetia with a tearful sniff. "Clementine is dead!"

"Dead?" echoed Warwick. "Oh dear, how very unfortunate for her. Look, Mother Dearest, I can hear you're upset so why not pour yourself a stiff drink and I'll call you back as I too, need a stiff drink on hearing such terrible, terrible news!"

Replacing the receiver he turned to Vincent, busy with a doggy chew, and said gleefully. "It looks as if we'll soon be able to say *arrivederci* penthouse for a while, Vincent, my loyal friend, and be living it up in a palazzo instead. This means you'll have to be fitted out for a pair of special doggy water wings seeing walkies over there could be a tad different! More *swimmies* than walkies in fact!'"

Taking a sip of his quickly mixed martini, Warwick said solemnly. "Silly Aunt Clementine. It just goes to show what happens to those people used to living in Venice when they decide to visit a run-of-the-mill town or city. They forget to look to the left, then to the right, then to the left again, before stepping from the pavement. So, thank you, dear silly Aunt Clementine, for, if all goes as it should, your palazzo is now my palazzo!"

Warwick gave a start as his private landline began to ring again.

"Please don't tell me it's Mother Dearest seeing A, I have barely had a drink myself and, B. I distinctly said I'd call her back. Grr!"

"Yes, Mother Dearest!" he snapped on answering.

"It's not your mother, it's your father!" boomed Percival. "How *dare* you upset your mother with some stupid rhyme suggesting your Aunt Clementine should have looked where she was going!"

"Err..."

"Don't err me, young man! For not only was your aunt *killed* by a wretched taxi the wretched taxi never even stopped! According to the police the taxi had been reported stolen the day before and later found abandoned near The Colosseum." Percival gave a snort. "Typical of today's youth! Steal a vehicle, go for a joyride and then some poor unfortunate soul suffers the consequences!"

Sounds to me like a deliberate Nero than a Nero miss, thought Warwick with a grin, but thought it best not to say so to his incensed parent.

"As I said to Mother Dearest, I am *so* sorry to hear about poor Aunt Clementine's sudden - and sad - demise."

"No, you're not! Not at all!" roared Percival. "You're most probably already working on a list of reprobates like yourself you'll be inviting to the first of your endless bacchanales in your newly acquired palazzo!"

Unable to restrain himself Percival added with a further roar. "A bloody queen in his castle at last!" before slamming down the phone.

"*Oh, my Papa!*" crooned Warwick à la Eddie Fisher, "*How very right you are! Not only a queen in my very own palazzo, but Venice's newest, rising* star!" He gave a chuckle. "Dear departed glamorous Peggy Guggenheim, art collector *supremo*, how you would have loved meeting *moi!*"

A SUMPTUOUS VILLA - PARIOLI NEIGHBOURHOOD - ROME

"Well done, Nicollo," grinned Paulo Pablo handing the scruffy little man a wad of lire. "I knew we could rely on you."

"Always, Signor Pablo. Always!" replied Nicollo Cristofari, a revered stuntman, known for his many other clandestine talents. "Anytime you need anything similar done, you only have to ask Nicollo!" Giving a slight bow, he added a soft "*Arrivederci* Signor, Signorina" before turning on his heel and leaving the salon.

"Someone should tell Signor Nicollo that even the most talented stuntmen-cum-hitmen need to take a shower now and then," snickered Sophia. "A walking advert for Aramis or its equivalent he most certainly is *not*!"

"Forget his personal hygiene, Sophia, and think of him as the bearer of good news instead for, thanks to odorous Nicollo, Clementine Lorenzzo, former wife and your stepmother, is no more!"

Sophia gave a theatrical sigh before saying mischievously. "Pity about the palazzo having slipped through your nimble fingers as I would have enjoyed staying there on the odd occasion."

"*Puah*!" retorted Paulo. "We already have this magnificent villa here in Rome *plus* the villa on Sardinia. So, count your blessings, as they say."

Giving his daughter a smile he said with a chuckle. "I wonder what Clementine would have thought of the film had she been able to attend the premiere?"

"Knowing how dizzy she was she would have loved it," snickered Sophia. "The story of a wily Casanova diddling a dotty old woman out of all her money and possessions and then dumping her on a desert island? *Fantastico*! I can just imagine Clementine saying to one of her geriatric friends. 'Huh, stupid woman. I'd like to see someone try that with me! I'd soon send them packing!' Which let's face it, Papa. That's exactly what we did!"

"Well, as Stephano used to say when his school lost at soccer. 'You can't win them all'!"

"Papa. Are you thinking what I'm thinking should Warwick choose to ever stay in the palazzo for any length of time?"

"If you were thinking of the odorous Nicollo's parting words 'you only have to ask Nicollo', I most certainly am! So, have no fear, Sophia dear. Aldo

Valenti, an affable gondolier. receives a monthly stipend for reports of any sorts regarding the goings-on at Palazzo Lorenzo. As a matter of fact, I spoke to Aldo earlier and informed him the palazzo was about to find itself under new management."

"You mean mismanagement," tittered Sophia.

"Under *gross* mismanagement, and to keep us informed," chuckled Paulo.

"And you're quite sure, Papa, there's no chance of a glitch in the divorce agreement, settlement, whatever?"

"No, no chance at all. Sophia. We parted amicably - or so Clementine thought! - and, as far as I'm concerned, that's a segment of my life that is now nothing more than a sordid memory. However, on a more cheerful note, let's think up something really fiendish for Nicollo to organise regarding our English nemesis."

"A Viking funeral Venetian style, perhaps?" giggled Sophia. "With dear Warwick being burned alive in a gondola instead of a ship."

"Good thinking, daughter dear!" replied Paulo with a grin. "If dear Stephano is looking down on us, he'd be doubly proud of his innovative sister!"

A LAVISH DUPLEX PENTHOUSE - CHELSEA HARBOUR

"Well, Vincent, my friend, it looks as if those doggy water wings are going to be put to use much sooner than your magical master thought. Another wings of significance importance will be your pilot's wings as we'll soon be flying, yo-yo style, between Venice and London." Warwick gave a giggle. "So, not only water wings but pilot's wings as well."

Much to Warwick's indignation, Vincent's response was a wide yawn followed by a pungent, silent snoopy.

"Pucking Hell! Vincent! If *that's* your answer, maybe you'll remain England bound as I am quite sure I could find a willing Italian replacement at the drop of a gondolier's ribboned hat!"

He glanced at his vintage Cartier watch. "Lois and Superman should come a tapping on the door any second from now . . . and yes, here they are. Right on time as always."

"*Buongiorno,* Louis and Clarke," he crooned as the two men entered the study.

"*Buongiorno,* Signor Warwick!" replied Louis and Clarke in unison.

"Aha! You speaka da Italian," tittered Warwick. "How fortunate!"

"A few words picked up on a holiday spent at the Lido in Vencie," giggled Louis.

"The Lido in Venice?" cried Warwick, clapping hands. "It gets better and better as I am about to become the owner of a rather gilded palazzo in Venice where I trust you, in your *very* distinctive way, will accompany *moi* should I decide to spend some quality time there."

Noting their puzzled expressions, headed nonchalantly. "At present there is *un uomo* named Dario in charge of the palazzo, but I am sure the three of you will adapt, get along, whatever, as Dario's continued presence is vital when yours truly and your good selves are not in residence."

"It sounds wonderful, *signor!*" exclaimed Clarke.

"*Magnifico!*" giggled Louis.

"Good! Then that's settled," said Warwick smugly. "Now, all I'm waiting for is a phone call and, in anticipation of this important call, be prepared to fly to Venice with *moi* and a contrite Vincent the day after tomorrow. As well as being on a canal the palazzo also boasts a pool so, at times, Speedos and flip-flop can be worn! *Capiche?*"

LADBROKE SQUARE

"So, this wealthy old aunt of his, a Countess no less, gets run over and killed on a visit to Rome and now wretched Warwick is now the owner of a palazzo? How very convenient," mused Andy.

"And say so all of us," chuckled Pegg. "However, for once I truly feel that the dreaded Warwick is blameless. First of all, the tragedy occurred in Rome, and even Warwick, with all those grimy fingers in all sorts of rancid pies - and I speak from experience - doesn't have access any such pies to really scavenge in."

"So, what are you suggesting?"

"Apparently the old girl was in Rome for the premiere of her ex-husband's latest film. According to Warwick there was a great deal of friction there, particularly after the ex-husband's son - her then stepson - 'died in a mysterious accident'. Quote, unquote." said Pegg. "So, maybe a finger, grimy or otherwise, should be pointing in another direction. According to hearsay, ex-hubby and his daughter never stopped blaming the ex-wife. A prime example of 'what if'. What if they *hadn't* been invited to stay in Tuscany et cetera."

"Yes, that's all very well, but regardless of rumours and what people think or say. Warwick is now the owner of a fucking palace," replied Andy.

"He is indeed," agreed Pegg. Taking a sip of his martini, he added with a chuckle. "When they said Venice was sinking, I had no idea it was said in anticipation of the possible arrival of such a pollutive new resident!"

PALAZZO LORENZO

"I feel as if I've just stepped into a fairytale," cooed Louis.

"Makes a change from feeling *this* old fairy's tail," tittered Clarke as he and Louis stood on the main terrace admiring the spectacular Canaletto-like vista.

"Oh, you! I can see the spirit of Casanova has already go you despite us having only arrived a few minutes ago. *Lover!*" giggled Louis.

"You *wish!*" snorted Clarke. "But then, you never know!"

"Uh-uh," muttered Louis. "Signor *Basso Profundo* approaches. I have to tell you. Clarke, no matter what Warwick says, I do *not* like Signor Dario one little bit. Talk about *un uomo* with a carrot up his you know what!"

"Only a carrot." Whispered Clarke. "More like a field of carrots!"

"Signori," rumbled Dario on reaching the giggling couple. "Signor Warwick wishes to see you in the grand salon. Please follow me."

"See us in the grand salon?" simpered Louis. "Lawks a mussy! We haven't even had a chance to unpack seeing we've been standing here *enraptured* by the wonderful view!"

"Please yourselves, signori," rumbled Dario deadpan. "After all, I am merely an employee of Signor Warwick and sadly no longer major domo and confidante to the Contessa Lorenzo."

"If that isn't a prime example of 'put it in your pipe and smoke it'," murmured Clarke, "then I don't know what is."

Giving Dario a stony look he said with a tight smile. "Thank you, Dario. As we have no idea as to where the grand salon is currently lurking, perhaps you would be so kind as to show us the way."

"I see trouble ahead," sang Louis softly as they followed Dino.

"No need to worry as ahead rhymes with dead," sang Clarke equally as softly.

"Ooh! That was *so* wicked!" tittered Louis. "Imagine what Warwick would say if he heard you say such a thing? Why, the poor young man would simply pass out! I *know* he can be difficult, but he's a sweetie at heart. We'll never know what that dreadful one-night stand said to him, but poor Warwick was upset for days."

"*Buongiorno*, Signor Warwick," they chorused on entering the grand salon. A scowling Dario having promptly left on showing then in.

"My, oh my, Signor Warwick," tittered Louis. "Talk about a quick-change artist! I *love* the striped top and the baggy trousers. *Very* gondolier! All you need is a ribboned, straw hat! Hee-hee!"

"Thank you, Louis," chortled Warwick. "Now pray tell *moi*, what you two gentlemen think of your new *casa* for the next few weeks?"

"*Bellissima!*" crooned Clarke. "*Molta Bellissima*! Talk about a dream come true in a positive dreamscape!"

"Good Hades, Clarke. For a dreaded moment you reminded me of that awful Yawn Williams man and his ambitious lark! A dream come true in a positive dreamscape? Whatever next? Delicious spaghetti I will never forgetti?"

Once the giggles and titters had died down, Warwick said with a conspiratorial smile. "Gently does it, but I do need you two gentlemen to take over the general running of the palace which means finding and rapidly training a new houseman who can look after matters when you are *not* here. As for Dario, he can puck off and join his family in Liguria, or wherever it is they *vivere*. The sooner the better: such as next week!"

"Hear! Hear!" cried Louis.

"*Brilliante!*" crooned Clarke. "Blooming *brilliante!*"

"It's a pity your Ginger cannot do a Vincent and become a frequent flyer between London and Venice," giggled Warwick. "But what's to stop you, Clarke, bringing a furniture rest or three to perch on a windowsill and watch the gondolas go by. A change from watching boats on the Thames, wouldn't you say?"

"Oh, no need to worry about Ginger, sir, as he's hopelessly in love with Mrs Bert, the head porter's wife, and she with him. She has now taken to not only spoiling him with endless delicious titbits but giving his ginger coat a daily brushing. A luxury - dare I say it - *purr*-fecto!"

RANCHO PLATA, PLATA, PLATA

"Latest report from across the ocean is that our friend is presently preening and prancing around his new abode Palazzo Lorenzo, in Venice," snarled Kurt as he, Joel, Sebastian and Delilah sat enjoying cocktails by the Olympic size swimming pool.

"Which goes to show how wise we were in *not* setting fire to the palace while the old countess was in residence, or even if she wasn't," boomed Sebastian. "But now that *he's* the owner and could even be there, maybe it's time to think a second La Fenice once again! Haw! Haw!"

"I thought we'd all agreed to let sleeping dogs - or curs - lie for the time being," said Delilah.

"An' so we shall, lil' darlin'," boomed Sebastian. "But that don't mean we have to stop talkin' about the great day! Haw! Haw! Haw!"

"Is it only me or do we all think he had something to do with his aunt's fatal accident?" questioned Joel.

"No, definitely not," said Kurt firmly. "After the countess divorced that slimeball of an actor, Warwick knew that he was back in favour and legally informed that once again the sole inheritor of the old woman's palace, money and possessions, so why get rid of her? After all, she was well into her eighties, so why upset the apple cart by deliberately getting rid of her?"

"So, who then?" said Joel.

"Why, that conniving actor, of course," replied Kurt. "With her being in her eighties and he, a much sought after matinee idol in his forties, I can assure you there was no love lost there. Not only is Paulo Picasso or whatever he calls himself still in mourning for his dead son for whose death he holds the old countess responsible, but he also has the support of his equally conniving daughter who openly blames the countess as well."

Taking a swallow of his martini, Kurt added matter-of-factly. "If I am correct - and I *know* I am - next on their hit list will be Warwick which means that we may have the pleasure of another La Fenice after all!"

CAPE TOWN

"Welcome to Cape Town, *lekker* Larry!" rumbled Amos taking hold of Larry and giving him a hug. "*Eisa*! Am I glad to see you!"

"Likewise!" cried Larry burying his head against Amos's massive chest. "I've been counting the seconds until I arrived and now, here I am and here *you* are! Fabulous! Fantastic, and anything else meaning wonderful!"

"The car's right outside," grinned Amos. "Pikki, my driver, can't wait to meet you!"

"Pikki? Should I be jealous?" trilled Larry.

"Somehow, I don't think so," replied Amos with a deep, belly laugh. "On meeting Pikki I have a feeling any such thoughts will sail right out of the window! C'mon, let me take care of your suitcase and follow me."

On stepping out from the air-conditioned airport into the blazing sunshine. Amos said with a wide grin. "The lady standing by that gleaming red Range Rover over there is my devoted Pikki, your would-be competitor."

Approaching the smiling Hattie McDaniels lookalike, Amos said in a whispered aside. "Pikki's my driver, my housekeeper and most of all, my dream mama."

"Pikki's your *mother*?" exclaimed Larry. Stopping midstride.

"Not my real mama: my imaginary mama," grinned Amos. "If I could have *chosen* my mama. I would have chosen Pikki as she's everything a son could wish for, and more."

Inroductions made, the cheerful three set off for De Waterkant.

"Larry, if you look to your right," said Pikki in a rich, melodic sing-song voice. "You will see that even Table Mountain is busy preparing a special welcome dinner for you this evening."

"Table Mountain? A special dinner for me?" quizzed Larry staring in the direction of a cloud topped Table Mountain.

"The clouds you can see nestling on the top are not an everyday occurrence," laughed Pikki. "But when they do appear to settle there, the local people always say that Table Mountain is wearing a tablecloth. In other words, for your special dinner tonight."

"Wow!" giggled Larry. "Not only a special dinner, but a *uniquely* special dinner served on a mountain! I *love* it! I love it *almost* as much as I love my *Meneer* Amos Agja!"

"If you love him more than I do," sang Pikki, "then you must really love my adorable Amos!"

28

A SUMPTUOUS VILLA - PARIOLI NEIGHBOURHOOD - ROME

"That was Nicollo ringing to say he and Signor Mancini - who he's nicknamed Signor Esca - are on their way and should be here at any minute," chuckled Paulo.

"*Buono,*" said Sophia. She gave a titter. "As we will be speaking English, I must remember to call the gentleman Signor Mancini and *not* Signor Esca which means bait in Italian! I have a bottle of Nicollo's favourite Pinot Grigio chilling nicely but, should Signor Bait - oops! Signor *Mancini* - prefer something stronger, there's grappa or even Strega on hand along with everything else."

She gave her father a mischievous grin. "I can't wait to meet Nicollo's Signor Mancini and, if Aldo's reports are correct that Warwick is guaranteed to drop into Harry's Bar for a drink or two each evening where - surprise, surprise - our Signor Mancini will casually strike up a conversation with him: it couldn't be more perfect."

Sophia couldn't resist a giggle. "Little will dear Warwick realise that their meeting will lead to such an unpleasant ending. Ah, and here they are!"

Spinning round to greet the arrivals, she said breezily. "Nicollo, hello! And you, sir, can only be Signor - oops! English, Sophia! - *Mr.* Mancini!"

If the circumstances were different, lucky Warwick is what I would have said, thought Sophia eyeing the smiling Roaul Bova lookalike. *Poor you on discovering that your Mr. Dream Man is, in fact, your executioner!*

HARRY'S BAR - VENICE - TEN DAYS LATER

"*Buonasera*," said the dazzling Raoul Bova lookalike to Warwick as he slid smoothly onto the bar stool next to him.

"Good evening," replied Warwick curtly. "You'll have to excuse me, but I don't speak Italian."

"Good evening, then," smiled the man. "Your first time in Venice?"

"No, I live here," replied Warwick, his antennae on full alert. *Too smooth and too obvious, Signor,* he thought. *You're either one of Salamander's minions or else you've something to do with that pucking Larry Pinkerton and the others. Ever since lousy Larry appeared and then disappeared, I'm suspicious of all you smooth talking mountebanks. Apart from Vincent, Louis and Clarke, I trust no one.*

"Lucky you," replied the man. Proffering his hand, he said with a whiter than white smile. "Ronaldo Mancini, visiting from Rome."

"Enjoy your visit. *Mr.* Mancini," replied Warwick ignoring the proffered hand. "Now, if you'll excuse *moi*, I'd like to continue with my musings."

As Pablo and his daughter said, a right cheeky bastard, thought Mancini withdrawing his hand. *But that can soon be amended.*

On his return to the palazzo Warwick immediately summonsed Louis and Clarke.

"I had a rather obvious approach made whilst at Harry's Bar by a man calling himself Ronaldo Mancini," he said. "After all the recent happenings I've been exposed to, especially after Mr. Pick-up Pinkerton, if anyone approaches you, especially a good-looking Raoul Bova lookalike, and starts a conversation, do *not,* under any circumstances, mention whom you work for or where you stay. *Capiche*?"

"We both well and truly *capiche,* Mr. Warwick," said Clarke in a sonorous voice. Glancing at Louis, he said matter-of-factly. "And I can assure you Louis and l will do our utmost to spare you the indignity of another Larry, sir."

About to respond with a furious "What do you mean by the indignity of another Larry", Warwick held his tongue and said instead. "Yes, Clarke. Another very unpredictable and therefore *dangerous* Larry!"

"Leave it to us, Mr. Warwick," replied Clarke with a reassuring smile. "After all, Venice does have a myriad of canals."

"It has indeed," tittered Louis. "So, goodnight, sir. Or, better still, *buona notte* and pleasant dreams."

"Leave it to us? Good night and pleasant dreams?" repeated Warwick after the couple had left. "Oho! Messrs. Louis and Clarke. Do I get the encouraging feeling that the two of you are more aware of what your employment may involve than I thought?"

Looking at Vincent asleep on a nearby chair, he said with a giggle. "Yet somehow, I am not at all surprised. After all, when you come to think of it, what's to stop a Darby and Joan turning into a Fred and Rose West. Not a canal, that's for sure!"

*

The next evening Warwick duly returned to Harry's Bar with Louis and Clarke taking a seat nearby several minutes later. On seeing Mancini enter the bar, Warwick gave the two a discreet nod and a thumbs-up.

ROME

"Any word from Mancini as yet?" asked Paulo in a phone call to Nicollo.

"Nothing as yet, Signor. However, he did approach Signor Warwick night before last and although he had been seriously rebuffed on his first approach, he said not to worry as its early days."

"*Grazie,* Nicollo," said Paulo before adding snidely. "However, next time you speak to Mancini, please remind him that my daughter and I have no wish for these early days to become distant days."

"Si, Signor. I'll tell him."

VENICE

Three days later a startled gondolier was duly shocked when his gondola bumped into a body floating in one of the many canals.

DE WATERKANT - CAPE TOWN

"You must be getting truly bored by our endless *welkoms* Larry, but *welkom* again," said Serendipity with a throaty chuckle.

"*Dankie,* Serendipity," replied Larry with a grin. Taking hold of Amos's giant hand, he added sincerely. "And when I say I am really, *really,* happy being here with you all, I mean it. You're all just wonderful. *Meneer* Agja especially!"

"Thank you, Larry, you deserve it!" replied Serendipity. "And now, some exciting news for you and Amos as your first commission as a team has come through."

"*Great!*" exclaimed Larry. He gave a chuckle. "As much as I enjoyed it all, I have to admit I was becoming a touch bored with sunbathing and gorging myself on those delicious, fattening *koeksisters*!"

"So, Serendipity, tell us more about this new commission?" rumbled Amos, all business, once the laughter had died down.

"It concerns a Vokkie Verschuur who owns several diamond mines in the Free State. He claims one of his more senior employees is stealing uncut diamonds and he needs us to find the guilty party and make sure they never steal again. I've confirmed a meeting between Verschuur and the two of you tomorrow. The meeting will take place as his office in Johannesburg. He is sending his jet" - she gave a chuckle - "very early I'm afraid, to collect you. You'll then be taken by helicopter from O. R. Tembo Airport to Sandton City, which means so you'll only be away from Cape Town for a couple of hours."

"Has Verschuur any idea as to who the thief may be?" asked Amos.

"Yes, one of his directors. A woman named Melanie Meibosfontein," replied Serendipity with a smile. "Not only a director but an ex-mistress who was recently replaced by a very young and much prettier nubile version of herself."

"The name of this much younger, prettier replacement?" tittered Larry.

"You won't believe it, but her name's Gloria *Digger,* as in gold digger, need I say more?"

"How serious a lesson a lesson is Miss Meibosfontein to be given or taught?" rumbled Amos.

"I'll leave that to you blokes," replied Serendipity. "All Vokkie Verschuur said was that you were to make sure *Juffrou* Meibosfontein will never wear diamonds again on her fingers or toes! But he'll tell you more plus discuss strategies and fees when you meet tomorrow."

"Which means instead of being *Melanie* Meibosfontein, she'll be known as *Stompie* Meibosfontein," giggled Larry,

"*Stompie* as in stumpy?" chortled Serendipity. "Goodness, Larry! Your hold on Afrikaans gets better by the day!"

OFFICES OF V.V. VERSCHUUR & SON
JOHANNESBURG CBD (CENTRAL BUSINESS DISTRICT) - THE NEXT DAY

"Verschuur and Son?" whispered Larry as he and Amos rode the elevator to the sixteenth floor.

"Living it up in Down Under," snorted Amos. "Apparently, he sees himself as another Sidney Nolan as opposed to a tiresome sponger."

"I'm surprised daddy hasn't asked Serendipity to give his errant little boy a severe spanking," tittered Larry.

"Oh, I'm sure he will," replied Amos matter-of-factly. "He and Serendipity go way back. See Verschuur Junior as an accident to happen!"

"Ouch! Whatever happened to family fidelity?"

"Who knows? We may even be given the answer by Papa Verschuur this very morning." Amos glanced at the glowing numbers above the door. "We're almost there. Now, promise me, love of my life, that you'll be on your best behaviour!"

"Good morning, Mr. Agja and Mr. Pinkerton," simpered a Miss Marple lookalike as they stepped out from the elevator. "Welcome to V.V. Verschuur and Son. I am Hettie van Wyk, Mr. Vokkie's personal secretary. Mr. Vokkie is waiting for you in his office. Please follow me."

It seems to me that in South Africa you're welcome everywhere despite being invited to carry out a mutilation or even a murder, thought Larry with an inward snicker. *So, it'll be interesting to hear what mein papa has up his sleeve!*

"Welcome! Welcome!" croaked Vokkie Verschuur, a pale, wizened Tikoloshe lookalike. "I take it the humdrum - hee-hee - Hettie has offered you a coffee or something equally insipid. Hee-hee!"

"She did indeed, thank you," replied Amos visibly taken aback by the snide reference to his secretary. "But we're literally floating in the delicious coffee we were given during out flight here, so I'll say no, but thank you. Larry?"

"As, like Amos, I am also a floater," said Larry deadpan. "I too will have to say no thank you."

"Good, *baaie goed,*" croaked Verschuur. "Now, I appreciate you need to get this little get together over as quickly as possible so that you can both get back to doing what you do best; so, cards on the table as it were. Hee-hee!"

Gesturing to the two to take a seat, Verschuur perched nimbly perched on the edge of his desk and said in a continuing croak. "You already know what you need to know so, what *I* need to know is what you are planning to *actually* do to Melanie Meibosfontein and how much I have to pay you, cash of course, to do whatever you decide to do. Once I give you the okey-dokey, I don't wish to hear another word. Okey-dokey?"

Amos quickly described what they had planned for Melanie's comeuppance and ended by naming their fee.

"Agreed," croaked Vershuur without hesitation. Turning he reached inside one of the desk drawers and took out a tumbler and a bottle of Van Ryan's brandy. Pouring a hefty dollop he added with a yellow smile. "Join me? You're more than welcome. This will be the third of my daily dozen - hee-hee - strictly medicinal, of course, as I couldn't get through a day without the aid of *Meneer* Van Ryan's finest! Hee-hee-hee!"

Staring at Amos and Larry as if waiting for their response to his offer of a drink (both shook their heads indicating no), Verschuur then, with a leer, reached into another drawer and pulled out a velvet box.

"Here, for you two," he croaked. "Don't be shy. Serendipity told me all about the two of you, how you met et cetera, and your wedding plans. Live and let live I always say - my blerry son being the exception - so please accept this as both an extra bonus and wedding present."

"Err . . . I don't know what to say, Mr. Verschuur," stammered Amos while Larry sat looking dumbstruck.

"*Ag,* Amos, may I call you Amos and Larry? It's just a little something wishing you both the best of luck and a happy future." Holding out the box he added with a mischievous croaking. "Have a look. There a two diamond encrusted rings for your ring fingers. Serendipity gave me the approximate sizes. As I said to her, it was the ring finger sizes I needed. Not your *cock* ring sizes, as I'm never *that* keen on giving away my diamonds! Hee-hee!"

*

"Well, talk about at atomic surprise," giggled Larry as he sat admiring his sparkling finger as he and Amos were being helicoptered back to O.R. Tembo Airport. "Maybe we should invite croaky old Vokkie to the wedding."

"I already did, while you were out having a pee," rumbled Amos. "Something else you need to know. As we will have to travel to Australia to deal with Verschuur Junior, croaky old Vokkie, as you called him, suggested we combine the contract with our honeymoon with him footing the bill for all!"

"I can't believe it!"

"There's more," added Amos with a grin. "Croaky old Vokkie suggested after we introduce ourselves to Frikkie - that's Junior's name - we invite him to join us on a trip to the Great Barrier Reef where he conveniently disappears while checking out six hundred or so corals. Needless to say - among the souvenirs we bring back, there will have to be a couple of *Frikkie* souvenirs as proof for croaky old Vokkie!"

"But before we jet off to the Great Barrier Reef in pursuit of Frikkie and enticing him to take up permanent residence amongst the colourful coral, I take it we will be attending to the light-fingered Diamond Lil?"

"You and your way with words," chuckled Amos. "*Yebo,* to use one of *my* words, we still have Miss Melanie to deal with. We can discuss this on the flight back as Vokkie gave me all the necessary details."

"Again, whilst I was peeing, I take it," snickered Larry.

"*Yebo,*" chuckled Amos. "At the moment she's staying in Grahamstown in the Eastern Cape."

"Grahamstown? Isn't there a university there?"

"*Eisa!* Not only are you learning to speak Afrikaans but you're starting to learn your South African geography as well. *Ja,* Rhodes University is in Grahamstown."

"Please don't tell me Diamond Lil is there posing as an unobtrusive student?" chortled Larry.

"No. She has a friend there who owns an antique shop - not a jewellers' - and who she visits on a regular basis. I was surprised to learn Melanie Meibosfontein is still employed by V. V. Verschuur and Son, but Vokkie made it quite clear that while we're trimming her greedy fingers and toes, we explain why we are doing so."

"So, where does this exquisite manicure take place? Grahamstown or Johannesburg?"

"Oh, most definitely in Joburg. And rather than being found bleeding while spreadeagled on a bed of diamonds, we'll place her on a bed of broken glass. To quote Vokkie. 'It's a blerry sight cheaper than the real McCoy!'"

"Nasty," murmured Larry.

"*Yebo*, my love, but that's what we are. Nasty."

"So, once again. When?"

"Vokkie says she'll be back in Joburg the week after next and, like today, he'll send the jet for us when we need it."

"*Yebo! Yebo! Yebo!*" carolled Larry giving Amos a high five.

A COSY APARTMENT - HILLBROW - JOHANNESBURG - LATER THE SAME DAY

"All I can say, Mr. bloody Vokkie Verschuur is that your humdrum Hettie is about to have the last laugh or, better still, a *dynamite* of a last laugh! You, Vokkie Verschuur are, without a doubt, one of the most evil of all men without any respect for anyone: anyone at all!"

Eyeing her reflection in the mirror above the faux fireplace, Hettie van Wyk raised her glass of sherry in a toast. "You'll never learn, will you, that intercoms need to be switched off, especially during one of your wicked, clandestine conversations."

Reaching for her burner phone Hettie tapped in a Grahamstown number. After a no-holds-barred conversation, she hung up and waited for a moment before tapping in a number in Sydney, Australia.

TWO DAYS LATER

"As I always open your post, I'm not quite sure what to make of this, Mr. Vokkie," murmured Hettie handing Vokkie a sheet of paper. "It's a letter of resignation from Miss Meibosfontein. Effective as from now."

"Show me!" snarled Verschhur reaching for the sheet of paper. Glancing at the contents, his pale wizened face - if possible - paled even further. "Have you got the envelope?"

"Yes, Mr. Vokkie. Right here."

"Postmarked Port Elizabeth," hissed Verschuur. "The devious bitch has obviously left Grahamstown so try her flat."

"Will do, Mr. Vokkie," replied Hettie not bothering to hide her smirk. "I'll get onto it right away."

Five minutes she returned to Verchuur's office and said in a puzzled voice. "I couldn't get any reply from Miss Meibosfontein's phone, so I tried the head porter." Pausing to take a deep breath, she added dramatically. "Apparently, she was there briefly yesterday. Not only did she pack several suitcases but, before leaving with these - she'd asked him to get her a taxi to take her to the airport - she had a brief meeting with an estate agent. According to the porter the flat is now up for sale."

"*What?*" exploded Verschuur. "Did he say who the agent was? Have you spoken to the agent?"

"Please, Mr. Verschuur, I'm merely a humdrum secretary, not Wonder Woman!" snapped Hettie. "I've only just got off the phone from speaking to the porter! Anyway, it would be pointless speaking to the agent who, like a doctor, I'm sure, would never reveal any details regarding his client."

Eyeing the wizened little man literally double up with repressed fury, Hettie added through pursed lips. "In my humdrum opinion, Mr. Verschuur, it looks to me as if Melanie Meibosfontein has done, as they call it on TV: a runner!"

29

SYDNEY - AUSTRALIA

"Good morning!" sang Larry cheerfully. "May I speak to Mr. Frikkie Verschuur, please."

"Who's calling?" twanged a heavily accented male voice.

"Larry Pinkerton from Cape Town, South Africa. Mr. Verschuur won't know me, but I've been told about his paintings by a friend of mine and, as I'll be arriving in Sydney tomorrow on a business visit. I was hoping to meet Mr. Verschuur, view his latest paintings and more than likely buy one or two for myself."

"Well, you could have a bit of a problem there, mate, as Frikkie is now somewhere in Myanmar or else Thailand on what he calls a look-see and could be away for a couple of months."

"Myanmar and Thailand on a *look-see*?" said Larry in disbelief.

"Yeah, a look-see for inspiration and all that shit."

The twang added cheerily. "The names Whacker and I'm Frikkie's flatmate. Sorry I can't be of more help. *Fuuuuuck!*"

"What?" gasped Larry.

"Nothing to make you shit your pants, but bloody Vokkie, Frikkie's cat, has just scarfed half my fucking supper. I gotta go!"

The line went dead.

Whacker Crosby, a wild-haired, Edward Scissorhands lookalike turned to Frikkie and said with a grin. "Your ancient girlfriend was right. That was one of your old man's hired galahs hoping to speak to you but, as you heard me say, you've gone walkabout either around Myanmar or Thailand."

"Brill, Whacker! Effing brill. The old bastard simply doesn't give up. does he?"

"Maybe it's time he was given a taste of his own medicine," said Whacker spooning lamb stew onto their plates as a totally disinterested Vokkie lay sound asleep nearby.

"Yeah, but how? Easier said than done,"

"Your ancient Pussy Galore, good old Hettie, surely she must have some old galah . . ."

"I wish you'd stop referring to hitmen as galahs," cut in Frikkie good-humouredly. "As I keep telling you, where I come from a gala means a social occasion."

"So?" replied Whacker as the two burst out laughing.

DE WATERKANT - CAPE TOWN

"Talk about a total fuck up," grizzled Larry on putting down the phone. "First of all, Melanie bloody Meibosfontein does an *The Invisible Woman* act and disappears into thin air, and now it looks as if Frikkie fucking Verschuur Junior has done the same!"

"What do you mean by 'done the same'?" questioned Amos.

"According to Mr. Whack Job, his *mate*, who answered, he's taken himself on an inspirational walk either around Myanmar or tantalising Thailand." Giving Amos a grin, he added wryly. "I have to admit I *was* rather looking forward to doing a Tom Daly among the coral reefs."

"Instead of getting your Speedos in a twist, we still have Warwick in our sights."

"*Out* of sight, you mean," scoffed Larry. "It is just as well Serendipity has that sugar guy in KwaZulu-Natal wanting a couple of rival planters given a non-too sweet - ha bloody ha! - seeing to, otherwise I'd most be probably having to sell myself to even the lowest bidder!"

"Then it's just as well I have a few rand stashed away for such an emergency," rumbled Amos.

"Are you suggesting that I'm now so used and abused by a certain Mr. Agja and so well past my sell-by date that no one will look at me?" said Larry in feigned indignation.

"Something like that," replied Amos with a grin. "Now, on a less sordid note, why don't I treat you to an elegant dinner at The Nellie. See it as a sort of sweetener before you have to walk the streets."

"Dinner at The Nellie!" exclaimed Larry. "*Wonderlik*! It'll give me a chance to wear my new *daasie*-patterned underpants!" (The Nellie being the name used by the locals when referring to the exclusive Mount Nelson Hotel.)

"I thought I'd invited a certain Larry about to be Pinkerton-Agja to dinner, not a bloody rock rabbit!" rumbled Amos leaning over to give Larry a kiss.

*

"Can you get that, Larry, *assemblief*!" yodelled Amos. "I've just got out of the shower and dripping wet. It's sure to be Serendipity as she said she'd be calling first thing."

"Your word is my command, oh mighty chief," carolled Larry picking up the phone. "*Goeie môre,* oh goddess of the Nile," he crooned.

"Unfortunately, it's not Cleopatra," said a brisk female voice. "I take it I'm speaking to Mr. Pinkerton and *not* Mark Antony."

"Err... who am I speaking to?"

"It's Hettie van Wyk, Mr. Pinkerton. Don't be surprised. After all I *am* Mr. V.V. Verschuur's loyal humdrum secretary and therefore aware of your telephone number."

"Err... Miss van Wyk, and yes, this *is* a surprise. Err... how may I help you?"

"I need a meeting with you and Mr. Agja," said Hettie in a no-nonsense voice. "I will be flying to Cape Town this morning, courtesy of V.V. Vercshuur and Son, so as to attend a relative's birthday party this evening in Constantia. Therefore, I suggest we meet at four o'clock in the café at the Alphen Hotel there."

"May I ask what this is about?" said Larry, signalling frantically to Amos as he entered the sitting room.

"You may, but I am not prepared to discuss why I need to see as all will be revealed when we *do* meet."

"And if Mr. Agja and myself decide not to meet you?" replied Larry a touch sharply.

"Let me just say, Mr. Pinkerton," purred Hettie. "I am in possession of several recorded copies of Mr. Verschuur's conversation with Mr. Agja - you were in the toilet at the time - regarding Miss Meibosfontein and Frikkie. Mr. Verschuur's son. Therefore, my answer to whether you meet me or not, is simple. If you don't wish to meet, then I have no alternative but to hand over one of the recordings to the police."

"Err . . . could you please hold on for a second, Miss van Wyk, while I speak to Mr. Agja."

"No, I am not prepared to 'hold on', Mr. Pinkerton. However, I expect to see you both at four o'clock as stipulated. Until then, goodbye, Mr. Pinkerton."

"Bloody Hell!" exclaimed Larry. "That was Vokkie Verschuur's archaic secretary. Did you manage to catch anything of what she was saying?"

"I sure did," muttered Amos. "Okay, let's meet *Juffrou* van Wyk and if she makes any attempt to blackmail us, she won't be returning to Joburg. In other words, she won't only be attending a birthday party but her farewell party as well."

ALPHEN HOTEL - CONSTANTIA

"So that's it, in a nutshell," purred Hettie. "You do to Mr. Verschuur what he was planning on you doing to Melanie Meibosfontein: the only difference being you cut his throat instead of cutting off his fingers. Again, as with Melanie, you leave him lying stark naked, on a bed of glittering broken glass inside his office.

"Thanks to Miss Humdrum van Wyk, Melanie Meibosfontein is now safely in Rotterdam and no doubt being comforted and consoled in the grasping arms of *Meneer* Lucas Pieters, her diamond dealer.

"As for payment, Mr. Verschuur has always been somewhat careless with any deliveries of diamonds, cut or uncut, to him in person so it wasn't unusual for him to leave pouches or containers unsupervised on his desk." Hettie gave a giggle. "Miss Meibosfontein wasn't the only one helping herself to the odd diamond or two. Which means I can either pay your agreed fee in cash or diamonds. It's entirely up to you."

"Cash," rumbled Amos. "It has to be cash."

Hettie gave a cat that got the cream type smile. "From your prompt reply I take it we have a contract?"

"What about the tape or tapes?" snapped Larry.

"You shall have a copy as soon as the deed is done," replied Hettie primly. "As for any other copies, I'll hold onto these as a girl always needs a safety measure, wouldn't you agree? I mean, should either of you agree to have a go at humdrum Hettie, *drums* will roll. Now, I have a birthday party to attend so I'll bid you farewell."

Giving a stunned Larry and Amos a smile, she added mischievously. "Oh, before I forget and before you have to remind me. Your deposit. Knowing your fee for redecorating Mr. Verschuur would be slightly higher than that agreed for the redecorating of Miss Meibosfontein and that you'd be wanting cash - and how right I was - you may or may not have noticed on your arrival, the holdall beneath my chair. In other words, a bit more than fifty percent of your deposit, in cash as anticipated."

Rising briskly to her feet, Hettie said with a smile. "You have all the entry codes et cetera and as soon as poor Missy or Posie, the cleaning ladies, trip over or hit Mr. Verschuur with a hoover, the balance of your agreed fee will be delivered to your house in De Waterkant. Enjoy the rest of your evening."

Without any further ado, Hettie turned and left the café.

"Bloody Hell!" snickered Larry after Hettie's no-nonsense exit. "You can forget *humdrum* Hettie for, as far as I'm concerned, we've just met Miss *Hurricane* Hettie! Before we say anything else; I need a drink and *then,* only then, will I be able to discuss her outrageous stratagem."

Drinks duly ordered and served, Larry leaned back in his chair and said contemplatively. "So, love of my life, do we, or don't we? Do we do what Hurricane Hettie has already part paid us to do to Vokkie Verschuur, and then do to Hurricane Hettie what we've already been paid by Vokkie Verschuur regarding Melanie Meibosfontein?"

"I can't see any alternative," said Amos. "Once a blackmailer, always a black mailer, and this, I can assure you, is only the beginning. However, to keep Madam Hurricane under control why not a double bill as it were. Vokkie Verschuur within a couple of weeks and, once we've received the balance of the agreed fee for old croaky, it's then *totsiens* Hurricane Hettie!"

"I could say well blow me down, but all I'm prepared to say is 'hear, hear, loud and clear'," tittered Larry. Giving Amos a wink, he added slyly. "I can hardly wait to read the ensuing poems!"

"*Ja*," rumbled Amos. "One titled *Totsiens Fokken Vokkie*, and the other, *Vegvlieg* - fly away - *Orkaan* - Hurricane - *Hettie*, or something worse!"

A LAVISH DUPLEX PENTHOUSE - CHELSEA HARBOUR - TWO WEEKS LATER

"Good morning, Medea dearest; or is it an MM morning," tittered Warwick.

"Definitely a Medea morning," replied Medea with a throaty chuckle. "You sound bright and breezy and full of vim! So, spill the Heinz as certain lower mortals would say. You obviously have a Yul B-type question or puzzlement to titillate my always alert mind!"

"I have indeed, Medea. A problem stemming from an unpleasant happening whilst in Venice and something which needs taking care of. A case of *arrivederci Roma*."

"I take it you're referring to Mr. Movie Star who so upset your Aunt Clementine and who you hold responsible for her death."

"*Esattamente!*" crooned Warwick before going on to explain about the intrusive Signor Ronaldo Mancini and his unexpected midnight swim in an isolated canal. His unexpected swimming instructors being none other than Louis and Clarke.

"Obviously, Medea, dearest, the problem of Signor Celluloid and his doting daughter will not go away unless I - we - *make* it go away."

"I have a sublime contact in Rome who goes by the name - don't laugh - Napoleone Bartolozzi. Napoleone - or Nappi as his friends call him - having had a mother who feel passionately in love with actor Herbert Lom who starred as Napolean in the film of Tolstoy's *War and Peace*," replied Medea. "Need I say he'd be perfect casting!"

"I take it your Signor Nappi is a touch more zappy than crappy," tittered Warwick.

"Oh, definitely much more zappy than crappy," assured Medea. "Think of a tow-haired Jamie Dornan, Italian version. Now dear, be a good little Warwick and let me have *all* details regarding your about to fade out movie star and his dismal daughter. Once I have all, I'll give Nappi a call and then get back to you. I have to warn you he doesn't come cheap."

"Tut, tut, Medea, you know *moi* better than that. Like your glamorous or handsome self, I'm a firm believer in the old mantra that nothing cheap is ever cheerful."

"I'll call you back as soon as I've spoken to the sinister signor."

"*Grazie,* Medea dearest. As for you much appreciated introduction to Signor Nappi, may I suggest, on my return, lunch at Cecconi's followed by an extravagant totter across the road to Tiffany's for a thank you bauble."

"Sounds exactly my cup of Lapsang Souchon," crooned Medea. "As I said, I'll call you back. Kisses! Mwah! Mwah!"

LADBROKE SQUARE

"Well, he's back," chuckled Andy in his daily catch-up call to Pegg. "A sure-fire case of palazzo to penthouse! Can't be bad!"

"So, it's back to the paranormal or, maybe as he's now a bona fide wannabe Principessa, maybe he'll have other things on his stultifying mind such as a hefty gondolier or two," quipped Pegg.

"Poor bloody gondolier is all I can say," snorted Andy. "Knowing how oblivious Warwick can be to any sort of criticism, it wouldn't come as any surprise if he and Vincent turned up at Peggs and simply say 'hello, we're back'!"

"God forbid," chuckled Pegg. "However, thanks for the warning and, like good boy scouts and a girl guide, Trish, Coli and me, will be prepared!"

"In the meantime, if anything untoward happens I'll bring you up to date when we join les girls for dinner."

A LAVISH DUPLEX PENTHOUSE - CHELSEA HARBOUR

"Darling, it's the lovely Medea in MM mode this sunny morn. I've spoken to Nappi and, typical Nappi, he said, without any hesitation, name the two bull's-eyes!"

"So, I take it we're on?"

"As on as we'll ever be. However, you must be patient, dear. Again, to quote Nappi. 'Rome wasn't built in a day, but Napoleone Bartolozzi's alternative should only take a week or two'."

"I'll be as patient as I can be until I run out of martinis," chortled Warwick. "Meanwhile, Vincent sends woofs. Speak to you later, glamorous *care*-taker! Haha!"

30

A SUMPTUOUS VILLA - PARIOLI NEIGHBOURHOOD - ROME

"*Buongiorno*, Papa," yawned Sophia on entering the elaborately decorated dining room clad in a Versace dressing gown and wearing Versace slippers.

"*Buongiorno, Tesoro,*" murmured Paulo barely glancing up from his copy of *Il Giorno*. "Nice getup."

"It is, isn't it," cooed Sofia. "Surely you must remember buying the gown and slippers for me before your last trip abroad?"

"My dear Sophia, as I never *stop* buying lovely things for my even lovelier Sophia, how can you expect your doting Papa to remember every bauble or article of glamourous apparel he buys you!"

"Love you, Papa!"

"Love you. *Cara* Sophia. Yes, Giovanna?"

"Excuse me, Signor Paulo, but there's a gentleman here to see you," said the housekeeper after knocking discreetly on the door.

"A gentleman to see me at this time on a Sunday morning?" said Paulo irritably. "Did he give his name?"

"*Si*, Signor Paulo. He said his name was Signor William Tell."

"Signor William Tell?" laughed Paulo. "Whatever next. Please show Signor *Tell* into the dining room, Giovanna. But, before you do, ask him if he's had breakfast and if he says no, offer him an apple! Haha!"

"Signor Tell, Signor," murmured Giovanna stepping aside to let a suitably disguised Napoleone carrying a holdall, enter the dining room.

"*Buongorno,* Signor Tell," sniggered Paulo on eyeing the insignificant-looking man. "How can I help you? As you can see there are no apples in the bowl of fruit on the table so, maybe a plum off the top of my head instead? Haha! Please take a seat and then explain who you are and why you are here."

"I must apologise at arriving here, at your beautiful home, uninvited," simpered Napoleone, "but I was speaking to one of your colleagues the other day. A Signor Foni?"

"Signor Foni? Doesn't ring any bells. However, what were you and this Signor Foni talking about and how did my name happen to come up."

"We were talking about first editions, Signor Pablo, and Signor Foni suggested I contact you as your interest in first editions was unparalleled."

"My interest in first editions?" scoffed Paulo. "The only interest I have is how much money my films make, Signor Tell. Not useless, dusty first editions!"

"Oh, dear, then I have been embarrassingly misinformed, Signor," simpered Napoleone. "I can only apologise for my intrusion and wasting your valuable time. Oh. dear, dear, *dear*!"

"Please wait, Signor Tell," carolled Sophia. "The holdall you have with you, I take it contains several precious examples of the books you were referring to? While I appreciate the books may be of no interest to Papa, may I have a quick look?" She added coquettishly. "I'm Sophia. Signor Pablo's daughter."

"It would be my pleasure," said Napoleone with a smile. Brushing aside his dull, unruly hair (a wig) complimented by a pair of furry false sideburns, he peered at Sophia through horn-rimmed spectacles and said softly. "As it will be for Warwick."

Ignoring Sophia's puzzled expression, Napoleone stooped to unzip the holdall and pull out a repeating crossbow.

"Who needs an apple, Signor Pablo!" he said cheerfully before firing an arrow into Paulo's forehead followed by a second arrow into Sophia's brow.

Looking at the two corpses, Napoleone reached for a pastry and took a bite. "Mm, nice," he murmured, his mouth full. "And would you believe it, apple filling as well!"

Ten minutes later Giovanna's terrified screams rent the air, disturbing the tranquillity of the villa and its hushed surroundings.

A LAVISH DUPLEX PENTHOUSE - CHELSEA HARBOUR

"Elucidate!" crooned Warwick.

"At least you didn't crow masturbate," chortled Medea. "As predicted, Nappi has come up trumps. I'm not sure what he's actually done but he asked me to tell you that an apple a day does *not* keep Nappi at bay!"

"An apple a day does not keep Nappi at bay?" repeated Warwick. "What the Hades is that meant to mean? He sounds almost as bad as Amos Agja and his poems!"

"No doubt Nappi will *elucidate* when he's here next week," chortled Medea. "I take it you *will* be able to join us for dinner. By you, I mean you and Vincent, of course."

"Join you for dinner along with the pleasure of meeting Jamie Dornan-cum-Napoleone?" warbled Warwick. "Keeping in apple mode, all I can say is that not even an unripe Granny Smith could keep Warwick and Vincent away!"

"Ha! Talking about an unripe Granny, why do I get the feeling it will be *my* turn to pen a poem," said Medea with a throaty laugh. "A poem titled: *Medea, get your gun!*"

AN IMPRESSIVE ARTIST'S STUDIO - GLEBE PLACE - CHELSEA - SIX DAYS LATER

"So, do tell, William Tell," chortled Warwick on being introduced to Napoleone. "I wish to know every excruciating, sordid detail of the now posthumous Pablos' demise."

"Sorry, Warwick, but I do not mix business with pleasure," replied Napoleone smoothly. "We're here for what I trust will be an enjoyable dinner so, let's keep it that way. Enjoyable."

Get you, Nappi Napoleone, thought Warwick visibly bristling at Napoleone's response. *You may see yourself God's gift in the good looks and carry out departments, but Warwick Laudanum-Standton does not appreciate being spoken to as if he's a nobody.*

Waving to where Medea was busy chatting to her other guests, he said pithily. "I am sure you will find Medea's dinner party even more enjoyable seeing I will not be part of it!"

About to turn away he added with a tight smile. "As Vincent always goes where his beloved master goes, he too will be leaving."

"Is it my aftershave or something I said?" asked Napoleone giving a bemused Medea a questioning look.

"Oh, forget it," replied Medea. She gave a throaty chuckle. "It's no surprise Warwick never puts on any weight as he's always flouncing out before sitting down to the majority of dinners he's been invited to. No doubt he'll be on the phone first thing, oozing charm and inviting us to lunch as if nothing had happened."

"Is he always so touchy?"

"I think touchy is putting it far too kindly, Nappi, dear," replied Medea drily. "Think flammable instead."

"I liked his dog," said Napoleone, equally as drily.

"Hmm. Unfortunately, I think that Vincent, like his master, could also a touch flammable. However, let's forget about my dearly departed guests. Now, another more pleasant surprise, Nappi dear. You said you were determined to see *Wicked,* the musical, I managed to get tickets for Monday night!"

"Now *that,* Medea, is *truly* wicked!" replied Napoleone, giving Medea a high five.

*

As predicted, a supposedly contrite Warwick telephoned early the next morning.

"My sincerest apologies, Medea, dear," said Warick crisply, "but your friend Napoleone wasn't at all what I expected: nor was he at all forthcoming when I brought up the subject of the departed Pablos."

"Not to worry, Warwick, dear. As I explained to Nappi, you've been under a lot of pressure lately and therefore simply to ignore your sudden walking out."

"And what was *his* response?"

Medea couldn't resist a throaty laugh. "Let's put it this way. He liked Vincent."

"Well, I suppose that could be seen as a good sign," snickered Warwick. "His liking of Vincent eventually making its way to Vincent's adorable lord and master! Now, another reason for calling so early. If you are free, would you and *Nappi* care to come here, the penthouse, for lunch It'll make Louis's evening as he knows you enjoy the extravagant, uber calorific dessert he always concocts especially for you!"

"Darling, we'd *love* to! I say we, because knowing my difficult friend, Warwick, I did say to Nappi you'd be on the telephone first thing this morning for a kiss and make up and then invite us either to lunch or dinner!"

"Did anyone ever tell you, Medea dear, not only are you a lovely Medea-cum-Michael, but a beautiful psychic bitch as well?"

"Constantly, darling! Constantly!"

DE WATERKANT

"I appreciate we've only been back for two days, but I feel we should waste no more time in getting back to Joburg and deal with Verschuur," announced Amos. "What's more, we'll take your Toyota seeing my red Range Rover is a bit noticeable."

"Driving? Why not fly up?"

"Because that would leave a paper trail, Larry!"

"Sorry! I wasn't thinking," replied Larry sheepishly. "Of course, you're right. Stupid me!"

"As instructed, as soon as we've dealt with Verschuur and left him lying in sacrificial form on a bier of broken glass - another reason we won't be flying as a suitcase full of broken glass could be regarded as a touch suspicious - we contact Hettie van Wyk, collect the balance of our fee and get the hell out of Joburg. We'll allow *Juffrou* van Wyk to wallow in her triumph for a week, tops, and then we drive back to Joburg where it'll be a simple case of wham, bam, *totsiens* mam!"

*

Reports of business magnate V.V. Verschuur's brutal murder made headlines along with extensive television and radio coverage.

An exclusive television interview with Miss Hettie van Wyk, V.V. "Vokkie" Verschuur's loyal secretary for nigh on thirty years, showed a frail, distraught elderly woman holding back her tears and barely able to speak. On expressing her horror at the brutal attack on her former employer, Hettie ended the interview by staring bravely at the cameras and saying in an anguished whisper.

"Who could ever do such a terrible, terrible thing to such a dear kind and caring man!"

What Miss Hettie van Wyk did not say was that earlier, the day before, she'd handed over a considerable amount of money to two men for a job, well done.

"So, do we, or don't we?" asked Larry.

"Nah, unless we hear differently, let sleeping bitches lie," replied Amos. "We've enough to pay for that beach house we checked out at Knysna and, as for the advance we were paid for the now missing Melanie Meibosfontein, let's spend that on refurbishing and decorating the beach house and maybe a trip to Kenya! I've always been keen to go on safari."

"Is that due to a yearning for seeing yourself in the role of a big black hunter?" lisped Larry.

"Why? You bored with your current big black hunter?" rumbled Amos reaching for Larry and giving him a smacking kiss.

"Bored by my big black hunter?" carolled Larrry. "*Yebo*! Deliciously bored in the nicest, possible way. Talk about a thriller driller or a big black hunter shunter!"

A LAVISH DUPLEX PENTHOUSE - CHELSEA HARBOUR

"Darling, we're here! And here we'll stay until lunch is over!" crooned Medea as she and Napoleone stepped from the elevator. Medea, a vision in a purple shantung trouser suit with a matching turban and sporting a pair of porcupine-like purple stilettos added mischievously. "And we promise, talons on our fickle hearts, that we won't flounce out until we've finished whatever delicious dessert Louis will have created for me today!"

"I'm part of the double promise," laughed Napoleone, his handsome face wreathed in smiles. "And, as a double promise we won't: two bottles of Dom Perignon to doubly seal our vows!"

"You *angels*!" crowed Warwick, followed by an exuberant "Mwah! Mwah!" of air kisses. "Please come through. We're lunching al fresco on the terrazzo as it's such a *favolosa* Sarah Miles type day!"

Noting his guests puzzled expressions he added blithely. "A tribute to Miss Miles in the film *White Mischief*, and to partly misquote her memorable line, 'Not another pucking beautiful day'. Haha! Now, as I said, do come through ... Oh, Clarke, as you can see my guests have arrived bearing gifts. Would you please put these two bottles of fizz into the wine cooler."

Turning to face a smiling Medea and a bemused Napoleone, he said cheerfully. "Before Clarke disappears; bellinis or mimosas for starters? Or, if you're feeling brave, a white bear?"

"White bear?" repeated Napoleone looking somewhat taken aback by the state-of-the-art décor of the sitting room and the spectacular view.

"Champers and vodka," carolled Warwick. "A wicked, wicked potion! Do try one!"

"Why not?" replied Napoleone. Without turning to Medea, he said in a whispered aside. "Tell me, is he always like this?"

"Always, darling!" replied Medea in a matching whisper. "Always a bit OTT, rather like the décor. Now, promise to be a *good* and brave Nappi, as you said you would, for the next couple of hours!"

Warwick could not have failed to notice the busy whispering but chose the moment to cover Vincent's muzzle with kisses instead.

Glancing at the two, Medea added with a throaty gurgle. "The icing on the cake, as you will see, is Vincent who sits on his own chair next to Warwick while we have lunch, and frequently fed titbits by his master! Nota bene, this only happens at the occasional lunch when Warwick deigns to lunch in, but never at dinner!"

Napoleone was not only well-behaved and brave for the next couple of hours but, completely overwhelmed by Warwick's personality and perspicacity, invited him to lunch, *sans* Medea, the following day.

A laughing, unfazed Medea, laughingly blamed the oversight and Napoleone's rash decision on Louis' dessert. An orange, tangerine and pineapple salad swimming in Cointreau and white crème de menthe.

SCALINI RESTAURANT - WALTON STREET - THE NEXT DAY

"I trust you approve of my choice of restaurant?" asked Napoleone with a heart-stopping smile. "As I am not as all familiar with your city, Medea suggested this restaurant for our lunch."

"I *adore* Scalini!" crooned Warwick. "One of my favourite restaurants! Their *Milanese di vitello* is to die for! Not that I'm willing to die just yet! Haha!"

"I should hope not," replied Napoleone smoothly. "As it would be a great pity,"

"A great pity, Napoleone?" replied Warwick archly. "Is that because you'd miss *moi*, or, from what I'm told, Vincent?"

"Both, actually," chuckled Napoleone. "Now, as you obviously know this place, I take it you'll ne ordering your favourite *Milanese di vitello*, I'll do the same, including what you suggest for a starter. I take it you'll agree if I order a bottle of Pinot Grigio to go with our meal?"

"I *adore* Pinot Grigio, as you must have noticed from the amount of Pinot we *all* guzzled at lunch yesterday! But, for starters, may I order a martini?"

"Of course, Warwick; and I'll have the same," replied Napoleone turning to face the smiling wine steward.

"So, tell me, Napoleone. You very kindly filled me in - ha - after lunch yesterday, regarding the demise of the dreaded Pablos so, being frank, why the unexpected invitation to lunch today? Care to explain?"

"There's nothing *to* explain, Warwick. I have never met anyone like you before so, not only would I like to get to know you, I would also like to - as you would say - puck you after lunch, if you're willing."

"Puck me *after* lunch if I'm willing?" repeated Warwick feigning shock. "Goodness, Signor Napoleone! Do we really have to wait until *after* lunch? Why not simply leave those drinks *and* the restaurant, so that we can hot foot it back to Chelsea Harbour and get down to it!"

He gave a giggle. "After all, it's not as if *anything* on the menu here could ever compare with what I have in mind for both a starter and an intercourse!"

A LAVISH DUPLEX PERNTHOUSE - CHELSEA HARRBOUR

"I take it you'll be joining Vincent *et moi* for dinner," cooed Warwick snuggling up against Napoleone's massive, hirsute chest.

"How could I say no?" chuckled Napoleone.

"However, I should warn you, Louis and Clarke are prone to giggles and winks on seeing an unexpected guest. In your case a series of 'I told you so' winks', and smirks."

"I'm sure I'll cope," replied Napoleone giving Warwick a kiss on his tousled head. "Which means I'm ready to face the *musica*!"

*

"So good to see you again, Mr. Bertolozzi, and so *soon*," giggled Clarke as Napoleone and Warwick entered the dining room.

"Likewise, Clarke," replied Napoleone with a dazzling smile. "But, as I said to Mr. Warwick, who could resist another delicious meal prepared by the talented Louis."

"My, you do have a way with words, Mr. Bertolozzi," giggled Clarke. "I'll be sure to tell him, Hee-hee!"

"Me, a way with words?" chuckled Napoleone. "When it comes to the usage of words, I'm sure you'll with me, Clarke, that Mr. Warwick heads the list!"

"Oh, I do, sir! I most certainly do," sniggered Clarke on exiting the dining room.

Looking at Warwick sitting opposite, his face golden in the candlelight, he added matter-of-factly. "Tell me, Warwick, have you ever considered writing a book? Not your autobiography, the pages would simply burst into flame, but a novel. Maybe a detective novel? It would certainly keep you busy and, better still, keep you out of mischief!"

"It's strange you should say something like that," replied Warwick in all seriousness. "I was only saying to Vincent a few days ago that seeing he's such a clever pooch, maybe I should write a book about him. Something along the lines of *Vincent, The Dog Detective*."

"*Genio*! Why not?" exclaimed Napoleone. *Vincent, The Dog Detective* would be great!"

"Better still, why don't I set my first pooch detective novel in Venice?" enthused Warwick. "Something along the lines of *Vincent, The Dog Detective. The Mystery of the Missing Gondoliers*."

Reaching for Napoleone's beefy hand he added with a mischievous grin. "It gives Vincent *et moi*, the perfect excuse to visit Venice within the next few days seeing we were only planning on going there over Christmas. I say the next few days because not only will I be able to work on the first chapter or so, it will also enable us to soak up the atmosphere along with the odd gondola and gondolier! Haha!"

Eyeing Napoleone, he added hastily. "Joking, only joking! "I know you'll be back in Rome but why not, if possible, join us there for a day or two, and, better still, have a look at what I have written. A sort of lover-cum-editor as it were."

"I'd be both honoured and flattered to assist you and Vincent in every possible way with your first *Vincent, The Dog Detective* novel," said Napoleone with a broad smile. "I take it you know people in the publishing world?"

"No, which means I'll most likely self-publish." Warwick gave a chuckle. "What's more, I shall *fill* the library at the palazzo and the study here with copies: regardless of the cost. Back to you joining us in Venice, will you really be joining us?"

"*Assolutamente*! Plus, I'm looking forward to pucking in your palazzo and, if it is anything like pucking in your penthouse, then all I can say is that there *is* a heaven on earth!"

"A revelation for both of us!" crooned Warick. Turning to Vincent he said in what he considered his best doggy voice. "Did you hear that, Vincent? You are about to become a famous pooch! Maybe even another *Lassie* or *Rin-Tin-Tin*! So, how about a woofed, 'well done, Warwick!"

PALAZZO LORENZO - VENICE - A WEEK LATER

"So, what did you think of my first chapter?" asked Warwick nervously. "Be kind, Nappi. If you honestly believe I *do* have any talent, say so, and if you think I should take up knitting instead: again, please say so."

"On reading the first chapter of *Vincent, The Dog Detective. The Mystery of the Missing Gondoliers*, I was - no bullshit, nota bene - I was well and truly hooked and cannot wait to read what happens after Vincent is asked by the Contessa Marmellata to find Borsite, her missing, personal gondolier," said Napoleone with a reassuring smile.

"You really mean that?"

"I really mean it." Looking at Warwick, Napoleone added softly. "Apart from writing this book, with more to follow, what else would you like to do?"

"What else would I like to?" murmured Warwick. "I'd like to do, once and for all and then no more, something unforgettable to three people in particular before calling it a day. David Pegg is out for if anything happened to him it would upset Peggs, his school for guide dogs, which would never do. However, when it comes to the likes of Kurt Cameron, Sebastian Salamander, and pucking Larry Pinkerton, they're still on."

"Right. So, how about we do this. While you continue to work on your novel either here or back In London, I return to Rome and from there arrange for your three unforgettable happenings to simply happen. End of grudges and end of story. If this means I can have you and Vincent, of course, to myself, then take it as done."

Napoleone gave a sigh. "I have to be honest with you, *Caro* Warwick. I am *not* a fan of your London but, whenever you visit *Bella Italia*, albeit Venice or my more modest apartment in Rome, I will be there."

Warwick, his face impassive, sat studying Napoleone for a full minute before saying softly. "Take is as done, *Caro* Nappi. If I was putting this down on paper I would have written: *Yes, woofed Vincent, his stubby tail wagging with delight!*"

THE WORLD KEEPS ON TURNING

KNYSNA - WESTERN CAPE

Residents of the popular coastal town with its pristine beaches were shocked to hear about the vicious attack on Mr. Larry Pinkerton who had been staying in his and his partner's newly acquired beach house while supervising the decorating. Mr. Pinkerton had been found, bound and gagged, by one of the workmen arriving at the site. To the workman's horror, on removing the gag he realised Mr. Pinkerton's tongue had been cut out.

"At least people will now be spared from having to put up with that irritating lisp," chortled Warwick on being given the news by a smiling Napoleone.

RANCHO PLATA, PLATA, PLATA

Sebastian and Delilah Salamander were wakened by an enormous explosion accompanied by a great flash and a rumbling, crumbling sound as Sebastian's replacement oil derrick, collapsed.

Sebastian, apoplectic with rage by the happening, suffered a major stroke which saw him as a shadow of his former self and confined to a wheelchair for the rest of his days.

HOUSTON - TEXAS

Kurt Cameron returned home to find a cryptic typed note left by Joel for him.

Sorry, Kurt, it read. *Unlike Big Arnie, I won't be back.*

Joel Ford was never seen or heard of again.

"Now you see him, now you don't," chortled Warwick on being given the news by a smiling Napoleone.

JOHANNESBURG

Hettie van Wyk, revelling in her new role as Chairperson of V.V. Verschuur and Son (Frikkie, via long distance, having happily approved the promotion), sold her modest Hillbrow apartment and moved into a palatial mansion in exclusive Sandhurst accompanied by Cyril Shafto, a muscular, young man and permanently resting actor as well as her man of the moment.

According to hearsay, Hettie and Cyril have also been spotted in Monte Carlo, Paris. London and Las Vegas.

PALAZZO LORENZO - VENICE

Much to Warwick's surprise and delight, his self-published. *Vincent, The Dog Detective. The Mystery of the Missing Gondoliers,* went on to become a top international bestseller.

Without hesitation, Warwick went on to write a sequel. *Vincent, The Dog Detective. The Secret of the Golden Oil Derrick.*

Encouraged by Napoleone whom he wittily billed as his, "Swoon and Prune, Svengali", a third exciting tale involving Vincent, The Dog Detective, was quick to follow.

As a result, Vincent, the unsuspecting hero of Warwick Laudanum-Standton's bestselling books, spends his time jetting between London and Venice in a private jet named Lone Star One.

Thanks to Napoleone, Dario is back in his former role at Palazzo Lorenzo as man of all seasons while Louis and Clarke, along with Ginger, remain in London looking after the penthouse.

"They'd never admit it, but dear Lois and Superman are much happier overlooking the Thames than the Grand Canal," chortled Warwick. "Their preference being able to carol 'Hey, sailor!' instead of 'Hey, gondolier!'"

*

As Vincent, The Dog Detective woofs at the end of each of his novels. "All's well that ends well, and so woof all of us!"

Not Bad, Bubba!

Robin Anderson

ABOUT THE AUTHOR

Robin Anderson, a successful independently published author and a former internationally acclaimed interior designer, was born in Prestwick, Scotland, but spent his childhood and teenage years in the former Southern Rhodesia (now Zimbabwe) and South Africa. Before attending Rhodes University in the Eastern Cape, he hosted his own radio programme in Rhodesia (where he was duly dubbed "The Golden Voice of Teenage Half Hour"!) and worked as a reporter on The Bulawayo Chronicle (still going strong!) during his gap year.

Leaving South Africa, he spent the early sixties working with interior design companies in Paris, New York and London. He set up his own London-based design company - **RAD** - in 1970. Commercial ventures have included such names as Gulf + Western and the former Merseyside Development Corporation (the total refurbishment of the magnificent Royal Albert Dock in Liverpool) and private clients including Ivana Trump; actress Coral Browne and husband Vincent Price (fondly referred to as Mr and Mrs Horror), impresario Mark McCormack, Australian film producer Rebel Penfold Russell, and author and theatre producer Sally Burton.

Although interior design has been Robin's first interest, he has never stopped writing.

The former designer-now-author lives in a spectacular Chelsea apartment "overlooking endless lush private gardens" which he shares with Miss Abel Mabel Mortis: a glamorous skeleton of questionable years with a penchant for metal studded leather bondage collars.

To read more about Robin please visit his website:

www.robinandersonauthor-ott.com

BOOKS by ROBIN ANDERSON

www.robinandersonauthor-ott.com

AUTOBIOGRAPHY

Never a "Craft" Moment

NOVELS

Regina
Red Snapper
Sebastian & Seline
Versus
The Gallery
Divoon Daddy
Neos Helios
Amo, Amas, Amassive
Ceruse - A Cover-Up Extraordinaire
The Grin Reaper
The Go Blow Go Bar
Bobette - The Ups & Downs of a Total (Male) Tart!
Jan Unleashed!
Still Life - The Resurrection
Bruised Fruit
Defunct Gristle
Paul Dot Go
Crisp & Golden
Too Good to be Trué
I Give You My Heart
The Evil That Men Do - The Evil I Have Done
High Jinks in High C
Five Caballeros
Et Tutu, Brute?
Pillow Squawk
Pits, Privates, & Feet
Leo, Lulu, Lobie, & Mae
81 Today! (Payback)
Sitting Not So Pretty
Not Bad, Bubba!

LA DI DA DI BLOODY DA! series

La Di Da Di Bloody Da!
Trannys to Tiaras!
Maharajas, Mystics & Masala!
Wow! Pow! & Persuasions!
Oysters Aweigh!
Triple Oh Heaven!
Rootin' Tootin' Khamun!
Aliens & Arabesques - Blast Off!

TREYTON TEMPLETON series

The Omnipotent
Colosseum
Who Scares Wins

NOVELLAS

The Burning Bush
Bel Ragazzo - Beautiful Boy?
Swallow Dive

SHORT STORIES

6 + 6 + 6 - Eighteen Tales of Textual Titillation (Volume One)
6 + 6 + 6 - Eighteen Tales of Textual Titillation (Volume Two)
She Married a Zombie Truck Driver & Five other "Trucking" Tales
Three on a Match Plus Three

CHILDREN'S BOOKS

Four Zimbabwean Adventure Tales
The Adventures of Tumble the Clumsy Tree

PLAYS

The Burning Bush

A WARNING BELL

Archibald Ambrose Amberley (Archie to a few discerning friends), having "dropped off" the Principessa Ginevra De Maria (Ginny the Gin to a few discerning friends) at her apartment overlooking Grosvenor Square, "dropped in" - as per usual - to his favourite Berkeley Square nightclub for his "as per usual" goodnight flute of fizz in the always charming company of The Widow.

Nodding a "thank you" to John, the beaming barman, as he automatically placed a flute of Veuve Clicquot champagne on the bar, Archie (a Theo James lookalike) glanced left, then right, then left again before staring straight ahead.

"No grateful, grovelling geriatric here tonight," he muttered to what he could see of his reflection in the mirror backing viewable between the bottles lined up on the numerous shelves. "But, as the always optimistic Scarlet O'Horror was known to say, *Tomorrow is another day!*"

"Excuse me," rumbled a spine-tingling baritone voice. "Do you mind if I sit next to you or, more importantly, would you mind if I adopted you?"

"Wha . . . what did you just say?" spluttered Archie, a mouthful of champagne literally showering the smiling suntanned, silver-haired, uber-handsome Mexican actor Demián Bichir lookalike poised as if to slide onto the adjoining barstool.

"I *said* would you mind if I sat next to you followed by would you mind if I adopted you," replied the man with a dazzling, whiter than white smile.

Gathering himself together Archie said with a tighter than tight smile. "Please sit where you wish: *sir*; albeit next to me or else on one of the other unoccupied stools. The choice is yours. As for adopting the desirable me, I think not, seeing I am already spoken for. If you must know, I live with the love of my life, Miss Cleodora Cuddles. A highly jealous and hideously possessive cat."

"Hmm, interesting," rumbled the matinee idol on legs sliding onto the adjoining stool. "In fact, *most* interesting seeing *I* live with Santi, a highly over-sexed tomcat - or thinks he is - despite being neutered." Proffering a manicured, suntanned hand, he rumbled disarmingly. "Alfonso Hernández."

"Archibald Ambrose Amberley," murmured Archie as he leant across and planted a smacking kiss on the smiling man's parted lips and said cheerfully. "Okay, Alfo! Now we've done the de rigueur surprise, surprise intro, how are you, dear friend? It's been *ages*. Yesterday, wasn't it?"

"Last night, actually, as the mighty Hernández's tender *la barra* keeps reminding him," chuckled Alfonso. "Talk about a squeeze on his *nueve pulgadas*! Ah, thank you, John," he added as a large martini was set down in front of him, "and another champagne for Mr. Amberley, please."

Turning his attention back to a snickering Archie, he said matter-of-factly. "After you left me, how did the other performance go?"

"Obviously there is no comparison to what I always refer to as the dashing Senor Hernández's standing ovations of which there were four."

"Only four?" chuckled Alfonso. "I find that *hard* to believe. As donor of this so-called *cuatro,* I could have sworn there were more!"

Archie took a sip of champagne. "As for the *other* performance, as I just said, there was no comparison to Senor's earlier standing ovations. Nevertheless, there were several curtain calls or, as you, my dashing eight inches plus, prefer to call them, several anguished curtain cries!"

Not Bad, Bubba!

Robin Anderson

Printed in Great Britain
by Amazon